Bell Bridge Book titles from Diana Pharaoh Francis

The Diamond City Magic Novels

Trace of Magic

Edge of Dreams

Whisper of Shadows

Shades of Memory

The Crosspointe Chronicles

The Cipher

The Black Ship

The Turning Tide (coming soon)

The Hollow Crown (coming soon)

Shades of Memory

Book 4 of the Diamond City Magic Novels

by

Diana Pharaoh Francis

Bell Bridge Books

Bell Bridge Books
PO BOX 300921
Memphis, TN 38130
Print ISBN: 978-1-61194-837-0

Bell Bridge Books is an Imprint of BelleBooks, Inc.

Published in the United States of America.

We at BelleBooks enjoy hearing from readers.
Visit our websites
BelleBooks.com
BellBridgeBooks.com
ImaJinnBooks.com

10 9 8 7 6 5 4 3 2 1

Cover design: Debra Dixon
Interior design: Hank Smith

:Lmsa:01:

Dedication

To Laurie Henneman, Mike Briggs, and Sue Bolich—friends gone too soon. You will always be missed.

Chapter 1

Gregg

WINDOWLESS WHITE walls, white floors, white toilet, white sink, white table. The room was unrelentingly white. Though Gregg assumed he was being monitored, he saw no signs of cameras or microphones. His rival in crime— Savannah Morrell—had imprisoned him in this incessantly white box and left him to stew. Stripped of everything but his clothing, he had no idea how long it had been since he'd been kidnapped.

The room offered no weapons. The bed was bolted to the floor, as was the table and the lone chair. The toilet had no seat or lid, and the faucet was motion sensitive. Only his mattress, the toilet paper, and the white cup could be mobilized, and while he could make a knife of the latter, it would have done him little good. No one came.

Nulls or binders deadened his traveller magic. Food arrived periodically. It arrived inside his table, which was attached to the wall. The tabletop rose, and within was a compartment accessible through a narrow panel along the wall. The meal arrived, and warned by the smell, Gregg ate, then shut the table again so that the panel could open to permit the removal of his dirty dishes.

Though plentiful, the food tasted like rehydrated camp slop. Gregg counted meals, even though he knew it meant little to the division of the day or night. He paced and performed a regimen of muscle-building exercises to keep himself ready. He slept in short bursts only when forced to by exhaustion. Mostly he spent his time staring at the sterile walls, mind spinning helplessly.

Somewhere outside this prison, his brother, Clay, was being tortured by the FBI. Or maybe the long week had passed, and he'd been released. Or maybe he'd broken, and they'd locked him in a supermax for the talented.

Gregg knotted his hands in his hair and let out an agonized moan. If he could, he'd kill Savannah for getting in the way of his saving Clay. God, he hoped Riley had made it clear of the trap. His brother's girlfriend had been with him when Savannah's thugs had closed in. He'd sent her running into the night. She was smart and had skills. Surely if Savannah had captured Riley, she'd have taunted him with it already. He had to take comfort in that. He had no other choice.

Thirty-six meals later, he received the newspaper. It came folded beside his paper plate. All the dates had been blacked out. He flattened it on the table and read the headline: *Marchont Research Facility Annihilated.* His chest exploded like he'd been punched. He knew that place. It was a secret FBI facility, and the one he figured housed Clay for interrogation. His breath coming in short pants, he scanned the article.

A magical explosion had not just leveled the compound, it had left nothing more than a black hole in the ground. A grainy picture of the scene splayed over the entire top half of the paper, with insets of blackened bodies and melted debris. The burn extended up the surrounding hills, leaving behind ridges of slag and ash. One hundred and twenty people had been declared dead or missing.

The article explained that the place had been attacked, though no one knew who might have done it. The reporter speculated that the explosion pointed to domestic terrorism or a Tyet hit.

Gregg stared at the pictures. Surely Clay had escaped. A scornful laugh wedged in his throat. God, how naïve and stupid! Clay had been held as tightly as Gregg was being held now.

Unless—maybe this had been a rescue. If Riley had escaped Savannah, if she'd organized an escape mission . . .

It wasn't possible. Resourceful as she was, she didn't have the means. Hell, she didn't even know Marchont was an FBI compound. She was practically a babe in the woods when it came to Tyet business.

He found himself sliding to the floor, rolling onto his side as he curled into a ball. Scalding tears ran down his face as he wept, the sounds he made ugly and harsh.

No one came.

Later he read the article again. Then again. Three more times until he noticed the little box on the back page in the "Too late for regular publication" box. It listed an update. A helicopter discovered abandoned a few miles away. It belonged to Hollis Aviation. Investigators were following up.

Gregg crumpled the paper in his fists, hope lighting in his gut. Taylor's helicopter. That meant she'd been there, with Riley. That meant it was possible they'd got Clay out before—

For the first time in hours, his brain shifted into gear. Had they caused the explosion to cover their escape? Had Clay done it himself? But up until the FBI had arrested him, he hadn't known he even had a talent. And even if he had known, he didn't make fire. At least, Gregg didn't think he could. His brother had moved a mountain as a child, before trauma had sealed that memory away in his brain. He hadn't created one lick of fire. Neither could he imagine Taylor or Riley sacrificing so many lives. It wasn't their natures. So what had happened? Who had wanted that building demolished beyond recovery? And why?

He paced. More food came. Another sliding panel opened, revealing a small shower. How long had it been since it last opened? He'd guess at least three or four days by his smell. He went inside gratefully. He washed and put on the clothes left for him inside the table. This time he was given a pair of gray sweatpants and a red Denver Broncos tee shirt.

More food, several more showers, no news. No contact. He fought to keep sane. He stretched and did exercises until his body shook with exertion and sweat ran in runnels from his skin. He made himself perform math equations out loud, if only to hear his own voice, if only to break the crushing silence.

He could do nothing about the smothering white.

And then, when his beard had grown nearly an inch, a different panel slid open to reveal a hallway with a pale blue carpet and flowered wallpaper between white Greek pilasters. Graceful tables held vases of bright flowers. Mirrors reflected the light of small crystal chandeliers.

A slender, dark-skinned man waited with two bruisers at his back. His mouth curved an unfriendly smile. He held up a heavy silver cuff. "Mister Touray, I am Dembe Heinu. Put this on, if you please."

Gregg eyed it balefully, then snapped it around his wrist. He didn't have to ask to know it was a null.

"If you'll just raise your arm, now?" Dembe held a small padlock.

Gregg did as requested, watching as the other man slid the shank through the loop on the cuff and clicked it home.

"I am to tell you that should you attempt to escape, the Micha Center will be destroyed. A large high school cheerleading competition happens there today. The death toll would be eight thousand at a minimum. You should also know that explosives have been placed at two dozen other sites throughout the city. Should you successfully escape, every hour will see further deaths until you return to our custody."

"You suppose I care about other people's lives," Gregg said tightly.

"*I* suppose nothing," Dembe said. "If you will follow me."

He turned and strode away down the wide corridor. Gregg fell in behind, with the two bruisers bringing up the rear. Tentatively, he reached for his magic, but as he suspected, the cuff nulled his power. Not that he'd dare an escape.

He didn't doubt for a single second that Savannah would follow through on her threat. She didn't mind blood on her conscience. He snorted inwardly. As if she even had a conscience. She was cold-blooded, ruthless, and devious as hell, not to mention ambitious and greedy for power. She liked holding other people's lives in her hands. She liked knowing that they depended on her to keep breathing. She liked it when they knew it, too. Most of all, she liked wielding that power. She'd left a lot of corpses in her wake over the years and wouldn't shy from adding to the body count.

They passed a number of doorways, then took a set of white marble stairs upward to a wide gallery scattered with clusters of furniture and capped by a coffered ceiling. An enormous fireplace dominated one wall, with floor-to-ceiling windows revealing a gorgeous view. The lights of the snow-covered city clinging to the side of the caldera below glimmered like stars against the velvet night.

On the other end of the gallery, Dembe led Gregg around a wall and through a wide archway. Here was a comfortable salon, with white couches and a fully-stocked bar along one wall. The windowed walls rounded outward and rose to curve overhead. He sighed as his deprived senses drank in the world.

"Welcome, Gregg. Would you care for a drink?"

Savannah Morrell rose from her wingback chair. She stood no more than five feet tall, though silvered pumps lent her at least four more inches. Blond hair curved around her face in a smooth cap. Her pale face was flawless, her clothing chic. She smelled of expensive French perfume.

Gregg hated her with all his soul. For weeks before his capture, he'd been hunting her, trying to find a hole through her security to kill her. Now here he stood within a few feet, and he might as well be on another planet, as much good as his proximity did.

He made himself relax. He needed to play the game if he wanted to find an escape. "I'd take a scotch."

"That's right. You like a good single malt, if I recall. Dembe, pour him a Macallan, if you please. It is quite good, I'm told. The usual for me."

She motioned for Gregg to sit in a chair and sank gracefully back into hers. Her legs were clad in silk stockings, her body sheathed in a long-sleeved cashmere dress the color of blood rubies. She said nothing, waiting as Dembe prepared their drinks and set them on the table between them.

"Leave," she said with a wave of her fingers.

In a moment, the two of them were alone. Savannah picked up her glass and sipped, making a pleased humming sound. "It's lovely outside, is it not? The new fall of snow makes the world seem fresh born."

"And yet we both know the world beneath the snow is crawling with maggots," Gregg drawled, swirling his scotch.

"We must take it as we find it."

"Or change it to suit ourselves. Is that not what you've in mind?"

She shrugged, a liquid movement full of feline grace. "You must admit that you plan the same."

"Except I want to save the city. Shut down the violence and the corruption."

She laughed. "Call it what you want, it's still running the city to suit yourself."

He forced a half smile, lifting his drink to his lips and taking a large swallow. The whiskey was smoky and woodsy, running down his throat in a delicious burn.

"You didn't kidnap me to discuss our competing views for the city," he said. He wanted to ask for news of Clay, of the explosion, but refused to give her the satisfaction. That, and she'd use it against him. Savannah could spot weakness a mile away, and she never hesitated to take advantage. When she went to war, she left nothing on the table.

"Direct as usual," she said with a curve of her red lips. "Very well. I want the Kensington artifacts in your possession, including the vial of his blood. Turn them over to me and no one will be harmed. Don't turn them over, and . . ." She shrugged and looked out the window, lifting her glass to her lips.

Fire bloomed in the night. Orange, red, and yellow swelled and burst into bright flowers. A few seconds later, another explosion, then another, and another. Six in all. Gregg leaped to his feet, coming to stand inches from the window, shocked horror yanking the air from his lungs.

He whirled. "What the fuck have you done?"

"I've made a point. Sit down. We're not done negotiating."

Chapter 2

Riley

"HOW THE HELL am I going to help you if you won't even stay in the same room with me?"

I was yelling. I don't know if it was more from fear, frustration, or fury. With incredible restraint, I did not pick up the chunk of petrified wood sitting on the shelf beside me, and I did not sling said hunk of rock at Price's head. I did stay in reach to keep my options open.

"If I stay in the same room with you, I'm going to kill you. Is that what you want? What will you do then? Haunt me?"

Price's voice emerged through clenched teeth. He faced me from the doorway across the room. As usual since we'd come to the safe house, he was in the middle of running away as soon as I came in the room. This time I'd tried sneaking into his bed in the dead of night, but the instant he became aware of me, he was off like he had a dog biting his ass.

"You can kill me from a football field away," I pointed out, quite reasonably. "Probably a lot farther. Your logic is completely stupid."

"God dammit, Riley. This isn't a fucking joke," he said, plowing shaking fingers through his shaggy black hair.

I wasn't sure when he'd combed it last. The rest of him looked about as bad. He'd always been lean, but now he looked gaunt. He'd lost a good twenty or so pounds in the last couple weeks, and his sapphire eyes looked bruised and sunken. His cheeks had hollowed, and his lips pulled flat in an angry line. He wore a pair of low-slung pajama bottoms, exposing his chest. I could count his ribs. It hurt to see his pain, to see him struggling so hard. The FBI had arrested and tortured him, and though they hadn't broken him, they'd done unspeakable damage to his mind and soul.

I loved this man so much I'd risked my life, my family's lives, and committed a dozen felonies to break him out of FBI custody. He could push me away all he liked, but I'd be damned if I'd let him take a road trip into hell without me. That meant tough love.

I lifted my chin and glared back at him. "I never said it was a joke. But you clearly aren't getting anywhere with your strategy, and we're running out of time. Aren't you the slightest bit worried about finding your brother?"

The last was a low blow, but I was getting desperate. I felt like he was slipping through my fingers and no matter how hard I tried to hold on, he just kept getting farther and farther away.

It didn't help my anxiety that I felt less than useless. I couldn't help him, and I couldn't leave him, not without taking the chance that his worry for me would drive him over the edge. That meant sitting on my hands while both of my brothers and my sister, Taylor, risked their lives to find Touray, who'd been kidnapped while Price was in prison. Price's obnoxious brother had sacrificed himself so I could get away when we were both being hunted by the Tyet bitch-queen Savannah Morrell. But since going back to the city nearly two weeks ago, neither Taylor, Jamie, or Leo had been able to find him.

But I could, if I were there.

Everybody leaves behind a unique trail of energy wherever they go. As a tracer, I can see it. I can even see nulled trace, which most tracers can't. In fact, I can do a lot of things most tracers can't. Or I could before I overloaded my magic channels saving Price and escaping afterward. In the two weeks since, I'd recovered a lot. I figured I was maybe at sixty to seventy percent of normal. I probably couldn't go jumping into the spirit world or do any major magic tricks, but I didn't need to. Right now, I only had to locate Gregg, and looking at trace didn't hurt that much. It wasn't just for Price. I owed the bastard. Plus, finding him meant taking my family out of the line of fire. For the moment, anyhow.

At my words, Price flinched like I'd punched him in the gut. His face went gray. I held myself still, just barely. God, but I wanted to wrap myself around him and hold him tight. But even if he'd stay in the same room with me, he wouldn't risk letting me touch him. Not after last time, when a simple kiss had turned into a roof-ripping storm. Luckily, Jamie and Leo had still been here and used their metal magic to fix it.

Price's newly rediscovered talent was immense. And seriously scary. He could control wind and air. But it seemed like he was always wrestling for control of it. He was terrified it would get away from him and cause a disaster. When he was a little kid, he'd been kidnapped, and that's when his power first flared up. He'd knocked half a mountain down, destroying villages and killing who knows how many people. After that, he'd blocked his talent and his memories of it. Until the FBI had tortured him, he didn't even know he had a talent.

"Christ, Riley! Don't you think I'd be turning Diamond City upside down to find him if I didn't think I'd end up wiping it off the map in the process?"

"Then let me try to help you—" That's all I got out before he cut me off.

"I won't risk hurting you."

"And I get no say? That's not going to work for me. I'm a grown-up. I get to make my own damned choices."

He glared, his jaw jutting stubbornly. "Not this one. This one's mine."

"What if you never find enough control? Where does that leave us?" My chest ached with unshed tears, but I kept my voice even. He didn't need to know how scared I was of losing him. It already felt like he was halfway out the door.

Anger flushed his cheeks red and glittered in his eyes. "It leaves you alive. That's all that matters."

It wasn't, but he wasn't going to listen. My stomach tightened into a ball of lead. I only had one card left to play. It would piss him off. No, it would devastate him.

I squeezed my eyes shut. I didn't want to force him. I didn't want to push him where he didn't want to go, even for his own good. Who was I kidding? What right did I have to tell him or anybody else what was good for them? I didn't even know what was good for me most of the time. But the cold hard truth was that if I wasn't doing any good here, I needed to go back to the city. Without him. I could help there, and here I was useless.

I let go of a long breath and squared my shoulders, opening my eyes. I gave a decisive nod. I could do this. I opened my mouth, and my phone buzzed in my pocket. Saved by the bell. I grabbed for it. I checked the caller ID. My best friend, Patti. Her diner served as my unofficial office, so people came there or called when they needed me.

"What's going on?"

"How are you?"

"Good."

Silence. "I see you're still a crappy liar. Are you going to tell me about it?"

I made a sound halfway between a laugh and a sob. I glanced at Price and then turned and went back through the kitchen and up the stairs, out of earshot. "Things here are rough." Understatement of the century.

"How's Price?"

Frustrated. Obnoxious. *Frustrating.* "Dammit, Patti, I don't know what to do. Every time I try to get within ten feet of him, he takes off like his ass is on fire, afraid to hurt me. How long can we keep doing this?" I gritted my teeth and took a breath. "Never mind. I'll figure it out somehow. How are things there?"

"A young couple came in a little while ago. Names are Emily and Luis. They were pretty flipped out. They've got a missing teenager and need you to find her for them. Said you knew them."

I didn't even think about my reply or what Price would say. Emily and Luis had risked their own lives to save mine the night that Touray was captured. If not for them, I'd be locked up somewhere and Price would still be in prison. I owed them, and I wasn't going to let them down.

"I'll be there as soon as I can."

"Are you sure that's a good idea?"

After freeing Price, I'd overloaded my magic so bad that just tracing hurt. I'd only tried something more demanding once, and that had dropped me like a sack of onions. I'd stayed unconscious for a good hour. Luckily, Price didn't know about that little hiccup. But I *could* trace, and that's what they needed from me.

"I'm sure."

"What about Price?"

Now that was a problem. I'd been about to threaten him with leaving in the hopes that his worry for me would convince him to let me help him, but I'd never meant to go through with it. Now I had no choice.

"He'll understand."

She snorted. "Right. Good luck with that."

"I'll call you when I'm coming into the city. Can you let Emily and Luis know I'll meet with them later tonight at the diner?"

"I can."

"Okay, then—"

"What the fuck was that?" Patti's voice turned razor sharp.

"What? What's going on?"

"I don't know. Ground shook and it sounds like a bomb went off. I'll get back to you."

She cut the call before I could ask anything else. For a second I froze, uncertain what to do. Then I shook myself. Whatever had happened, I could find out on the way back. Right now I had to tell Price I was leaving and get on the road.

I sent a quick text to Taylor, Leo, and Jamie to make sure they were all right, and then went to confront the lion in his den. Again.

I started back downstairs, then veered off toward our bedroom. Well, my bedroom, because Price refused to share it with me. I wasn't dressed for outside. Hopefully, by the time I was, I'd have figured out how to break my news to him.

I strode across to the spacious walk-in closet. Inside, I stripped off the comfortable fleece pants and tee shirt I'd worn to bed, exchanging them for clean underwear, a pair of jeans, and a long-sleeved henley. None of the clothes were actually mine. Jamie and Leo, who'd built the safe house, had stocked it with a variety of sizes in men's and women's clothing in case guests hadn't had time to pack. I had definitely *not* had time, and even if I had, my stuff would still be somewhere back on the mountain near what used to be the FBI facility.

I pulled on a pair of heavy wool socks, then grabbed a lightweight gray Patagonia jacket guaranteed to keep me warm down to minus thirty degrees, along with a pair of snow pants made of the same stuff.

I returned to the bedroom. Price stood in the doorway. His body was tense, like he was burning for a fight. He probably was. Curls of air swirled restlessly around me. His control was slipping.

"What are you doing?" He jammed his fists into his pockets.

I hesitated. He was riding a knife edge between control and nuclear meltdown. Was I really going to push him off that edge? I had no choice.

"Getting ready to head back to the city."

His face hardened, and his sapphire eyes turned nearly black. "That's not funny."

"It's not supposed to be. Patti called and Emily and Luis need me to trace a missing girl. You remember I told you about them. They were at that restaurant when I got trapped by Savannah Morrell's thugs. If not for them hiding me and helping me to escape, I'd be at her mercy right now." I hesitated. "There's something else. Just before Patti hung up, something happened. She said it sounded like a bomb went off."

His jaw worked. The slow curl of air around me quickened. He swallowed convulsively.

I answered his protest before he unlocked his jaw to make it. "I'll be fine."

"You don't even know if the FBI is hunting you."

"The Marchont compound was wiped out, and Leo and Jamie shut down communications before anybody knew we were breaking in. Nobody knows it was us."

"They found your sister's helicopter. Do you really think the entire Hollis clan disappearing at the same time doesn't look suspicious? Then there's your father. What's to keep him from saying something? He's got no reason to keep quiet."

My father. The man who'd messed with my brain and set bombs inside my head to kill me if I started trusting anybody like Price with the secrets of my talent. The bastard had abandoned me and the rest of the family ten years before and then popped back into our lives the night the FBI arrested Price. I still didn't think it was a coincidence.

"He's got no reason to say anything," I said, pretending I believed it.

His brows rose, and he gave a harsh bark of laughter. "You don't know that."

"And I can't sit on my ass doing nothing because the world's a scary place. Emily and Luis need me and I'm going to help them." I scraped my teeth across my lower lip. "You can come with me."

"You know I can't." His voice was strangled.

I nodded. I did understand. His time with the FBI had given him a serious case of PTSD. Well, the FBI and the recently recovered memories of when his bitch of a mother had taken him to South America at the ripe old age of *three* to exorcise the magic out of him. The result had been a lot of dead people and Price suppressing his magic and all memory of it. Now he fought bad guys in his dreams. That's what had driven him out of our bedroom at first. One night he gave me a black eye and a couple of bruised ribs before he came out of it. He'd moved out that night.

Of course I'd ignored him. We had heal-alls to fix the damage. No harm, no foul, and I could take a little pain. I'd suffered a lot worse.

The next night I'd crawled into bed with him, which makes everything that happened after that my fault. At some point he realized someone was with him, and not expecting me, he went into a primal "stranger danger" mode. Caught up in his memories, fears, and hatreds, he hadn't been responsible for what he did. And that was to suck the air out of my lungs with his magic and then seal up my nose and mouth so I couldn't breathe.

Luckily, he'd come to his senses before I died. Not before I passed out, though, and that had sent him spinning into overprotective land. Now he wouldn't stay in the same room, much less touch me. Anytime we crossed the physical boundary, his magic broke his choke hold of control. The last time we'd kissed, all the furniture and windows in the room had ended up shattered. I told Price that was because he rocked my world. He was not amused.

"It's okay," I said, which was a total lie, and we both knew it. It wasn't okay for either of us, but that couldn't be helped. It was time and past time for me to get back to Diamond City. Emily and Luis just provided a handy excuse to hit the road now.

"Dammit, Riley—" Price snapped his teeth together, the muscles in his jaw flexing as he looked up at the ceiling. White dents bracketed his lips and nose. The air in the room tightened, coiling and knotting until it felt like it had to explode.

"I should go," I said finally, when he didn't say anything more.

He didn't move.

"Price, you have to get out of the way."

The words opened a yawning pit of black fear inside me. It felt too much like we were breaking up. But then, maybe we already had. I couldn't help the resentment and bitterness that washed through me. It wasn't fair, but the last two weeks with him constantly pushing me away felt like he didn't care. Not enough. He feared hurting me. I got that. In the meantime, he was killing me, and he hadn't even noticed.

When he just kept standing there like a giant stump, I lost my temper. "What exactly do you want me to do? You won't let me help you. Fine. Your choice, but you don't get to tell me to stay here when I'm needed in Diamond City. Now, let me by. If I leave now, I should be able to make it home by early afternoon."

I held up a hand to stop him when he started to speak. "I know the spiel. This is when you say you aren't willing to hurt me and blah, blah, blah, round and round and we come back to where we started. That horse has been beaten to a pulp. The poor carcass can't take any more and frankly, I'm not feeling much better."

"Did Patti really say Emily and Luis needed you?"

I blinked. It took a second for the words to percolate through my skull and make sense. My mouth fell open. I considered sticking my fingers in my ears to see if they were working properly. Instead I stepped back, my chest hurting like he'd punched me. "Are you fucking serious? You think I'd lie about that?" My voice rose, and my eyes burned with tears of frustration and hurt. "You think I'd play mind games with you?"

He winced but didn't look remotely apologetic. "Riley, calm down—"

"Fuck you! I've got every right to be pissed. You push me away and then when I'm actually going to listen and go away and leave you the hell alone like you keep telling me to, you accuse me of lying just to get away from you." The words ratcheted out like bullets. "I *do not* lie. But you know what? I don't have to lie in order to leave. I can just go. Wanna see? Watch me."

I started toward him, fully intending to do whatever was necessary to make him move. At the moment, kicking him in the balls seemed like a fine choice.

"Don't do this to me, Riley. I can't—" His voice broke. "You mean everything to me. Hurting you rips me apart."

I made a sound of frustration and rage, stopping when the air around me firmed into the consistency of Jell-O. One way or another, Price was going to keep me away from him. Even as his magic escaped his control, it answered his primitive feelings.

"Watching you suffer is no picnic, either, but you know what? As long as we were swimming in the deep shit together, I was okay. But we aren't in it together anymore. You made your choice, and now I get to make mine. So get the fuck out of the way and *let me go.*" Despite my anger, the words nearly broke me.

"You could die," he choked, and now the winds broke free. A gale roared up, spinning through the room, knocking the pictures from the walls and flipping the blankets from the bed. I dropped my coat and snow pants and walked toward him. The clothing whipped through the air. Price's hands remained jammed in his pockets. A white film covered his eyes. When he was totally submerged in his magic, his eyes went altogether white. I wanted to keep him as far away from that as possible. At least until he had control.

"I can't watch them put you in a hole, too." His gaze skewered me with agonized desperation. The white in Price's eyes thickened until I could only see a shadow of his blue irises. I knew he was remembering the funeral we'd had for Mel only a few days after arriving at the cabin.

In rescuing Price from the FBI compound, my stepmother, Mel, had been killed. It had been an accident, one that Price had caused. None of us blamed him. He'd been tortured past the point of reason and simply wasn't responsible. But every time he thought about letting me help him, I knew he remembered Mel's broken body as we carried her out and her cold, white face as we lowered her into the ground.

My stepbrothers have metal talents. They were able to dig through the frozen, rocky ground to make a grave. Taylor, Price, Dalton, and I had built a coffin for her out of a supply of lumber in the basement. The whole thing had been a nightmare, and yet after, I was glad I'd had a part in laying her to rest. It gave me a chance to grieve and share my sorrow.

For Price it had been an unending nightmare. He was always going to feel responsible for killing Mel. Nothing any of us said could change that. And now he was imagining me in the wood box, me being lowered into a hole, me being covered by a mound of rock and dirt. Me being the one he'd killed.

Deep grooves fanned his mouth and eyes. All around us, the wind kicked higher. The window rattled, and the doors slammed and shuddered in their jambs. The two lamps on the nightstands turned into kites. Their cords gave way one after the other, and the ceramic smashed against the walls, the shards and cords whipping into the air with shoes, soaps, pillows, blankets, towels, and every other loose bit in the room.

I hardly felt the pain of things pelting my body. A trickle of warmth dribbled down my neck as something sharp cut just below my jaw. I reacted without thinking, driven by the knowledge that Price hovered on the brink of total meltdown. If he noticed he was hurting me, I didn't know what he'd do. Was there such a thing as a land-based hurricane?

I did the only thing I could think to do. The only thing that I wanted to do. I flung myself at him and wrapped my arms tight around his neck, pulling myself up to press my lips against his.

His body was all angles and stone against mine. At first, he remained stiff, his mouth pressed tight, as if his entire being refused me. Then in a convulsive moment, his arms clenched me in a brutal embrace. I could hardly breathe. I didn't care. For the first time in weeks, I felt like I was where I belonged. A heavy weight fell from me. I'd worried Price would never let me close again. That I'd never hold him or be held; that I'd never taste him again or feel him inside me.

His mouth opened. His kiss was desperate with need and hunger and want. Mine no less so. Not to mention a healthy dose of fear on both our parts. I clutched his head. Our teeth ground together, tongues jabbing and sweeping. Desperation is too little a word for what we felt.

My body felt electric beneath the sweep of his hands as they ran over my back and hips and back up. Abruptly he lifted me up. I wrapped my legs around his waist, pulling myself as close as I could. I wasn't going to let anything separate us.

All around us the wind whirled and grew more violent. The window shattered, and its glass thudded against the walls and ceiling, flung like ninja stars. We both stood in safety at the center of the vortex, a calm eye in the storm.

We continued to kiss with all the fury of our primitive needs. Crazy as it sounds, I wanted nothing more than to strip away our clothes and get down and dirty. I ached to feel the intimacy of it, to feel us be together the way we were supposed to be, skin to skin, soul to soul.

It wasn't to be. He twisted away, jerking his head back. His eyes had turned entirely to milk now.

"Help me, Riley," he said, his arms clenching around me. "Help me. I can't—" He broke off, his eyes squeezing shut. Then they sprang open again. "You can't go without me."

Tremors shook him as wild emotions crashed through him. He'd not dealt with anything since his talent woke. Every little emotion brought on an uncontrolled eruption of magic. He'd bottled up everything—his fear for his brother, his guilt for Mel, his worry for me, his terror of his own power—but now they were ripping free. I'd helped tear away the dam, and now I had to help him find a way to manage his feelings so he didn't tear apart the world.

I only knew one way to do it. One way that had succeeded before. Unfortunately, I'd died that time. Price had barely managed to revive me.

I pulled his head close, pressing my forehead to his. "Don't worry," I said. "I've totally got this."

One thing I knew for sure—I'd be damned if I was going to die before I made sure he was going to be okay.

Realization must have struck him. An electric jolt ran through his body, and his eyes widened. He opened his mouth to protest. I didn't give him the chance.

Chapter 3

Gregg

"JESUS CHRIST. What the hell have you done?" Gregg whirled to face Savannah, squeezing his glass so hard it shattered in his hand. It cut into his flesh, but he didn't feel it. His shock and horror overrode everything else. "There weren't supposed to be any explosions, not if I didn't try to escape."

"No, they were promised if you tried to escape. But that didn't mean other things wouldn't demand the need. I've now demonstrated my resolve," Savannah said with a cool smile as she swirled her drink. "You needed motivation to give me what I want and now you have it. If you fail to produce the artifacts within the next thirty-six hours, I will set off more. Every hour you are late after that, the cost will grow."

He stared, his mind racing. He had three artifacts, plus the vial of Zachary Kensington's blood. None were of any use unless she'd found the last two artifacts, plus Riley.

In the early years of Diamond City, the Wild West ruled. Prospectors poured in, looking to get rich quick. Hundreds of Tyets sprouted, turning the city into a perpetual warzone, but Zachary Kensington ended all that. He created a weapon to take down all the Tyets in the city and force a truce.

After that, he broke the weapon up into pieces and hid them. Thanks to Riley, Gregg had acquired three, along with a vial of Kensington's blood. He hoped Riley would be able to use the vial to trace Kensington's workshop and possibly locate the last two pieces, along with instructions on how to assemble and use the weapon. It was the same reason Savannah needed her.

Or maybe not.

Riley was the only tracer Gregg knew of with that level of ability. That didn't mean Savannah didn't have somebody else up her sleeve. The real question was whether Savannah already had the remaining two sections. If not, then he could afford to turn his over to her. That would buy him time to stop her before she razed the city. What were the odds she had the last two?

Savannah's cool voice broke into his musings. "Such a shame, really. I believe that one of the explosions destroyed an elementary school. Fortunately, as late as it is, the school was empty. Next time the children might not be so lucky, though." She arched a meaningful eyebrow at Gregg.

Every muscle his body tightened, and it was all he could do to keep from jumping on her and snapping her neck. He didn't want to ask, didn't want to give her the satisfaction, but he couldn't stop himself. "And the other targets?"

She smiled her triumph. She knew she'd found his weakness. One of them, anyhow. "A movie theater, a cafe, a medical clinic, a church, and oh, what was that last one? I just can't remember. Oh dear, was it a hotel?" She shrugged as if it didn't matter. "Being that it's so late, there may not have been too many casualties."

Gregg made a sound low in his throat. "God, you're insane."

"I am simply a businesswoman who knows what I want, and I'm willing to do what's necessary to get it." She rose gracefully and set her glass on the marble bar top before turning to face him.

"You should get going. The clock is ticking. You have thirty-six hours. It's more than you need, but then, traffic will be terrible after the explosions. And"—her eyes flicked to the cuff—"you're short on your usual resources. I'd wish you good luck, but the truth is, whether you succeed in your mission or not, I still win." She smiled, her expression cold as a penguin's dick. "You see, I want the artifacts, but watching you fail offers its own delightful pleasures. Besides,"—she gestured at the blue, red, and white emergency lights flickering all over the city—"it never hurts to remind people how much they should fear you. I do so love fireworks. I can always retrieve the artifacts later. I'm sure you've been keeping them quite safe for me."

"You're a fucking cunt," Gregg choked out through clenched teeth.

"And you, my dear, are a hopeless fool." She tossed her head. "Just think: if only you cared for the city as little as I do, I couldn't blackmail you into giving me the means to destroy the whole damned place." She bent closer, lips thinning. "Thanks to you, I'm going to own every living soul in Diamond City, including yours."

With that, she left. Gregg could hear her heels clicking across the floor, lending rhythm to her smug laughter.

She hated him with an insanity he could hardly comprehend. He'd done his best to get in her way, to choke her out of the city, and clearly she'd taken it personally. Was he really going to turn the artifacts over to her? He glanced back out the window. What choice did he have?

Dembe stepped inside the doorway, his face expressionless.

"Shall I see you out, sir?" he asked. He eyed Gregg's bleeding hand and went behind the bar to retrieve a white towel.

Gregg took it and wrapped the cloth tightly around the shallow gash in his hand. It wasn't bad, just messy.

Dembe motioned for him to follow and walked out of the room. Gregg paused to gaze once more out on the city, his lips pulling back in a snarl. He told himself he didn't have to decide what to do yet, but deep inside he knew he'd already chosen. And he still didn't know if Clay was alive or dead.

Chapter 4

Riley

PEOPLE DELUDE themselves all the time, thinking if they've done something once, that means they can do it again without any trouble. That's true for some things, I suppose. Like falling down stairs. Or breathing. Once you do either of those once, you'll pretty much know how to do it a second time. Falling down stairs doesn't take a lot of skill or talent. Just a willingness to fling yourself off the edge.

Moving my spirit into Price's body was everything and *nothing* like that.

As a tracer, I'd learned that if I dove down into my own trace and made a hole, I could leave my body and go into someone else's using their trace. I'd done it a few weeks ago with Price, ironically enough, to help him gain control of himself in the middle of a tornado he'd created. Apparently, learning how to control his talent wasn't as easy as falling down stairs either.

The unfortunate side effect of my sort of spirit travel, much like falling down stairs or playing with hand grenades, is death.

I'd died the last time I'd tried this trick, saved only by Price giving me mouth-to-mouth and CPR. Once I left my body, I lost the ability to keep it working. Here's hoping I got back before it became too much of a problem.

The first order of business was to sink down into myself to where my trace rooted inside my body. Once there, I told myself to shoot through into my trace as fast as possible. Once again, *myself* was a horrible listener and did no such thing.

The feeling of being inside my own trace was almost indescribable. Orgasmic, euphoric—like touching God.

I was engulfed in a crystal silence so profound that I ached. Chills ran through me. There's a feeling that druggies talk about, like they are as big as the universe and can feel every breath, every blink, of every soul everywhere. Now I knew what that felt like. I wanted to bask in the experience—soak it up, live on the peak of ultimate pleasure.

But . . . Price. Not to mention impending death.

The last time I'd done this, I'd been exhausted, running close to empty, and panicked. Now I was only one of those things. Surely that meant I could speed the process? We had to figure out why Price hadn't been able to maintain his control himself after I'd helped him the first time. I wasn't sure how many times I could keep doing this.

As many as it took, and I'd damned well learn to like it, I told myself. Because I'm no quitter, especially when it comes to the people I love. I'd even put my life on the line for Price's brother, Touray, even though he scared the shit out of me most of the time. It's what you do for family.

A thin wire of molten emotional pain pierced me, wrapping and tangling around me. Mel. My stepmother had died in the course of rescuing Price from the FBI. I hadn't yet let myself deal with the grief. I couldn't. Embedded deeply inside it was guilt—that she'd been there at all, that she'd involved herself for me.

I wasn't ready to accept her sacrifice. I didn't know if I ever would be. Which made me ridiculous and contrary, since I would risk myself, sacrifice for those I loved. I'd learned that from her. I shoved the thought away. Now wasn't the time to contemplate my total lack of logic. Do as I say and not as I do, and all that sort of crap.

Focusing again, I pushed out of my body, but not before taking four fast, deep breaths. Maybe that would help my brain last longer. The fact was, a tinker or heal-all could do a lot to help the body, but they couldn't fix a dead brain. Or stupidity, for that matter.

Once I shoved out into my trace, I needed to make a hole. This was easier said than done. Trace is part of a person's spirit. It doesn't want to be damaged. I hadn't let myself think about the long-term effects of putting a hole in your spirit. The last one I made seemed to have healed up. At least, I couldn't see where it had been.

I steeled myself against the pain I knew was coming, and gathered power. I let it build inside me, potent and hot. I concentrated, forming it into a knife. No, a scalpel. Sharp and precise. The next thing I had to do was harden my trace. Otherwise, it would bend away from the scalpel, or flow around it like water. Ready at last, I swiped with the scalpel.

I didn't remember it hurting this much last time. Maybe because I was already in such pain at that point, it hadn't seemed like too much more. Apparently I'm *not* fucking Wonder Woman or Superwoman or whatever, because I was finding out just how bad it actually hurt. Like swimming through a vat of boiling acid while cockroaches chewed on every inch of every one of my nerves.

Too late to stop, even if I wanted to. As I made the opening, an aura of emptiness flowed inside. A deadening, like a patch of barren ground in the middle of a meadow. Ignoring it, I pushed through the opening and into the spirit realm.

It was cold. Graveyard cold. Not that I really felt it. The pain continued and didn't let much else through. I was surrounded by an endless velvet night filled with brilliant streamers of flickering light. This was the land of the dead. This is where my mother lived. If you could say dead people lived anywhere.

I didn't look for her. I didn't have time. The space around me rippled and churned. It surrounded me, closing like a fist. Pressure clenched on me. All of a sudden, a demon-possessed woodchipper swallowed me. And I'd thought cutting into my trace had hurt. I didn't know what was attacking me, or if this was just what happened when you went unprotected into this realm. Something similar had happened before, though I didn't remember it being nearly so awful.

That was turning into a theme for this adventure.

I had no idea how to fight, so instead I launched myself into Price and hoped that would get me away. I followed his burgundy-blue trace back to where it connected with his spirit. This next bit was tricky. The last time I'd done this, he'd not reacted well.

I dove into the magic aura swelling around him. It felt incandescent. Everything else burned away as I sank into the flood of power. It crackled and danced over and through me. It didn't hurt. It invaded every part of me, prying and digging. I swam through it, following his trace, arrowing into that secret, private place where his spirit and body linked.

I felt his jolt and the instinctive revulsion at my invasion. I flung out my magic, pouring all my love, respect, and pride for him into it. I felt him turn into me, reaching out. The heat of him twined around me, cradling my spirit in delicate silk.

What the fuck are you doing? You died last time we did this.

I felt the horror and fear he was trying to hide. Of me dying, of him killing me. *I'm helping you.*

Hurry up, then.

The words smoked with the heat of his fury. He might be holding back his rage, but it still leaked out. All the same, he wasn't going to waste time on an argument. Not when we both knew my body was dying. Later he'd have a thing or two to say. Loudly. And with many bad words.

I pushed out into him, melding and weaving our spirits together so we were essentially one person. I wished I could have savored it, that intimacy, that sweet friction of us rubbing up against one another on a level where we needed no words.

I kept myself focused on my task. I needed to follow the flow of his power to its beginning within Price. It wasn't going to be easy. Power surged from every direction, buffeting and swamping me. I got caught in a whirlpool and spun before getting flung out and wrapped in coils of electric magic. I felt the strands of myself linked with Price snap and fray.

Shit. I twisted, searching for the headwaters of his magic. But it was everywhere around me and seemed to come from nowhere. I'd never experienced anything like it. He seemed to be made entirely of magic. I tried not to believe it. If that was true, if he was what he seemed to be, I couldn't help him.

I dove back down, drawing on my own magic to protect me. It wasn't enough. I was too thin, too woven into the fabric of Price. More threads of me popped and tore free of our melding. I felt myself starting to shred. I contracted, trying to reel in the flying strands, but the wild churn of Price's power pulled back.

I struggled, trying to keep my shock and fear from reaching Price.

What?

Of course. Melded together like this, I couldn't have hidden vaginal itch from him. I decided honesty was the best policy, especially since he'd know if I lied.

I can't find the source of your magic. You're different. You've changed.

What does that mean?

His entire being drew together, like he was tensing to fight. I could feel the sour pulse of fear and self-doubt running through him. Scared wasn't something he was good at. He was a doer; he made things happen, and he didn't fail. He'd never wanted to have magic. He'd been happy without. Only the FBI had ripped open the walls holding back his abilities, and now that power was out of control. Price was sailing blind on a storm-tossed ocean. He was going to crash on the rocks unless he could tear that blindfold away, unless he could find a way to pull the power back in. And he was out of time. Here, now, this was his stand. Guilt skewered me. He wasn't ready, but I'd pushed him to this edge. I'd been so sure of myself, so sure I could save the day. And now we were both going to pay for that arrogance.

Riley? Price prompted me.

It's not going to work like last time. I paused, not wanting to admit the rest. Guilt and embarrassment made me want to curl into a ball. *I don't know how to help you.*

A moment of bleak silence. *Then get out. Get back to your own body and get away.*

Trust him to think of me first. *I don't know that I can get away.*

Try. Hurry up.

Beneath his clipped, cold words, he burned with wild emotion. I felt him grappling with it, forcing it down inside, and layering them over with icy determination. Before I could even think, he turned his attention to untangling himself from me.

I wanted to grab hold and not let him go. But what could I do? I'd only get in his way. Maybe make things worse by stirring up his fears for me.

Your magic used to flow through you like a river. Now it's like you're made of it. It churns inside you like a hurricane—like six hurricanes playing bumper cars.

Fine. Now get the fuck out. The implacable order came with a hard shove.

I dug in my heels. *You don't understand.*

He needed to understand what he was. It was the only way he might figure this out. *You're an elemental. This magic isn't like a normal talent that feels like a tool in your hands. It's part of you, just like your heart or your liver. Fighting it only makes you weaker, makes it try to protect itself, the way the body will protect itself from infection.*

A profound silence followed. Elementals weren't just rare, they were practically unicorns. Most people didn't believe they even existed anymore, and the ones who did didn't think they were human. The few that made the history books had been considered messengers of God. Angels. Devils. That sort of thing, and rightly so. They were living magic. What they all had in common was they were dangerous, volatile, and their potential to lose control made them targets. Kill them before they accidentally or purposefully killed you.

I'll take it under advisement. His mental voice dripped liquid nitrogen. *Now leave.*

Reluctantly, I extracted myself from him, retreating through the maelstrom of his power and through the cold of the spirit realm. It took a lot more work than I expected. I felt flat and spent.

I wriggled back through the ragged hole in my trace. The brilliant of the silver and green had faded to been-wash-a-thousand-times gray. I was closer to death than life. I took a few seconds to close the hole I'd made. It sealed, but the spot seemed weak, and pain continued to leach from it. Hopefully it would heal up.

Back inside my own body, I kicked through the root of my trace. This time when the pleasure hit, I brushed it aside. I had no right to feel good when Price was fighting for his life—our lives.

I nudged myself out through my body. My flesh felt awkward and stiff. How long had I been gone? Two minutes? Less? More? I told myself to breathe. For a long second, nothing happened, then my lungs expanded with a jerk and I drew in a painful breath. Relief avalanched through me.

Price still held me upright. Sort of. I hung slumped in the iron circle of his arms, my head flopped against his chest. My legs were wet rope. A roar filled my ears. I was cold. Not just from having been technically dead. Icy air nipped at my exposed skin. Magic saturated the air and crackled through my lungs as I sucked in racking breaths.

Fun fact: rib-breaking coughs will help wake up a half-dead body.

Tingles prickled along my toes and up my legs, followed by a wave of heat. The same thing happened in my hands and arms, finishing at my head. I tried to stop coughing, but between the magic and not breathing for a while—not to mention the cold—I couldn't get the spasms to stop.

I don't know how long it took me to catch my breath and stop coughing. By then I was able to support myself on my own legs, though dizziness spun my brain in the opposite direction of Price's tornado. Or at least that's what it felt like.

The roof and walls of the room were gone. I was surprised we hadn't crashed through to the bottom floor of the house. The whirling wall was full of dust and debris so dense I couldn't see through it. I let my head fall back. Far above I could see a circle of crystal blue sky.

I finally looked at Price. His eyes were solid white. Creepy as that was, it seemed to be a sign of a powerful talent. Maya, the tinker who'd lately become my personal healer, had white eyes when she was deep in healing. On the other hand, mine didn't get any fancy colors, and I was the strongest tracer around. Cass's didn't either—she's a dreamer friend, and terrifically powerful. So either Price and Maya had more juju than either of us, or I don't know what. Maybe Maya was some sort of elemental, too. Maybe Price wasn't, but I was sure he was.

Price's lips moved, but I couldn't hear what he said over the roaring of the wind. I wasn't sure he was talking to me. His eyes stared straight ahead, locked on some invisible point.

"Price!" I tried to yell, but I barely scraped out a sound. I started coughing yet again. Once I managed to get myself under control, I didn't bother trying again.

I put my arms around him. He might as well have been a statue. I pressed myself tight to him, nestling into the crook of his neck. And then I started praying.

Chapter 5

Gregg

DEMBE LED GREGG to an expansive mudroom near the back of the house.
Benches and lockers lined the walls, with cabinets hulking beside the doors.
Dembe presented Gregg with a garbage sack containing his clothes, now clean,
and his boots. His weapons, cell phone, money, and jewelry were gone.

"Mrs. Morrell wishes you to know that you're a person of interest in the
Marchont building's destruction, since your brother was being held there. You
may wish to avoid the law," Dembe said as he opened the door. A couple of
men waited. They both wore heavy clothing for the outdoors with balaclavas
pulled down to expose their chins and goggles over their eyes. Both carried
compact assault rifles.

"This way," the gray-bearded one on the left said. He was the smaller of the
two. He motioned with the barrel of the gun for Gregg to follow along the
cleared brick path.

The cold sank its teeth into Gregg the moment the door opened. His sweat
pants and tee shirt did little to keep it out. He paused to fish his socks and boots
from the sack. When he'd pulled them on, he drew out his coat and slid it on.
His escorts watched impatiently. Before he could bend to lace his boots, the
taller of the two dug the muzzle of his gun into Gregg's kidneys.

"Let's go."

The smaller one led the way, the other bringing up the rear. Savannah's estate was up on the rim above the city, where only those with billions of dollars
could afford to live. The main house had thirty or forty bedrooms, at least as
many bathrooms, and expansive spaces for entertainment. A dozen or more
guesthouses cozied beneath trees within carefully manicured glades. Wood
smoke billowed from a few of the chimneys, scenting the evening air.

They walked to a long outbuilding screened by trees and magic. A golf cart
waited for them in front. One guard slid into the driver's seat. The second
motioned for Gregg to sit shotgun, then got in the seat behind.

They pulled out onto the winding drive. After about five minutes, they arrived at a set of gates large enough to let a semi through, though Gregg knew
from experience that it wasn't the main entrance. The driver muttered something into his collar and a pedestrian gate glamoured to look like the wall appeared just right of the gates and slid open.

"Get out," the back seat guard ordered.

Gregg didn't need to be told twice. He jumped out and started walking.

Savannah could very well be playing a game—letting him go so far and reeling him back in to prove her control. She definitely wanted the artifacts, but whether that desire outstripped her delight in toying with him, he didn't know. She reminded him of a cat determined to toy with her food before devouring it.

He slipped through the gate and out onto a wide swathe of unmarked snow. The gate thumped closed behind him. Sixty feet or so in front of him was a cleared sidewalk and a wide avenue. Goldengrove, if he had to guess. Which put him on the east side of Savannah's compound. He needed to go west.

As he scanned the area, he considered staying in the shadows of the wall, but his sweatpants would soak through in minutes. He'd end up hypothermic before he made a mile. At the moment speed mattered more than the shroud of shadow. He eyed the sweep of virginal snow before him. Getting to the road wasn't going to be easy, and he'd end up just as wet. Though the ground looked innocently flat, a broad drainage culvert ran just this side of Goldengrove. He'd sink to his neck.

Gregg rubbed a gloved hand over his mouth, then decided. Better to move than stand in place like a rabbit ready for the stewpot.

Turning right, he started in a diagonal path toward the culvert. He should be able to stop himself before bogging down in it. He'd head for Sweetwater Avenue, the next cross street. He'd be able to cross the culvert on the sidewalk there.

Before he'd slogged forty feet through the thick, heavy snow, his legs ached from just above the bottom of his thighs to his toes. The cold chewed through his flesh to his bones. He shifted gears, breaking into a lunging jog. His sweats pushed up at the ankle. The cold soon numbed his legs.

By the time he reached the road, he was soaked to the skin and his socks held his feet in a clammy embrace. The light wind cut through his wet pants like knives, and within moments of standing on the sidewalk, he began shivering. With a quick, sharp glance around himself, Gregg broke into a ground-eating jog, counting on the exercise to warm himself and the speed to move him out of immediate danger.

At the moment, Savannah was the least of his problems. She was always under surveillance by law enforcement and competing Tyets, including his own. Right now, the hostile eyes of his rivals watched him. The only question was whether his people or his enemies would pick him up first.

As he ran, Gregg scanned back and forth, digging into shadows, looking for hidden danger. He cast surreptitious glances behind him but saw no followers. Yet. He snarled. Fucking null. Fucking Savannah.

White street lights lit the avenue, turning the snow to diamonds. In the distance he could see the flash of emergency vehicles from the city below, accompanied by the subdued shrieks of sirens.

Diamond City had been built in the 1800s on the side of an ancient volcanic caldera that was riddled with diamonds, hence the clever name of the town. Three shelves composed the main parts of the city—Downtown, Midtown, and Uptown, all named with equal genius, imagination, and originality. Savannah's estate had built her compound on the rim overlooking the caldera, where only those with more money than God could afford the real estate. Gregg had the money, but no interest in wealth masturbation. He preferred Midtown, though he had houses peppered throughout the city. He found moving frequently and randomly made it more difficult for enemies to plot an attack, and some locations were better suited to certain business operations.

Headlights appeared on the avenue behind him. He looked back. The car turned off. Behind it, a gray Lexus, its lights off, leaped forward as the driver gunned the motor. The wheels slipped and whined on a patch of black ice in the intersection. The rear of the car whipped around, stopping when it had spun three-quarters of the way around, and it now faced away from Gregg. His people didn't drive Lexuses. Gregg turned and sprinted. Not far was a subway station, used almost entirely by Rim employees who could no more afford to live where they worked than they could fly to the moon.

He heard the Lexus right itself and rev its motor. It's lights came on, the driver giving up on stealth. Gregg skidded on a patch of ice, caught his balance, and continued to run. He wasn't going to make the subway. He eyed the walls to either side. Too high to climb. Where to make his stand? He needed cover. They'd surely have guns. His only chance to take them down was if he could get close enough to fight.

A roundabout in the next intersection contained a small copse of trees at its center. Snowplows had piled small mountains around it. A terrible place to hide, but with any luck, he could find a branch to use as a weapon and use the trunks to shield himself from gunfire.

Gregg hurled himself toward the roundabout. It was going to be close. The Lexus was coming on fast. Too fast. His lungs ached from the cold air, but his run had warmed his legs so that they felt like they might obey his commands. A bitter smile twisted his lips. Obeying was in their best interest. After all, if he died, they were screwed, too.

He reached the snow-piled wall just as the Lexus skidded to a stop behind him. Doors opened. Gregg scrambled up the berm. Yells bombarded him, but he wasn't listening. Any moment he expected bullets to rip into him. But none did. It appeared they wanted him unharmed, no doubt in order to have a blank slate to work with. No one liked to torture an already mutilated victim. Where was the fun in that?

He reached the top and skidded down the other side on his butt, not looking behind to see how many followed. Enough. Too many. It didn't matter.

The snow around the bases of the trees was deeper than he'd expected. A good three feet. Worse, the copse was well-manicured. The lowest limbs of the pines jutted a good four feet above his head. He couldn't make a move without being seen.

Gregg launched into the obnoxiously well-spaced trees, weaving around the trunks. Under the snow, his feet caught in bushes and rocks. That was an idea. If he could find a good rock to use as a weapon. . . . Either way, it was going to be close combat. His lips tightened in grim anticipation. He could live with that.

He heard yells and then someone sliding down into the bowl of snow with him. Shots rang out. Gregg frowned. Who was shooting? Maybe his people had arrived. Maybe his enemies were fighting over him like jackals. Maybe not everybody cared if he lived. He pushed all of that to the edges of his perceptions. Right now he needed to focus on the immediate danger—the person with him in the tree bowl.

The hunter was not quiet. Snow and bushes crunched, and he swore before the words cut off abruptly. Gregg peered around the trunk he'd ducked behind. His foe was coated in a layer of snow. He wasn't wearing a coat. He'd been in a nice warm car, after all. Good. Any punches Gregg landed would do real damage to the man's torso rather than be cushioned by a cozy layer of down.

The man held his gun up in front of his eyes, turning it and his head so his gaze didn't leave the sights. Well-trained. The fact that he kept to the outer edges of the trees indicated he knew what he was doing. He'd drawn the same conclusions Gregg had and wasn't going to make it easy for Gregg to close on him and wrestle the gun away. Nor was he going to stupidly walk into an ambush so Gregg could clump him on the back of the head. This was not the movies, and villains didn't commit idiocy just so the hero could triumph.

Gregg snorted inwardly. As if he were anything like a hero.

More shots. Gregg edged backward around the trunk of the tree, keeping it between him and his adversary as the other man rounded the copse. His feet and legs had gone numb again. At least the wall of snow surrounding them blocked the wind.

He shoved his hands into his armpits to try to keep them warm and contemplated his next move. He could let the guy capture him, and then work at a chance to disable him. Then he'd be armed, which could only help with escaping the rest of his pursuers. And if he waited much longer, his hands would be worse than useless.

Gregg stepped out from behind the tree.

"Hands up and stay still!" the other man shouted.

"Which do you want? I can't do both," Gregg called back, deciding that irritating the other man could only work in his favor. Angry people forgot to think; they made mistakes.

"Fuck you. Stand still. Hands up."

Gregg kept walking. "Come on, pal. Give me a break. I'm so cold my nuts crawled up my ass." He kept his voice conversational.

His captor gave a little sneer of a smile, but didn't lower his weapon. Gregg kept slowly stepping forward, eating the distance between them.

"That's far enough," the other man said when Gregg was eight feet away.

This time he stopped. They stood a moment, listening to the sounds beyond the wall of snow. Unintelligible voices. Thuds and movement. Gregg's captor never took his eyes off Gregg, nor did his weapon waver in the slightest.

After a long minute or two, Gregg let out a gusty breath, a white cloud blooming in front of him. "Look, I don't mean to tell you your business, but I think you're supposed to capture me. Which means"—he jerked his head—"getting out of here. Hopefully into a nice warm car?"

"Shut up."

A quick staccato of gunshots. They continued for several seconds. Gregg's captor's gaze flicked upward toward the rim of the snow wall. It was the best distraction he was going to get.

Gregg launched himself, hunching low. He drove his shoulder into the other man's stomach and plowed him to the ground. An explosion of breath. A muffled curse, the sharp bursts of gunfire. Squirming and punching. Gregg gripped the other man's wrist, digging his fingers hard into the tendons while pulling himself up to straddle his thrashing opponent. He smashed his fist into the man's temple and jaw. He struck fast and hard, his fist a jackhammer.

Blood poured from the other man's nose and mouth. His lips and skin pulped beneath Gregg's blows, and his left eye socket caved in. A moment later the beleaguered man slumped unconscious, his hand going slack on the gun. Gregg snatched up the Glock 17 and vaulted to his feet. He popped the magazine. Nearly full. He slammed it back and checked the chamber. Loaded.

Tucking it into his coat pocket, he lunged up the side of the snow wall. More than once he slid back down. His lungs pumped, the cold air searing. He dug his hands deep into the snow and pulled himself upward. At the top, he braced himself and elbowed up so he could peer over the crest.

He faced the opposite side of the roundabout. Several cars and trucks had parked haphazardly, doors flung open. A Ford F-250 with studded snow tires growled loudly, engine running. Adrenaline spiked. Gregg scanned the tableaux below. He counted eight living and six bodies. No telling how many were out of sight or how many were foes.

His gaze narrowed on the truck. That was his ticket to freedom. All he had to do was get there in one piece. Hell, he'd take getting there in a few pieces. He dismissed the idea of using the Glock he'd confiscated to pick off people from above. Shooting accurately downward wasn't easy, and once his targets became aware of him, he'd be a sitting duck in a carnival game.

Getting down unnoticed was going to be equally impossible. On the other hand, he didn't have much choice. If he kept himself flat and moved slowly, maybe he'd go undetected.

He grimaced. Unlikely. Still, he couldn't see any other likely option.

Wriggling and pulling himself up on his elbows, he crawled up on top of the berm. He sat on his butt and swiveled his legs around. He reached into his pocket to grip the gun. Iron bent easier than his fingers. Gregg drew the weapon. With a bullet chambered, the Glock was already half-cocked. Pulling the trigger would finish it and send the bullet on its way. He didn't dare put his finger into the guard. He could barely feel anything. He'd probably shoot himself.

Pulling himself with his heels, he scooted off the edge of the berm, laying back against the snow, digging his elbows in to help slow his descent. Fresh snow had fallen recently, and instead of sliding easily, he sank down into a marshmallow of snow.

"Fuck," he muttered through clenched teeth. They wanted to chatter. On the positive side, the bezel of snow helped disguise him from anybody not directly below him.

He worked his feet and arms, inching himself downward. A ridge of snow formed between his legs and stopped his progress. He rocked back and forth to flatten it. Unfortunately, his breath showed above him like a whale spouting in the ocean. God dammit. He reached under his soaked coat and pulled his shirt up over his mouth to contain the steam of his breath.

The battle below continued, punctuated by shouts, gunfire, and running foot-steps. Gregg clung to the sound of the F-250's continued rumbling. Hopefully some moron wouldn't put a bullet through the block before he had a chance to steal it. Someone was definitely shooting a hand canon. Maybe a .357, maybe a .44 Mag. Both could end his chances with the truck.

He wasn't surprised that no cops had shown up. They were too busy dealing with the carnage of Savannah's bombs—those who hadn't been paid off to look the other way. Nobody else would be stupid enough to step in the middle of a Tyet war.

That suited Gregg fine. He didn't want to be responsible for killing any innocent bystanders, and as corrupt as most of them they were, he didn't relish seeing any cops killed, either.

The downward side of the snow wall was about thirty feet. He'd nearly reached the bottom when he heard a loud clang, then sputtering and coughing as his best hope for escape died a slow death. He lifted his head and surveyed his surroundings. So far no one seemed to have noticed him. He scooted the rest of the way and rolled off, landing on the slick pavement on his hands and knees, the Glock still clutched in his right hand.

He pushed himself up into a crouch. Too fucking slow. The cold penetrated deep inside. Tremors ran through his arms and legs. He firmed his grip on his gun. The snow near his head exploded in a puff of ice crystals. He jerked back. He'd been seen. Twenty feet away was a Jeep. It sat sideways, the passenger door facing Gregg. No one seemed to have taken refuge around or behind it.

He pushed to his feet, the movement agonizingly slow. He broke into an uneven jog, ducking and zigzagging to make himself a difficult target. A hard blow hit his left calf, and he stumbled, his left leg buckling. He looked down at the hole in the back of his sweats and the dark stain of blood spilling from his leg. He was so numb, he could barely feel the pain. Driven by sheer will, Gregg shoved himself back up and staggered toward the Jeep.

He made it around the back end without getting shot again. He leaned against the rear, panting hard as the tremors in his body turned into palsy. He shoved the Glock into his pocket and tucked his right hand under his armpit. He didn't believe for a second that he could generate enough warmth to get better control of his hand, but he had nothing better to try. He wasn't giving up. He wouldn't give up if someone showed him a death certificate and told him he was dead.

Behind him, the gun battle continued unabated. A bullet pinged off the front of the Jeep, and he flinched. Beyond him, the avenue continued on, and in the distance, the lights of Diamond City rose from the caldera. More empty vehicles blocked the road in that direction.

He lurched forward toward the sidewalk. His leg throbbed with remote pain. Warmth trickled down the back of his calf and into his shoe. No time to bind off the wound. Hopefully, he'd find refuge before he passed out from blood loss.

Gregg had just made the sidewalk when a battered green Tahoe with a yellow stripe down the side and fat snow tires roared up beside him. He turned, reaching for the Glock. The back door swung wide, and Gregg found himself staring into the brilliant blue eyes of the last person he expected to see, the woman who made him hard every time he thought of her. Taylor Hollis. Riley's sister.

Chapter 6

Riley

WIND SHRIEKED, and I shivered. My backside was developing frostbite and my front side was sweating like I was in a sauna. Price radiated heat like the sun while pulling in frigid air from outside. Who was I kidding? He'd pretty much knocked down most of the cabin. We were no longer actually *inside* by any definition of the word.

He kept hugging me. Or anchoring me down so I didn't fly away. His grip hurt, but I wasn't particularly interested in becoming a kite, especially in the gale hurtling around us.

Talking was out. I couldn't have made myself heard above the din if I wanted. His power had grown and changed, morphed into something I didn't recognize. Elemental talents were off the charts powerful, and very few existed. Maybe because they killed themselves when their power erupted. Price had been über-lucky to manage a shutdown as a toddler. Now he had to find that strength or knowledge or whatever he needed to get it under control again.

I can't say when I realized that the wind was slowing. The change was hardly perceptible at first, and then it unraveled all at once, detritus raining down. An invisible air umbrella protected us from getting brained by a plummeting toaster or toilet.

At last the world went quiet. Price panted, his ribs bellowing under my arms. His head fell onto my shoulder. He started shaking, and his arms convulsed around me. I whimpered, my ribs creaking with the pressure. Instantly, he loosened them, raising his head again to look down at me. His eyes burned with an intensity I'd never seen before. Almost like he wasn't quite human. At least they were blue again.

"Are you okay?" His voice was little better than a scrape of sound.

"Could be worse," I whispered, my mouth dry. I was more shaken than I cared to admit. I held myself stiffly so the rest of me wouldn't shatter apart. "How about you?"

"Fucked up," he said, and then he kissed me. I tasted dust from both our lips. His hands knotted in the back of my shirt as his mouth claimed mine.

Some kisses are sweet, some are exploring, some are sheer lust. This one wasn't any of those. It was demanding and punishing and desperate and raw. I gave as good as I got, my own emotions stretched to their limits. Because next time, he might not survive. We might not survive. And I was sure there would be a next time.

He must have felt the same. His hands slid up under my shirt and up over my breasts and then around to sweep up and down my back. I did the same, moaning into his mouth as I touched satin skin over taut muscle. He hitched me closer, if that was even possible.

I wasn't ready when he tore his lips from mine. I made a sound of protest, and he kissed me swiftly again and then pressed his forehead to mine.

"I don't want us to be separated again," he said raggedly. "Bad shit happens when you go off on your own. I'm going back to Diamond City with you or I swear to God I'll chain you down here."

I snorted and gave a weak laugh. "Good luck with that. There's no *here* left."

He cupped my face between his palms, tipping my head so I could meet his gaze. A storm still raged in the depths of his eyes, a sign that he'd always be fighting for control. He rubbed his thumbs across my cheeks. "I'm serious."

I raised my brows, irritation returning. "Are you saying I need a body-guard?"

"Yes. No. Dammit, Riley, I'm saying that whatever happens to you, I want to be there. I'm not trying to rescue you or keep you from going off on crazy adventures—"

"You don't want to keep me from doing insane things?"

"Of course I do. But if you're going to be committing stupidity, I want to be by your side. I *will* be at your side."

I bit my lower lip hard. I wanted to believe him, but that was a promise he couldn't make. Not when he'd already promised his brother he'd join the family business. That made Touray his biggest priority, and sooner or later, Price was going to have to choose between us. No matter how he felt about me, I couldn't imagine I'd be the winner. I tried to smile and failed utterly. "Okay."

He scowled. "What's wrong?"

I made lips turn up. I probably looked demented. "Just wondering if I get to go to the bathroom alone."

"Dammit, Riley, I'm serious!"

"I know. I'm not objecting." I just didn't believe it.

"So what's wrong?"

"Nothing."

"Bullshit. Talk to me. Don't shut me out."

Like he had for the past two weeks? I didn't say it, even though it burned on the tip of my tongue. Finally I shrugged. "Everything's good. I'm happy you're coming back with me. We should probably get on the road."

His lips pulled back from his clenched teeth. "Fine. But I'm not done talking about this. Count on it."

I decided a change of subject was in order. "You shut down your power. Does that mean you've figured out how to control it?"

"Control is a strong word. I'm pretty sure I can open and close the spigot. Anything else is a crap shoot at this point."

"You'll learn."

"If I don't blow us all the hell off the face of the earth first."

"I'm not worried."

"Makes one of us."

He was still staring at me like he wanted to crack my head open and look inside. I averted my eyes, looking around at the damage.

We still stood on the second floor, but the walls were gone and most of the rest of the second story. Plumbing pipes stuck up in the air like skeletons. Our room was near the stairway, which was probably the most solid part of the building. Or so I guessed, since it was still standing. I figured we could probably get down them, so long as we made the jump over the four-foot hole between us and it.

"You don't do things halfway, do you?"

"No. I don't." A meaningful look, and then he finally looked away. "I'll owe your brothers some money."

"Worry about them later. Let's get on the road."

We picked our way to the hallway. I tested the floor and scooted forward until I stood on the edge of the hole. I glanced down. Below us was the living room. It looked mostly intact, except for fallen debris from the walls and ceiling. I leaped and landed on the other side, scooting over to the stairs so Price could follow. We descended the stairs, testing each tread before putting weight on it.

I couldn't help but think that the wreckage reflected my inner turmoil. I blew out a breath. I hadn't lost Price yet, and I wasn't going to spend all my time mourning what might never happen. *Yeah right*, a little voice in my head said. *You should be so lucky.* I told it to fuck off and grabbed Price's hand.

THE ROADS WERE decent. Flakes of snow fell, but the incoming storm would be a weak one. We had four-wheel drive, snow tires, and chains, plus a couple of charms to help with the rubber gripping the road. Price drove. That was fine with me. I knew how, but I spent most of my time on the subway, the bus, a bicycle, or my own two feet. Recently, thanks to Price, I'd become enamored of snowmobiles.

After a while, I sensed that Price wasn't being quiet because he was concentrating on the road. He was brooding. I decided that his thoughts were on his kidnapped brother.

"Morrell isn't going to kill him," I said, not for the first time. Also completely unhelpfully. What did I know? Savannah Morrell was a psychopath as far as I could tell, and that made her completely unpredictable.

"I know," Price said, also not for the first time. "But there's a lot of territory between healthy and dead, and Savannah knows just about every square inch of it."

"He's strong. He'll get through it."

"Doesn't make me feel better."

"I know."

"Anyway, I wasn't thinking about him."

I was silent a moment. "Oh."

"You ready to tell me yet what's bothering you?"

No, but he wasn't going to let it go until I did. I leaned against my door. "Reality sucks."

He frowned, darting a glance at me. "What's that supposed to mean?"

I sighed and looked out. The sun had started turning the sky gray. Snow mounded on the mountain sides and blanketed the trees on either side of the road. "When Touray and I end up on opposite sides, I'm going to lose you."

There. The elephant in my world.

Price stomped on the brakes, and we screeched to a halt. Thank goodness for really good road clearing. He jammed the SUV in park and twisted to give me one of his patented death glares.

"What. The. Fuck. Is that supposed to mean?"

I flicked a look at him and then turned my attention to the road ahead. And another metaphor for my life. "Just what I said. It's going to happen, it's just a question of when."

"That doesn't have to be true," he shot back. "You two don't have to be at odds."

"I have two words for you: Kensington artifacts. He's going to want that weapon. Hell, he's going to need it to take down Savannah."

"You want her gone, too."

I rolled my eyes. "You know it's inevitable that we'll lock horns. Maybe it won't be the artifacts. Maybe it will be another disagreement. Then you'll have to choose sides and you've already joined the business. Plus he's your *brother*. You can't let him down."

"But I can let you down?" Price's voice was as cold as glacier ice.

"I'm not saying you'll want to, but what's the choice? Like I said, reality sucks."

He faced away from me, his hands gripping the top of the steering wheel, knuckles turning white. Abruptly he jammed the SUV into drive and took off. I waited for him to say something, but the miles reeled away—and nothing. Finally, I turned back to looking out the window. My stomach ached, along with a knot in my throat.

I'm not sure how far we'd gone when he broke the wall of silence between us.

"I'm not going to lose either one of you," he said, grimly.

I wasn't worried about him *losing* me. I was worried about when he'd toss me aside.

"Riley?" he prodded when I didn't answer.

I bit my lower lip, tasting blood. "Sure," I said, because telling him he was delusional wasn't going to help. "You'll find a way."

Chapter 7

Gregg

GREGG WONDERED if he'd been shot in the head and was hallucinating. The last person who ought to be here was Taylor.

"Come on," she ordered, reaching out a hand.

He staggered toward her. Seeing the difficulty of his movements, she hopped out to help him inside. She held a mini Uzi and focused her attention behind him, shooting a short burst.

"Get the fuck in before you get hurt," he growled.

"You first."

Since the faster he moved, the faster she'd get the hell out of the line of fire, he did as told. Even though he hurried, his bullet wound and his half-frozen limbs made him clumsy and far too slow. Taylor grabbed his waistband and gave him a shove. He fell half across the green vinyl seat and half on the floor. She pushed his feet up out of the way as she clambered up onto the seat and slammed the door, sending a spike of blinding pain through his wounded leg.

"Go!"

But the driver had already hit the gas. They fishtailed and straightened. Taylor hooked her hand under Gregg's arm and helped him up onto the seat. He slumped awkwardly against the door, trying to breathe through the tide of agony. She scanned him critically.

"Got any leaks?"

"Bullet in my left calf."

She set her weapon between them on the seat and twisted to grab a first-aid kit from the back. She popped it open and fished out a woman's maxi-pad, along with a pressure bandage and a pair of medical scissors. She closed the box and set it on the floor.

"I need your leg."

Gregg didn't let his expression change as he twisted and lifted his foot. It hurt like fuck. She took it and set his heel on top of her knee. She cut a slice up his pants leg and peeled it away, flipping it back up over his thigh. She bent to look, her mouth pulling down.

As she worked, Gregg scrutinized her. She looked as beautiful as ever, despite the circles under her eyes and the tense line of her mouth. Her hands moved deftly and surely.

"Hold this for me," she said, taking the wrapping off the pad and pressing it to the bullet hole.

Gregg bit back a hiss. He sat forward and held the pad in place while she bound the bandage around it. When she was done, she lowered his foot back to the floor, wiping her fingers on her jeans, leaving dark bloody streaks.

He pushed himself more upright against the door.

"Do you want a painkiller?"

He shook his head. "No."

Taylor nodded as if she'd expected as much.

She eyed the driver. "Give me one of those heal-alls."

"Can't," Gregg said, holding up his arm. "Nulled."

Taylor frowned at it. "Did you escape or did Morrell let you go?" she asked.

Gregg hid his surprise. Again, he'd underestimated her. He wouldn't have thought she'd think Savannah letting him go was an option.

She turned away, looking outside, scanning ahead and turning to look behind. He knew she'd been a pilot over in the sandbox for private military groups. He had as much data on her as was available. He'd never been able to put that tough-as-nails pilot together with the fashion plate she usually portrayed. But she used the Uzi with comfort, and skill and she had that hypervigilance of someone who'd spent time getting shot at. Not to mention her dressing of his wound had been quick and efficient, with no qualms about the gore.

He flicked a glance at their driver. His brows furrowed. It couldn't be . . .

"That's Dalton," Taylor confirmed, once again seeming to read his mind. She gave a little shrug. "He's on our side for the moment."

The man in question cast a hard look over his shoulder at Taylor. His silver eyes were ringed with blue. Tinker mods.

"*Our* side?" Gregg asked, picking his gun back up and holding it ready in his lap, his gaze fixed on the man in front of him. Dalton's hair was long and black and bound in an elastic at the base of his neck. His neck was darker brown, revealing what Gregg imagined was likely Native American heritage.

"The side of the angels," she said with an ironic glance. "What else?"

He eyed the back of Dalton's head. The bastard worked for Taylor's and Riley's father, who was an enigma all on his own. Gregg had dug hard into the man's background and come up with next to nothing. Sam Hollis was a ghost. Except that he was very much alive and he held Dalton's leash, making the latter man supremely dangerous. His motives were unknown, except the last time Gregg had seen him, the man had been in the process of kidnapping Riley.

He sucked in a thin breath between his teeth. Was she alive? Was Clay alive? Was he free? He wanted to ask, but he wasn't sure he could handle the answer. He wasn't sure he was ready. So long as he didn't know for certain, Clay could be okay. *And if he were okay, wouldn't he be here instead of Taylor and her treacherous companion?*

The thought sent saw blades ripping through his gut. He swallowed, clenching his teeth. He refused to lose his shit. Not now. Not with Savannah to deal with. Not with witnesses to his pain.

Deciding he didn't want to reveal anything in front of Dalton, Gregg ignored Taylor's question. "Where are you taking me?"

"Safe house, unless you've a mind to do your thing and travel off somewhere."

"Can't. I'm nulled."

"Where is Riley when you need her?" Taylor murmured.

Present tense. Did that mean—Gregg could no longer hold back the question any longer "Is she okay? And Clay?"

Taylor shrugged. "As well as can be expected, all things considered."

Gregg drew a shaky breath and let it out, rubbing a hand over his face. Relief flooded through him. He closed his eyes against the burn of tears. *Alive.*

He looked at Taylor again. "What happened?"

"Long story," she said. "But your brother found his talent. Or maybe it found him."

He didn't know how to react to that. Her tone said it wasn't a particularly good thing Clay had come into his talent. "What is it?"

"Wind. Air. He does things with it." She waved her fingers.

"What kind of things?"

"Big." It was all she was willing to say, and from the look on her face, the memories weren't pretty.

Gregg bit back the rest of his questions. Distraction was a bad idea right now. All three needed their wits about them to keep from being discovered and tracked. Unless Dalton was driving them right into enemy hands, which Gregg wouldn't put past him.

"How do you know you can trust him?" he asked, jerking his chin at the man in question.

Taylor looked at Dalton, who kept his eyes fixed on the road. She didn't answer for a long minute. Gregg didn't know if she was considering her words or scrabbling to find an answer.

Finally, she spoke. "I'm not sure I do."

From his seat against the door, Gregg could see Dalton's knuckles whitening on the wheel. The Tahoe sped up fractionally. Not the answer Dalton had been wanting. But his reaction was interesting. He was emotionally invested in Taylor, whatever game he was playing. That he *was* playing one, Gregg was certain. The bastard worked for her father, who had set mental blocks in Riley's head to kill her if she tried to reveal certain of her secrets. The man nearly succeeded in killing her. Whatever Sam Hollis was up to, it was a deep game, and as one of his trusted soldiers, Dalton was hip deep in it.

"Should get that off him before we head back," Dalton said suddenly, his voice a low, rocky growl. "Might be a tracker inside."

"*Almost definitely* a tracker inside," Gregg amended.

"Who's got seriously tight security and will let us in?" Taylor asked.

"Hotels," Dalton replied. "Security binders and nulls would suck the juice out of that little thing." He made a turn and hit Marconi Avenue, leading down to one of the tunnels from the Rim into Uptown.

"How about the Pavilion? It's close," Taylor suggested.

"We won't get close in this bag of bolts," Gregg said. "Walking up won't help either. They'd take one look at us and throw us off the property. We'd never make the first security circle."

"Got another suggestion?"

Taylor's look was challenging and none too friendly. She'd never been his biggest fan. She blamed him for the kidnapping and torture of her former fiancé. She had some cause, Gregg had to admit. He hadn't kidnapped or tortured Josh, but he had stolen him from the real culprits, intending to keep Josh prisoner until he gave up the information he had on the Kensington artifacts. The same artifacts Savannah had her panties in a wad for.

He'd also barged into her hangar and home, beefing up security when it was clear her relationship to Clay, Riley, and himself made her a target. She'd been none too thrilled about that.

Gregg closed his eyes and swallowed, his head starting to feel thick and cottony. Blood loss, he supposed. Maybe shock. The chill was wearing off, and his skin flared with fiery heat. He rubbed his hand over his mouth and focused. "A bank could work. Wouldn't need to be open. In fact, better if it's not."

Taylor scowled at him. "Are you going to pass out?"

As if it were his fault. "Maybe."

She grimaced and looked behind the seat again. Gregg heard a zipper and some rustling. When she sat back in her seat, she held a piss-yellow bottle of Gatorade. Taylor twisted off the cap and handed it to him. "Drink it all."

"Yes, ma'am." He swigged it. Warm and way too sweet. But he needed the fluids and electrolytes, so he guzzled the rest.

Dalton swerved down an alley as they came up on a line of backed-up traffic. Drivers and passengers stood in the road and on the sidewalks as they gazed toward a fire that was maybe three miles away at most.

Which explosion was it? The elementary school? The recital? There was no way to know. Gregg ground his teeth together. Somehow he had to stop Savannah. Without letting her have the artifacts. Whether he gave them to her or not, a bloodbath was inevitable. No, there had to be a way to handle her without giving access to yet another weapon.

What did she care about? Not her husband, Whit. At least not enough to give up her ambitions for his safety. She had no children. She had a brother somewhere, but had never shown an interest in him. He could hit her in the wallet, but she had money coming out her ass. It would take a lot to bring her to her knees that way, more than he had time for, maybe more than he might be capable of. That left physical harm. That was his best hope, but she had incredible security. Getting to her would take a war he might not win, and if he did, it wouldn't be before she leveled the city. He'd been trying for months to kill her with no success. Now he had all of thirty-six hours to get it done.

Once again he ran a hand over his mouth, scowling.

"What?" Taylor asked.

He twisted to face her. "What?" he echoed.

Her mouth tightened in impatience. "What's that look on your face about?"

Gregg cut a glance at Dalton. "Considering the future," he said.

"And it's not so bright?"

He gave a grim smile. "What do you think?"

"These explosions tonight have something to do with you, don't they?" Dalton asked from the front.

Gregg scraped his teeth over his lower lip. He wanted nothing more than to punch the other man in the back of the head and toss him out of the Tahoe. The man was trouble. Gregg had had Dalton imprisoned in a set of cells impossible to escape from, and Dalton had done just that, along with Percy Caldwell, the man who'd tortured Riley and who was responsible for the Sparkle Dust trade in Diamond City. The drug was instantly addictive and turned its users into wraiths—literally. They slowly faded from the skin inward until there was nothing left of them. Gregg still had no idea how the two men had escaped, and he dearly wanted to know.

Both Taylor and Dalton waited on his answer. "It was a message, yes."

"Which was?" Taylor prompted.

"Do what Savannah says or she'll level the city."

Taylor stared at him, her mouth open. Dalton eyed him in the rearview.

"She's serious?" Taylor asked finally.

"What do you think?" Gregg said, bitterness filling his mouth. He wanted nothing more than to spit. The Tahoe's windows were manual, otherwise he'd have rolled his down and done just that.

"She's insane," Taylor murmured, slumping back against her seat.

"She's a sociopath," Dalton corrected from the front seat.

Gregg bit his tongue before he could tell the silver-eyed bastard to go fuck himself. Not that he was wrong. Savannah *was* a sociopath.

"What does she want you to do?" Taylor asked, her voice thin but unwavering.

Gregg eyed her appreciatively. Beautiful, smart, and brave. She was sturdier stuff than he'd thought. He pulled himself away from thinking about her. Taylor was off-limits. They were practically related, for one. She despised him, for two, and for three, he wasn't interested in anything more than a quick fuck. Those reasons neatly put Taylor on his "Don't Touch" list. Didn't mean he couldn't admire the scenery, though.

He flicked a meaningful look at Dalton and then back to Taylor. He gave a firm shake of his head. He wasn't going to reveal Savannah's demands to the bastard. Gregg wasn't even sure he wanted Taylor to know.

She let out an annoyed breath and turned away. "Where are we going?" she asked Dalton.

"Mercury on the south side. Should be able to get there. It's far enough from the explosions."

Gregg nodded approval of the choice. He had accounts at the bank. The Uptown south branch would have excellent security and be very visible, to pacify any fears of the wealthy clientele they served. Their security web started a good five yards beyond the building. They had multiple rings of binders and nulls to suck the energy out of any active spells. That made it difficult for some clients who either had to deactivate all spells they carried or worry about them being destroyed. But a bank would be negligent not to protect itself from hostile magic. Since you couldn't predict what a thief might use in a robbery, it was better to lock down everything. Besides, a bank without certain levels of protection wouldn't get deposit insurance, which meant they wouldn't get customers.

The rest of the ride was silent. Gregg suppressed the urge to ask about Clay and how they'd broken him out of federal custody. He'd wait until he had Taylor alone, or better yet, talk to Clay himself. He damned well wasn't going to say anything in front of the bastard in the front seat.

Dalton pulled up next to the bank parking lot. An iron fence surrounded the grounds. A guard shack stood within the closed gate, a flickering light inside indicating a guard was watching TV.

"There," Taylor said, pointing as they rolled around the corner at the back of the bank.

Dalton pulled over and shut off the engine and lights. He thrust open the door. "Let's make this quick."

Taylor jumped out, slinging the strap of the Uzi over her shoulder. Dalton held another. Gregg opened his door and eased out on his good leg, staggering a little as he stood up. He left the Glock on the seat. He didn't trust Dalton not to put a bullet in his back, but he couldn't do what was needed with his hands full.

Fire roared up his leg as he took his first step. His knee started to buckle. He locked it, issuing a string of profanity in a low voice.

"Quiet!" Taylor ordered in a harsh whisper against his ear. She smelled of gasoline, smoky cinnamon, and something spicy, like cardamom. She hooked her hand in his armpit and pulled him forward. Dalton walked just to the side to have a clear line of fire behind and ahead.

They went around the front of the car, feet crunching on the snow and ice. On the other side, a berm of snow rose three-quarters of the way up on the other side of the fence. It had drifted through the bars so that the hill on the near side was just as tall. Getting close enough to the protection spells to take off the null would be a matter of stepping over the three or four feet of iron fence protruding from the top. The hardest part would be avoiding the close-together spikes on top.

"Keep an eye out for security," Taylor told Dalton in a low voice. If the bank guard looked up from whatever show he was streaming and checked the camera feeds, he'd be sure to come running, along with all his security friends.

Dalton took up a position on the sidewalk with a clear line of fire toward the corners of the building and the street.

"Are you going to manage this?" Taylor asked Gregg, pressing close so he could hear.

"No choice," he said, trying not to lean on her as they stepped up on the bank of snow.

He sank about a foot before hitting an ice crust. Those would be layered beneath like frosting on stacked cakes. It was the nature of winter in Diamond City. Snow followed by sunshine and melting followed by freezes. Rinse and repeat.

Taylor kept her hand under his arm, steadying him when his leg refused to hold him. Gregg gritted his teeth, willing strength back into it. When they reached the fence, she slung her gun behind her.

"You ever been lifted up onto a horse?" she asked.

He scowled at her. "No. Why?"

"Bend your knee at a right angle with your foot behind you. Like that." She gripped the calf of his bent leg. "You jump and I'll lift. Trust me. This works."

He didn't have much choice. Turning to the fence, he grasped the top bar just below the spikes. Those were wicked, with rapier points and four razor edges on each flared flange. Set in rows of three, they meant business. He had to clear them or be gutted.

"Ready?" Taylor didn't wait for his reply. "Jump."

He thrust himself upward. Taylor's jackknife lift gave him surprising loft. He went over head first, kicking his feet up as he cleared the spikes. Almost cleared. Searing pain swiped down his wounded shin.

Gregg sprawled facedown on the other side of fence. His mouthful of snow helped suppress the loud expletives crowding his tongue. Not wasting time, he forced himself upright, staggering toward the building.

He didn't feel security web. Riley would have. At the thought of her, relief that she was alive cascaded through him. She and Clay. Riley was the key to the puzzle of the Kensington weapon. He just had to convince her to help him. His jaw knotted as he remembered Savannah and his deadline. A darkly pragmatic part of him wondered if it would have been better if Riley had died. Savannah wouldn't have the tracer she needed to find Kensington's long lost workshop and the instructions on putting the weapon together and using it. Then again, Savannah was awfully sure she could use them, and he didn't think she was counting on Riley. Just as well. It would devastate Clay to lose Riley, and Gregg wasn't about to do that to his brother.

"Done?" Taylor called in a low voice.

Gregg staggered backward nearly to the fence and reached for his power. It filled him like a dog seeing its master for the first time in a month. He let it go, and nodded.

"Done." He eyed the fence. He wasn't getting over without help. But then, he didn't have to.

He opened himself to the dream plain. Colors swirled among shapes that stretched and collapsed then split into a thousand tatters and melded with something else. This was creation, or as close to it as anybody on earth would ever get. It stretched out in every direction, as big as the universe, as big as life itself.

Gregg dove in, focusing on the patch of sidewalk next to the Tahoe. Around him, the scene formed. With a twist of his mind, he stepped out. Fell out, really. His leg collapsed. He'd have crashed to the ground if he hadn't caught himself on the door of the battered SUV.

Taylor whirled, then joined him, bounding over the snow like a deer. She wrapped her arm around his waist and yanked open the door. With a helpful shove, she pushed him onto the seat and followed after. By that time, Dalton was back behind the wheel and dropping into gear.

Gregg leaned back against the seat. His leg throbbed and burned. He swallowed back the bile that rose in his throat. He didn't have time for pain. He had work to do.

He sat up just as Taylor leaned over and dropped a necklace over his head. She slipped the pendant under his collar next to his skin.

"That should take care of you," she said, then reached behind the seat for a towel that had seen better days. She wrapped it around his leg.

He eyed her with raised brows.

"Don't need you getting blood everywhere," she said, and something in her voice made it sound like it was his fault he'd been shot and had cut his leg to ribbons.

Gregg said nothing. Worms of healing magic rooted through him, finding any damage and fixing it. It was a noxious feeling, but better than bleeding to death. He leaned back and shut his eyes, waiting for the heal-all to finish its work.

"Clay's really okay?"

His question was met with an ominous silence. "He's having difficulty with his talent."

He twisted to look at Taylor. "What does that mean?"

She gave a shrug. "Just what it sounds like. He's having trouble managing it."

Gregg scraped his teeth over his lower lip, trying not to swear at her. Better he talked to Clay.

"Where is he?"

"Out of town."

"Son of a fucking bitch. Give me a goddamn answer!"

She shook her head. "I'll give you his number when we get to the safe house. That's the best I can do."

Because she didn't trust him. No more than she trusted the bastard behind the wheel. He couldn't blame her, even though he wanted to wring her neck.

"How long until we get there?"

"Depends on traffic." She gestured at the flashing lights, to soften the nonanswer.

Gregg blew out a harsh breath and closed his eyes again, the worming feeling intensifying around the wound on this leg. He could have just travelled to one of his homes, but he needed a better weapon than a handgun, and he needed intel.

"How long has Savannah had me?"

Another ominous silence. "Almost three weeks."

"Fuck."

"Yep."

"All right. Tell me what's been going on. Tell me everything."

Chapter 8

Riley

PRICE AND I MADE it to Diamond City in just over seven hours. We drove along South Rim Road of the massive caldera that provided a perch for Diamond City. It poured like an architectural avalanche down one side on three major shelves plus the rim level. The caldera was as deep as the mountain above used to be tall. The bottom was full of snow, with an ice-covered lake and a river running through it. Snow-sugared forested peaks rose up all around, and tall cedars and pines crowded up against the road.

Lead clouds humped low in the midday sky, and flurries of snow threatened another storm later. The inside of our vehicle remained quiet and tense. Price's face might as well have been carved from rock. He hadn't said more than a handful of words since we left the safe house near Durango, and I had stopped trying to make conversation. I wasn't sure if he was mad because I recognized the truth of the situation, or because I'd assumed he'd choose his brother over me. I still couldn't imagine him doing anything else.

We could see emergency lights strobing as we circled around to the city. It looked like a red, white, and blue disco party.

"This looks bad," I murmured, then remembered that my brothers had equipped the crew-cab truck with a police-band radio. I flipped it on. Within minutes we'd learned that hours before there'd been a series of six explosions in the city. The hospitals were overwhelmed, as were the emergency response teams. Price and I exchanged a look. I pulled out my phone and dialed Patti first.

She picked up after two rings. "We're fine," she said. "It's gridlock out there. Not sure how you're going to get into Downtown. See you when you get here."

She didn't wait for an answer but hung up. The diner must have been busy.

Next I dialed Taylor. She didn't pick up. I dialed Leo, then Jamie. Same thing. My stomach coiled into knots.

"They aren't answering," I said, even though Price could clearly tell that was the case.

"Do you have Dalton's number?"

I gave him a startled look. To say Price didn't like Dalton was like saying seals don't like polar bears. He despised the man, and for good reason: Dalton used to be—and probably still was—my father's loyal henchman. I knew he owed Vernon for something big, like saving his life. He'd helped rescue Price on Vernon's orders, and then joined up with my Scooby squad because of the experiments he and Taylor had discovered in the FBI building where Price had been held for torture. Experiments that Vernon had also known about, which put the two on the outs. He'd become Taylor's shadow. Calling him was worth a try.

He answered before the first ring finished. "Yes?"

"Taylor and my brothers aren't picking up. Is everything okay?" I spoke fast and sharp. I didn't like Dalton much either. Yes, he'd helped break Price out of the FBI torture chamber, and yes, he'd been working to protect me before that. But he'd also tried to kidnap me. *And* he worked for my father. Supposedly he didn't work for Vernon anymore, but I'd believe that when monkeys flew out my ass.

Dalton's hesitation didn't bode well. I bit my tongue so I wouldn't swear at him to hurry the hell up.

"There have been developments."

I managed not to reach through the phone and rip his head off. "Explain."

"Mr. Touray is free. We are taking him to safety now."

"Free?" I clenched a hand on Price's arm. "He escaped? He's okay? Is he hurt?"

Dalton didn't answer. I heard the sounds of fumbling, and then Taylor came on the phone.

"He's been shot, but we gave him one of Dalton's healing pendants."

"You're taking him to the safe house in the Bottoms?"

"Unless he travels off on his own."

Price was shooting me looks, his expression burning with hope.

"Touray's free. He's going to be okay," I told him. Then to Taylor, "How did he escape?"

"He didn't."

"Then how——?"

"I don't have the full story."

"Okay. We're coming into the city now. I've got a trace I need to do and then we'll meet you at the safe house."

"*Can* you trace?"

That's my sister. Direct and to the heart of the matter. Since she'd know if I were lying, I didn't bother. "Think so. It hurts, still, but this can't wait. I shouldn't have to do anything more than a trace, though."

"Good. See that you don't. If you die, I will not forgive you. If I can, I'll meet you at the diner later."

With that, the phone cut out. I made a face at it and slid it back in my pocket.

"What did she say?" Price's hands were tight on the wheel. The air in our vehicle pressed hard against me, as taut and tense as he was. I rolled my window down to see if that would cut the pressure. It did, but it also froze me to the bone.

"Sorry." He rolled my window up again, and though a breeze continued to blow through the vehicle, I no longer felt like I might suffocate.

I repeated my terse conversation. He sagged back against his seat in relief.

"Thank God." He thought a moment and scowled. "What did she mean——

Gregg didn't escape? Why would Savannah let him go? Or maybe someone in her organization did it?"

"No idea. We'll find out soon enough. But first we have to get to the diner. It's a fucking mess down there."

We pulled into an overlook near the southern entrance into Diamond City. A smoky haze made it tough to see any details of the city. The stench was bad. Chemical and rubber and wood and tar. Breathing it gave me a headache and made my throat hurt.

"We're not going to get to the diner until late tonight in this mess." Price crouched at the edge of the overlook. "Subway will be down. If there's a chance of tunnel collapse—natural or not—protocol is to close it. We're going to have to hoof it if we want to get anywhere."

I nodded and pushed to my feet. "Better get started, then."

He tossed me a glance. "Or we find a bike."

That was code for "steal a motorcycle." He sure as hell wasn't talking about the pedal variety. "Sure," I said, helping him up. "Let's go."

Archer Highway, the southern artery into the city, was a six-lane road. It was backed up all the way to the Rim. A parking structure on the west side offered a place to stash the truck. We locked it, invoking the stay-away charms tied to the mechanism with an extra sweep of one finger, before shouldering our packs and heading out to the road.

A red neon sign for the subway station just below the parking structure flashed *Closed*. That made me happy. I hated being underground. Or in small spaces like elevators. Just going into my basement turned me into a gibbering idiot. I'm not a coward. I use the subway and elevators whenever I have to. I just prefer with all my soul not to.

It was cold enough outside that people sat in their cars with the motors running. Sooner or later they'd run out of gas. I wondered what they'd do then. Of course, they'd probably need bathrooms long before that. I didn't let myself think about how they'd solve that problem.

Finding a ride wasn't going to be so easy. Any bikers who might have been caught by the gridlock had just ridden between the stopped cars and gone about their business. All the same, we had to find something. The diner was still a good forty miles away.

Price is a strong man. He's got a whole lot of muscle and hardly any fat, but he doesn't spend a lot of time walking, or jogging for that matter. And he was barely recovered from a first-class torturing. We'd gone about three miles when he began to slow down. I was kicking along at a rapid pace. I walked just about everywhere unless I was in a hurry. In the summers, I used a bicycle. The winters, I grabbed an occasional cab or, more likely, I suffered through a subway ride. I hadn't done a lot of walking in the last few months, but my body hadn't forgotten how, and my joints and muscles only ached a little until I warmed up.

"You okay?" I asked.

"I'm upright and breathing," was Price's sardonic reply.

"Got any ideas where we're going to find a bike? There's a shop about ten miles or so from here. We could head for it. Break in."

He shook his head. "Once we hit Downtown, we'll find something. Bikes are a lot easier to have in the city, not to mention less expensive and easier to park."

A few miles later, we reached the long, sloping ramp into Downtown. It went through the Jeffrey Michael Howe tunnel, aka the JMH. The tunnel snaked back and forth in four lazy curves. A sidewalk ran alongside, and more than a few people had been killed walking it. Demands for a covered stairway to Downtown had been met with inaction. Tonight, though, traffic wasn't an issue. Breathing was. Well, that and being in a teensy tiny tunnel.

Motors continued to run, filling the zigzag space with carbon dioxide clouds. The areas without a direct opening to fresh air would be bad. "This could get dicey," I said. "We need to go quick."

"At least it's downhill," Price said. "Lead the way."

I broke into a fast jog. Luckily, the sidewalk wasn't icy. I wasn't going to slip and fracture my ass. Behind me, I heard the reassuring thump of Price's feet. He had a longer stride than I did, so I put on a little more speed.

By the time I'd reached the second turn, I'd forgotten what oxygen tasted like. My mouth and nose were filled with cloying fumes. My lungs ached from trying to sort oxygen from the miasma. I didn't think the motorists were in any real danger, unless they had asthma problems. Vents in the tunnel ceiling every twenty feet or so allowed some of the exhaust to escape. I slowed whenever I passed under one.

At the bottom, I flung myself outside and braced myself against the wall. My lungs bellowed, and I gasped. Price leaned beside me, his face flushed and sweat gleaming along his cheeks beneath his knit hat.

"I may have just developed stage ten emphysema," I said before breaking into a hoarse cough that sounded a lot like a donkey braying. If that donkey smoked a dozen cigars a day for fifty years.

"Is there a stage ten?" Price panted.

"There is now."

After we managed to gulp enough oxygen to breathe normally again, we speed-walked down into a nearby residential area. Lights were still working here. People stood in clusters on street corners and in apartment parking lots, staring off toward one of the emergency sites and talking rapidly.

We sidled up to one group. "What happened?" I asked.

A dark-skinned man wearing a heavy flannel jacket lined in fleece glanced at me with suspicion. "An explosion. Six of them. Where the hell have you been?"

"We just drove in from Mesa," Price lied. "Haven't been listening to the radio. What was blown up? Was it terrorism?"

A woman about the same age as the man, her arms folded tight just above a swelling belly, shook her head. "News says it was Carre Elementary, Sacred Heart Church, Café Trevor, Keyes Inn, the Andrea Movie Complex, and the Wallace-Lees Medical Center." Tears rolled down the woman's cheeks, and the man pulled her into an embrace. "What kind of monster would do this?"

"Damn sure someone ought to pay," an older woman said, a scarf covering her curlers. She wore a print dress, with heavy tights, and sweater pulled over it.

Another man snorted. He was wiry and small, with long brown hair and glasses. "Cops don't care. Tyets drop money in their pockets like Vegas gambling machines and they pay out in favors and cover-ups. Isn't going to be any justice. You can bet one or more Tyets will be hitting back. Gonna be a war. Be a smart time to get the hell out of the city."

I pulled Price away. His body was rigid, his hands clenched into fists. He shook with rage.

"Whoever did this is going to pay and pay hard." He spoke through clenched teeth. "I'll make sure of it."

"We," I reminded him. "We will make sure of it." I spoke quietly, but my blood burned, and if I could have, I'd have dropped the bombers into a wood-chipper and watched them scream.

He glanced at me and gave a short nod. We both knew that there was nothing we could do right now. It was going to take research, planning, and man power.

We wandered through the gridlock until we found a residential area and a likely target in the shape of a pair of bikes parked under a carport beside a tidy blue pillbox of a house. Snow mounded on the front lawn of the house and blocked most of the driveway, except for a cleared path from the carport to the street and another to the front door.

"What now?" I asked. I could pick a lock, and back in the storage cabinet in my house I had a couple of spells to open electronic locks. But when it came to vehicles, I was about useless, except for maybe cheering Price on. I just didn't have experience swiping them.

Priced glanced at the sky and then up and down the street. The sun had already begun to set, but there were people still on the sidewalks and moving in and out of their houses.

"We need to wait until it's darker and it quiets down. There's a steak house a couple miles from here. Let's go get something to eat and warm up."

I wanted to argue, but I was freezing and starving, not to mention thirsty as hell. When he took my hand and slid it inside his coat pocket with his, that warmed me more than just about anything else could have done. I squeezed his hand.

We returned around three hours later, after a good meal. I felt a lot better and the exercise of the day, while making my muscles ache, also felt good. It was good to be outside. Price had been quiet, but he'd managed to find ways to touch me all along—holding hands, nudging up against my leg with his, rubbing his shoulder against mine.

The street of our target house was empty now, and flickering lights inside a couple places revealed TVs. Hopefully everybody was glued to the news reports and wouldn't notice us.

"Wait here," Price ordered, striding under the carport. He carried himself like he had a right to be there.

After about three minutes, he wheeled one of the bikes out of the driveway and kept going up the street. All I knew about the machine was that it was a Honda, which I read off the orange gas tank. It looked older, like it had been well used. Price waited until we were two blocks away before he pulled out his pocket knife and set about hot-wiring the ignition. A minute later, the bike started with a rumbling growl.

"Nice work."

Price threw his leg over the seat with a grin, reaching out to steady me as I slid on behind. I wrapped my arms around his waist.

"Ready?"

I nodded, and he hit the accelerator, shifting gears smoothly.

Even aboard the bike, it took us another three hours or so to get to the diner. We kept running into roadblocks and detours, and a couple of times stopped to help push stalled cars off the road. A lot had run out of gas, and the owners had walked away to find warmth. By the time we arrived, it was nearly midnight.

Despite being closed for two hours, lights still gleamed inside. This area was pretty well protected from the electrical issues plaguing much of the rest of the city. A copshop was right across the street, with a hospital a couple miles away. The whole area was on a side system with its own backup generators fueled by magic.

Price went around behind the diner and pulled into the parking lot, stopping by the dumpster. He shut off the bike. I slid off. My face ached with cold. I'd pulled my coat up as high as I could, but the chill of the wind crept beneath and burrowed into my bones. Price swung his leg over the seat and stood, pulling his gun from his pocket and thumbing back the hammer. He didn't do unprepared.

I drew my own weapon, holding it at my side as he went to the door. He depressed the handle. It didn't open.

"It's locked," he told me.

"We could go around front."

He shook his head. "Better we stay out of sight. Knock and let them know we are here."

I pulled my right glove off with my teeth and gave a couple of sharp raps against the steel. We waited. Price shifted so that he stood behind me with clear views of both the parking lot and the door. He lifted his gun, pointing toward the street. I didn't question him. At the moment, we were fugitives from both the law and most of the criminals, which meant about sixty or seventy percent of Diamond City was hunting for us. Assuming they knew we were alive.

Preparation paid off when a figure stepped into the alley opening. I recognized him immediately.

"What are you doing here?" Price called out coldly, not lowering the barrel of his gun.

The gunfire sounded like the quick pop of popcorn or firecrackers. Price shoved me against the door, slamming hard into my back. The breath went out of me with a whoosh.

I heard at least a dozen quick shots, and the ping of bullets striking the dumpster and building.

Sudden silence.

All I could hear was Price's ragged breathing in syncopation with my own. The air hung preternaturally still. Price must have used his talent to block any more shots.

"Are you okay?"

"Are you?"

"I'm fine. Tell me, are you hit?"

"I don't think so, but the way you knocked me against the door, I might have a broken rib."

Hesitation. "I didn't touch you."

I looked down at myself. I couldn't see a hole in my jacket, but then there didn't have to be one. If I'd been shot, it would have struck me in the back. Nothing said it had to come back out. I did notice a feeling of wet warmth and a tickling trickle beginning along my spine.

I heard Price's breath suck in and then felt pain explode like fireworks in my chest as my brain finally caught up to me having a bullet drill through me.

"Shit, not again," I mumbled. A wave of dizziness, and then my leg bones disintegrated. I felt myself falling and then endless cold.

Chapter 9

Gregg

DALTON WOVE THROUGH the city, dropping to the Downtown shelf through the Excelsior Tunnel. Almost immediately they ran into gridlock. Sirens wailed and red, white, and blue lights strobed across the area. A heavy cloud of acrid smoke hung low overhead.

"Park it," Taylor said to Dalton. "We'll walk."

Parking was easier said than done. Nothing moved. Dalton swerved up onto a sidewalk and then into an alley, scraping between a lamppost and a BMW with a metallic screech. The owner of the Beamer would not be happy.

Inside the alley, he found the entrance to an underground parking garage. Above sat a squat tower, the first floor filled with businesses, the upper floors devoted to apartments. Dalton pulled into a slot marked *Customer Parking Only*.

Taylor popped open the rear of the Tahoe and fished out a loose jacket made of Thinsulate and slid it on, hiding her Uzi beneath. She handed Gregg a knit hat and a pair of gloves. He'd lost his. He couldn't remember where.

"Don't have socks, I'm afraid," she said as she passed him a packet of chemical hand warmers. "Break those and stuff them in your shoes. Should help."

He did as told, shoving them down to his toes. It wasn't comfortable, but he'd gladly exchange a couple of blisters for warm feet.

Another car entered the garage, and they each stiffened, watching as it pulled into another slot. A woman sat inside. She gave them a thumbs up as she talked into her phone. Apparently, she'd thought Dalton's sidewalk trick worth emulating.

Taylor and Dalton rifled through the rest of their gear, stuffing some into a pair of backpacks. Before she could put hers on, Gregg grabbed it.

"I'll carry it."

She scowled at him. Before she could rip him a new asshole, he shrugged. "You've got the Uzi and you know where we're going. It's smarter to have you unencumbered."

Her lip curled slightly, but she nodded. "Fine." She cast a glance at Dalton. "Ready?"

"Let's move," he replied.

She headed up the parking ramp exit. Gregg fell in on her right and slightly behind. Dalton brought up the rear. That made Gregg's entire body itch. *Never put your back to your enemy.* Not that he had a choice at the moment.

He overtook Taylor just outside the entrance. "Where are we going?"

"Safe house, like I said."

"I don't have much time."

She darted him a sideways glance, then went back to scanning their surroundings. She kept close to the wall, her Uzi held ready against her stomach. "Got a party to get to?" she asked.

"A funeral is more like it," he said.

"Care to explain?"

He glanced over his shoulder at Dalton. "It's a little crowded for my taste."

"Suit yourself."

Taylor crossed the street, slipping between cars like a shadow. Gregg and Dalton followed closely.

"How far?" Gregg asked on the other side.

"Few miles, then a few miles more," she said with a taunting smile this time.

"Jesus fuck," Gregg muttered. "I don't have time for games," he growled.

"Then shut your pie hole and walk faster, or use your talent and Tinker Bell off somewhere else. We won't miss you."

By God, he was tempted. He grimaced. "I need to hear what's been happening since I was taken, and I could use some weapons and clothing before I get back."

"Then stop dawdling."

The sidewalks were mostly clear of ice, making progress easier. Gregg paid attention to the signs, marking their journey on a mental map. They were heading north, staying close to the escarpment dividing the Downtown shelf from the Midtown shelf.

They'd gone about four miles when Taylor abruptly turned into Royer Park, a three-hundred acre expanse of meadows, trees, and bushes. On the east side was a pavilion for musical performances and Shakespeare in the Park. Beside it were baseball diamonds, a soccer field, and large dog park. Those took up maybe a fifth of the park. The rest was a nature preserve—untended and wild.

Taylor strode up under the trees, pushing between bushes and slogging through drifts of snow.

"If this is a shortcut, it stinks on ice," Gregg pointed out.

She ignored him. Her silence made him want to shake some words out of her. Or force them out with spankings and other pleasurable punishments. He snorted inwardly. He didn't have time for idle distraction, no matter how enjoyable it promised to be. He caught himself up short, a bit unnerved that he had to keep reminding himself that if he fucked Riley's sister, Clay would have him by the short hairs. She was hands-off. *Look, but don't even think of touching.*

He'd have to convince his cock of that. But just at the moment, he decided watching her sweet ass swinging along in front of him was a reasonable compromise.

Finally, they stopped. Brambles and bushes crowded the path, and wind whistled in the branches of the cedars looming overhead. Before Gregg could ask what came next, Taylor ducked down, pushing aside the branches of a holly bush with a stick. She slipped under.

Gregg heard a grating sound. What the hell? He crouched, copying Taylor as he used his branch to shove aside the prickly leaves. Underneath was a hollow place about two feet by two feet wide. A hole gaped in the ground. Gregg crawled under the bush and looked inside. A ladder led downward. Darkness filled the hole.

"Taylor?"

"Shut up and get your ass down here," she called, her voice little more than a whisper.

Gregg swung down, wrapping his gloved hands around the outside of the ladder and clamping his feet likewise on the outside, and slid down. The drop was about twenty feet. He hit bottom with a sudden jolt that jarred his bones and made his teeth clack together. He stepped aside as a shadow blocked the light above. Dalton slid down in the same manner as Gregg, landing with catlike grace. Before he'd made it halfway, the hatch above started to slide shut.

The inky blackness lasted only a moment. Strips of small lights came alive along the floor and ceiling. They stood in a small hollow about fifteen feet across and twenty feet long. Just ahead of them was a track that vanished into dark tunnel mouths on either side. Sitting on the track was a cigar-shaped vehicle. It looked like the bastard child of a Coors can and an Airstream trailer. Both ends had consoles with buttons and levers. Between were eight bench seats, each wide enough to hold one person.

"Get aboard," Taylor said, going to the left side. She grabbed a handle set above the empty window opening and slid inside, feetfirst. She dropped into the seat behind the console and began flipping switches and pressing buttons. White lights flickered alive along the underside of the car's canopy. The interior matched the polished steel exterior, except for the dark blue upholstery cushioning the seats.

Copying Taylor, Dalton lifted himself and slid feetfirst inside, taking the last seat, farthest from Taylor. Gregg just stood agape.

Taylor twisted to look at him. "I thought you were in a hurry."

"What the hell is this?"

"Private subway," she said, flashing a grin at his shock. "Now get aboard or we'll leave your ass here."

He didn't doubt that she would. He grabbed a handle and swung himself inside. He'd barely sat down before Taylor flipped on five brilliant headlights and the car started rolling.

"Keep your body parts inside," she called. "Tunnel gets tight."

With that, the car shot like a bullet into the darkness. Gregg's heart leaped into his throat at the sudden acceleration. The wheels made a slight whirring sound, but otherwise the silence was complete.

"Here comes the tricky part," Taylor said. "Hold on to your butts."

With that warning, the car tipped downward and spiraled around and around like water spinning down a drain. Gregg gripped the windowsill to balance himself as centrifugal pressure pushed him against the wall of the car.

He was dizzy by the time they straightened out. They didn't slow down. If anything, they increased speed, shooting off in a straight line that seemed impossible. Unless—"Are we *under* the Bottoms?"

"Very good, Mr. Touray. You get a prize," Taylor said, not looking away from the passage ahead.

The tunnel walls whipped past. He had no idea how fast they were going, but it couldn't have been less than seventy miles per hour. They'd gone another twenty minutes when they started to descend again. The slope reminded him of a roller coaster's plunge, except it went on for a full minute. At last they flattened out and began a long, steep climb. They never slowed down. The car was powered by spells cast by powerful mages. Questions popcorned in Gregg's brain. Who had built it? Who did it belong to? Taylor and Riley's family? How had they done it? When? Why? Where did it go?

At the top of the grade, the tunnel split. They glided into the right-hand passage, curving in a lazy arc. After another ten minutes or so, they slowed to a soft halt. As they arrived, lights along the platform burst the darkness. The cavern was nearly identical to the previous one, except for a walking passage that led off to the right.

Taylor shut down the car, snapping off the lights before grabbing the handle above the window and swinging through. Gregg and Dalton had already disembarked. Gregg eyed the other man through narrowed eyes. Dalton stared back, expressionless. Blue still ringed his silver eyes. Gregg wished to hell he knew what the other man could see. Certainly infrared and heat signatures. But what else? Distances, short and far? Magic? Smells? The possibilities were many.

"Coming?" Without waiting for an answer, Taylor crawled up the rungs of the exit ladder with fluid grace, pressing her hand against a spot on the wall that betrayed no indications it was anything but a stone face. Instantly, a trapdoor slid away and a burst of chill, dank air washed down over them. Taylor climbed through.

Gregg waved at Dalton to follow. He didn't want the man behind him any more than necessary. Dalton gave a knowing smirk and clambered up.

They stood inside yet another tunnel. It had tool marks along the walls, indicating it had been part of a mine. Taylor shut the hatch and started walking into the darkness. She pulled a headlamp out of her pocket, donning it and turning it on. Dalton did likewise.

They hadn't gone far before they came to a branching. Taylor turned sharply down the left-hand passage, striding quickly. It wasn't long before he caught a whiff of fresh air cutting through the cave smell. His breath plumed white. Then suddenly they were stepping out of the cave onto ground smothered in pine needles and clots of snow. Close-growing cedars and firs stood to either side, their drooping limbs brushing his hair as he passed below.

The path wiggled and snaked, the wall of trees occasionally giving way to a towering boulder before resuming again.

The path kept going, breaking up as trees and bushes encroached. Most of the bushes trailed wicked bramble vines, making it unlikely that intruders would accidentally find their way through. Not that anybody spent time exploring the Bottoms. Those who came down to the bottom of the caldera stayed in the wart of a town where they could disappear from the law and buy the drugs and other illicit items they desired. The caldera bottom contained no roads. The only ways down were a walking path and the massive elevator system for the mines on the western wall. In the winter the caldera bottom filled with snow. In summer, it smelled fetid, the many square miles of boggy center surrounding the lake and river sweltering and swarming with biting bugs.

Taylor stepped off the path, through a niche between two sugar pines, and disappeared beneath a drooping curtain of winter-blackened vines. Dalton followed and then Gregg. Thorns scraped his cheek and hooked on his jacket. It took a moment for him to disentangle himself. When he turned around, he found they'd arrived.

A small log cabin sat ten feet away. Trees grew close around it. Bushes and brambles peeked through the snow piled on the roof. The whole place faded into the forest like it wasn't even there. It took a moment for Gregg to distinguish the building from the disguising foliage. Someone flying a drone and looking for it would be hard put to see it.

"Christ," he murmured with no little admiration as Taylor opened the door.

He was reaching for his gun before he was aware of the why. Taylor's body stiffened, and she jerked back slightly, as if she'd been slapped. She hesitated on the threshold, then moved stiffly inside.

Gregg wanted to elbow Dalton aside, but the other man was hard on her heels, his weapon raised. Gregg brought up his Glock as he followed.

His two companions stood in the entry, buttery light radiating from lamps in the living room beyond. The smell of roasting meat filled the air, mixing with smoke from a woodstove. The air was warm and should have been inviting after their journey, and yet Gregg felt like he'd stepped onto a live firing range.

"What the fuck are you doing here?" Taylor demanded, fury radiating off her like summer heat off the pavement. "You're like a cockroach, turning up wherever you aren't wanted and—"

She broke off. Gregg edged to the left to look around her, his gun still raised. The living room beyond was far larger than the front of the cabin promised. It was filled with cozy couches and chairs, with a woodstove sitting in a stone alcove in the corner. A man stood facing the doorway, hands behind his back. He had silver-blond hair, slender, with tanned face. He smiled at Taylor, his blue eyes sleepy.

Across the room behind the unwelcome visitor was Taylor's eldest half brother, Jamie. A metal talent, he had fox-colored hair that was clipped short. He was slender but muscular, with blue eyes. He slouched against the wall, his mouth twisted in a mirror of Taylor's fury. Standing to the right of Gregg in the kitchen doorway was Leo, the younger of the two brothers, though older than Taylor. His dark hair was clubbed behind his neck, the chiseled planes of his face looking harsh.

Taylor glanced at her brothers, then back at the older man. "Tell me why I shouldn't just shoot you where you stand."

Gregg's brows rose. Today he was seeing layers to her he'd had no idea existed.

The other man smiled patiently.

"You shouldn't shoot me because I'm not here to talk to you. I'm here to talk to Mr. Touray." The man gestured toward Gregg.

Taylor shot Gregg a disgusted look. "Of course. Why wouldn't you two know each other?"

Betrayal and bitterness underlined her disgust, and Gregg almost pulled the trigger on the stranger for painting him with whatever shit the other man wallowed in. His jaw hardened. He spoke in a gentle singsong, tamping down his fury, letting it burn like a white-hot coal. "Mister, I don't know who you are or what business you think we have, but I'm not interested."

The stranger locked eyes with him, his expression innocuously bland. But Gregg had been swimming with sharks since he was a teenager. In the other man, he recognized the glint of mercilessness and savagery just under the surface.

"I beg to differ," the stranger said. "I've done you a service. I should think you would be grateful."

"Service? Mister, I don't know who the fuck you are and I sure as hell don't have any reason to thank you."

"Ah, but you do. I have delivered you from quite a pickle." He paused. "One hour ago, I killed Savannah Morrell."

Gregg's mouth fell open. Savannah dead? Relief lifted a weight off his back, even as his mind darted around, collecting potential ramifications. "Just who the fuck are you?"

"Vernon Brussard." The other man paused as if waiting for a reaction.

Gregg had heard the name, but couldn't place where or when. "Is that supposed to mean something to me?"

"In my former life I went by Samuel Hollis. Taylor and Riley are my daughters."

Gregg flicked a glance at Taylor, understanding her anger now. "You tried to kill Riley. Nearly succeeded."

He remembered something else. After he'd travelled through the dreamspace with Riley and her spirit had been ripped away from him, she'd been lost for hours. Later they'd figured it must have been her father who'd dragged her off. The images she'd seen while in his clutches had implicated Gregg in her mother's murder. Some of her first words upon returning to her body had been to tell him she didn't believe Gregg guilty of that murder.

"You tried to convince Riley I killed her mom."

"Yes."

Gregg didn't know what he expected from Brussard, but the ready admission wasn't it.

"All in the name of protecting my daughter," he added.

Taylor made a strangled noise in her throat. "Your hypocrisy is unbelievable. You nearly killed her, you self-satisfied jug of dickjuice."

Gregg couldn't help his smirk. Taylor's stint as a mercenary company pilot in the sandbox had given her an excellent command of the more colorful elements of the English language.

Brussard ignored her, focusing on Gregg. "You and I have business to discuss."

"Do we?"

"We do. Perhaps you will put your weapon down and we can speak." He looked at the other four occupants of the room. "Privately, if you don't mind."

"It is our fucking house," Jamie said in a bored voice that did little to disguise his tension.

Brussard didn't reply, merely looking at Gregg as if expecting him to clear the room. He finally lowered his weapon. Whatever the man wanted, Gregg needed to hear it.

"Please," he said aloud to the three siblings, never breaking Brussard's gaze.

"Are you fucking serious?"

Gregg winced at the outrage and betrayal in Taylor's voice. Abruptly she marched to the door, flinging it wide so that it banged off the wall. Dalton followed, but she stopped him.

"Leave me the fuck alone. Besides, your master is here. Don't you want him to scratch your belly? Maybe give you a treat? Go on, puppy. Go heel."

She stormed away, and Dalton stepped back inside and shut the door, his face a mask of indifference. His damned silver eyes gave away nothing. If eyes were windows to the soul, then Dalton's soul was a machine.

"Let's go, Leo," Jamie said, grabbing his jacket to follow Taylor. Leo paused on the threshold, giving his stepfather a pointed look. "We'll be back soon. Don't get too comfortable."

The door shut again, leaving Dalton, Gregg, and Brussard. The latter looked at his henchman.

"You're not wanted either."

"I don't work for you anymore."

Brussard's face flattened in annoyance. "Nor are you welcome, here."

He snorted. "More welcome than you." He glanced meaningfully at the doorway.

"Is this a hill you're prepared to die on?" Brussard's words lacked force, but Gregg believed the threat. Not that Dalton would die easy. He'd proven he had skills not to be underestimated. But it seemed he'd decided the battle wasn't worth it. Wordlessly, he went to the door and stepped out.

"Let us get down to business," Brussard said, sitting in a stuffed chair and crossing his legs. He gestured to the chair opposite. "Please sit."

That he played host in the house rankled, given how much the man's children clearly despised him. Nevertheless, Gregg obeyed. He held his gun in his lap. Brussard made no comment about it. Instead, he folded his hands and examined Gregg.

"Savannah released you."

Gregg didn't respond. He'd never been able to establish spies inside Savannah's organization. At least none long enough or close enough to her to do any good. For Brussard to know she'd freed him meant his spies were well situated. Gregg made a mental note to rake through his own people for Brussard's moles.

The other man examined his sleeve, brushing away an imaginary wrinkle before fixing his gaze on Gregg. It was laser sharp and acutely observant.

From the dossier Gregg had developed on Riley, he knew Vernon—formerly Samuel Hammond Hollis—had disappeared over ten years ago, and hadn't been heard from since. No doubt that was when he'd changed his name to Vernon Brussard.

"Savannah was smart. Canny. Well liked in certain circles."

Which? Gregg didn't ask. Questions revealed as much as they demanded. He merely lifted his brows as if to say "get to the point."

"Her ambition, however, led to an unhealthy obsession with the Kensington artifacts. Of course, she couldn't be allowed to have them."

"Of course," Gregg agreed sardonically when Brussard paused to wait for a response.

"Bloody as her techniques could be, they were frequently effective. After this morning's bombings, it was deemed likely that you would turn your artifacts over to her."

Brussard paused again, but Gregg merely waited patiently without speaking, making himself stay outwardly relaxed. Who had deemed it likely? How could Brussard know about the three Kensington artifacts he'd collected? Did he also know about the vial of blood?

"The bombings have brought unfortunate attention to Diamond City. To allow her to continue in that vein would have been troublesome."

To *whose* attention and troublesome for *whom*? Brussard's carefully crafted sentences gave nothing away. "If you're trying to convince me that killing Savannah was a good idea, I'm not arguing."

The real problem was the vacuum. What happened now? Who would take over? Her husband? Possibly, but Gregg didn't think Whit had the balls to run the organization. More likely there would be infighting with someone rising to the top, while other Tyets chewed off pieces of Morrell territory and business. Once news of the death made the rounds, it would be a feeding frenzy.

Brussard picked invisible lint off his pants leg. "I merely wished for you to understand the logic that went into the execution order. There are those who would like to see the violence in Diamond City ended. It is believed that your own goals coincide with such a project, and I am here to offer you resources to achieve that peace, in whatever fashion you deem appropriate. Those resources would include man power, magic, and finances. You would have a blank check."

Gregg cocked his head, not allowing his surprise to show. "What's in it for you—for these people you say you represent? What are you going to want from me?"

"Sustained peace. Nothing more."

"Not the artifacts—presupposing I have them? No favors? No telling me how to go about conducting my business?"

"I understand the offer seems too good to be true, however I assure you, it is quite real."

"If I refuse?"

Brussard smiled, but it didn't reach his eyes. "Why would you? Your beloved city will be the center of a Tyet war if someone does not take control now. Did I forget to mention that you would also receive the necessary funds to rebuild and repair the city? In time, you'd be able to establish elected officials who answered to you. You could protect this city and its people for the foreseeable future."

"There must be something in it for you. Or the people you work for."

"There is." Brussard stood, clearly not going to explain any further. "I can give you twenty-four hours. If you aren't willing to take the city in hand, another will be selected. I hope you will make the right choice." A smile flickered across his lips. "It would be unfortunate if you did not."

With that, he went to the closet at the front door and withdrew a long cashmere overcoat. He slid it on, followed by a gray fedora, leather gloves, and a scarf. He nodded to Gregg, who'd stood to watch him.

"I'll expect your answer by"—he glanced at his watch—"this time tomorrow."

"How do I reach you?"

Brussard put a gloved hand into a pocket and withdrew a phone. He tossed it to Gregg. "The number's programmed in."

With that, he opened the front door, leaving Gregg standing alone, his mind whirling. He was off the hook for the artifacts, but a blind bargain with Brussard and whoever he worked for would be insane. At the same time, Savannah's death would mean the chaos of succession and dozens of factions fighting to get a bite of her empire. That was on top of a city already on the verge of exploding into war. The feds would move in, and maybe the National Guard, if they weren't already on their way. If he was going to keep a lid on things, he needed to get to work and *now*, but he didn't have the resources to handle every front all at once. Not with all the bloodsuckers diving in for a piece of the action. Given time and the ability to make surgical strikes—he was more than prepared to take on all the wolves wanting a bite of the city. But this was going to be full-on war.

He eyed the phone in his hand, then thrust it into his pocket. Before he decided anything, he needed to find out what had been happening during his incarceration, and he needed to talk to Clay.

TAYLOR AND HER brothers returned after a half hour had passed. Jamie came in first, followed by Taylor and then Leo. Taylor looked spitting angry, but she crimped her mouth in a tight line and said nothing. She glanced at him with stormy eyes.

"You're still here? Shouldn't you be out starting a Tyet war? Maybe drown some kittens on the way?"

He bit back a caustic response. "How do I reach Clay?"

She went into the kitchen and came back with a phone, tossing it to him. "Riley's number is programmed in."

All three looked at him with obvious dislike.

"What did Vernon want?" Leo asked, folding his arms and propping himself against the wall.

"To tell me he'd killed Savannah. And to make a deal."

The three siblings exchanged a smoking look. He thought they'd pepper him with questions about the nature of the offer, but they didn't. Neither did they comment on Savannah.

He wanted to ask them questions and make some calls before heading out, but clearly he'd worn out his welcome. He doubted they'd be forthcoming. Besides, urgency gnawed at him. With Savannah gone, he had a narrow window to get a bite on her territory before other Tyet lords learned of her death and the buzzards descended.

Taylor's next words nearly gave him whiplash, going from angry to generous. "You can clean up before you go. We've got some clothes and a shower."

Leo rolled his eyes at her offer, and Jamie made an irritated sound.

"What? He sacrificed himself for Riley."

"And you pulled his ass out of the fire tonight," Leo said. "We're even."

"Sure, but first we'll wash him and dress him before kicking him out the door. Riley would want us to."

Jamie sighed but didn't disagree. "I'll get food started."

Leo eyed Gregg balefully. He opened his mouth to say something, but then shut it, shaking his head before following his brother. "I need a drink."

"Make me a double," Taylor called and then gestured for Gregg to follow her down the hallway. She went into a small bedroom on the left. She pulled open one side of the folding closet doors to reveal shelves full of clothes. "You should find something to fit you," she said, then brushed past him and out of the room. She opened a linen cupboard on the opposite wall. "Towels along with whatever toiletries you're likely to need. Bathroom is next door."

She waited for him to step aside so she could return to the kitchen. He didn't. Her jaw tightened. She shifted her weight. It was slight, but the warning was clear. She was ready to fight. Not that he was worried. Except maybe that he might hurt her. The idea of getting a chance to put his hands on her sent an electric shock to his balls. He ignored it.

"Excuse me," she said in a clipped voice.

"Why don't you tell me what's crawled up your ass and died?" he asked, unmoving.

"I got my period," she said. "PMS is a royal bitch."

"Bullshit."

"Is it? Too bad for you, then. It's all you get."

"What can you tell me about Brussard?"

"You know all you need to. He tried to kill my sister. That should be plenty."

The urge to grab her and shake a straight answer out of her was almost more than Gregg could contain. "God dammit, this isn't a fucking *game* you're playing. I can't protect you and your family if you shut me out."

Her eyes flattened. "If you're in bed with my father, then we can't trust you. Hell, I don't know that we can trust you even if you're not playing yank and tickle with him. So until I know different, you get the cone of silence. And to be very clear, we can take care of our own damned selves."

Her entire body defied him to push her, to try to force the information out of her. God, but he wanted to. Instead, he stepped aside. "Maybe your brothers will have better sense."

She brushed past him, smelling of the outdoors, sweat, and hint of exotic perfume. "Sure. You give them a shot. See how far that gets you."

HE SHOWERED quickly and dressed in a pair of black jeans and a black tee shirt under a gray fleece. He pulled the sleeve down over the padlocked null bracelet. He'd have to wait until he could get to a pair of bolt cutters to get it off. Neither Jamie nor Leo seemed in charitable enough moods to take it off for him.

Dalton had returned while Gregg was showering. He sat at the far side of the wood dining table in the kitchen. They eyed each other with mutual animosity.

"When are you leaving?" Leo asked, sprawled in another chair and sipping a glass of bourbon.

Gregg grabbed a chair and twisted it around to straddle it. "Tell me about Clay's escape from the FBI."

Taylor started the tale, telling how they'd broken in and how Clay had an un-controllable magic cascade after seeing his bitch of a mother, and how she'd betrayed him. Gregg's brain exploded with hatred. He'd kill the bitch if she wasn't already dead. He hoped to hell she was.

He shuddered at the idea of Clay going into cascade. Riley had managed to bring him out of it, which was a miracle. He squeezed his eyes shut. He'd come so close to losing his brother.

His stomach tightened. What if he'd had Riley killed when he'd planned to? When Clay had first hooked up with her. His brother would be dead. Period. No one else could have brought him out of cascade. Thank God for Riley. He said it aloud as he opened his eyes.

"You won't find any of us arguing that point," Jamie said.

He'd hardly spared a glance for Gregg as he cooked, but that didn't mean Jamie hadn't been paying close attention. Riley's half brothers made their living as metal artists, crafting jewelry and sculptures. But they were neither soft or stupid. The two men carried themselves with the same kind of watchful readiness that their sisters did. They always expected trouble. Was that something Brussard had impressed on them? He'd seen Leo create weapons and shackles in mere seconds. Their power was impressive, but was eclipsed by their mental toughness, their cunning, and their willingness to get down and dirty.

"I'm so sorry about your mother," Gregg said, his voice low, words inade-quate for what they'd lost. Riley wasn't the only one who'd sacrificed for Clay. He hadn't believed that Riley could pull off a rescue. But she had, with the help of her family, who'd put their lives on the line for Clay. Gregg owed them more than he could ever begin to repay.

For a long moment, nobody spoke, then Taylor picked up the story again, telling how Riley had seen a massive trace line of dead in the hills and another line of living coming down to the compound. His mouth fell open when she described the null Riley had built to not only null out their trace as they laid it down, but much of what they'd already left behind. It wasn't possible. But then, a lot of what she did was impossible, and he had a feeling that with the re-strictions of living off the grid and in the shadows, she'd barely scratched the surface of her talent.

"Does the FBI or anyone else know that Clay's alive? Or your part in things?"

"We had to abandon one of my helicopters near Marchont," Taylor said. "So they know at least I was up there. They've seized our properties, so they have to have something. I'm sure it doesn't help that we've all vanished. No official warrants have been issued that we know of, but then, we aren't all that well connected."

"I'll see what I can find out through my sources."

She nodded. "Good."

"Anything else happen I should know about? While I was in Savannah's cus-tody?"

"Until today—the usual. Murders, thefts, Tyet skirmishes, and everybody wondering about you. I'm sure you're going to be fighting interlopers and insurgents for a while."

Right about then, Jamie started dishing out the meal on four plates. Good as it smelled and as hungry as he was, Gregg was sure he wasn't getting an invita-tion. He stood.

"What are the chances I can get one of those automatic rifles?"

"I'll get you one." Taylor left.

"Expecting trouble?" Leo drawled.

"I'm always expecting trouble."

"Traveller like you—you're going to land in home territory. Should be safe enough." His eyes glinted. "Or maybe you think you've got a rat infestation."

Gregg gave a caustic grin. "You know how it can be when the cat's away."

"Sucks when a criminal can't trust his criminal buddies. Who'd have be-lieved it? I'm shocked. Utterly shocked, I tell you."

Jamie chuckled at his brother, setting the plates on the table. "At least he never has to worry about who's out to get him. Everybody is."

Before Gregg could answer, Taylor returned. She handed him the weapon with a couple of extra clips. Her gaze hooked on the padlocked null.

"You guys want to do something about that?"

"But he looks so good in shackles," Leo protested.

She gave him a dry look. "Don't be petty."

"I like being petty."

Gregg started when the null around his wrist wriggled. He pulled up his sleeve to see it better. The padlock was gone. Now the bracelet was a thick, solid band with no visible way to get it off. As he watched, words inscribed themselves across the top: *I'm the ugly brother.*

"That'll make it easier for us to find you," Jamie said, passing Gregg the phone.

"I'll be surrounded by magical security. You're not going to get through it."

"Sure. If you say so," Leo replied, winking at his brother.

Gregg sighed inwardly. He'd have to have his head of security beef things up. But damn, he wished he could get these miscreants on his payroll. He had a feeling once they gave their loyalty, it stayed given. They couldn't be bought. He'd have to take comfort in knowing that at least he wouldn't be fighting against them. He had no doubt they could cause him serious headaches.

There wasn't much else to say, and while he wanted to go to Clay, their reunion would have to wait. He'd decided long ago that the city mattered more than himself, more than any one person, no matter how important they might be to him. Gregg had to get back into the driver's seat of his organization and figure out just what he was going to do with Vernon Brussard's offer. To start with, he'd have to learn just who the fuck the man was, who he worked for, and what he wanted. And then—

He wished to God he knew what happened then. Hopefully, it wasn't Armageddon.

Chapter 10

Riley

I HALF EXPECTED TO wake up as a new resident of the spirit realm. How many times could I get shot and not die? At least twice, apparently, because I woke up flat on my back on the diner's main counter.

I opened my eyes and groaned, swallowing my nausea at the sensation of healing magic worming through my wound.

"Riley?"

I twisted my head to see Taylor. She had hold of my hand and was squeezing it so hard, I thought maybe I'd get gangrene. I frowned. Was she supposed to be here? Had I whacked my head too? "What are you doing here?"

"We got done at the safe house and came here to see you." She clipped off her words, blinking fast. A tear escaped, and she angrily brushed it away.

I blinked at her, letting my sludgy brain absorb her words. "We? Leo and Jamie are here, too?" I sounded stoned. Even I could hear it.

She shook her head. "Dalton came with me. The boys had some other things to take care of."

"Oh." I let that sink in. "Where's Patti? And Price?"

"Right here." Price's voice on the other side of me sounded wire thin.

I twisted my head to find him standing beside me. Worry and tension radiated off him in palpable waves. Tremors shook him, and sweat beaded on his forehead. He held my other hand in both of his.

"You okay?" I asked him.

He snorted and then held still like he feared if he did anything at all, he might shatter. "You got shot."

It sounded accusing. "I didn't mean to."

He gusted a sigh, his grip tightening. My bones might have actually creaked. "Of course not."

"Who did it, do we know?"

He gave a faint shake of his head, his jaw hardening. "They won't hurt you again, though."

The grim chill in his eyes told me he'd made sure of it, and I was willing to bet he'd used the wind to do it. That was a positive sign. He'd controlled his talent. Unless he'd also leveled half the city to do it. I decided I didn't want to know yet.

I glanced around for Patti. She stood just beyond Price, her arms folded, her eyes narrowed. Her cheeks were pale with hard slashes of red indicating fury. When our eyes locked, she stepped forward and jabbed her finger into my thigh to punctuate her words. "You do not get shot. Ever again. Do you understand? I will so kill you if you do this to me again."

"Okay. Maybe you could tell the bad guys that, too. I'd like them to stop shooting me."

She let out an unwilling laugh. "I'll take out an ad in the paper."

"Please do."

The wormy feeling was starting to let up, and the pain I'd been feeling went with it. I sat up, Price and Taylor helping me. I realized then that I had a healing pendant around my neck and four more wrapped around each of my wrists and ankles. Overkill much? My head spun with wooziness.

"Make the room stop," I said, closing my eyes.

"You lost blood. Dalton's pendants can't help with that," Taylor told me.

I nodded and then looked around. "Where is he?"

"Outside. Patrolling."

I'd have to thank him. Again. I had no idea where he kept all the pendants stashed or how he kept such a good supply of them, but they'd sure come in handy more often than I cared to admit.

My brows crimped as my brain started working more clearly. I remembered Dalton stepping into the alley and Price demanding to know what he was doing there. Then the shooting started. "Who shot at us? And here of all places? I mean, how did they know where to find us."

"Not *us*," Price grated. "You. I was the bigger target and more out in the open. They aimed at you."

I blinked at him. "Why?"

"Vernon was at the safe house," Taylor said, as if that was an answer.

My head whipped around. "What? How? Why?"

"He was there when we got back with Touray. Wanted to talk to him. Privately."

"What about?"

"Touray said he wanted to make a deal."

"For what?"

"Didn't say. Wouldn't have believed him if he did. Vernon said he killed Savannah Morrell."

"What? When?"

"Had to be after she let Touray go."

I squeezed my eyes shut. None of this made any sense. Maybe I *had* hit my head. I couldn't have heard that correctly. "Did you just say she let him go?"

"She expected him to bring her back the Kensington artifacts. She blew up half the city to motivate him."

"Fucking hell."

"Amen to that. Anyway, sometime after we picked up Touray, Vernon had her killed."

"Why? And why now?"

"Wish I knew."

I tried to bring my brain back to the present. "You think he had me shot, don't you? Why would he?"

"Who knows how he thinks? He tried to kill you before. Maybe he figured it was time to finish the job."

I tried not to let that hurt. I already knew that everything I thought I'd known about my father was a lie. That he was a cold-blooded bastard and that he didn't love me or Taylor or anybody else. Still, an ached bloomed in my chest, and a lump hardened in my throat. Parents were supposed to love their kids. What was wrong with me that he wanted to kill me? Hell, what was wrong with *him*?

I swallowed and shoved all thoughts of Vernon aside. He wasn't worth my time or energy.

"Let's get you down," Patti said, taking charge. "You need to clean the blood up and change."

I realized that my shirt was clammy against my back. Ew.

Taylor and Patti removed the nulls from my wrists and ankles, but left the one on my neck.

"To make sure," Taylor said.

"How long before Emily and Luis get here?"

"They'll be here anytime," Patti said.

Price pulled me off the counter and into his arms and carried me upstairs to Patti's apartment. I had my own room and clothing there.

Price didn't set me down until we were in the bedroom. Then he shut the door and started stripping me. He never said a word. He turned me to face away and pulled off my coat, my shirt, and unfastened my bra. His fingers ran lightly over my back, like he wanted to be sure the wound was gone.

"How do you feel?"

"Tired, but no pain."

"Okay."

His arms came tight around me, and he pulled me hard against his chest as he buried his face in the crook of my neck. We stood that way for a good five minutes. I covered his hands with mine and pressed against him. I didn't bother to point out that he was getting blood all over his own shirt. He wouldn't have cared.

Finally, he loosened his grip. "You should get cleaned up," he said hoarsely.

I turned in the circle of his arms and pressed my lips against his. "I love you."

"You're going to break me."

I didn't know what to say to that. "I'm sorry."

He nodded, his hands tightening on my hips. He let go. "You'd better get in the shower."

TAYLOR AND PATTI were waiting downstairs. Ben, Patti's partner and cook, made delicious things in the kitchen.

Seeing me, Patti dropped the cleaning towel and bottle of bleach spray she'd been holding and came over to hug me. She smelled of coffee, bacon, and her favorite perfume. The scent of home. I squeezed her tight.

She let me go at last and stood back. "You've lost weight. What have you been eating?" She looked at Price. "You're not any better. God, let you two go off by yourselves and you forget how to eat. I hope you remember how to tie your shoelaces. Come on then, get sat down. Ben will put something together for you."

She bustled away up the hallway and into the dining area. I groaned even as my mouth watered. Ben's food was to die for, and Patti made the best coffee on the planet. We weren't getting out of here until we'd eaten our weight in food. Just at the moment, that sounded perfect.

"I hope you're hungry," I said to Price. He still wore that brittle look, like it was everything he could do to keep himself from shattering apart. I took his hand, standing on tiptoe to kiss his cheek. "I'm okay."

"For now."

I gave him a steady look. "It's not going to get any better. This is our lives."

He scraped his teeth hard over his lower lip. "I'm not sure I'll survive."

"I'll try to understand if you need to bail." Even though that would kill me faster than any bullet.

He pulled me tight against him. "Never going to happen." He bent to give me a fast, hard kiss, and then pulled me toward a seat.

"Not there," Patti said. "In the back. More private and no windows."

She shepherded us into the overflow dining area beyond the stairs. We went through the double doors under the stairway and into a large room. Booths with red vinyl seats and gray tables lined the sides. Chrome and gray tables with chrome chairs and red vinyl cushions made a checkerboard in the middle.

I scooted into a booth. Price sat beside me, and Taylor sat opposite. Patti handed out coffee cups. She set a jug of cream on the table and a sugar shaker, and then sat down beside Taylor.

Just then Dalton came in. "Perimeter is clear," he told Price before grabbing a chair and sitting at the end of the booth. He cocked himself so he could see the door. Patti poured him a coffee. He murmured thanks.

"So, we don't know who shot me or how they know I was here, except Vernon is looking like a good bet. Is that about right?" I stirred cream and sugar into the black elixir that was Patti's coffee. I did it one-handed, since Price had my other one tangled in his, and that was just fine by me.

"Did you see anything outside?" Taylor asked Dalton.

He shook his head. "Found some brass. That's about it. Nothing to tell us who was behind it."

"But we all know it was Vernon," she challenged, a belligerent edge to her voice.

"Could be. I don't know."

Her lip curled. "Don't you?"

He gave her a long look. "Could be him. But better to work on facts. There might be another player stepping up and if we don't consider it, we take a chance of getting blindsided. And maybe somebody else gets shot. Maybe somebody gets killed."

It was all said in a mild tone, but the rebuke was clear. Taylor flushed and bit her lips together. I thought she'd explode at him. But then she just nodded.

"You're right."

Her willingness to be reasonable in the face of her well-deserved hatred of Vernon surprised me. Dalton made sense, even if it annoyed the fuck out of me. I'm not sure I'd have been willing to admit it.

He nodded back at her without even a flicker of a smile to indicate triumph that he'd won the point. Good thing, too, or she'd probably have decapitated him.

I could feel Price getting antsy. Antsi*er.* A breeze had started up in the closed room. His iron control was slipping. I leaned my head against his shoulder and tightened my fingers on his.

"Easy," I whispered. "We're safe."

"For now."

"Now's all that counts. Try to relax."

He snorted, but took a slow breath and let it out, forcing his shoulders to relax. The breeze settled. I decided to change the subject.

"What happened with Touray? How did he get free?"

Taylor described retrieving Price's brother. Dalton sat silent, nodding once in a while. His gaze was restless. It skipped from each of us to the door, around the room and back to us in an endless circuit. The colors at the outer rims of his silver irises cycled from orange to green to blue and back to silver. It was damned creepy.

It wasn't long before Ben dinged the bell. Patti jumped up and dragged Dalton with her. It took them both two trips to haul all the food. Only newbies to the diner ordered. Patti gave the rest of us what she thought we needed. If you refused the offering, your next meal or twelve would be inedible. I'd never had a bad meal in all the years I'd been eating there.

She deposited bowls of baked potato soup in front of me and Price with a basket of crusty bread and crock of honey butter. Dalton got a steak smothered under mushrooms and onions and accompanied by a mound of garlic green beans and rosemary mashed-potato patties. Taylor received a halibut sandwich with a mound of onion rings and a Caesar salad.

Patti glared at me and Price. "Eat it all. Don't dawdle."

I dug in, knowing this was only my first course. Taylor paused between bites to finish the story on Touray, and then switched to an update on us.

"Far as we can tell, the FBI is still sticking with the story that Price died in the explosion. Mom's been declared missing." Her brow clouded with the memory of Mel's death. She visibly forced the memory away. "I don't know if they actually believe any of that. They've seized all our houses and businesses, so chances are they don't believe the story they're selling. Haven't seen hide nor hair of Arnow since we got back, so she's been zero help with FBI intel."

"I bet Vernon knows where she is," I muttered, glancing at Dalton from beneath my brows.

He stared back. "I can ask," he said after a few moments.

"Why bother?" Taylor asked. "It's not like he'd tell the truth. Even if he did, we couldn't trust him. It's pointless."

That assumed that Dalton *would* tell the truth, which I highly doubted.

Dalton's lips tightened like he knew what I was thinking, but he stayed silent. As usual, his expression revealed nothing. I wondered if he practiced that bland look in the mirror.

"Anyhow, we've been staying off the radar. I expect that now that you two are back and Touray is free, that's likely to change."

I nodded. None of us planned to hide forever. Just long enough to rescue Touray and then go to war. Touray was determined to gain control of the Tyets in the city and force a peace. Only now that Savannah Morrell was dead, I wasn't sure what would happen. Maybe without Savannah in the picture, he could control the Tyets without a lot of carnage.

Regardless, I had to help Emily and Luis and then go find Arnow's missing people like I'd promised. 'Course, Touray might have different plans for Price, and that meant mine were based on maybes and mights. At least we knew who'd set the bombs and that she'd got her just deserts.

"What do you think Vernon wants with your brother?" Taylor asked suddenly, tipping her head to the side as she eyed Price.

He shook his head, his mouth tightening. "Whatever it is, I doubt it's good for Gregg. Or the rest of us."

"He has an endgame," Dalton volunteered suddenly.

We all looked at him.

"What does that mean?" I asked when I'd overcome my surprise. It was like having your cat suddenly spout words. Highly unexpected and almost surreal.

Spots of red bloomed along his high cheekbones. He didn't like the attention. "Your father plots. Always. He has something he wants and everything he does and has done is to get it."

"What does he want?" Taylor demanded, facing him, her eyes blazing.

"He's never told me," Dalton said, setting his silverware down on his plate and resting his hands on the table. "But it drives him relentlessly."

I snorted. "That's one word for it. Pathologically obsessed is another." So it was two words. He could sue me. "Why are you telling us this? Or is this part of one of his plans?"

Dalton's face hardened, his nostrils flaring white. "I do not work for him anymore."

"Of course not," I drawled and rolled my eyes. None of us were that gullible.

He sat back in his chair, folding his arms and tipping his head back. He'd not shaved recently, and five o'clock shadow highlighted the hollows and contours of his jaw. He wasn't exactly handsome. He wasn't ugly either. More like he'd been roughly carved from rock, and the artist hadn't had time to refine the blunt line of his nose, the sharp slants of his cheek bones, or the uncompromising jut of his chin. Combine that with the eyeball tinker mods, and he was not at all reassuring to look at.

His next words about made me fall out of my chair.

"What can I do to prove myself to you?" His gaze gathered us all in, including Patti, who'd run off to retrieve more meals and now arrived with two heaping platters for Price and me. Hamburgers this time, loaded with all sorts of goodies like cheese, bacon, deep-fried onions, and avocado. "All of you," Dalton added, to be sure we got his point.

I shoved aside my empty soup bowl and grabbed my hamburger platter. Patti sat beside Taylor again, purple-black nails on the tabletop. Happy little skulls in pink decorated each one.

The room got quiet. I wondered if any of the others were trying to think of something. I was, which shocked the hell out of me. Was there anything he could do to convince me to trust him?

"Killing Vernon might be a start," Taylor said finally.

Dalton gave her an inscrutable look. "If that's what you want."

Sold! To the two daughters of the bastard! But I didn't say it. I'd killed and Taylor had, too, but we hadn't murdered. Besides, if someone was going to kill dear old dad, we deserved the first shot.

Taylor exchanged a look with me, her brows raised as if she also wanted to say yes. I gave a regretful shake of my head. Dalton caught it.

"Then what? I'd really like to know. I'm sick and tired of living in limbo."

I gawked. He was pissed. Like pin-pulled-and-about-to-detonate mad.

"Honestly? I don't have a clue," I said after swallowing the enormous bite I'd taken. "I admit that it would be nice to know that you aren't going to hamstring us the first time we aren't paying attention, or lead us into a trap, or kidnap us," I said, with emphasis on the *kidnap*. After all, he'd already tried that with me on behalf of Vernon. Supposedly for my own good. God, but I hated that phrase.

"And you?" he asked Taylor.

She shook her head and then shrugged.

"Could have a dreamer look in his head," Patti suggested.

I choked on my coffee and snorted it through my nose. I wiped my face with my napkin and looked at Dalton, who actually appeared to be considering it. I wouldn't. I hated dreamers. The only one I trusted was Cass, and only because she'd saved my life and pulled Vernon's fuckery out of my head. She'd proven herself.

That caught me up. I distrusted dreamers about as much as I distrusted Vernon and Dalton. But her actions with me had made me trust her. Why couldn't I trust Dalton's recent actions?

It came down to Vernon. He played the long game, and we couldn't trust that he wasn't cementing Dalton into our lives in order to fuck with us later. He'd messed with my head ten *years* ago and disappeared to let the seeds he'd planted grow. Hell, he'd married Mel after my mom's murder, and from what I could tell, their entire marriage was part of his plan. Bastard.

"Would you let someone have a look?" Taylor asked Dalton.

His lips thinned to a straight line and his entire body stiffened like he was about to take a blow. "Yes."

I have to admit that all four of our jaws hit the floor. Even so, the cynical, self-protective gremlin in the back of my head couldn't help wondering if Dalton was willing because he was so confident in Vernon's brainwork. That he was sure Cass wouldn't be able to see any tampering.

If so, he was betting on the wrong horse. I'd bet on Cass against my dad any day.

The front doors chose that moment to rattle. Patti leaped out of her chair and scurried into the front room. If a woman wearing five-inch-high Converse wedge heels could scurry. Who thought that was a good idea, anyway? Hey! Let's put monster heels on athletic shoes!

The front bells jingled as the doors opened, and a minute later, Patti led in Emily and Luis. Emily looked washed out despite the caramel color of her skin. Her eyes were puffy and bruised, like she'd been crying. Luis had his arm around her waist. His expression was stern and a little desperate. My experience was that as a rule, most men didn't know what to do with a crying woman, and Luis wasn't an exception.

"Riley!" Emily launched herself at me. Price had scooted out of the booth to let me up. She grabbed my hands in a frigid grip as she looked pleadingly at me. "I need your help. Please." She closed her eyes and swallowed, then gave me a watery smile that was more like a grimace. "My cousin, Cristina, is gone. We think—" She broke off and bit her lips together as tears started flowing again.

Luis came up behind her and put his hands on her shoulders, pulling her back against him. It was a brotherly move, comforting and supportive. "Cristina disappeared last night from her bedroom. She didn't leave a note, but took some clothes, a toothbrush, comb, makeup. We think she's run off with this guy she's been sneaking around with. She's fifteen. He's twenty-three and a bad guy. Mixed up with a lot of illegal stuff. Rumors say he's killed people. He beats his girlfriends. Some disappear when he's done with them."

With his explanation, Emily had straightened. She pushed the loose strands of her black hair behind her ears with shaky fingers, her chin coming up. "Crissie's a good girl," she said. "We didn't know she even knew him. Aunt Rosa and Uncle Steven would have grounded her, taken away her phone and laptop. She's been e-mailing and FaceTiming him." She bit her lips, fury darkening her eyes. "She sent him pictures of herself." Her voice dropped to a whisper. "Without clothes." She started fumbling with her purse. "Please, you've got to find her before he . . . he . . . hurts her."

I was pretty sure Emily was about to try to pay me. Not a snowball's chance in hell I'd take money from either one of them. "Have you got something that belongs to her?"

Emily looked up at me, her hands going still on her purse, hope breaking through the despair on her face. "I've got this," she said, taking a charm bracelet from her pocket. "I don't know why she left it. She loves it."

I took it from her and dropped into trace view. Everybody has a trace—living or dead. It's as unique as a fingerprint. A person's trace is laid down everywhere they've been and on everything they've touched. Most tracers can only see the ribbons for maybe a couple of hours at best, before the traces fade away. Not me. I don't even know if there is a limit on what I can see. That may or may not have something to do with being in the Kensington blood line, a fact I'd only learned recently from my dead mom. My life is a bad horror movie.

Dozens of ribbons wrapped the bracelet. More than dozens. Anybody who'd ever touched it left trace behind. All the same, picking out Cristina's was pretty easy. Hers tangled them all, weaving through and around, making a massive tangled knot around the bracelet.

Her trace showed lime green with hodgepodge splatters and streaks of magenta. It was vibrant and healthy, so whatever else she was, Cristina was alive. I said so. Emily made a noise and pressed her hands to her mouth, relief making her cry again.

"You can find her?" Luis asked.

I looked at Price. "Ready to go?"

He nodded, his expression taut. He'd gone into cop mode.

"We'll all go," Taylor said.

I shook my head. "No." I held up my hand before she could protest. "The fewer the better, right now. We have to find out what we're up against—if we're extracting a starry-eyed girlfriend or a scared victim. If we need help, I'll call. I promise. But I have something else I need you to do."

"What?" She looked skeptical, like I was just trying to keep her out of the way and safe.

Taylor's a highly skilled pilot and has mad fighting skills, plus she's smart as hell. All the same, the rest of the family had gotten into the habit of pushing her to the sidelines like she didn't have anything to contribute since she didn't have a magical talent. When Price had been taken, she'd given me a come-to-Jesus meeting about that. I was working on changing my habits, but she still didn't trust my motives. The truth was, I hated sending her anywhere dangerous, but I didn't have a choice these days. We lived in a dangerous world, and hiding in a closet from all the bad guys wasn't an option for any of us.

"Vernon knows about all the safe houses. He helped plan and build the tunnels and he obviously remembers how to access them. We need to move our headquarters to my place. He doesn't know where it is and he doesn't know about any of the entrances or tunnels leading in. We need food and water supplies, weapons, ammunition—anything you can think of."

"Expecting a siege?" Patti asked.

I shook my head. "I don't even know what to expect, but if we have to lay low and hide out for a long time—whether from the FBI or Vernon or anybody else—we need to be ready. I also need you to work on getting all the stay-away charms and protection spells renewed. Have the boys work on the tunnels. All of them. We need to booby-trap all of them so Vernon can't use them, and we need to be able to remove the booby traps if we need them. Maybe have them shut down the cars. I don't know. Leo and Jamie can figure it out."

Taylor's skeptical look had turned thoughtful. "We'll want to bring in some furniture too—beds especially. We might need to expand your place."

"Then we will. The boys built it, they can expand it easily enough."

"I'll get on it."

"Be careful," I said.

She laughed. "I think that advice is better given to you. I've been in a war zone and you're the one who keeps getting shot."

"Then let's both be careful." I looked at Dalton. "Watch her back."

His jaw knotted. "I always do."

"What about us? What should we do?" Emily asked. "We could come with you. Crissie might listen to us."

I took her hand. "Go home. We'll call if we need you. I promise she's all we're going to focus on until we get her back, okay?"

She nodded, turning her hand to grip mine tightly. My heart ached for her. This was the reason God had given me this talent. I was supposed to help the helpless, to find the stolen and lost and bring them home.

"What's the asshole's name?" Price said. "Where does he live? Hang out? Who does he hang with?"

He had a pad of paper and a pen. I had no idea where he'd pulled that from. Maybe Taylor had given it to him.

"He goes by the name Ocho," Luis said. "His real name is Michael Lawson. Spends a lot of time down in the Calvera neighborhood. He's got a pretty big crew. They scrounge work from local Tyet bosses. They'll do anything for a buck. They like the rough stuff."

"Any particular place they like to go?" Price asked.

"The Hard Luck Bar. Pino's Griddle. Some warehouses and stores that are closed up."

Price wrote things down before he looked at Luis again. "You know a lot about this guy." It wasn't a question, but his comment demanded an answer.

Worry carved age into Luis's handsome face. He had big brown eyes, black hair he wore in a short ponytail, and a normally dimpled white smile. Now he bit his lower lip. "My cousin runs with Ocho."

"Your cousin? Have you talked to him? Does he know anything about Crissie?" Price pounded out the questions like hammer strikes.

"He told me to mind my own business and stay out of the way or I'd get hurt." Luis's arm tightened around Emily. "I told him to fuck off."

"What does Ocho look like?"

Luis described a young man with a rangy build. He had short brown hair and a soul patch. His left arm was a complete tattoo sleeve, while his right arm was mostly bare except for two knife scars on his forearm. He wore a heavy gold chain with the number eight hanging off it.

Price took the description down, then looked a silent question at me. He was done. Did I want a turn? I gave a micro shake of my head, and he turned back to the agonized couple, handing Luis the pad of paper. "Give me your phone numbers."

Luis wrote them down and returned the pad.

"We'll find her," I said.

Emily nodded, and then Patti led them away. I heard the bells jingle again and then the doors clack shut. Patti swept back in.

"Finish your burger," she ordered me. I'd managed about half of it before Emily and Luis had arrived. I started to protest, but she cut me off. "You don't know when you're going to eat again. Half the city is shut down. Stoke up now while you can."

I couldn't argue with her logic, though the burger tasted a lot like newspaper now. Price and I sat back down. Taylor and Dalton were already done. I waved at them.

"Go on. You've got work to do. I'll call when I have news."

Taylor nodded, then looked at Price. "Take care of my sister."

"I'm not letting her get into trouble."

I snorted. Try and stop me. "I'm sitting right here. *And* I'm perfectly capable of looking after myself, thank you very much."

"I'm not saying you aren't capable," Taylor said as if explaining things to a particularly slow child. "I'm saying you don't bother. I wish you had a healthier sense of self-preservation."

I grinned. "If only the bad guys weren't such meanies."

She glared at me. "It's not funny."

"Well, you know the saying: If you can't laugh in the face of danger, you'll end up in the loony bin."

"I don't think that's a saying," Taylor said, rolling her eyes.

"It should be."

"*You* need to be in a loony bin."

"Maybe next week. I'll see if there's time on the calendar between finding missing girls, fending off psychotic fathers, fighting and surviving a Tyet war, and doing that job for Arnow."

Taylor grinned and headed for the door, followed closely by her grim shadow.

Patti slid into the seat across from us. "What do you need from me?"

The way she said it, I could tell it wasn't as simple a question as it seemed like on the surface. This wasn't about the next few hours or days. It was about how she was going to fit into my new life. She didn't want to be on the sidelines. She loved the diner, but she loved me too, and she didn't like not being involved.

I decided I'd answer the less obvious question, since I didn't want her to kick me in the head. She's got several black belts in different ways to kick ass and had demonstrated several times that she could do just that. Since I was a quick learner, I felt this was the smartest choice.

"I don't know," I said honestly. Price shifted beside me, alerted to the serious turn of the conversation by my sober tone. "Things are up in the air."

"That's crap," Patti snapped.

"Not crap. With Touray free and Vernon on the scene, not to mention all the other players in the game, I have no idea what's going on. None of us do." I sighed in frustration, drumming my fingers on the table. "Right now, we're playing catch-up."

Her blue eyes glittered. They were lighter than Price's, and often shifted to more gray than blue. "Don't feed me a line of shit. I'm not a mushroom and I don't plan to eat crap and live in the dark."

"I know. I'm not asking you to. I'm just saying I don't know what the fuck is going on and until I can get more pieces together, I won't have anything like a full picture of how I fit, much less how everyone else fits. Trust me on this, though. Whatever Taylor says, I'm not stupid enough to walk into the middle of the minefield, and I'm over working alone. I have no intention of shutting you out."

She digested my words, her steely gaze not letting me look away. "Okay. I'll be patient. For now. But I'll expect an invitation to the table. I don't want to hear everything second or thirdhand anymore. I'm sick and tired of my best friend running off to fight battles and I don't get to hear anything until days or weeks after. That's going to stop now."

"I hear you," I said.

"Good," she said, standing up. "Now give me a hug so I can clean these plates and you go find that poor girl and bring her home to her family."

She came around the table and hugged first Price and then me. "Don't let her kill herself," she told him over my shoulder.

"I won't."

I pushed back and looked at both of them. "You, too? I mean, I'm not *that* bad."

"Yes, you are," they said in unison.

"You aren't any better," I groused a few minutes later when Price and I were headed for the bike. "You got arrested and tortured and then nearly died when your talent exploded. Twice, if you count earlier today. And that doesn't even take into account when Savannah shot you. I've only been shot twice."

Price started the bike. "If you want it to be a contest, then you'll lose. Let's see. Leaving aside getting shot twice—though the first time got you into my bed, so I can hardly complain about that—what else is there? Oh, right. Getting burned all over your arms with cigarette butts. Having your thumb cut off. Having your brain nearly fried and almost dying as a result. Trying to save me from my magic—you did actually die that time. Then there was when my magic blew up in the cell. I nearly crushed you under a pile of rubble—"

I stood beside him, not yet having gotten on the bike. I rubbed his shoulders as he broke off and looked away. Mel *had* been crushed. Not his fault. He'd been out of his mind with pain, both physical and mental. Part of his torture had been hallucinations that I'd come to rescue him. Plus he'd kept the rest of us all safe until he'd emptied himself of power. Mel's death had been an accident, pure and simple.

"And there's another one," I said, poking a gloved finger into his chest, not willing to let it go yet. "You got shot by your mom."

"And you got kidnapped, exposed to Sparkle Dust, and then you nearly froze to death, then overloaded with magic when taking down that null wall. And you came close to dying three or four times when the FBI attacked my brother's building and your sister's ex-boyfriend tried to kill you, plus you took on Savannah." He frowned. "I know there's more. What am I missing?"

"Okay," I said, raising my hands in defeat. "Fine. You win. I'm a walking target. But as I recall, all that happened after you forced me to work for you in the first place. So really, it's your fault."

"Because you never got into danger on your own before that? Didn't you tell me you got stabbed—?"

Not a road I wanted to go down. If he knew how many close calls I'd had, his head would probably pop off. It was a good thing that tinkers didn't leave behind scars when they healed people, or I'd be in trouble.

"All right. I surrender. We're wasting time. Let's go."

I made it sound like he was the one who'd started the argument and caused the delay. My inner six-year-old had to have a little win. I ignored his shit-eating grin as I slid onto the seat behind him and wrapped my arms around his waist.

This time I won't get near dying, I told myself as Price put the bike in gear.

I should have remembered the old saying about best laid plans and all that.

Chapter 11

Riley

CRISTINA'S TRACE led south and east to Calvera, a depressed neighborhood with high crime.

I wasn't willing to confess it to Price, but I couldn't maintain contact with the trace dimension for very long. Just touching it ached bone deep, and every time I checked for her trace, the pain increased. Clearly, my attempt at helping him manage his power had made my situation worse. All the same, it was a small price to pay if we could get Cristina home safe and sound.

Price wove through the lines of traffic. The snarls had not lightened at all, even though midnight approached. Emergency vehicles continued to howl and careen up onto sidewalks and any clear space they could find. More than once, the first responders activated road-clearing magic that shoved vehicles to the sides of the road, sometimes crushing them. If the people inside were smart, they'd know to abandon the vehicle as soon as they saw the lights coming.

After a while, the businesses and buildings around us began to look tired and worn. Trim sagged from porches, and rust chewed at the siding. Our bike made the only noise. If we wanted to be stealthy, we were out of luck. Trouble was, we needed to be able to case the situation without anybody noticing.

Price pulled into a small parking lot in front of a bodega. He switched off the motor, and we both got off. Price started to wheel the bike toward a notch between the little grocery and a sandwich shop. I grabbed his sleeve and pointed toward the corner. He hesitated, then nodded for me to lead the way.

I was familiar with this part of town. I'd had jobs that brought me to the area, but more than that, I'd walked every inch of the city, memorizing it so that I would never be lost, and never without some sense of where to run. I like escape routes. They've come in very handy in my line of work.

At the corner of the bodega and the one-lane street beyond, I turned left up a rise. The sidewalk disappeared after about ten steps, and the snow had never been cleared here. It had been mashed down and refrozen who knew how many times. The lumpy bunches of ice and snow were enough to turn my ankle. At least I didn't fall on my ass.

We reached the top of the rise. I went left again. On the right stood a couple of duplexes, looking neat and tidy despite their obvious age. To the left was a post office. Now closed, collapsible steel scissor gates blocked the front. I pointed to the end at the two blue mailboxes bolted to the concrete. Behind them was a little patch of bushes and a cedar tree. As hiding places went, as long as we got back before the post office opened in the morning, the chances of someone finding and stealing the bike were low.

We followed Cristina's trace on foot. I could tell when we stepped into Calvera. We'd reached a whole new level of poor and run-down. Graffiti plastered the buildings. Boards covered half the windows, and bars protected the other half. Mounds of snow piled against buildings and over the roofs, pushed aside by the plows clearing the roads. Most of the streetlights didn't work—whether because they'd burned out naturally or someone shot them out, I couldn't tell. Bars, strip joints, and bodegas dominated the sparse businesses. The first two outnumbered the last by about five to one from what I could tell.

Everything about Calvera screamed nobody cared. It wasn't worth anybody's time or effort. Police didn't patrol here. Ambulances had to be paid huge bounties just to drive inside. The businesses that survived either paid for protection from the local Tyet boss or went under. Even the homeless stayed out of this area. The Bottoms was starting to look safer than Calvera, and that was saying something.

Price drew his gun. "We've got to be careful."

By which he meant *I* needed to be. I gave him a sideways look. "Because we weren't already being careful."

"How about this, then—try to behave yourself."

"Define behave."

He groaned exasperatedly. He bent and gave me a fast kiss, his lips gone almost before they touched mine. "Don't get dead. How's that?"

"*That* is something I can definitely get behind."

During our conversation, a breeze started picking at my hair and coat. I wondered if Price meant to have summoned it up. Maybe it was perfectly natural. I decided not to ask. At the moment, I preferred blissful ignorance and to focus on the job.

The Calvera neighborhood was big and sprawling. It was in an old area of Downtown, where the Calvera Mining Company had built a company town way back before Diamond City was even getting started. The CMC had brought in thousands of workers and pretty much turned them into slave labor. They got paid less than they needed to live, guaranteed by making workers rent company housing and shop in the company store. Pretty quick the workers ran up debt they could never pay off, ending up in perpetual service to the company.

The CMC was in the business of making money and didn't give a shit about its employees. There were always more downtrodden waiting to be sold a bill of goods about a desperately needed steady job. A lot of people died—in the mines, from machine accidents, and from illness. Some even froze to death in the winter when they didn't have enough firewood to get through the cold.

Another mining company eventually bought out CMC's claim. Over the years, the neighborhood had seen some attempts at renovation, but mostly it was a sad, dilapidated place. Most people here still worked in the same mines begun by CMC. The houses here were the same shacks the CMC had originally built, which meant they were now Frankensteined with scrap wood, metal, and whatever leftover bits the residents could scrounge to cover holes and keep out the weather. If not for the dole, the residents couldn't survive. But every month they got a check for living in the city. The dole came from a fund created by the mine owners to make it more "affordable" to live in the city so their workers would stay. The payments were a bargain for mine owners and barely an eyelash of their massive profits.

Gangs cropped up here out of the people's desperation to belong to something, to have control, a future. Calvera was a fertile ground for recruiting Tyet soldiers. And why wouldn't it be? Walk away from a dead-end place and a dead-end life and get money, weapons, and the prestige—the security—of being stronger than someone else. From all indications, Ocho was working his way toward just that life. Hopefully we could get Cristina out before she became a casualty of his ambitions.

We kept to the shadows. A cat galloped across the road in front of us. I jumped. Price gave a low chuckle. I caught glimpses of tiny little red eyes reflecting in scraps of light. Rats. Most of the city had magical suppressions in place for vermin. Not Calvera. This was vermin heaven. There weren't enough cats in the world to handle the offerings.

Price kept a step ahead of me. I'd drawn my gun and kept an eye on our flanks, pushing and tugging on his arm to guide him after Cristina's trace. Since going on foot, I'd wrapped it around my wrist to keep on track. My head pounded, and I'd started to get chills. If we didn't find where Ocho had her soon, I'd have to tell Price. Not something I looked forward to.

We passed an old motel on the opposite side of the street. Though clearly closed, club music pulsed into the night from within. Clusters of people stood outside, smoking and dancing. A couple embraced against the building, so drugged up they could barely keep to their feet.

We stuck to the shadows on the other side of the potholed road. Nobody noticed us until the rear door of a van parked just ahead of us flung open and a half-naked man staggered out. His shirt was unbuttoned, revealing a chest full of tattoos and scars. He was buttoning his pants, saying something to whoever remained in the back of the van. We stopped dead, hoping he wouldn't see us. But we were out of luck.

"Who the fuck are you?" He pointed at us. "Gordo!" he shouted. "We got us trespassers!"

The motel boiled into motion. Price and I started running. We hit a cross street and dodged left, sprinting like Death himself was chewing our asses. The mob behind us revved engines, even as the rapid snap of footsteps followed us.

We didn't see the giant pothole filled with shadow. We hit it at the same time, both expecting to land on pavement. Instead, we dropped a good six inches into a tiny skating rink of smooth ice. We crashed together as we fell. I heard an ominous snapping sound, and then my head exploded and that was all I knew.

I WOKE TO BRIGHT lights and a dozen hammers banging around inside my skull. My mouth was parched, and my shoulder and knees ached. It took about a second for my memory to come back. My eyes popped open.

I found myself sitting on a wooden chair. They'd tied my hands around back of it, the bindings pulling painfully on the tendons in my shoulders. Across from me, similarly bound, sat Price. His head hung forward. Blood spattered his shirt. Relief poured through me. He was breathing.

I scanned the surroundings and stopped when I saw the face of a young man, though his blue eyes held experiences far older than his years. He looked like he wasn't quite old enough to drink, with dirty-blond hair, a square jaw, square shoulders, square hands, and probably square feet. He clearly lifted weights. He sat on the edge of a vinyl-covered dining table, the metal legs groaning under his weight.

"Welcome back to the land of the living, Dollface," he said conversationally. He reached up to scratch his bristled cheek as he cocked his head to the side. "What brings you into my neighborhood?"

"We're looking for someone," I said, and winced. I touched my tongue to my lower lip, which had split and swelled. I moved my jaw back and forth, an ache rolling upward to add to the pounding in my head.

His brows rose. "Who?"

"A girl. Fifteen. Runaway. Her family thinks she's in trouble."

He considered me a long moment. "You're telling the truth."

I shrugged, which wasn't all that easy with my hands pretzeled up behind me. That's when I remembered that ominous cracking sound. I wriggled around. I hurt, but not broken-bone hurt. I glanced again at Price. It must have been him. "What did you expect?"

He smiled lazily, and it was actually charming. "Don't get a lot of do-gooders here."

"I bet. So are you going to keep us tied up? Can we go?"

He eyed me again, then gave a regretful shake of his head. "Tell me more about this girl. How are you going to find her? Who has her?"

"And if you're allies with an asshole who'd take a fifteen-year-old girl from her family, what then? Kill us?"

He wouldn't, because I'd drag us into the spirit realm before he could.

"Business is business."

"Yeah, well, your business sucks. People matter, you know."

Again that long solemn look. "I know."

"He's going to hurt that girl. Beat her, rape her, kill her. Do you want that on your conscience?"

Our captor sighed. "Who?"

There wasn't any point in holding out. "Goes by the name Ocho."

He gave a silent "ah," clearly unsurprised.

"An ally," I said with no doubts at all. "You keep shitty company."

"Yes, I do," he said, standing and going to a dented-up refrigerator. It used to be green, but now looked dirty gray. He reached in and took out a bottle of water. He twisted off the lid and came toward me. "Want some?"

I wasn't proud. I nodded. He tipped it gently. I hissed as it hit my swollen lip.

"Sorry."

I just pushed a little forward and gulped. Icy cold ran down my chin and dripped onto my shirt, but I didn't care. I drank half before pulling away.

"Thanks."

"No problem."

He returned to his perch, scrutinizing me again. "You look familiar. Why do I know you?"

"Maybe you caught my centerfold issue in *Playboy.*"

The corner of his mouth quirked, his gaze running over me and back up. "I wouldn't have forgotten that."

He went quiet, waiting for me to speak. I could have kept my lips shut forever. I'm good at doing exactly what other people don't want me to do, but I didn't have time to waste. Maybe I could convince him to let us go.

"I'm a tracer. I've been in the papers."

He got that "aha" sort of look and nodded. "That's it. You're really good, too, right?"

I blew out a breath. "Yep."

"And him?" He nudged his chin toward Price.

"Don't take this the wrong way, but you really don't want to piss him off," I said.

"Is that a threat?"

"Didn't I say don't take it the wrong way? And there you go, doing exactly that. When he wakes up, he's going to be in a lot of pain if that cracking noise I heard was one of his bones like I think it was. He's also going to be afraid for me. He'll totally freak out. When he freaks out—" I shook my head. I wasn't going to tell thug-boy Price's talent, but I had to convey the danger. "You'd be smarter to let us go. At least untie us and let me try keep the shit from hitting the fan."

Once again, thug-boy studied me. His hair fell across his eyes. "You're telling the truth," he said again.

"What are you? A human polygraph?"

He grinned. "Just good at reading people. Have to be. It's the only way to stay alive." He dug in his pocket and pulled out a blue pocketknife. He flicked it open and came around behind me, slicing through the ropes. I awkwardly swung my arms around in front of me, groaning as blood ran back into my hands.

He went around and cut Price free. "What's his talent?" he asked as Price's hands fell down to dangle beside him.

"Better you don't find out." I stood. I ached from the fall and getting tied up. I stiff-walked over beside Price and lifted his head. A knot lumped on his right temple. A bruise circled his left eye. Damn. I should have asked Dalton for a couple heal-alls. Note to self: put together a danger pack for my adventures and include heal-alls. I pulled Price's hands up into his lap and gently rubbed the back of his neck.

"Gimme some water, will you? Do you have a towel? What is your name, anyhow?"

He grinned again. "Tiny."

"You can't be serious."

"My uncle called me that. It stuck. Better than the real one."

"'We called the dog Indiana,'" I muttered under my breath, and then snorted. How did dangerous situations always bring out the snark in me?

Tiny opened the refrigerator again and took out another water. He grabbed a handful of fast-food napkins from the counter and handed them to me.

"Thanks." I poured the chilled water onto the napkins and then sponged Price's forehead and cheeks, then moved to the inside of his wrists. It took a few minutes before his lashes fluttered, and his slack body stiffened with consciousness. He let out a moan.

"We're okay," I said, gripping one hand as I rubbed his neck with the other. "Hear me? We're okay."

I repeated it until his eyes opened and he lifted his head. Sweat shone on his forehead and grooves cut deep along the sides of his mouth. His gaze locked on mine, searching for confirmation. Sapphire blue. I breathed a sigh of relief. He still had his power under control, then.

He grimaced and then scowled. "What happened? Where are we?" He twisted to look around, body going rock hard when he caught sight of Tiny. "Who the fuck are you?"

"He goes by Tiny," I said. "We're his captives and he is friends with Ocho."

"Allies," Tiny corrected. "Not friends."

"What's the difference? You're in bed together."

Price looked at me again. "You've got an odd definition of being okay."

I tightened my hand on his. "We're alive and breathing."

"And captive to some wannabe Tyet thug."

"Gotta have goals," Tiny said. He seemed perfectly relaxed as he watched the two of us.

I didn't sense any active magic on him or in the room.

"Jesus fuck," Price said as he started to stand. He fell back into the chair. His face had gone white.

"Your leg? I heard bone crack when we fell. Which one?"

"Right," he said through crimped lips.

"Sucks," Tiny said unhelpfully.

"I don't suppose you've got a tinker handy?" I asked.

I was surprised when he gave another of his grins. "Could be."

"What do you want?" I demanded, tired of the game. Every second we dawdled gave Ocho a chance to hurt Cristina. Seeing Price in pain wasn't helping me one bit.

"For what?" Tiny had a slow way about him, almost Southern, as if he could wait. He had the patience of a sniper.

I decided not to lose my temper and kick him in the balls. "What do you want to heal him? To let us go?"

"What do you have to offer?"

"Name it. I'll get it." And I would, too. No matter what I had to do.

That seemed to catch him up. His expression sharpened, and sudden urgency thrummed through him. As fast as it appeared, it evaporated and he shook his head. "Nothing you've got to give."

"Try us," I said.

"I want Calvera. I want to run it. I want Ocho and the rest of the bloodsucking horde out of here. I want money to rebuild, to give the people here real lives. I want to keep the shit like what happened out in the city last night out of here."

I stared at him, then looked at Price. "Holy shit, he's your brother from another mother."

Despite himself, Price smiled. "Heaven help us."

"You think I'm funny?" Tiny's expression had gone steely, and despite his youth and easy manner, a mass of rage, protectiveness, frustration, and ambition seethed. A warrior ready to protect his home and his people with whatever means necessary. He really was just like Touray.

"No, not funny," I said. I looked at Price. "Do you want to call or do you want me to?"

He grimaced. "Better you. He can chew my ass later in person."

"As long as he leaves something for me to grope. I like your ass."

"I'm sure he'll take it under advisement."

"What the hell are you two talking about?" Tiny interrupted, frowning as he looked back and forth between us.

"Give me a minute," I said, digging in my pocket for my phone. It was gone. I looked at Tiny. "I need my phone."

"Who are you calling?"

"The guy who can get you what you want."

That caught him up short. "Right," he said, sucking his teeth in disgust. "For people who want my services, you sure are playing it stupid. I don't mind dropping you down a mineshaft. After the rats got done with you, there wouldn't be anything left to find."

I held out my hand. "Just give me my fucking phone."

We played the who-would-blink-first game, and he went down. I'm nothing if not stubborn. I was the champion in the family, and Mel, Jamie, Leo, and Taylor were no slouches. Tiny dug in his back pocket and produced my burner phone.

I punched in Taylor's number. She answered on the first ring.

"What?"

"I need to talk to Touray."

Silence met my announcement. But where Jamie and Leo would have badgered me for information, Taylor stuck to business. "I'll text you his number. Give me a second."

The phone went dead. A few seconds later, the blue message light began blinking. I dialed the number. My mouth was oddly dry. For some reason, I was nervous.

He picked up just as fast as Taylor had. "Touray," he growled.

"Riley."

His shock lasted about a split second. "What's wrong? Where the hell are you? Is Clay all right? What's going on?"

It annoyed me that he immediately assumed something was wrong. Not that I could do anything about it. He was right. "We're with a potential . . . partner," I said, looking at Tiny.

I could feel his attention sharpening, drilling through the phone. I resisted the urge to take a step back. Like that would help. "Partner?"

"He wants to take control of Calvera," I said. "Clean it up, get rid of the bad eggs, and restore the community."

"What the fuck is going on, Riley? Because I don't have time for this shit. The city is wrecked and your father—"

"Vernon? Taylor said he showed up. What did he want?"

"To make a deal, which is why I don't have time for games. *Tell me what's going on.*"

"We're working a trace. Got captured. Price has a broken leg. We're negotiating for a tinker and freedom."

Touray's voice went molten and quiet. I'll admit I cringed a little and was very glad he was not in the same room. I glanced around the dingy walls, half expecting to see him appear out of nowhere. He was a traveller, after all.

"Explain."

"You know about the trace job?"

"I am aware that you took one. I do not know the details." His words were carefully clipped and formal, and I could hear the taut wire of his patience stretching thinner with every second.

"Story short: missing girl lured by her boyfriend who's a known rapist and killer. They've holed up in Calvera. We got here, got jumped, captured, and Price's leg broke. We need a tinker and some man power. Tiny here is willing to help if the trade is worth it. Maybe you should hear his terms," I added and passed the phone over to Tiny before Touray could ask anything else.

"Hello?" Tiny said warily into the phone.

The room pulsed and crackled with sudden magic. Neither Price nor Tiny would be able feel it. "Shit," I said, and then a furious Gregg stepped out of nowhere and trained his gun on Tiny.

Tiny's face paled. I didn't know if it was the gun or if he recognized Touray from the papers, or if it was just that a super scary man had appeared out of nowhere. Touray's gaze swept over Tiny, who'd lifted his hands, then around the room, over me, and landed on Price.

"You look like shit."

"Looks like Savannah took good care of you," Price answered. "Maybe she could give the FBI a few lessons."

I hadn't really thought about the changes in Price over the last few weeks. I studied him. He was leaner than before, like every bit of fat had burned away, leaving only carved ripples of muscle. His hair had grown out a little and flopped in his eyes. Those were haunted and so much older than before. He still moved like a panther, graceful and dangerous, but much of the veneer of civilization had flaked away.

On the other hand, Touray looked about the same as always, though his normally short hair looked a bit shaggy. His eyes were as black and turbulent as ever, giving me the heebie-jeebies. They reminded me of cold and unforgiving shark eyes, and they promised hell unleashed if you crossed him. Savannah Morrell might be lucky she was dead. The rest of him was as usual: broad shoulders and thick slabs of muscle and he radiated a violent, barely contained energy.

In a word, the man was terrifying, and I won't lie: even though I was his brother's girlfriend and supposedly we were family now, I was still scared shitless of him. Not that I was going to let him in on that secret.

"I don't bargain with men who are holding my brother prisoner," he snarled at Tiny.

Oh goody, I didn't rate a mention.

"Now, if you want to live, you walk us out of here."

"I'm not walking anywhere," Price said. "Not with this leg. Anyway, I think you might be interested in working with Tiny to clean up Calvera."

Touray glared at Tiny, his gun trained on the younger man's chest. By this time, Tiny had collected himself. He still held his hands up, but his expression had gone back to that wary carelessness. I'd be willing to bet that look worked in his favor a lot. Nobody would take him very seriously, and then he'd strike.

"You want to clean up the neighborhood?" Touray asked with a hefty dose of skepticism.

"I'm *going* to," Tiny retorted.

"How?"

"That depends on whether you're going to give me what I need, Mr. Touray."

Ha! Tiny *had* recognized him. If Touray was surprised, he didn't show it.

"What's in it for you? Or do you just want a clear field to run your own operation?"

"Gonna have to raise money somehow."

"So extortion?"

Tiny shook his head. "I'm not going to see this place eat itself alive again. My crew will take jobs from the outside, do some smuggling, money laundering, credit card scams, steal identities—the usual. Most of it can be done in virtual space. Might set up a porn site. I won't outright refuse anything. It's going to take a lot of money to rebuild the neighborhood and keep the peace. I'll do whatever's necessary."

A thought poked my brain. I was watching the birth of a Tyet lord.

The two men had their own little staring contest, or maybe it was one of those movie love moments. Either way, at the end of it, Touray lowered his gun, though not so far he couldn't have a bead on Tiny in a nanosecond.

"All right," he said. "Show of faith. Bring in your tinker and fix up my brother."

"And if I do?"

"Then you get the resources you need."

Tiny looked skeptical. "Just like that? No rules or conditions?"

"Of course there will be rules. You'll have to make sure you look after the neighborhood and protect the people. You'll be the law here. You'll have to keep a tight rein on your soldiers so they don't get it into their heads that they can shake people down just because they work for you. You're going to report to me and if I need you, you're going to show up and fight for me."

Tiny shook his head. "No deal. I'm not wasting Calvera blood on your causes."

"My *cause* is Diamond City," Touray said, striding forward to stand in front of Tiny, who actually looked like his name for once. Touray prodded the other man in the chest with a blunt finger. "What you want to do for Calvera, I'm going to do for the whole fucking city. If I need your help, you're going to give it, no questions asked." He stood back. "Take it or leave it."

"If I say no?" Tiny's voice rasped, but he'd managed not to pee himself. Touray often had that effect on people.

"Then we're back to you walking us out of here." Touray twisted his head to glare at Price. "I'll carry you if I have to," he snarled before Price could object again.

On the positive side, he didn't say he'd travel Price out without me. 'Course, he needed me for the Kensington artifacts. If not—I wouldn't want to bet on my chances.

Tiny rubbed a thoughtful hand over his mouth and jaw. Finally, he stood up and held his hand out. "Deal."

Touray clasped his hand. "Now call your tinker to fix my brother's leg."

"I'm the tinker," Tiny said with a sly grin. "I specialize in fixing and breaking bodies."

He crouched beside Price, circling his hands around Price's left calf. I could feel the surge of magic as the healing began. Price's hand tightened on mine. It wasn't pain. Healing always felt gross—like worms wriggling around in your flesh. I watched Tiny like a hawk, but the truth was, if he wanted to rip open an artery or explode Price's heart, we wouldn't know until it was too late. Touray would put a bullet between Tiny's eyes, but Price would still be dead.

There was no reason for Tiny to back out of the deal and a whole lot of good reasons for him to stick with it. Still, I was holding my breath when he dropped his hands.

"That should do it."

I let out my breath, and Price stretched his leg out and stood. He nodded. "Feels good. Thank you."

"Not that it would have needed healing if your people hadn't attacked us," I said to Tiny.

"Down, girl," Price murmured, tugging me against him.

Touray watched our exchange with a hooded look. "We need to talk," he said, his gaze gathering both of us up.

"After we get Cristina," I said.

Touray's brows winged down. "One girl isn't worth the whole city."

"I'll remember to tell her parents that when we find her body and I have to explain why we didn't get to her in time. You want to save the city? Then maybe we start by caring about the people," I said acidly, pushing out of Price's hold. I looked at Tiny. "Where's the rest of our stuff?"

He went out the door and came back with a battered cardboard box. On top lay our coats, and inside contained the rest of our possessions, including our guns. I shoved my arms into my coat, ignoring Touray. Price came up behind me and took his coat in silent support. Partners. He knew I wasn't going to back off from rescuing the girl, and I didn't think he was willing either.

"The city's on fire and the two of you are out to rescue a stupid girl who ran off with a shitty boyfriend," Touray said scathingly. He grabbed Price's arm, pulling him around. "Clay, you know this is stupid. Our organization has been without leadership for weeks. We've likely got traitors in our midst, and this Vernon Brussard is making threats that I'm afraid he can keep. There is no *time*."

Price didn't bat an eyelash. "I know you want to protect the people of Diamond City. That's your calling. Always has been. Cristina is one of those people. Just because she's just one single naïve girl doesn't make her any less valuable than anybody else in the city. I know the big picture is bad, but you've got to remember the small picture. Every life matters, even idiot teen girls."

My chest swelled at his words. He'd said what I felt but hadn't been able to put in words. That mentality is what had driven his career as a cop. He looked after the small picture—the individuals.

Touray blew out a breath and dragged his hand through his hair. A familiar habit he shared with Price.

"Fine. We'll get her. Fast. Then we get out of here and figure out how we're going to handle this mess."

That's when I realized that Touray wasn't angry that we were helping Cristina. He was angry about his own sense of vulnerability and confusion. He didn't have a plan for his next steps, and that was driving him nuts. He was a man used to being in control, but he'd been imprisoned for weeks. He got free, only to find his beloved city bombed and my father apparently making threats. He didn't know what changes had happened to the uneasy Tyet truces in the last weeks or who was in charge of what. He didn't know who to trust except Price.

I hid a smirk. I could almost feel sorry for him. Price came with a boatload of baggage. Touray wasn't going to get just Price; he was going to get me, Taylor, my brothers, plus maybe Dalton and even Arnow. He couldn't scare us into obeying him.

This could get *very* interesting.

Chapter 12

Gregg

URGENCY CHEWED AT Gregg's stomach as he watched Riley and Clay gather their things. He didn't have Savannah's deadline hanging over his head anymore, but Brussard's threat continued to haunt him. After travelling home from the safe house, he'd caught up on events and started getting the word out to his people that he was back in the driver's seat. More than a few of his "faithful" hadn't seemed very pleased at the news. He was going to have to seriously evaluate his organization for spies and traitors.

He'd called in the people he was almost certain he could trust and gotten an update of events during his absence. The report wasn't good. Several allies had turned on him and taken control of some key businesses. Luckily, he had plenty of cash, gold, and diamonds stashed away in case of civil war.

Savannah had actively started prying apart his hold on a diamond consortium, as well as undercutting his relationship with some of the more powerful players in town. Without someone to tell his people what to do, they'd acted independently, some looking out for his interests, others stealing from the candy jar. That was the problem with criminal organizations—they were full of criminals looking out for themselves.

The complexities had taken hours to sort out before he'd felt he had enough of a handle on events to start shooting orders designed to grab back control and reassert his dominance. Disappearing again to traipse after Riley and Clay would not generate a lot of confidence.

He snorted inwardly. So much for no one person taking precedence over the city. As soon as Riley had said they were captured and Clay was hurt, he'd launched himself into dreamspace. Total reflex and instinct. Clay was his only family, and Gregg couldn't bear the thought of losing him. He'd lived in agony the last weeks trying to believe that Riley had done as she'd promised and rescued Clay from the FBI's torturers.

It turned out she'd done a hell of a lot more than that by stopping Clay's power cascade. He owed her more than he could ever repay. If he'd lost Clay, he would have lost himself, lost that touchstone that reminded him why he gave a damn about cleaning up Diamond City. He'd have been an empty shell of a man.

Clay had changed since being in the FBI's clutches and finding his power. It wasn't just that he'd lost weight, or that his eyes now held a dark, bitter knowledge. When he looked at Riley, that bitterness softened and the love there burned like the fires of creation. She was clearly his anchor in the storm.

She'd changed as well. Riley had been tough before. More than he'd ever expected. She might look like a gypsy vagabond, but she had a backbone of titanium and a will of steel. She didn't back down, and she didn't give up. Thank God, because from what Taylor and her brothers had told him, it was Riley and Riley alone who'd pulled Clay out of the cascade and saved his life. He couldn't begin to imagine how. If anybody had asked him yesterday, he'd have said it was impossible.

Riley wore a new air of maturity. Everything tentative or uncertain about her had burned away. She carried herself with a confidence she'd lacked before, and she wasn't afraid to make demands and give orders. She'd become a leader rather than a lone wolf.

What really hooked Gregg's attention was the way each of them moved with an almost supernatural symmetry. Their awareness of each other seemed virtually psychic, as if they were connected at a cellular level. The touches, the looks, even the words—all of it seemed to convey more meaning for them than outsiders could see or understand.

And he was an outsider.

The realization sent a spiral of loss through Gregg's chest. He'd lost Clay. He mentally slapped himself before the thought finished crossing his mind. It wasn't true. But his bond to his brother had shifted. Clearly Price held Riley more dear than anyone else, even Gregg. Not that he could fault his brother. He envied the connection Clay and Riley shared. He knew he'd never have it. He'd never allow himself to have it. If he found a woman to love, she'd have to understand that she'd always come second to the city. He'd committed himself heart and soul years ago. It was his first wife and would always own the best of him. For better or worse.

Tiny had stepped out and now returned. "Crew's getting ready. Ocho's on his home turf and he's got himself plenty of muscle."

Riley eyed Gregg. He shook his head before she could make the suggestion. "I could travel to the girl, but the chances of that going well are pretty slim. She went willingly with this Ocho. If I try to grab her, she'll fight. If there are others around, I'll likely get shot. She might too, in the crossfire."

"Then it's the old-fashioned way," Riley said with a smile.

"I really don't like it when you smile like that," Clay said, frowning at her. "You're up to no good."

"I'm just thinking how nice it will be to meet Ocho face-to-face."

Clay shook his head. "I could almost pity the guy."

"Like I'm the scary one." Riley snorted. "Look at the two of you. You're bad cop and worse cop, only more like bad monster in the closet and worse monster under the bed."

"Which am I?" Gregg asked.

Riley considered him, then shook her head. "I take it back. You're the full-on bogeyman. Tiny here can be in the closet."

Gregg felt something loosen in himself at her easy banter. She was family. He'd called her that, but only because she belonged to Clay and that meant she was precious. But he was just beginning to realize claiming her as family meant more. He had a sister. Someone who would tease him. It had always been just him and Clay, and Gregg had always been the guardian. He'd protected Clay, and they'd always been close, but never in this way. He smiled with real pleasure for the first time in a long time. His smile widened as Riley looked taken aback.

"Wow," she said. "I'm a little scared that being the bogeyman puts a happy smile on your face, but okay. I'll take it." She looked at Price. "How worried should I be? Is he going to play that game with me like the kids in *The Parent Trap*, where they tied their father's girlfriend up, covered her in honey, and sent a bear in to visit her?" She looked back at Gregg. "You aren't getting rid of me that easy. Hell, you aren't getting rid of me at all. Kill me and I'll haunt the fuck out of you."

That earned her a genuine laugh, and Gregg found himself wanting to hug her. The impulse died when Clay set a possessive hand on her shoulder and slashed a cutting look at Gregg.

"You don't have to worry about my brother doing you harm," he said in a flat voice.

Before Gregg could react, Riley patted his hand. "Down boy. He's not going to do anything to me. He's loves you too much. And besides, if he did, he'd have to deal with Taylor and my brothers and I'm pretty sure he'd rather yank his own balls off."

Gregg laughed, smothering the hurt of his brother's doubt. He deserved it. They both knew it. He was nothing if not ruthless. But he'd claimed Riley as family, and that meant he wouldn't hurt her.

"This is all very entertaining," he drawled, "but we're on a countdown clock, so we should probably stop wasting time."

Riley's eyes narrowed as she glanced between the two brothers. "Actually, I could use a pit stop. Tiny? Want to show me the bathroom?"

The younger man nodded and led her out the door.

She looked back over her shoulder. "Take your time." The door clicked firmly shut behind her.

Clay shook his head and looked at Gregg. "Subtle."

"As a weed wacker," Gregg agreed, grateful to get a few minutes with Clay. He strode forward and pulled his brother into a tight hug. "God, I thought I lost you." A hot knot rose in his throat.

"Not a chance," Price said, hugging him back.

After a moment, they stood back.

"How bad was it?" Gregg needed to know. Whatever his brother had gone through was on his head. He'd *known* Clay could be a target for his suppressed talent. His brother had been totally in the dark.

Clay's attention turned inward, and a shadow passed over his expression, followed by a cocktail of emotions: pain, rage, fear, and guilt. "I beat the crap out of Riley. I nearly killed her," he said finally, his voice gravelly. He clenched his hands.

The air in the small kitchen *moved*. It swirled, turning from a mere hint of wind to a stiff breeze in seconds.

"What the hell?" Gregg tensed, whipping his head back and forth.

"It's me," Clay said in a strangled voice. His jaw was knotted, and sweat gleamed on his forehead. "My talent. Wind. Give me a minute—"

He grimaced, and his entire body clenched with effort.

"What can I do?" Gregg asked. Taylor, Leo, and Jamie had told him about Clay's destruction of the FBI compound, but even so, he'd discounted their story. They'd blown it out of proportion. Except they hadn't.

Clay said nothing, bowing his head as if under a great weight. He sucked in a deep breath and held it. Slowly the breeze gentled and stilled. Clay let out the breath with a gust and staggered to the wall, leaning back against it, his chest bellowing.

"I'm still working on control," he panted.

"You did all right," Gregg said, keeping the worry out of his voice. "You'll be a great kite-flying partner."

Clay glared. "When have you ever in your life flown a kite?"

"Lack of wind," Gregg said, relaxing as Clay's breathing steadied and his hands stopped shaking. "But now I could be a champion."

"The wind always blows here. Anyway, I don't think there are kite-flying competitions."

"There are hot dog-eating contests. There must be some for kites."

Clay straightened. "Enough with the fucking kites."

"Fair enough," Gregg said, sobering. "Taylor, Leo, and Jamie told me what happened when they got you out. They don't hold anything against you." Nothing. Not their mother's death or Clay using Riley for a punching bag. Obviously, she'd forgiven him, too. Or more likely, knowing her, she'd not needed to forgive him. She'd probably blamed the right people—the FBI torturers.

"They might not, but I do," Clay said flatly.

"I would, too." They exchanged a look of understanding. Both measured themselves on how well they protected those in their care. As far as Clay was concerned, he'd failed. Worse, he'd betrayed the woman he loved. That would chew at him until his dying day.

"If it weren't for her, I wouldn't be standing here," Clay said. He shook his head when Gregg nodded. "Not just breaking me out. I cascaded. They told you that? What they didn't tell you, what they don't know, is that Riley died." His teeth scraped white dents over his lower lip. "I almost couldn't bring her back. She gave her life for me. Stupid, stupid woman," Clay muttered, his shaking hands revealing the depth of his emotion.

And now Gregg knew exactly how much he owed Riley. He reached out and put his hand on his brother's shoulder, squeezing tight. "It *is* surprising," he said in a light voice that belied the hot emotion within him. "Personally, I'd think she should have cut her losses and gone on to the smarter, better-looking, richer brother."

A smile flickered across Clay's lips. "You couldn't get her attention if you stripped naked, put a bow around your neck, and sprawled on her dinner table. Though I admit, I'd pay to see that."

"You're probably right. She's clearly got questionable taste. I wonder if insanity runs in the family? Dear old dad is quite a piece of work. He's made me a proposition that I'm not sure I can refuse. I'm going to need to hear everything you and Riley have on him."

Clay's lip curled. "He's as trustworthy as a scorpion," he said. "That's the main thing you've got to know."

"I already figured that much out."

Just then, a light knock sounded on the door, and Riley stuck her head in. "We're coming up on dawn. We should get going."

She stood aside as the two men trooped past. Gregg paused long enough whisper in her ear.

"Thank you."

She grinned at him, and he was startled when she slid her arm through his. "Not bad for a stupid, irresponsible, moronic, ungrateful child," she said, reminding him of an argument they'd had just before all hell had broken loose and Savannah had captured him.

"I should probably say sorry for that."

"Probably. But you won't. And I probably won't apologize for what I said about you being a control freak Neanderthal," she said as they stepped out of what appeared to be the manager's living quarters of an old motel, following Tiny and Clay. The rest of the motel curved away in a one-story half-moon facing the street. There were probably no more than a dozen units. Dim lights lit the windows, and shadow figures stood in clusters along the sidewalk in front and in the parking lot.

"A control freak Neanderthal?" he asked. "I don't remember that."

"You might not have been there. Or I might not have said it out loud."

"Ah. Well, I appreciate the nonapology."

"I aim to please."

"What now?" Clay asked Tiny.

"Ocho likes a place in south central Calvera. It's an old skating rink that he's fixed up as a clubhouse and his headquarters."

"How many people will he have?" Gregg asked.

Riley pulled away, and he found himself missing her touch. He'd never experienced that kind of easy companionship with a woman. He didn't really have friends, and the women he slept with were either professionals or shallow, short-term lays with no strings.

"Personnel changes. With a new girl to celebrate—probably fifty or sixty. Ocho would want to throw a welcome party."

The sour look on Tiny's face indicated what he thought of the sort of party Ocho would throw.

Riley had gone very still. "New girl? Is he going to use Cristina as a party favor?"

Tiny shrugged. "Hard to say. Wouldn't be the first time."

The muscles in Riley's jaw knotted, and her lips pulled flat. She looked ready to commit murder.

"Let's get on it," Clay said.

Tiny turned and whistled. The men and women lounging in the shadows scattered, and the sounds of engines firing cut through the morning darkness.

"This way," Tiny said, leading them around to the other side of the manager's office. Parked next the building was a battered Jeep pickup. It had once been a pistachio green, but between the dents, scrapes, and rust, it looked more brown than anything else. It looked at least fifty years old, if not older.

It had only two doors, with the shift on the floor. "Gonna be tight," Tiny said. "Sorry."

In fact, he and Gregg would take up most of the tape-patched seat. With the temperature hovering in the single digits, riding in the back would be chilly.

"Not any worse than the bike," Riley pointed out to Clay.

He grinned. "We can huddle together for warmth."

"Sounds like a good plan." She vaulted into the back of the truck. The tailgate hung down over the bumper. Clay jumped up after her.

"You sure?" Gregg asked. He looked at Tiny. "How far is it?"

"Five miles or so," he said, jingling his keys in his hand.

"We'll be fine," Clay said, sitting down with his back to the cab. Riley went to sit beside him, but he pulled her down between his legs and put his arms around her, pulling her back against his chest. "Let's get this show on the road."

Tiny and Gregg got into the cab and shut the doors. They closed surprisingly quietly. The engine purred.

"People judge books by the cover," Tiny explained, putting the Jeep into reverse and backing out into the street. The suspension was tight, and they bounced hard over the ice ruts. "People underestimate me when they see me coming in this."

"Not for long," Gregg observed as they pulled out onto the empty street, followed by a line of other vehicles. None had their headlights on. Ocho wasn't going to get a warning that they were on their way.

"How so?"

"Taking over the neighborhood means becoming the guy in charge. You'll be very visible. And a perpetual target. You ready for that?"

Tiny shrugged. "It takes what it takes."

Gregg didn't have to ask if Tiny knew what he was getting into. He'd been like the boy once. Still was. Neither was going to let anything get in the way of doing what they needed to do.

"I don't want you fucking with my people," Tiny said, turning a corner. "Once things are under control."

"I don't know what you mean."

The other man gave a short laugh. "You're Gregg Touray, head of one of the biggest Tyets in the city. What you need, you take. I've given you my allegiance, but I'm not giving you the people of Calvera. They aren't kindling for your ambitions."

"Noted," Gregg said. He and Tiny were very much alike.

It took a matter of ten minutes to reach their destination. Acrid smoke from Savannah's explosion fires thickened the early morning air and scraped at the back of his throat. They parked a few blocks away from Ocho's headquarters in a school lot. Pink had started to wash across the eastern sky. They wouldn't have the cover of dark much longer.

"She's close," Riley said as she jumped down off the back of the Jeep. "Plus a lot of other trace. Fifty or sixty may be a conservative estimate."

Gregg watched her. She stared ahead as if she could see through the buildings separating them from Ocho's hideout. Her body vibrated with angry energy. Keeping her safely out of the fray wasn't going to be easy. Nevertheless, Gregg was determined. Clay looked ragged enough without putting him through that kind of worry. Nor could Gregg afford to lose her skills.

Gregg counted Tiny's crew. Thirty, plus him, Clay, and Riley. He could work with that. "What's the layout on the skating rink where Ocho's holed up?"

"It's a big rectangle. Front entrance at one end with wide steel doors with glass inserts. A ticket window. A few windows on the bottom floor where there were offices and a few more above those. A side door near the rear, then a big double access door with a ramp in the back. Another side door up near the ticket window, where the snack bar was. There are windows down the other side, but they are boarded up. Not a lot of free access."

"So it's a fortress," Gregg said. He gaze roved to Clay and then back to Tiny. "This is your turf. Thoughts?"

"We have to move fast," Riley inserted before Tiny could answer. "The bastard's already had Cristina too long."

"That leaves waiting them out," Tiny said. "Best bet is to set up a diversion in the front so that you can sneak in the back."

Gregg nodded. That had been his thought, too.

"What do you have in mind?" Clay asked.

Tiny grinned. "Ocho's got a fine restored big-block Chevelle and a Harley he's real proud of. He keeps the bike inside, but if someone started fucking with his car, he'd be pissed enough to come out and stop it. He's not the only one of his gang with a sweet ride, either. We light up a weenie roast with some Molotovs and they'll come running quick. Once they do, we'll pick off all we can."

"Where do they park?"

"Around front mostly, but some are in back."

"So if you hit both ends with some cocktails, then a small group of us can go inside and retrieve the girl while they're busy with you," Clay said. He nodded. "Let's do it."

Tiny waved at one of his lieutenants, ordering him to start siphoning fuel into glass beer bottles every vehicle seemed to have. Nice and handy for the makeshift fire bombs. Gregg could see dozens of beer bottles sitting in boxes on the trunks of cars and the tailgates of trucks. Most of the vehicles had hoses extending from their gas tanks. Soon the smell of gasoline saturated the air. "You came prepared."

"We always come prepared. How many of my crew do you want to go inside with you?" he asked Clay.

"Eight. They can flank us and push Ocho's assholes out to you. Create a cross fire."

Riley's face tightened in clear disapproval, but she didn't say anything. No doubt she feared for the girl, but Clay was an expert at this sort of thing, and as far as Gregg was concerned, his word was the last word.

"How long before you can be ready?" he asked Tiny.

"Ten minutes. Maybe fifteen. We'll fill everything we brought."

He turned away and joined his crew, pulling aside five men and three women who would accompany Gregg and Clay.

"You should take cover here," Gregg told Riley.

Her brows rose. "That's not going to happen."

"We don't need you to find the girl. We'll find her and bring her out."

She rolled her eyes. "Where do I start? First, fuck off. I don't take orders from you or anyone else. Second, Ocho might decide to take Cristina out of there and we'll need to track them fast. Third, I'm not some useless ornament for you to hang on your rearview mirror. You don't like it, you can shove your head up your ass. Oh wait, it's already there."

"You're a liability," Gregg declared, anger bubbling inside him.

"How so?"

How could she not know? Clay would implode if something happened to her. Clay would implode if anything happened to her, and she needed to accept it. He said so.

She stared at him a long moment, then turned deliberately to look at Clay. "Why don't you deal with this? I'm done."

With that, she stalked away.

"She's a liability?" Clay shook his head. "Brother, you're treading on thin ice. She's my partner, and not just in bed. She can handle herself. I don't like her risking herself, but I've had to get over it. Riley's not going to back off, any more than you or I would."

"I know she's capable enough. But she ought to—" Gregg broke off. He wanted nothing more than to chain the stubborn woman to a tree until this was all over. He had plans for her, plans to take down his enemies and control Diamond City. Not that Clay needed to know that right now.

"She ought to?"

"Have more respect for how you feel."

"And I have to respect how she feels." Clay's look was pointed. "If I'm not going to stay out of trouble, how can I ask her to? All I can do is have her back." His expression hardened, turning bleak and unforgiving. "I know exactly what it's like to lose her. I'm not going to let it happen again."

"I don't get it. The brother I know would lock her in a cell before he let her risk herself like this."

Clay's lips flattened. A sudden breeze lifted his hair and gusted through the parking lot, swirling powdery snow into ghostly shapes. "I try something like that, I lose her. Guaranteed. My only choice is to help her, or she'll dive into trouble without me—maybe without telling me."

Gregg nodded. "Got it," he said, pretending conviction he didn't feel. He was going to have to figure out a way to sideline Riley. Maybe not tonight, but hell was about to break loose in Diamond City. He promised himself he'd find a way to keep her off the front lines. Even if she weren't Clay's lover, the strength of her tracing talent made her too valuable to risk. If he was ever going to get ahold of the rest of the Kensington artifacts, he needed her alive and well.

If that meant locking her up, he was willing. He doubted Clay would be too angry with him.

She stood a short distance away, watching Tiny's soldiers plugging the gasoline-and-diesel-filled bottles with strips torn from thrift-store sheets and shirts before setting them carefully into boxes. In less than ten minutes, the cocktails were ready to go, except for dousing the wicks with the gallon bottles of cheap vodka that Tiny's people produced from the trunks of cars and truck boxes. Gregg lifted his brows when he saw them.

"You certainly came well stocked for a cocktail party."

"Not my first," Tiny said. He eyed Gregg. "Sure would like it to be my last."

Gregg's jaw tightened. He'd spent too many years trying and failing to get Diamond City in his grip. That had to change. Savannah had been his greatest competition. With her dead, he had a narrow window to grab control of the city before someone stepped up to replace her, or other Tyet organizations moved in. That meant he was going to have to wade a whole lot deeper into the cesspool of Tyet politics and violence. It also meant he was going to have to take Vernon Brussard up on his offer. Much as he hated not knowing the price tag for the bargain, he'd do it, if that's what it took to make his city safe.

"Next time you'll have better than Molotovs," he said, knowing full well that Tiny wanted an end to the fighting, not better weapons. Right now, the best Gregg could do was the latter.

Tiny scowled, but said nothing else.

A short time later, the incendiary bottles were divided up between the vehicles, glass clinking as they shifted together in the boxes.

"You should get into position." Tiny glanced at his watch. "Be ready in ten minutes. We'll hit front and back and draw them out."

He scanned over his crew. Gregg figured Tiny had around forty soldiers, give or take, all armed to the teeth.

"You're going to want to hurry. Once Ocho figures out this is a full-scale attack, he'll retreat into the rink and start trying to pick us off. We'll make sure no one will get out, then bring the fight inside. You'll want to get out before that. He's about to find out he's done in Calvera."

Tiny's face was set with brutal determination. If Gregg had doubted the kid's dedication to the job he'd taken to protect the neighborhood, that doubt faded. Whether Tiny could handle Ocho. . . . Gregg was a good judge of character and ability, and he'd bank on Tiny any day, even without seeing Ocho. This kid had the makings of a born leader, and failure wasn't an option for him.

The sky had lightened, though the low pewter clouds blocked the sun. Shadows clung like ghosts to the buildings, bushes, and trees.

After checking their watches to mark the time, Clay and Gregg fell in beside Riley and followed Tiny's eight assigned soldiers around the side of the school. Behind spread a broad level field five feet deep in snow. The last thaw and freeze had created a thick crust beneath a few inches of newly fallen powder.

They clambered up on top and jogged across. Gregg wrenched one leg when his foot broke through. He stopped and yanked himself loose before overtaking the others.

On the other side of the field ran a line of evergreen trees, the bottom branches cut up high enough to walk beneath. Beyond ran a fifteen-foot berm of snow pushed up from the snowplows. A notch had been dug in it, likely to allow children to pass through on their way to school.

They followed Tiny's soldiers through, coming out on an ice-packed sidewalk. Just up the street on the left was a gas station and carwash, both currently closed. Across from them was a strip mall with a beauty place, a dollar store, a butcher, and a German/Mexican delicatessen.

A gleaming, lemon-peel sun peeked out of the clouds. The street and sidewalks were empty except for a handful of parked cars. They trotted across to the other side, then down the length of the berm on the other side to the plowed entrance. They hooked inside, weapons raised as they scanned for enemies. Nothing. Foreboding prickled down Gregg's back. It couldn't stay this easy for long. He flexed his fingers on the grip of his gun. His heart hurried faster, pushing adrenaline through his body.

The parking lot angled from the back along the side of the cinder-block skating rink in an L shape. Evergreen trees rose at intervals across the lot, and bushes grew in a scraggly, overgrown belt down the long side of the building. A smaller berm of plowed parking lot snow paralleled the bushes. Whoever had cleared it had done a half-assed job of it, too. The pavement was invisible beneath a six-inch-thick layer of rutted ice and compacted snow. Gregg doubted it would melt on its own before June.

They scuttled across the wide-open expanse, depending on the cloudy twilight to conceal them. Gregg counted cars in the rear parking area. Just under three dozen. Several junkers in the back corner humped beneath mounds of snow.

They scrambled up over the eight-foot-high hill of snow and down the other side. No one had bothered to clear the sidewalk, and the snow had been trampled to form a lumpy walkway. Bright-colored graffiti rose three-quarters of the way up the forty-foot cinder-block walls. The eleven intruders shuffled down to the rear exit door to wait for Tiny's diversion.

A mess of cigarette butts, used condoms, beer cans, bottles, and candy wrappers littered the ground. Yellow ice pooled around them and halfway up the berm. The stench of ammonia from the piss made Gregg's eyes water. Tiny's contingent whispered disgust. Clay's hand chopped through the air to shut them up. At least there weren't any guards. Gregg was willing to bet his right hand that if any had bothered to stand watch in the night, they'd quickly gotten lazy and retreated inside for warmth and entertainment.

He glanced at Riley, who bounced on the balls of her feet. "We still got a reason to go inside?" Blunt, maybe even harsh, but if the girl was dead, there wasn't any point in risking their lives.

"Yes." She didn't bother to look at him.

He fought to keep himself from using their wait to grill her about Vernon, even though her memories of her father were suspect, given the traps he'd set in her brain.

After getting back home and taking care of immediate business, Gregg had run Brussard's name through a number of channels and discovered that Vernon Brussard was a ghost. He didn't pay taxes, he had no social security card, no passport, no driver's license, no birth certificate, no work record, no arrest record, no credit record, nothing. As far as government bureaucracy was concerned, the man simply did not exist.

That in itself was confusing. Most people who disappeared reinvented themselves with forged documents, stolen birth records, and so on. They established their new identity with careful precision, making it nearly impossible to penetrate. Some people developed multiple aliases that would survive deep background checks.

Not Brussard. That worried Gregg. The man wasn't stupid, so he hadn't overlooked creating a new persona. The fact that he felt he had no need to establish one meant he was confident it didn't matter. He'd never have to answer for it. That took a lot of power and a lot of connections.

And that meant Brussard's threat had teeth. Big teeth.

The sounds of revved engines and shouting broke the morning's serene silence. From the front of the building, Gregg heard gunshots and a small explosion followed by cheers and breaking glass. A line of vehicles wheeled into the back parking lot. Tiny's crew lobbed cocktails from windows and the backs of trucks. Crash after crash. Smoke and flames billowed up. More shouts sounded, and then gunshots rang out.

"Time to go," Gregg said, but Clay was already at the door. He pressed his back flat against the wall, holding his gun ready in his right hand as he reached for the handle with his left. He depressed the thumb button and gave a little tug. To Gregg's surprise, the door opened a crack.

"Stupid fucks," he muttered.

"Arrogance," Riley said from behind their scruffy companions. They held their weapons high and ready, demonstrating more training than Gregg had expected. "Who'd dare attack the big bad Ocho in his own house?"

Clay pulled the door wider and slid between it and the jamb. He scanned the interior, then jerked his head at his companions. Tiny's crew flowed inside with Riley and Gregg bringing up the rear.

Inside was a cave of colored lights. Strings of them stretched above like a massive spiderweb, with more dangling down the walls. They were the only light in the cavernous space.

The rescuers had entered near the back of what had been the sunken skating surface. A half wall curved around the rink at the far end, and beyond was the former snack bar, which now served as a kitchen.

The wall ended a quarter of the way around the rink. A faded orange carpet-covered platform surrounded the rest of it, six inches above the skating floor. The entire skate surface was littered with clusters of odd bits of furniture, rugs, cushions, and televisions. A squatters' haven. The place stank of unwashed bodies, sex, pot, and popcorn and fried chicken from the kitchen.

Clay turned to Tiny's eight-man crew. "You'll take point. Up this side"—he gestured to the left wall—"then sweep across to clear the floor. Incapacitate everyone. Don't leave anybody able to bite your asses."

Tense nods. They trotted up the side of the rink. Each carried at least a handgun, a couple had AR-15s. All of them had knives for quick, quiet work. Gregg exchanged a look with Clay and then glanced at Riley. Did she understand Clay's orders? Did she know that this was about to turn into a bloodbath?

He couldn't tell. Her face was a taut mask. She practically vibrated with impatience.

The line of Tiny's soldiers began their silent purge of the people who had not been drawn outside by Tiny's antics. They wended through furniture and fast-food boxes and towers of stacked beer cans. A discordant mix of TV channels and video game sounds coupled with the muffled pops and bursts from outside gave them an eerie soundtrack. Gregg kept one eye on them and one eye on Riley. Her expression never changed as the soldiers stopped to silence Ocho's dregs. Drugged out of their skulls, probably. Or passed-out drunk. One shouted, and Tiny's soldier leaped on top of him. Silence.

Riley's mouth tightened, but no other reaction. Good. Maybe she was figuring out what war really meant. Maybe she was ready to do what was necessary to clean up the city and stop the bloodshed.

"Where is she?" Clay whispered.

Riley pointed toward a wall of doors on the opposite side of the rink. In between were glassless picture windows covered in plywood. Some of the doors were open. They hustled across the rink behind Tiny's string of soldiers.

A shirtless man sprawled on a pullout couch bed. Though one of Tiny's eight soldiers had clubbed him in the head with a gun butt, he remained alive. A woman sprawled beside him, her mouth open, her breathing harsh between her lips. She bore no wounds.

A lot of people didn't have the stomach for killing women, even drugged hags involved in kidnapping little girls. Gregg was one of them, but he could get past his squeamishness and do what was necessary. He lifted his gun, then lowered it again and reached for his knife.

"No," Riley said. "Leave them."

Gregg shook his head. "It's too risky."

She rolled her eyes at him. Infuriating. "We won't be here very long and if they were going to wake up or stir themselves to do anything, they would have already."

He was shaking his head before she finished. "No."

"Then we'll tie them up."

"We don't have time."

"And we have time to stand here and have this argument? Because I'm willing to stay here until you accept reason."

Gregg didn't need her permission, and he damned well wasn't going to let her boss him around. With a quick twist of his wrist, he drew his knife, stabbing them in quick succession, first the man and then the woman. He cleaned his knife on a dingy sheet and resheathed it.

Riley made a frustrated sound. "Asshole."

"True enough, but I'm alive and I mean to stay that way," he said. "You can thank me later."

"In your dreams."

"Look at it this way. Some of Tiny's crew will live because these two died."

"What were they going to do? They were unconscious."

"Unconscious people wake up. They weren't innocent people, Riley. They were thugs. If I didn't kill them, Tiny would have. Me doing it guarantees they won't wake up and surprise us from behind."

Before Riley could argue, Clay intervened. "Enough. It's done. Get moving."

They reached the other side of the rink without encountering any other bodies, alive or dead. They joined Tiny's soldiers as they stepped up on the carpet-covered floor between the skating floor and the line of rooms.

"What now?" one of the men asked. He was in his early twenties, with a black five o'clock shadow. He cradled his AR-15, barrel tilted to the floor, his gaze ricocheting around the room as he looked for trouble.

"You four split up and take the front and back doors. Keep Ocho's people from coming back in as long as possible. We'll find the girl," Clay said. "Hopefully the ones you didn't put down in here don't wake up and bite you in the ass."

Five O'Clock Shadow glared at his companions, apparently unaware that they'd left live threats behind. Several of them looked away shamefacedly.

"Grace, Aldonado, Ruiz, Kim—take the back. The rest of you—with me." The two groups split away.

"Which door?" Clay asked Riley, not wasting time.

"Up here," she said, already leading the way. Ragged and threadbare holes pocked the thin carpet covering the platform. The soles of Gregg's shoes stuck in places. He didn't even want to think about what he was stepping in as he brought up the rear. Riley arrowed to the first door nearest the front of the rink, pausing outside to glance at her two companions.

Clay pushed Riley behind him and took up a position on one side of the door. Gregg stepped to the other side, his gun held high. He nodded. Clay twisted the knob and thrust the door open. It bounced off the interior wall. The stench of smoke, sex, greasy food, and sweat rolled out in a choking cloud. Gregg launched himself through the doorway, scanning back and forth, his gun raised and swiveling with him.

Against the right wall sat two lamps on a plastic set of drawers. Their bulbs were red and cast a lurid light over the rest of the room. The walls had been painted black and then graffitied. A target had been painted on the plywood panel covering the window. A half dozen knives sprouted from the splintered wood. On the opposite wall was a king-sized water bed sitting high on a pedestal. Mirrors had been glued to the ceiling above.

The head of the bed was piled with pillows, and the bookcase headboard was filled with overflowing ashtrays, water pipes, syringes, rubber tubing, and a cache of weapons. The girl was nowhere to be seen.

Clay pushed in beside him, blocking Riley's entry. "Where is she?"

Gregg moved farther in to look down the side of the bed and froze "Here," he said, finding himself staring down the barrel of a black snub-nosed .38 revolver.

Cristina had scrunched herself up into a ball between the bed and a wooden chair in the corner. Purple bruises splotched across the right side of her jaw and around her neck. Her left eye was black, and her lower lip was split. She held the gun up in surprisingly steady hands. Her dark eyes glittered with hatred and panic.

"She's here," he said, his own gun trained on her. He didn't blink. The slightest twitch, and he'd shoot. Better her dead than him.

Riley climbed up on the bed. Gregg held out a stopping hand to keep her from blocking his line of fire.

"We're here to help you, sweetheart," Riley said softly.

Cristina's gaze didn't flicker from Gregg. She gave a tiny shake of her head. "Don't believe you," she whispered.

"Emily and Luis sent us. I'm Riley Hollis. I'm a tracer. We're here to take you home."

"Why is he pointing a gun at me?"

"Because you're pointing one at me," Gregg said. He grimaced and drew up his magic. He thinned himself, sliding halfway into the travel dimension. He could still hold the gun, but it wasn't all that useful. It was half out of the world too, and that made the dynamics of combustion in the chamber strange. Still, a bullet wouldn't kill him as long as he maintained the shift. He lifted his arm, pointing the gun up at the ceiling. "Satisfied? Can we get out of here before we all get killed?"

A ripple ran through Cristina's body, and her eyes looked haunted. God dammit. Whether or not Ocho had touched her, he'd stolen her innocence, her sense of safety. Kids thought they'd live forever, that their bodies couldn't break. Ocho had taught Cristina different, and probably a hundred girls besides. Cruel bastards like him and Savannah and victims like Cristina were the reason Gregg would never give up on his mission to clean up the city. Plenty of money could be made without hurting innocent people.

The look on his face must have revealed his disgust and hatred. The girl's eyes widened, and she pushed back against the wall like she could make herself disappear inside it.

"Hey," Riley said, pulling the girl's gaze away from Gregg. It was only a moment, but time enough for him to pounce forward and wrap his hand around Cristina's and shove the gun upward.

She jerked her finger and the gun went off, the sound exploding in the small space. The bullet hit the drop-tile ceiling and went through, clanging against something metal.

Cristina let out a strangled sound and started kicking, banging her free fist against his shoulder and head. Gregg had left the travel space, and her blows stung against his ear and cheek. When he didn't let go, she curled her fingers and started clawing at him. He shook the gun out of her hand. It fell with a thud. He twisted her to face away from him and wrapped his arms around her waist, lifting her off the ground, her feet dangling.

"Easy now," he said against her ear. "Nobody's going to hurt you anymore."

She either didn't hear him, or didn't believe him. She braced her feet against the wall, shoving backward and twisting. When that had no impact, she wriggled and kicked, her heel catching Gregg's knee and the other his shin. He dumped her onto the bed. She started to scramble up, but stopped when she saw Clay blocking the door. Riley slid off the other side of the bed and Gregg picked up the revolver.

Cristina panted, her body tight as a coiled spring.

"Look," Riley said in a gentle voice, the kind you used for scared dogs. "I promise we're here to take you home. Emily and Luis asked me to find you. We'll take you to them, but you need to hurry. Right now, Ocho and his crew are distracted. That's not going to last long. We can take you out of here walking, or we can carry you out, but we are not leaving you with a shitbag like Ocho. Which do you want to do? You've got about three seconds to decide."

A heartbeat passed. "What about the gun? I want it back."

Riley looked the question at Gregg. He didn't like it, but he understood the girl's need to be able to protect herself. He offered it to her, butt first.

"Try not to shoot one of us."

Cristina eyed him, her dark brows winging together. She took the gun slowly, as if expecting a trick. She wrapped her fingers around the grip, then looked at Riley. "I'm ready."

Clay looked out, then swore and yanked himself back in. "We've got company."

"How many?" Gregg asked.

"More than is healthy." Clay gave another quick look. "Six. But if they overwhelmed the four soldiers we sent up there, more will be coming—and fast."

Cristina made a whimpering sound, but then clamped her teeth tight. Tough girl.

Yelling broke out, and with it came the pelting of feet. One voice rose above them all, shouting orders for more ammo, weapons, and to secure the rear of the rink. Had to be Ocho. He sounded pissed, but he'd kept his cool.

"Put the injured down on the skate floor. Secure the side doors—make sure no one comes through them." He called off names. "Help up front. Make sure no one comes through." Another set of names were told to go in back.

Clay pushed the door shut. He and Gregg exchanged knowing looks. They were trapped.

Cristina looked at each one of them, her face taut and pale. "What do we do?" she asked, her voice shaking and desperate. "How are we going to get away?"

Chapter 13

Riley

FROM THE MOUTHS of babes. How the hell *were* we going to get out? I glanced at Gregg. He was a traveller. He could take them one at a time. Maybe. The last time he'd pulled her through travel space, Vernon had kidnapped her spirit and nearly killed her. Again. Sometimes I wonder why the man hadn't just worn a condom instead of having a kids.

"Take the girl," Price told Touray. "Get her out of here."

"I'm not leaving you two on your own."

"Damned right. Get your ass back here quick."

Clearly Touray didn't like the idea. He looked like he'd prefer a good case of diarrhea. Apparently, he figured he didn't have a choice, because he grabbed Cristina and they vanished.

"What now?" I asked.

Price had that cold, calculating look he got when he was at war. Like he'd stripped away all his emotions. If he hadn't been on my side, I'd have been nervous.

"We wait for Gregg."

A minute ticked by. Then another. Then it was five. He should have been back in under a minute.

"He's not coming back," I said finally.

Price nodded. With his robot face on, I couldn't tell if he was pissed or worried or both.

"We have to get out of here," he said.

Well, that went into the "no shit, Sherlock," category. *Can I have dumb questions and dumb answers for two thousand, Alex?*

"So we just sashay across the rink and walk out?"

Price glared at me. "You think this is funny?"

"I get snarky when I'm terrified. Sue me. Whatever you want me to do, I will. Just tell me."

"You must be scared all the time," he grumbled. "Here's what you can do: don't get shot, don't get hurt. Can you do that?"

"Sure. Where's my bulletproof bubble suit?"

A fleeting grin flashed across his lips and vanished. "The longer we wait, the more time they have to settle in. We need to go while they are still distracted."

The air in the room had begun to swirl. It cooled the nervous sweat on the back of my neck. Whatever his demeanor said, Price was getting agitated.

"I could take us through the spirit realm," I offered.

"Do you think can?" he asked. "I've watched you all night. Every time you picked up Cristina's trace, you nearly doubled over in pain."

So much for hiding it. "I can manage if I have to." I hoped. Trying to help Price at the cabin had unraveled a lot of the healing I'd done over the last couple of weeks.

"I don't suppose you'll leave without me."

"I don't suppose I would," I said, folding my arms and glaring at him. "I'm not leaving you to get killed."

"I don't plan to let them kill me."

"Then you can plan not to let them kill either of us, because you're stuck with me."

He must have decided that arguing would be a waste of time. He peered through the crack he'd left in the door. His back stiffened, and the air in the room tightened so that it was hard to breathe.

"Get up against the wall, and stay close," he said. We're going with Plan B."

We had a Plan B? I didn't have time to ask what the hell it was. I jumped behind him and pressed against the wall.

I hadn't felt any active magic since we'd arrived inside the skating rink building beyond some small wards and a few other minor magics. But it only stood to reason that Ocho and his crew had to have talents. I felt it sparking up all around us—all different kinds of talents as people flooded back inside the building.

I heard the tromp of feet coming closer, along with babble and shouting. Maybe they'd walk on by. It's not like Ocho needed a nap right now, and the room wasn't good for much else besides assaulting helpless girls. I wondered if Cristina would have worked up the nerve to shoot him. Probably. She was tough.

Some of the feet thumped past. I held my breath. Maybe it was a false alarm and we wouldn't be discovered. Yet, anyhow. But we couldn't be so lucky. The door started to push open.

Price didn't wait. In one fluid move, he grabbed the intruder by the hair, yanking him up against his chest and pressing his gun to his captive's head.

"Ocho, I presume?"

"Fuck you, asshole." Despite his words, Ocho held himself still. He stood a few inches shorter than Price's six foot two. His hair was glossy, black and he wore it in a ponytail. His face was wide and angular, his eyes black as his hair.

"Drop your weapon," Price commanded, grinding the barrel of his gun against Ocho's scalp. "Now."

The other man let the AR-15 fall. It thumped on the floor. I wondered how many of his people had noticed Price grabbing him. Where the hell was Touray? Nothing short of the Second Coming would have kept him away. I took a steadying breath. We didn't need him. We could do this on our own.

I tried to believe it.

"I'm going to have your balls for breakfast," Ocho declared. "I'm going to castrate you, and then I'm going to cut you open and watch your guts fall out on the ground. Then I'm going to find your family and rape all your women and kill all your men and shit on their graves."

Clearly he didn't understand the rule that says don't piss off the guy with the gun to your head. I thought everybody knew that one. Seemed like common sense. Like, don't stick your hand in a fire or don't try to breathe water. Ocho was quite clearly a nut job. Or maybe he had tricks up his sleeve. My stomach twisted, and I tightened my hand on my gun.

"You are going to order your people to let us walk out of here. If anybody tries to get in our way, I'll drop you like a bad habit," Price said roughly. "Understand?"

I hoped Ocho's people were loyal, and he didn't have some understudy dying to step into the part of gang leader. If so, using him as a shield might turn us into targets. Leaky targets.

"Sure thing, *cabrón*. Let's get it on."

I wished Ocho sounded the slightest bit nervous. As it was, he seemed eager. I exchanged a look with Price. He didn't like it any more than I did. Not that we had any choice. I gave a little shrug to tell him I'd follow his lead. He grimaced and then pushed Ocho into the doorway.

"Let's go. Tell your crew to stand down."

Ocho gave a low laugh, cut off by Price's gun jabbing into the soft hollow between his neck and jaw. "Tell them."

"Everybody!" The wiry man called out, his cheeks flushed red, though whether from anger or humiliation, I couldn't tell. Neither was good for us. "These *cabrones* want you to put down your guns or they'll kill me!"

Silence fell around us and rippled outward. I heard clicks of hammers cocking, and a gun fired. The plywood window covering thumped and rattled as the bullet struck. Price jerked Ocho's head back and dug the barrel of his gun harder into his jaw.

"Do that again and he dies," he said, his voice carrying.

I could almost hear some of them considering their options. I doubted all of them wanted to see Ocho keep breathing, but apparently some did.

"All right," a woman called out. "Go ahead."

"Does she mean shoot him or walk out there?"

"Let's hope they want him alive."

"I suppose it's too much to hope for that they actually put their guns down."

Price didn't bother with the obvious answer. "Stay close behind me. We'll keep to the wall and go out the front. It's closer. Make yourself as small as you can.

"Can you do anything? With your talent?" I didn't want to be more specific in front of Ocho. Even though he struggled, Price had begun to get the hang of using the wind.

"I'm not ready to bet our lives on my control. Being tired doesn't help."

Fair enough. I had a lot of practice with my talent, and I knew from experience that fatigue made everything harder. Neither one of us had slept in over thirty hours, and both of us had been seriously injured. Magical healing didn't fix the physical exhaustion that came with trauma, or in my case, replace lost blood.

"Ready?" Price asked.

"Right behind you."

Price eased out of the doorway. I gripped his belt with one hand, pressing myself close. I felt like a coward hiding behind him, but following his orders was the intelligent thing to do. Especially since the air in the room had . . . tightened, pulling taut like a bungee cord stretched to the max. I wondered if Price realized he was doing it. I thought about the tornado in our safe house—was it only yesterday? He'd gained control over himself, but then his power had been triggered by our argument. How would it erupt now if one of us got shot?

Hopefully we didn't find out. Just the thought of the danger he was in right now made my chest cramp with fear. I took a deep breath. Losing it now wouldn't help. I'd panic later, when we were safe. Where the fuck was Touray?

We eased down the wall. Ocho started yelling something, but his voice disappeared in a rasping gargle.

"None of that, now," Price instructed, the muscles of his arm flexing as he tightened his hold around Ocho's neck. "Step it up, Riley," he said to me. "The natives are getting restless."

I guessed they were, because we hadn't gone five more feet before all hell broke loose.

The lights went out, creating a total blackout. At the same time, Price started tussling with Ocho. I heard grunts and stamping feet and a crack like bone, and then Price's gun went off. I squawked and ducked. I wanted to be small. Screams and shouts erupted throughout the skating rink. My own clogged in my throat, and then I heard Price yell my name. My heart hammered back into motion. He was alive. I dragged in a ragged breath. I opened my lips to answer, but at that moment an electric shock sang through me, and I made a bubbling sound.

When we were kids, my brothers had tricked me and Taylor into grabbing ahold of an electric fence. This was like that, only more intense. Every hair on my body stood on end. Sharp-edged ribbons of energy throbbed through me, prying at the molecules of myself.

"Riley!" Price shouted again, and now the air around me tightened, spooling tighter and tighter with every passing second.

"I'm here," I gasped, but between the compression from without and the AC/DC-river inside, the words came out disgustingly whispery, and I couldn't tell if he heard. I reached out to find him. Something thumped against my side, and I grunted, twisting away from the pain, my face smashing up against the wall. My nose took the worst of it. Jesus fuck, but it hurt. Blood ran from it and down my lips and chin.

In that moment, the lights came on again. Lucky for me the skating rink wasn't well lit, or I'd have been blinded. I almost wished I was. Price's arm thrust straight in the air, his hand welded to his gun. He still had his arm around Ocho's neck, but the other man had twisted around and now pummeled Price's stomach and chest with sharp jabs. Price grunted and kicked out, knocking

Ocho off his feet. The other man dropped and hung from Price's hold on his neck. He scrabbled for footing. Price twisted and thrust out his leg to keep Ocho from regaining his balance.

His hand and gun remained upraised. They seemed to be stuck fast in the air. Maybe a binder spell of some kind? His biceps and forearms bunched as he fought the invisible hold. He let go of Ocho's neck and threw himself back and up, turning his prison into leverage. He kicked out, hitting Ocho in the jaw. The other man came off the floor as he flew backward. He landed flat on his back. His head bounced, and he lay still.

"Riley!" Price spun toward me, reaching out to yank me to my feet. He planted a hand on my back and shoved. "Run!"

Uh, no. First, we were surrounded, and second, there wasn't a snail's chance in a beer bath that I'd be abandoning him to save my own ass. I staggered forward and then swung back around and pulled on my power. I might as well have shot myself up with acid, and not the good hallucinogenic kind. The pain was instant and burned my raw channels. I couldn't hold it.

The loosed magic flailed wildly, lashing me with electric whips. Welts rose on my skin wherever it landed, some of them turning bloody as the energy cut into my flesh. One slashed across my forehead, and warmth trickled down my face. If I could have used the burst of uncontrolled magic as a weapon, I would have. Unfortunately, it targeted me.

I brushed the blood away from my mouth to breathe better, no doubt making a mess of myself. I probably looked like a killer out of a slasher movie. Jason Voorhees's daughter, maybe, or Michael Myers's sister. The one he didn't manage to kill. Some movie magic would come in real handy right about now to get us the hell out of this mess.

Price still hung by his arm in empty air. Definitely a binder spell of some kind. I couldn't release him, and the fact that he wasn't yet riddled by bullets was only because he was caught and Ocho would want him to die slow. I guess I wasn't as much of a threat. I still had my gun, but it wasn't going to do me a lot of good against dozens of enemies. Other than that, I didn't have any magical help on me. I hoped to hell that Touray had a damned good reason for hanging us out to dry.

Chapter 14

Gregg

AT THAT VERY moment, a very pissed-off Gregg found himself being tossed on the back seat floorboards of a Cadillac Escalade, his arms bound to his sides and tape covering his mouth. The thugs who'd taken him had hung a null around his neck to prevent him from travelling. The door slammed shut, and his two captors got inside.

They'd been waiting for him. How the hell they knew he was coming, he couldn't begin to imagine, but they'd damned sure been ready for him. He'd travelled to the Diamond City Diner. The security nulls hadn't been activated, which should have tipped him off, but he was in so much of a hurry to get back to Clay and Riley that he hadn't paid attention. Gregg had planned to dump the girl off on Riley's friend Patti and leave. But the moment he'd stepped out of dreamspace, someone had clocked him.

Gregg twisted over onto his stomach. He braced his head against the floor, gritting his teeth against the throbbing ache pounding through his skull.

Balancing his weight on his head, he inched his knees up under him. Once he had enough leverage, he heaved upward and flung himself sideways onto the seat. He sat up straight and surveyed his captors. The driver was white, forty or so, with short, stubbly black hair surrounding a bald spot; he had rough skin and meaty hands. He was built like a tank. The passenger was younger, maybe late twenties, early thirties. He was dark skinned with short dreadlocks. If anything, he was bigger than the hulk of a driver.

The fucker probably had a glass jaw.

Urgency slammed into Gregg. He'd left Clay and Riley surrounded by an army of thugs. He clamped his teeth, thinking. The null around his neck hung on a heavy chain, the kind you might get at a hardware store. The null itself was an industrial-sized nut. Maybe he could bend down and shake it off over his head?

He didn't get the chance.

Dreadlocks turned. In one smooth motion, he lifted a stun gun and shot it. The barbs caught in Gregg's coat. Paralyzing fire flashed through him. His back arced, his muscles went rigid. He couldn't move. His entire body had short-circuited. Dreadlocks watched Gregg impassively as the electricity continued to pump into him, then abruptly let go of the trigger.

Gregg's body went from stone to quivering jelly in a heartbeat. He melted sideways onto the seat, gasping to fill his lungs. He felt like a mule had kicked the air right out of him.

Dreadlocks made a show of shucking the used module and replacing it, then rewound the wires. When he was done, one eyebrow twitched up as if asking whether Gregg understood the message, then he turned back to face the windshield, losing interest in his prisoner.

Adrenaline pumped through Gregg He didn't so much hurt as he felt disconnected from himself. After a minute or so, the sensations passed. He didn't waste time. He scooted forward, dangling his head down over the seat. The null hung down to the floorboards, but the chain caught around the base of his skull. He shook his head, and it rode up behind his ears.

He jerked his head up and down, trying to work the chain over his head. Before he could, a hand grabbed his collar and dragged him upright, shoving him against the seat.

Dreadlocks faced around, his expression mildly annoyed. He leaned over the seat, grabbed Gregg by the hair, and yanked him close, then smashed a fist against his jaw. The punch felt like getting hit with a cement bat. Once, twice, three times, and everything went black.

GREGG CAME BACK to himself as he was being dragged backward through a doorway. Dreadlocks and Ham-Hands gripped him under each arm. His heels bumped across the threshold and slid over black marble floors. He blinked away dizziness, but someone seemed to be drilling a hole down through his skull. He lifted his head groggily. His teeth felt loose, and his lips and jaw were swollen. Breathing through his nose was nearly impossible. Thank goodness someone had removed his tape gag.

They passed through two more doorways before the two thugs dropped him onto wooden armchair. The impact jolted through his head and sent a railroad spike through his ear. He bit back a groan, refusing to give his captors the satisfaction of seeing him suffer.

Instead, he made himself sit up and examine the room around him. The place was elegant and masculine, with modern steel and glass furniture, gray wallpaper, and a white-and-black patterned rug. A black and crystal chandelier hung overhead. An ebony desk sat opposite to him with an abstract painting in the colors of an impending summer storm hanging just behind. Sitting at the desk was Jackson Tyrell.

He didn't look as powerful or menacing as he should, as he was. In fact, he looked a lot like a butcher or baker awkwardly clad in an expensive suit. He had a round, jowly face with thin gray hair combed over his bald pate, broad shoulders, and a well-tended stomach. He sat back in the chair, a cup of coffee held in a pudgy, thick-fingered hand, watching Gregg through the steam. His eyes were calm and clever. He got right to the point.

"I have an offer for you." He frowned. "Are you able to comprehend what I'm saying, Mr. Touray? Your brain isn't scrambled, is it?"

"No more than yours is," Gregg said, the words slurring through his swollen lips. He watched Tyrell steadily, his right eye not fully opening. He had no doubt that whatever happened in the next few minutes would determine whether he walked out of here alive or dead.

Tyrell smiled. It did nothing to warm the chill of his eyes. "Good. I'd rather not have to find a replacement for you."

Gregg lifted his brows "Do tell. I wasn't aware that I might need replacing."

"The pieces on the chessboard can't know the plans of the master who moves them."

"I don't play chess," Gregg lied.

"Not everyone has the mind for it."

"Why am I here?" Gregg couldn't help the anger heating his tone.

"The delay necessary to politely arrange a meeting wasn't acceptable. Time is of the essence."

"Is it, now? And me with *such* a full schedule."

For the first time, Tyrell took real notice of Gregg, his eyes narrowing. "Your calendar has been cleared," he said. "You are *entirely* at *my* leisure. Time is of the essence," he repeated.

That repetition told Gregg that despite his calm exterior, Tyrell was stewing. It would almost be worth it to tell the bastard that he had all the time in the world, but Gregg suspected that he didn't. Not if he gave the wrong answer to the other man's so-called offer.

"You know who I am?"

"Who doesn't?"

"Good. I won't need to convince you of my sincerity or willingness to take action."

Gregg said nothing in response to the none-too-subtle threat.

Tyrell continued, not expecting a reply. "I am taking a stake in the Diamond City trade. You're going to head up operations for me, beginning with uniting your business with that of Savannah Morrell and establishing order. You will have immediate access to ample resources, but I expect prompt results. Do you have any questions?"

The similarity to Brussard's offer was striking, except this was no offer. It was a do-or-die order. But why? Why Diamond City and why now? He wondered what Brussard would do if Gregg took Tyrell's offer. The man claimed to have serious resources. Could they compete with Tyrell's? Maybe Gregg could pit them against one another and cut them both down while they were occupied with each other.

"What's your endgame?" Gregg asked, pleased at the flicker of respect that flashed in Tyrell's eyes.

"It is of no relevance to your task."

Gregg hadn't expected any real answer. He was playing for time—enough to think of a way out of this.

"Time line?"

"With the resources I will give you, five days should be sufficient to unify the businesses. A bonus to you if you succeed before that."

"Should I expect obstacles from the outside?" Enemies that Tyrell brought to the table. Brussard, maybe.

The other man's mouth flattened. "A smart man always expects obstacles."

That was a ringing yes. Gregg didn't bother asking what would happen if he refused. He'd be rotting in a landfill before lunchtime. Nor did he ask what would happen if he betrayed Tyrell or fucked up. At the very least, he'd get to witness the death of Clay and all his friends , and then he'd end up in a chamber of horrors somewhere getting tortured and begging to die. Tyrell's reputation preceded him.

Gregg eyed Tyrell, keeping his expression neutral. The swelling helped. "All right," he said, because there was no other way out of the room, no other way to get the damned null off his neck. Or back to Clay and Riley. How long had it been since he left them? Were they even alive? If they weren't, Tyrell and his goons had bought themselves a one-way ticket to hell.

The other man's eyes narrowed. Gregg had given in too quickly. He was expecting more of a fight. But Gregg wasn't done.

"I'll run your Diamond City operation, but the city belongs to me. I get the last word on what happens here and no interference."

Tyrell sipped his coffee and set it aside again, nodding. "So long as my needs are met, I see no issue with that."

"You find a way to wipe every law-enforcement file clean of my brother and the Hollis family—from local LEOs to Homeland Security and everything in between. I want them left alone. Permanently. No one bothers them—not you, not the cops, not the government."

A tip of the head. "I can do that."

It was a risk, telling Tyrell he cared enough about certain people to protect them, but there was a strong likelihood he'd assume it had everything to do with Riley's talent and the Kensington artifacts, which wasn't entirely wrong. And Tyrell would already know about Clay.

Tyrell continued to wait, his flat gaze picking Gregg apart. He was expecting more. Probably money demands. Gregg wasn't interested in money. He owned his own diamond mines, plus many other lucrative ventures.

"Shut down the Sparkle Dust trade," he said, watching Tyrell to gauge his reaction.

A flicker of something. Knowing. Irritation. "I'm afraid that's out of my reach. I have no stake in the SD trade."

A lie, Gregg was sure of it, but it helped gauge the extent of Tyrell's desire to hire him, though hiring wasn't quite the word Gregg would use. Forced labor was more like it.

"All right, then. How about you tell me exactly how your men knew where I was going to be travelling to and when?"

Tyrell smiled approval. He leaned back, reaching for his cup and stroking invisible wrinkles from his crisp gray shirt with the other hand.

"I'll tell you what. You get the consolidation done within seventy-two hours, and I'll give you the details."

That was a point in his favor. Gregg had expected an out-and-out refusal.

"Nothing else?" Tyrell asked.

The question felt like a test, like there was something he was leaving on the table, something Tyrell expected him to demand, maybe even wanted him to.

But what? If he didn't get his shit together, Tyrell would make him regret it. The man didn't respect weakness.

He considered. Tyrell was playing chess, a game of strategy. What if Gregg played into Tyrell's lowest expectations? He wanted Gregg to be smart and interesting in the game, but what if that didn't happen?

"Ninety percent of revenue from Diamond City operations," he said.

Tyrell's expression didn't change. Nonetheless, Gregg felt his disappointment and disgust. Money was so prosaic.

"Ridiculous. You can take thirty percent. That's more than fair."

Gregg shook his head. "Ninety or nothing." The demand was absurd, and he knew it. Once again, it gave him a chance to learn things about Tyrell.

Interest gleamed in Tyrell's eyes. "Do you think you're worth it?" he asked.

"Doesn't matter if I do or not, does it?"

"I like a man who knows how to measure himself."

"I like a man with ambition," Gregg said. "A man who spends his time playing with yardsticks doesn't push the boundaries."

"A measuring man also gets the job done."

"Then go find one. I know how big my dick is."

Tyrell smiled again. "I also like a man who is confident. I hope you aren't exaggerating your worth."

"*You* kidnapped *me*," Gregg pointed out. "I didn't apply for this job. If you don't know who and what I am, that's on you. You don't like my terms, then find someone else."

Tyrell nodded slowly. "Very well. Ninety percent. That should more than suffice for you, I should think."

Tyrell wasn't in this for the money, just as Gregg had suspected. He was up to something more in Diamond City. But what? And why now? And more importantly, what would the effect be on the city? Tyrell wasn't going to let any cats out of any bags, so Gregg would have to find out on his own.

"What does this have to do with the Kensington artifacts?"

Tyrell's brows rose, and a faint look of avarice flickered across his expression and vanished. "It depends on how things play out."

Gregg scowled. "And if you decide you want them?"

"We will talk."

Which meant making Gregg cough up the artifacts. "And if we can't reach an agreement?"

"I'm confident we will."

"Are you, now?"

Tyrell smiled, this time with his teeth showing, like a shark. "Quite. Now then, you have little time, so we'll get you on your way." He tapped a button on his desk. A moment later, the door opened, and Gregg's two captors reappeared.

"From now on, Bruno and Randall will accompany you and follow your orders as well as guard you from harm."

"I have bodyguards."

Tyrell laughed. "Not good ones. First Savannah takes you, then I do. You need looking after and Bruno and Randall are second to none."

Gregg didn't bother to tell him he'd walked into Savannah's trap on purpose.

"Now then. There's one last thing to do before you leave. Please pardon my barbarity."

Before Gregg could ask what he meant, Tyrell took something out of his desk drawer and came around in front of Gregg. He held a weapon, somewhere between an ice pick and an upholstery needle, the long point about six inches long. He held the wooden bulb end in the palm of his hand and as Bruno and Randall gripped Gregg's shoulders, Tyrell drove it down through Gregg's thigh. It hit bone. Fire erupted. Gregg lunged upward, only to be pushed back down by Ugly and Uglier.

"Jesus fuck! What the hell?"

Tyrell took a tissue from a box on a nearby table and wiped off the steel, dropping the bloody tissue in the trash. He bent and again touched the console on his desk.

"Yes?" came a male voice over the speaker.

"Join us in the rehab room."

Tyrell turned back to Gregg. "It's necessary that there be a clear erasure point for the dreamer. No worries. I've a healer on standby to take care of it. He won't be able to deal with your other wounds, of course. You would wonder why they didn't exist but didn't remember being healed."

"Dreamer?" Gregg repeated, his mouth going dry. "Erasure point?"

"Yes. To facilitate our dealings, a dreamer will implant certain compulsions. One will be to report your progress to me daily, though it will seem like your own idea."

"What else?" Gregg demanded, steel bands tightening around his chest. Fear.

"Nothing you need to worry about. You won't remember any of this conversation when you're through. Let's go."

Tyrell's thugs hoisted him up onto his feet. Blood stained his jeans and trickled down his leg. He limped along, his mind racing. This mind fucking was going to happen. He had no way out. The only way to fight it was to make himself ask questions later—to make himself account for something that he couldn't remember. That would create enough suspicion for him to get himself checked out. He just had to do it without Tyrell knowing. He was always wary of dreamer tampering, and had planned to get checked out following his release from Savannah. No doubt one of Tyrell's compulsions would stop him from doing just that.

Gregg started by biting his tongue hard enough to bleed. It wasn't enough. He might chalk it up to getting bashed in the head by Randall. Or Bruno. He wasn't sure which asshole was which.

His wrists remained bound behind him, and he still wore his jacket. Sweat stuck his shirt to his back. He tried to gouge a wrist under his coat sleeve, but his nails were too short to do more than make a scrape.

All too soon they arrived outside a steel door. Tyrell typed into a keypad on the outer wall, and the door slid open on a windowless room. Inside was a metal table with straps hanging along the edges. Gregg's stomach twisted at the sight. He threw himself backward, twisting and kicking. Bruno and Randall picked him up and shoved him inside. He sprawled onto the floor. The door slid shut behind.

"You can release him," Tyrell said.

Dreadlocks slid a knife through the plastic cuffs. Gregg's hands separated, and he leaped to his feet, swinging around to face the other three men, his hands clenching. He shook his aching arms to get the circulation going again. Unfazed by any threat Gregg presented, Tyrell stepped up and lifted the null from around his neck.

"There's a null field surrounding this room. You won't be able to travel." He dropped the chain into a basket on a wooden side table

Gregg reached for his magic the moment the null had come off, but ran into a wall blank of nothingness.

"Do keep your clothing as is," Tyrell said. "I don't want to have to redress you before you wake. At any rate, this won't take long. Boys?"

Bruno and Randall grabbed Gregg. He fought, but it was like wrestling with two buffalo. They shoved him facedown over the table, one of them holding him in place as the other hoisted his legs up, twisting and flipping him so he lay on his back. A few seconds later, the straps snugged into place around his shoulders and waist, followed quickly by more around his hips, thighs, calves, and feet. Finally the white goon fastened the last one over Gregg's forehead so he was forced to stare straight up at the ceiling. A bright light shined down from above, making his eyes water and producing black splotches across his vision. He squinted.

He twisted and yanked against his restraints. He wasn't going anywhere. Gregg mentally kicked himself for getting into this situation. He should have protected himself better. Been more careful, somehow.

He heard the door slide open again. He slid his eyes sideways, but couldn't see anything more than Bruno's or Randall's ass.

"Good, you're here," Tyrell said. "Be as quick as you can. Boys, step outside if you please."

After a moment, Gregg's view was unobstructed, but he still couldn't see the dreamer.

"You're going to stay?"

Gregg's eyes widened as he now recognized the voice. Vernon Brussard. Riley's father. What was he doing working for Tyrell? And what was the charade about providing Gregg with resources and giving him the opportunity to say yes and no? Hell, that deadline was still hours away, and yet here he was on a table about to be mind-fucked.

"I believe I shall stay this time."

"Please remember not to interrupt."

"This is not my first erasure, Vernon," Tyrell rebuked, a slight edge to his voice.

He walked past Gregg, his cologne pungent and expensive. Out of sight, chain clinked and rattled. The null Gregg had been wearing. Tyrell must have put it on. In order for Vernon to erase Gregg's memories, the binder field had to be turned off. Tyrell clearly didn't trust Vernon, putting the null on to protect himself from Vernon's magic.

"Get started."

Vernon gave a little sniff and then came into view. He stopped by the table, leaning over Gregg, tilting his head to face him better. "Relax. This won't hurt. You won't even remember it when it's over."

Gregg opened his mouth to lambaste the other man. To demand to know what the fuck was going on. Before he could speak, he felt his tongue grow thick, his jaw too heavy for him to even think of speaking. He glared hatred at Vernon. Clearly the bastard didn't want him talking—didn't want Tyrell to find out about Vernon's little extracurricular visit to Gregg.

Exactly.

Vernon's dry voice rippled through Gregg's mind. Goddamned, motherfucking dreamers.

Are you sure you want to be rude to the man digging into your brain?
Go fuck yourself.

Not a constructive or original response, but hatred and anger were the only way to fight the panic flaring in his gut. His greatest fear was to lose himself and not even know it. To have his mind tampered with, the way this same man had tampered with his own daughter's mind. Riley had nearly died fighting against the constructions Vernon had made in her brain. If not for Cass, the one dreamer on the planet Gregg had come to trust as much as he could trust any dreamer, Riley would have died.

When Vernon was through with him, he'd be Tyrell's willing slave and he'd never know things could or should have been different. The thought made him want to vomit. Instead, he gathered what little spit remained in his mouth tried to launch it at Vernon. His swollen lips doomed the effort. It wouldn't have made a difference. Vernon had already stepped back, reading Gregg's intent in his mind.

"Now, now. None of that." He glanced over his shoulder at Tyrell. "Everything still as we discussed?"

"Yes," was Tyrell's succinct response. "Get on with it."

His tone was sharp. Clearly there was animosity between the two men. Why else would Vernon betray him by secretly negotiating with Gregg?

"Relax. This won't hurt a bit."

Vernon leaned over Gregg. Butterfly wings flickered inside his skull. He clenched his teeth, sucking in a harsh breath. He wrenched at his bindings, to no avail.

I hope you are as smart as I expect you are.

What did that mean?

A sliding movement along his wrist and under his coat sleeve. Pain tracing a thin line. A cut, not deep, just enough to bleed.

Do try to figure out how you got that later, won't you? Otherwise, I'll have to rethink my plans.

If you don't want me to forget, why not just pretend to mess around in my head?

Tyrell is brilliant and he likes to randomly double-check the work of his employees. This must be done properly.

"Riley may be dead," Gregg blurted aloud. Maybe he could distract Vernon or delay him long enough to find a way to escape. A long shot at best.

The other man froze, skewering Gregg with a gimlet stare. "What did you say?"

"My brother and Riley—they were trapped in the middle of a gang battle. I was supposed to travel to pull them out. I ended up here. They were surrounded, about to be overwhelmed."

"What was that?" Movement and the soft clank of chain. Tyrell appeared beside Vernon. "What is he saying?"

Butterfly wings flickered inside Gregg's skull. Vernon's eyes widened and then narrowed, his nostrils flaring white, his mouth thinning into a flat line.

"You aren't lying."

"About what?" Tyrell asked.

"Nothing important."

"I'll decide what's important."

Something deep and dark moved in Vernon's eyes, but his voice remained even.

"He says that my daughter may be dead."

Curiously, he left out any mention of Clay. Gregg watched the interaction between the men.

"Oh dear. I hope not. Her tracing abilities could be invaluable," Tyrell said. "What has happened to her?"

He asked Vernon, not Gregg. More butterfly wings. The bastard lifted the details of the situation out of Gregg's mind with little effort.

"It appears she took a trace job finding a runaway girl who shacked up with a wannabe Tyet gang lord in south Downtown. Looks like she was in the middle of a firefight when our boy here travelled the runaway girl to safety. He was supposed to go back, but came here instead. Unless the gang took her prisoner, she is likely dead."

And so was Clay. The thought gutted Gregg, but the idea of losing his daughter seemed not to bother Vernon in the least. He spoke as if describing the events in a movie. No emotion at all. "I thought you had a watch on her," Tyrell said, shaking his head with obvious displeasure. "As soon as you finish here, I'll send someone to investigate. If she's alive, it's time to bring her into the fold where I can protect her. She's too great an asset to risk. Be sure to get the exact location from him for my team."

"Of course," was Vernon's tight-lipped reply.

"Be quick, then," Tyrell said, returning to his seat. "Oh, and be sure that he tells us about the girl after you're done, to avoid inconsistency. He can ask for my help."

Like hell he would. He'd jump into a pit of burning tar first.

You'll do it because it will be your idea, came Vernon's response. *You'll want to because I will tell you to want to.*

If he could have, Gregg would have ripped the man's throat out.

A gathering tension like pulling together a handful of ropes tugged in Gregg's brain. He twisted and fought the bindings with all his strength.

The last thing he heard was Vernon.

You'd better damned well hope you haven't fucked everything up, or I will turn your brains into pudding and put you in a Bottoms brothel where you'll be ridden like a mare in heat for the rest of your days.

"NOW THEN, I have other business to attend to. Is there anything else?" Tyrell asked crisply from behind his desk. Not waiting for Gregg to answer, he continued. "I expect speedy results, and toward that end, I've given you access to immediate funds. No worries about tapping it dry. You won't. I've also given you a roster of available talents you might want to utilize. I keep teams of travellers at my operations around the world. Anyone in my organization can be at your disposal within an hour at the very latest. Everyone is on standby. All the necessary information for personnel requests is provided in the files."

He pushed an electronic tablet across the desk. "I've also included a number of contacts that you may need, including my own." He glanced down at his watch. "You're on the clock. You should get going. Do not attempt to lose Bruno and Randall. It would be unfortunate for both them and you." He gestured at the black bodyguard. "Remove the null. We're done here."

Just like that. Summoned and dismissed, and Clay and Riley likely dead. The fury that burned in Gregg's gut exploded. "You're a fucking bastard," he said, lunging forward out of his chair. His bodyguards/captors grabbed his shoulders and dragged him back down, though what they thought he'd do with his hands bound behind his back, Gregg didn't know.

His mouth twisted into a snarl. "While I've been sitting here, my brother's likely been getting murdered. So help me God, if he's dead, I'm going to make you pay."

He'd caught Tyrell's attention. The other man leaned over the desk, gaze sharp and cold as winter ice.

Something like surprise flickered across his expression. "Your brother murdered, you say? Explain."

Gregg hesitated, but then decided there was no point in keeping it a secret. "His girlfriend took a trace job and they got into some trouble. I went to give them a hand and we were mobbed by a gang of street thugs. I travelled out to take the teenaged girl—the trace target—to safety. I was supposed to go back and travel them out as well. Only you grabbed me before I could." His lip curled. "The odds of their survival aren't good."

Tyrell nodded and reached inside his suit jacket, removing a phone from his breast pocket. "We will do something about this," he said as he pressed a button and put the phone to his ear. "Your brother's girlfriend is Riley Hollis, is it not?"

"Does it matter?"

"She's a powerful tracer. Perhaps the best." His attention hooked back to the person on the other end of the line. "Ready the team," he said. "You have ten minutes," and then hung up.

"Let me go," Gregg said. "Now. Ten minutes is too long." A deep rage boiled in his gut. Clearly Clay was of little importance to Tyrell, and on one hand, that was a good thing. It meant Tyrell didn't know Clay had an elemental talent. Those were rare as uranium and a thousand times more valuable. On the other hand, Clay being in danger likely wasn't what motivated Tyrell. He wanted Riley.

His new boss considered him through narrowed eyes. "I don't know that I want to risk you. Your death would cause me some headaches and rearrange my plans."

"Screw your plans," Gregg said. "I'm going to go help my brother and if he's dead because you held me here, then our deal's off." His lips peeled back in a vicious smile. "Not that you'll care. You'll be too dead to worry about it."

Tyrell pushed back from the desk. He walked unhurriedly around the desk and stopped in front of Gregg. His eyes had turned dark and hard, like a snake's. He put his hands in his pants pockets, his pose casual and yet menacing.

Gregg refused to be impressed. A dark wildness whirled inside him. A combination of desperation, rage, contempt, and an animal desire for freedom. No matter what Tyrell thought, Gregg was not going to be caged.

"I suggest you think carefully about your position," Tyrell said finally. "I do not tolerate treachery. The consequences for you would be catastrophic, and that would be unfortunate. You have potential. You could go far with me. The rewards are nearly infinite for quality employees."

Gregg sneered. "As long as we're making things clear—the only catastrophe you could possibly inflict on me is the death of my brother. This deal of ours hinges on him keeping to this side of the dirt. Not just that. If he lost Riley, it would destroy him and I can't have that either. Both of them and her family are totally off-limits to you. Anything different *I* will regard as treachery and I'll tear your world apart. Now cut me loose and let me go before it's too damned late, if it isn't already."

Another long moment of consideration before Tyrell nodded at the two men behind Gregg and stepped back, leaning against his desk.

A knife slid between Gregg's wrists, and they parted. His hands and arms ached, but he had no time for pain. In one movement, he tore the null from around his neck flung it aside, then snatched the knife from the white thug's hand. A second later he was flying through dreamspace, hoping to hell he wasn't too late.

Chapter 15

Riley

"GOD DAMN YOU, Riley. Why didn't you run?" Price demanded hoarsely over his shoulder. An impossible breeze swirled through the cavernous skating rink. Price's eyes were cloudy and turbulent. "If you'd have run, I could let my talent loose," he said. "Now I can't risk it."

I'll admit, his none-too-subtle accusation stung, but not because I didn't run. The truth was, it *was* my fault for taking the trace job, but I refused to accept I should have just abandoned him. Anyhow, the likelihood I'd have escaped was between slim and none.

"Do it anyway," I said. "What have we got to lose? If you don't, we're dead anyway, which isn't as romantic as *Romeo and Juliet* makes it out to be." The next words hurt me to say. "I can't help us. I tried."

Annoyingly, my voice cracked. My magic had never failed me before. No, it was me. I'd failed to handle it. I wiped a trickle of blood away before it dripped into my eye, surreptitiously brushing away the hot tear that escaped my custody. God, I was such a baby.

That's when Ocho woke up. He rolled onto his back, swearing loudly. He'd lost his Mexican accent. He sat up. The look he sent our way wasn't just angry. It was psychotic.

"I think you might have cracked his brain," I said to Price, trying to pretend I didn't want to pee my pants. I didn't have to ask to know what kinds of plans Ocho had for us. They weren't going to be pretty.

"I love you." I said it because it's what you say when you think you're about to die. My voice shook. I'd been kidnapped and held prisoner before—was it only a couple of months ago? Getting casually burned all over my arms with cigarettes had been beyond awful. I don't know how I'd survived it. This would be a thousand times worse. That is, if I let it happen. But I wouldn't. I'd fight until there was nothing left of me. I would *not* become Ocho's personal voodoo doll. Or blow-up doll, for that matter. I shuddered at the thought.

Price stiffened, and smoke practically poured out of his ears. He couldn't turn around to face me, what with us being mostly surrounded by bad guys with guns and magic and him trying to shield me even with his hand up in the air.

"What the hell is that supposed to mean?"

"I thought it was obvious. I love you."

"And you thought you'd mention it now."

No sense beating around the bush. "If I die I want to know I said it before I headed for the great white yonder or wherever I end up."

Now the breeze really kicked up. In point of fact, it was more like a stiff wind. The front doors rattled, and everything that wasn't nailed down inside the building started to wave, sway, and tumble.

"You aren't going to die," Price said in a flat voice.

"Because saying so makes it true." I don't know why I was needling him. Oh right. I was scared shitless, and the link between my brain and mouth had shorted out. Not to mention we needed him to let go of his magic. We really didn't have anything to lose.

Ocho chose that moment to snatch a gun out of someone's hand and level it at Price. "Stop it right now or I'll put a bullet between your eyes."

Randomly, I wondered if he was that good a shot.

The air in the room seized up. That menacing just-before-the storm stillness swallowed all sound. My fingers curled in Price's shirt. What could I do? I stepped around Price, aiming for Ocho's chest. I'm a good shot, but I wasn't going for flashy.

"Hey, Bozo! Or is it Zero? You aren't as scary as you think you are. Oh, unless you're drugging little girls and pimping them out."

"Riley." Just that one word squeezed out of Price. Agonized, demanding, pleading.

Ocho's hot gaze settled on me, followed by the barrel of his gun. My finger tightened ever so slightly on the trigger, but I didn't follow through. Not yet. The moment I shot Ocho, we'd get hit with a hail of lead from his companions. Who was I kidding? At any second it would start. My finger tightened.

A gunshot exploded the stillness. Mine followed a millisecond later, but I swear blood erupted from Ocho's head before I got my shot off. Somebody had decided to stage a coup.

The room exploded with ratcheting gunfire even as a whirlwind spun to life around me and Price. Make that a small tornado. All sorts of crap got sucked up in it almost instantly, and I couldn't see anything. I couldn't hear anything above the roaring wind.

I spun around, my empty hand reaching out for Price as I searched him for blood. I dropped the gun and tore at his coat. The black fabric didn't show a hole, but there was no way he hadn't gotten shot. I had to stop the bleeding. Hands closed around my wrists. The binding spell no longer held his arm up in the air. He dragged me against his hard chest, closing iron arms around me.

"Easy, Riley. I didn't get shot. Tell me you're not hurt. Please, baby."

It took a bit for the words to sink into my panicked brain. "I'm good," I said, even though I had no idea if that was true. I did a quick mental inventory. Who the hell was I kidding? Getting shot *hurt*. I definitely didn't have new holes. "No lead poisoning for me," I added. "What now?"

Once before he'd lifted us out of a big hole, aka, the basement of the FBI building, using his talent. He could sweep us out the front doors now. Couldn't he?

His arms trembled, like muscles trying to hold up heavy weights for too long. White lines bracketed his mouth and nostrils, and his neck corded with strain.

"I just—I don't know—" His teeth clenched together, his jaw knotting. He shook his head. "It's so strong and it keeps growing stronger every day."

I'd never heard of anything like that before. Talents erupted and didn't weaken or grow over time. But Price was an elemental, and that made his talent a wild card. "Can you hold this and walk? Just nod or shake your head."

Price's head jerked to the side. So that was a no-go.

"Push it out and let it go. Knock them down and let it go and we'll make a run for the front doors." Hopefully the walls wouldn't collapse.

I pressed my palms to Price's cheeks, trying to help him center himself. "Can you do it?"

A jerk of the head. This time in the positive.

"Then go."

His face twisted in concentration and pain, and then the calm eye of the whirlwind exploded outward. In the same moment, Price grabbed my hand and yanked me into a run.

Bits of loose ceiling tile rained down, along with other flying debris. I lifted my free arm to shield my face as we raced up the low ramp and through the old snack bar and past the counter where they used to rent skates. We dodged and leaped over people still stunned from the hard blow of the whirlwind. What glass had remained on the front doors had shattered, leaving toothy holes interspersed with plywood.

We ducked through one of the empty panes. The cold slapped my face. I sucked in deep breaths of needle-sharp air, adrenaline tearing through me. Price shot left toward the side parking lot. Belatedly, I remembered Tiny. Please God, don't let his crew shoot us.

I heard voices and shouting. Price and I launched ourselves up the big berm. We half jumped, half slid down the other side, only to find ourselves surrounded. Hands grabbed us.

"Let them go!" Tiny bellowed.

Our captors responded instantly.

I looked at the young Tyet lord in training. "Go in now. Ocho's dead, I think. Everybody else is temporarily flattened."

He didn't hesitate, barking orders. Seconds later, his small army rushed over the berm, leaving Price and me alone. My breathing gradually slowed, and my heart steadied. It felt good to have the mountain of snow at our backs.

Price took my hand. "We've got to keep going. We're done here."

I nodded, and we took off in a slow jog, careful not to fall on the rutted ice covering the parking lot.

We retraced our path to the school where we'd filled the Molotovs and kept going. A few more blocks down, we stopped. Price bent over, drawing deep, ragged breaths. He didn't let go of my hand. I rubbed his back with the other. Abruptly he straightened and pulled me into his arms. He buried his head in my neck.

"Dear God in heaven, you've got to stop doing that to me. My heart can't take it."

I didn't bother telling him the same thing. The chances of our lives getting less dangerous were about as good as the odds of the dinosaurs coming back. Zilch.

I didn't want to ruin the moment, but we were still on the clock. "We should get out of here," I said, gently pushing at his chest. "Find out what happened to your brother."

At the mention of Touray, Price stiffened, and the wind around us picked up, scouring the street and making the nearby trees toss. I could see fear in his eyes.

"Let's boost a ride," I said, twisting out of his arms. We should have taken one of Tiny's vehicles, but I had no intention of going back to get it. Just then, the sound of an engine broke the cold stillness of the morning.

We stepped into the shadows between a couple of juniper bushes and waited for the car to pass. It was one of those little boxy jobs that look like a loaf of bread on wheels. It went a couple of blocks down and turned into a dilapidated apartment complex. I looked at Price.

"Let's see what we can find."

The apartments looked like they'd been built in the fifties, with flat roofs and oversized windows. Three two-story buildings faced the street in a U shape. Out in front were rows of carports. The little car we'd seen had slid into a slot in front of the left building. A young woman still sat inside, her fingers tapping over the screen of her phone.

Convenient. We wouldn't have to break in and hot-wire a car. "Think she'll give us her keys if we ask nicely?"

"She doesn't get a choice." Price stalked along the line of parked cars.

The girl finished with her phone about the time we got to end of the carport. Oblivious to us, she fumbled in the seat beside her, bending down to pick up something off the passenger floorboards. She opened the door and got out. She wore blue scrubs and looked like she hadn't slept in a couple of days.

Shit. I did not want to steal from a doctor or a nurse or whatever she was. Of all the people on the planet who did not deserve to get carjacked, first responders topped the list. I didn't have much of a choice.

She slung a tote bag over her shoulder and reached for her purse. That's when we pounced.

"I'm sorry, but we need to take your car," Price said.

She gasped and spun about, eyes wide. She clutched her purse to her chest like a shield.

"What do you want?" Her voice squeaked.

"I want to borrow your car." Price held out his hand. "Give me your keys."

She shook her head, anger filtering into her fear. "I don't think so. I've just had the worst night ever and I'm not going to get my fucking car stolen on top of all of it. You can just go screw yourself."

Price just grabbed her wrist and twisted the keys out of her grip. "I'm sorry, but it's a matter of life and death," he said. "I'll return it, with a hefty rental fee. I promise."

"Right," she said. "Please. I'm not stupid. I'm fucked and I know it. The only reason I'm not screaming is nobody would come to help, so you can save yourself the buttering up. Cops won't do a damned thing either. So take the damned thing and get the hell out of my way."

I had to admit I liked her style.

She glared up at Price. She wasn't all that tall. Maybe five foot four. A little taller than Patti and just as feisty. "Well? Are you going to move, asshole?"

"Give me a pen and paper," I said.

"What?"

"Pen. Paper. Give them to me. You've got to have some sort of writing tool in that tote."

She shook her head and muttered, but dug into her tote and handed me a little spiral notebook with white kittens on the front and a pen from Carter's Garden Supply.

I flipped open the notebook and scribbled down my name and the number of the diner. I handed it back to her. "Call me. You'll get your car back and chunk of cash for your trouble and aggravation. I swear if someone's life wasn't on the line, we wouldn't be doing this."

"Right. I totally believe you." With that, she thrust past us and stomped away.

We slid into the seats, and Price whipped us out of the stall and back onto the main road in a matter of seconds. The car was a stick, and he drove it deftly.

"That was easier to accomplish than I expected." I switched the heater to high and sighed as warmth poured out of the vents. "Where are we going?" I asked, tipping my head back against the seat rest.

"Gregg's."

"Is that a good idea? I mean, he would have come back if humanly possible. That means someone got him. It probably happened at home—I can't imagine where else he'd have taken Cristina." My stomach churned as I realized that whatever had happened to Touray had put the girl in the cross fire. Had we rescued her from the frying pan just to dump her into the fire?

"All the more reason to go there."

"Unless whoever got him is waiting to get us, too."

Price made a growling sound, my logic annoying him. "What do you suggest, then?"

I dug in my pocket for my phone. "I'll call him."

Price didn't comment on what a ridiculous plan that was, for which I was grateful. What were the chances Touray would be able to pick up? If he'd been attacked like I thought, he wouldn't answer. Still, I hit the dial button.

As expected, I got his voice mail. I almost hung up without leaving a message, then decided I'd better. "We got out. We're okay. Call us. We're worried about you." I cut the call.

"Now what?" I said.

Price slid a swift glance at me and then back to the road. He was still on his way to Touray's. I closed my eyes, trying to think. My adrenaline had dissolved, and exhaustion pulled at me. I felt like a bag of wet cement. I could barely lift my eyelids, I was so tired.

"I need to sleep," I said, yawning. "So do you."

"I'll sleep after we find Gregg," came Price's clipped reply.

"We're not going to be much good if we—"

"Crawl in the back and sleep if you want," he snapped, cutting me off.

He swerved around a pothole. The tires spun and skidded on ice. The back end fishtailed.

"Kill us on the way and we aren't going to do him much good," I murmured. His "crawl in the back" dismissal annoyed me. Then again, if Taylor, Jamie, or Leo were missing, I'd be going after them like a crocodile after a wildebeest.

"Is there any chance of caffeine?" I braced my feet on the dash. It helped keep me from flying around the car with the twisty driving.

"No."

Short, sweet, and very final. Not that I really expected him to stop, but a vat of coffee would sure make me a lot more capable.

I leaned my forehead against my upraised knees and closed my eyes to relieve their sawdusty dryness. *Think.* Price needed me to be helpful. Touray not coming back meant he'd been forcibly kept away. The only other possibility was that another, more pressing disaster had reared its head. If it came down to a choice between the city and Price, the city would win.

God, I hated relying on other people. No, I corrected myself. I had no problem relying on Taylor, Leo, Jamie, Patti, and Price. Cass, too. I knew they'd come through for me no matter what. But Touray? His agenda didn't necessarily include keeping me and mine safe. His promises always had exception clauses.

It was only going to get worse. I needed his help to protect my family from Vernon, from the FBI, and from other Tyets, and yet he might throw any one of us under the bus for the sake of his goals. Noble goals, in their way, but I didn't want to get ground up into hamburger in someone else's war.

The knowledge sat like a ball of cold lead in my stomach. What other choice did I have? Touray had the power, money, and resources to keep us safe. Nobody else did.

"What are the chances Touray didn't come back because he had something more important to do?"

Price flicked a burning look at me. The air in the car swelled, and the front windshield cracked, sending zigzag lines across the expanse. The pressure against my ears hurt, and my chest felt like a giant was squeezing me in a bear hug. I rolled down the window. Frozen air rushed inside, but the pressure eased.

Price swore and pulled over. He sat a moment, staring straight ahead. His hands flexed and clamped on the wheel.

"Are you accusing my brother of abandoning us *on purpose?*"

I winced. Yes. "Isn't it possible?"

Price's eyes laced over with white. "I know you don't like Gregg, but God dammit, he's my brother and he could be fucking dead!" He slammed a frustrated fist into the center of the steering wheel. The horn beeped, a cartoon sound, totally at odds with his fury.

Regret burrowed through me. I hated doing this to him, but we'd promised to be truthful with each other.

"It's not that I don't like him," I said. "He just scares the ever-loving shit out of me most of the time. And it's not that I think he'd just walk away from us willy-nilly. I'm asking if maybe something more important came up. You know how he feels about the city."

Price opened his mouth and then snapped it shut. He shook his head. He knew I was right.

There was a bright side. "So if he had something more important to take care of, then he's probably all right," I said softly, putting my hand on his thigh.

His muscles bunched into stone beneath my touch. I pulled away, but he grabbed my hand in his, his fingers tightening.

"It's possible," he admitted, hope threading through his voice.

That's when my phone rang. I checked the number. Patti. "Hey."

"You should know that thugs dragged Price's brother away after he dropped off Cristina," she said without preamble. "Broke in here and tied me up, then waited for him. Thing I can't figure out is how they knew he was coming. I sure as hell didn't expect him."

Fuck. So much for the bright side. I glanced at Price. "Did they say anything? Got any idea who they worked for?"

"Nope. They hardly said a word."

"Is Cristina okay?"

"They didn't bother her. A few minutes ago, the two thugs left behind to guard us got a call. They cut us loose. I'm taking Cristina up to my apartment to clean up and maybe sleep."

"Can you call Emily and Luis and make sure she gets home?"

"Sure. What are you going to do?"

"How did they take him out of there?"

"SUV."

"We're on our way."

I hung up and repeated the conversation to Price. He was already pulling back onto the road.

"How did they know to be there?" I asked. "There's no such thing as telling the future."

"Maybe there is. People claim they can all the time."

"Crackpots and con artists."

"Maybe not."

I'd never heard of any legitimate account of someone reading the future, but then, ignorance wasn't exactly proof the skill didn't exist. The fact was, someone had managed to lie in wait for Gregg in a place he was not expected to be. The only logical explanation was that someone had seen the future and set the trap.

"They took him by car, so I should be able to pick up his trace," I said. If I could control my magic and stand the pain of it. But I had to try. I'd damned well better succeed, because I wasn't letting Price lose his brother because of me.

The traffic had eased up on the outskirts of the city, but Downtown was practically a parking lot. Despite the explosions, people still had to get to work, and between regular traffic and the backups caused by the explosions, we found ourselves in a gridlock of epic proportions. Which begged the question—how had the SUV that had taken Touray managed to get anywhere?

Maybe it hadn't gone far. Maybe he'd be close to the diner, and we'd be able to find him quickly. Hell, maybe the kidnappers were stuck in traffic somewhere.

"Do you think?" I asked Price, after explaining my logic.

"Seems reasonable," he said.

His voice had gone flat. He'd already vaulted to the worst-case scenario, which unfortunately had the best odds. I hurt for him. I rubbed my knuckles over the ache in my chest. What could I do?

"If they took him, then they wanted him alive," I said by way of being comforting. But we both knew from dreadful experience that staying alive wasn't a picnic, or even just a bad nightmare. Sometimes it was hell itself. All the same, better alive than dead, any day.

"Right," he said.

Price's tension ratcheted up with every breath. It wasn't long before he twisted the wheel and drove cockeyed into a small niche between parked cars. He drove the front end up on the sidewalk and shut down the car. Faster to walk than fight the traffic. I opened my door and met him on the sidewalk. That was crowded, too. Even so, people took one look at Price and gave him a wide berth. I let him clear the way, feeling a lot like a water-skier getting dragged behind a speeding boat.

All the subway exits were blocked with closed signs. No wonder the streets were so gridlocked.

We passed a coffee kiosk. The line ran up the block to the corner. I smelled the sweet manna of roasted beans. Someone walked away with a couple of steaming cups, and it took all my self-control not to grab one and run. I reached up to run a finger under my lower lip just to be sure I hadn't drooled.

I wasn't paying attention and didn't notice Price stopping. I banged into him and pinballed into a tiny little woman wearing a scarlet coat.

"What's your problem?" Then she took a good look at me and scurried away like her ass was on fire.

I must really look like a million bucks. Oh, right. My power had whipped me, leaving behind bloody welts. I probably looked like an extra off *The Walking Dead*.

In the meantime, Price had fished his wallet out of his back pocket one-handed. He let go of my hand, pulling out a fifty-dollar bill. He went up to the guy at the head of the line. The barista was just handing him a giant cup.

"I'll give you fifty bucks for that," Price said, holding up the bill.

The guy's eyes widened, and he held out the cup. "You got it, buddy."

Price made the exchange and passed me the coffee. I sipped from the cup and nearly orgasmed. It was just like I liked it. Sweet and creamy with an extra pop or two of espresso. I felt the caffeine running through me. My brain sparked alive.

"I will love you forever," I said.

Priced just grabbed my free hand and started off again. I figured we were about twenty-five blocks away from the diner. At least crossing streets was easy with the traffic barely moving.

I drank the coffee quickly, warmth flowing through me like liquid sunshine. I tossed the cup in a trashcan outside a vitamin shop.

I banged into Price again as he stopped dead. His hand clamped painfully on mine. I recovered, then someone plowed into me from behind, and I caught an elbow in my kidney, making me stagger into Price yet again. He gave about as much as a brick wall. Thank goodness I'd finished the coffee. I'd have hated to spill even one drop of the elixir of the gods.

"What's going on?" Before I could get around to see for myself, Price wrenched his hand free. He grabbed someone, and then they were hugging.

Touray.

Price pounded on his brother's back and Touray returned the favor. His face was bruised, his lips swollen. One of his hands held a chain with a heavy weight on it. Luckily not the one thumping Price like a drum. Apparently men, when overflowing with feeling, hit each other. Touray shoved back from Price. He spun to look at me.

"If you've got a null, use it now, then run. Call me and we'll come to you."

With that, he gripped Price's arm and the two disappeared.

I gaped at the space where they'd been. I wasn't the only one. Someone jostled me, and my brain kicked into gear. I started moving even as I activated the tattoo null around my belly button. I hadn't had the strength to make any nulls these last couple of weeks, but the charge on this one was still strong.

I started burrowing through the crowds, putting as much distance as I could between me and the spot where Touray had found us. Clearly whoever had taken Touray was after him. Just as clearly, he wanted me to get away from where the null cut off my trace so they couldn't find or follow me. Good plan.

Without Price, it was both harder and easier to speed through the throng. He didn't plow the way open, but I was able to slide into narrow slots between people, bumping and ducking as I went. More than a few called me names, but I just kept going.

I turned corners randomly, still working in the direction of the diner. It wasn't the smartest plan, not with Touray getting kidnapped there, but if the goons came back in search of him, they'd find Patti again, and I wasn't going to let her face them alone.

I put on a burst of speed, knocking between a trio of friends and then vaulting over a cement planter box and into the gutter. I dodged between the cars and ran down the center line.

Almost twenty minutes later I'd only managed to get about a mile away from the place where I'd last seen Touray and Price. My phone rang in my pocket.

"Yeah?"

"Where the hell are you?" Price demanded. "When did you plan to call?"

"From the diner," I said.

Silence. Disapproving and understanding at the same time. "We'll meet you there."

I didn't bother to tell him that was a bad idea. Whoever had taken Touray in the first place would likely look for him there. But since I had no intention of not going, I couldn't very well tell him not to go.

Since Patti had been literally tied up until maybe an hour ago, I was surprised to see that the diner was jam-packed, mostly with emergency responders and cops. Patti had a sign in the window that said their meals were free.

Touray and Price waited for me outside. Price zeroed in on me when I came around the copshop on the other side of the street—his once-upon-a-time home precinct. He strode across the street like a panther stalking its next meal. A harsh gust of wind came with him, picking up snow and swirling it into the air like dancing ghosts.

He swept me up and buried his face in my neck. He didn't say a word.

"I'm okay."

"You should have called. Right away."

"I know. But one cup of caffeine only goes so far toward getting the old synapses firing right," I said with a weak grin.

I stood back and looked over his shoulder at Touray. His eyes were like black holes, only instead of emptiness, his held a world of rage and hate.

"What happened?"

His jaw jutted, and he shook his head. "Not here."

I looked back at Price. "I need to check on Patti."

He nodded, and we headed back across the street. Touray fell in beside me. I felt like the meat in a lethal sandwich, which is a stupid metaphor and only goes to show how dull my wits were at that moment.

The noise of the diner wrapped us in cheerful welcome as we walked in. The glorious scents of breakfast made my stomach cramp with hunger. I did my best to ignore it as I looked around for Patti.

She bustled out of the back room carrying a tray loaded with dirty plates. "David," she called.

A dark-haired kid—probably just scraping eighteen—leaned out one of the swinging doors leading into the kitchen.

"Bus the back. Booth eight is going to need clearing in a couple minutes."

The kid ducked back inside and returned with a gray tub. Patti set the dishes she was carrying inside. She saw us and practically ran across the floor to pull me into a tight hug.

"Are you okay? They didn't hurt you?" I asked.

She shook her head. "Fine. Pissed as hell."

I glanced at my simmering companions. "You aren't the only one."

Patti's gaze swept me up and down. "You look like shit. Go upstairs and get cleaned up." Her gaze gathered in the two men. "You two can get started eating."

Touray opened his mouth to object, and she planted her hand in the middle of his chest. "I am so not in the mood for any more shit. You will sit. You will eat. My best friend has clearly been through hell and I'm not letting her leave here hungry, thirsty, or bloody." She glared at me. "Go."

Touray scowled, then shook his head in defeat. Smart boy. People underesti-mated Patti, a fact they often ended up regretting. She's a binder, if a relatively minor one, and she's a black belt in three or four different martial arts. She knows how to fuck you up, and she's willing to do it. She's doesn't take crap off anybody.

I headed up the back stairs to Patti's apartment. Price followed on my heels. I glanced over my shoulder at him, but didn't bother trying to convince him to sit and start eating. His forbidding expression said he wasn't going anywhere I wasn't. Patti knew better than to try to stop him either.

One of the bedrooms in Patti's apartment is essentially mine. I keep clothes, toiletries, shoes, and other necessities there. I left Price in the living room and went to the bathroom. After turning the water on in the shower to warm it up, I started stripping. It took longer than it should have. The wild brambles of magic had flailed through my skin as well as my hair, though oddly leaving my clothing unscathed. Unfortunately, the cloth stuck to my wounds. They hurt like hell to peel off.

Eventually I managed to get myself naked, though I felt like I'd been at-tacked by a horde of garden rakes. That's when I took a good look at myself in the mirror. Christ on a cracker. The zigzagging lacerations made me look like a badly made human quilt. I scowled at myself and tried to remember the past—what? Thirty-five hours?

First there'd been Price's out-of-control tornado at the safe house, and then we'd ridden the stolen motorcycle without a helmet, which partially accounted for the rat's nest that was my hair. Then we'd run into Tiny's guys, which in-cluded a conk on the head—I fingered the lump on my scalp. Then we'd gotten into it with Ocho's gang, where I lost control of my magic. That's where most of the blood had come from, the uncontrolled eruption engraving the long, scabbed-over lacerations on, well, mostly everything. Arms, legs, chest, back, head. I looked like I'd been in a fight with a knife-wielding octopus.

I reached behind me and shut the door. If Price saw how badly I'd lost my shit, he'd probably birth a hippo. Anyhow, it was all pretty cosmetic and didn't even hurt that much. Yeah, and as long as I was telling myself fairy stories, I was really a princess with a castle in the Alps full of talking dishes.

I pulled the tie out of my hair, and a whimper escaped my lips when several chunks of hair came with it. What the fuck? The knife-wielding octopus had given me a bad haircut. I turned my head in the mirror. I looked like a three-year-old had gone after my hair with a pair of scissors. Of everything, that pained me the most. I *liked* my hair. It was thick, coppery, and long. Emphasis on *was*. Now I was going to have to get it all chopped off.

I sighed and swallowed the unexpected lump in my throat. It was ridiculous to cry over hair. It would grow back, and it was *only* hair. *Pull up your big-girl panties, Riley, and get over yourself.*

I dropped the hair tie and my shorn locks onto the sink, and I stepped into the shower and moaned with pleasure. I stood there for a minute just letting the heat wash over me. The memory of Touray waiting downstairs spurred me to action. I was pretty sure if I took too long he'd come haul me out by my hair. Probably the short and curlies. Which might apply to the drapes as well as the rug, once I'd finished the chop job.

I choked back a hysterical giggle. I so needed sleep.

It took two washings and a heavy coat of conditioner for my hair to feel reasonably normal, or as normal as possible after getting weed whacked by magic. Somewhere in there I remembered to deactivate my belly null. The diner and apartment had excellent nulls. I should know. I created them.

I washed the rest of myself gingerly, then reluctantly shut off the faucet. The bathroom was so full of steam I couldn't see past the glass doors. I like a *really* hot shower.

I grabbed the towel I'd slung over the door rail and gingerly patted away the water on my skin before wrapping my hair in the thirsty cloth.

I slid open the shower door and stepped out. A shadow loomed in the steam, and I gave a little scream before I realized it was Price. He was leaning with his back against the bathroom door, his arms crossed, his expression somewhere between pissed off and "hey waiter, there's a roach in my salad."

"You gave me a heart attack," I said, casually reaching for another towel to wrap around myself. Maybe he wouldn't see the extent of the damage I'd done to myself.

He snatched my wrist before I could complete my plan. His gaze ran over me, and I clearly wasn't turning him on. He tugged me around so he could see my back.

"See anything you like?" I asked, wiggling my ass. Maybe I could sidetrack him.

His finger traced just below one of the lacerations running over my right shoulder to the middle of my back. "What happened?"

His voice was conversational, like he was talking about the weather. Not good. That meant he was feeling so much he'd locked it down so he wouldn't strangle me. At least he hadn't started a tornado. Yet.

"We were in a fight," I reminded him, hoping he wouldn't ask for specifics. But Price knew when a witness wasn't telling the whole truth.

"One of Ocho's people did this?" He clearly didn't believe it, but was playing along.

I really wanted to lie. I mean, really, what harm could it do? But we didn't lie to each other. Period.

I sighed. "No."

"Riley." He turned me back to face him. "What. Happened?" He spaced the words, his lips thin and tight.

I shrugged. "I told you I'd tried to use my magic but couldn't."

I pulled out of his grip and opened the door, abandoning the idea of the towel. I headed for my bedroom. I took a pair of jeans from the dresser, along with a bra, underwear, and a tee shirt. I dragged them on, trying not to flinch as they skimmed over my wounds, then dug for a pair of socks and slid those on too. All the while, Price glowered at me from the door.

Finally I faced him, folding my arms over my chest.

"I couldn't hold my magic. It hurts to use it. It got away from me."

He rubbed a hand over his mouth, considering, his sapphire eyes drilling through me. "Were you going to tell me?"

"Eventually. You've got enough on your plate without me adding to it."

He shook his head slowly. "Not how this works."

"It's not like you could do anything about it. It happened. I'm okay."

"Until you try to use your power again." He crossed the space between us, gripping my upper arms. Despite the harsh look on his face, his touch was gentle. "You can't shut me out. I want to know if you've got a hangnail. I want to know if you're hungry. Even if I can't do a damned thing about it, you need to tell me."

"Gotcha. Zit on my ass and you're the first to know."

He cracked a smile and gave me a little shake. "I'm serious."

I sobered. "I don't want to push you over the edge and make you lose control. You might never let me touch you again. Hell, you might decide we can't even be in the same room at the same time again. We've done that for weeks and I'm so done with it."

"I'm working on control. I'll do better if I don't have to worry about what you're hiding from me. Anyhow, I'm touching you now, right?"

He ran his hands up over my shoulders and down my back, gently tugging me against him. I melted, pressing my face against his chest and sliding my arms around his waist. I hid a wince as he touched one of the lacerations. I'd suffer a hell of a lot more than that just to have him holding me again.

I looked up at him. "I've missed you."

He nodded. "I've missed you, too." His face darkened. "I couldn't live with myself if I hurt you."

"I can take care of myself."

The corner of his mouth lifted. "Sure."

"If I get to rub my naked self all over your naked self, then you can have anything you want from me," I said, my hands sliding down over his ass.

He sucked in a breath, his arms tightening. "Don't tempt me. My brother is waiting for us and who knows what sort of shitstorm is about to hit."

"Just another day in the life," I said with a wry smile. I obediently let him go and drew away, averting my face to hide my disappointment and just a little bit of hurt. It's not that he wasn't right, but this was pretty much the first time he'd seemed like he actually *wanted* to touch me in weeks, aside from holding my hand in the truck on the way back to Diamond City. He'd withdrawn from me for good reasons. I couldn't say they weren't. But he seemed to be taking the loss of intimacy between us all in stride. It would have been nice if he could have at least acted like it was harder to let me go.

I sighed. I was being ridiculous. Sappy and stupid and totally high school irrational.

Time to get over myself. I squared my shoulders and marched over to the closet to find something warm to wear over my shirt.

I found a soft, fuzzy blue sweater on a shelf. I'd forgotten I even owned it. I pulled it over my head and turned around. I ran hard into Price. Before I knew what he was going to do, he yanked me close and began kissing me, and not a soft, sweet sort of caress, but a hungry, I-need-you-desperately sort of kiss.

I made a sound in my throat, halfway between a moan and a groan and pressed into him, my arms wrapping his neck. He slid a hand up behind my head to hold me as he impossibly deepened the kiss.

I held on, sparks whirling through me. I barely noticed the breeze that began to spin circles around us. I didn't care. I was on fire and wanted nothing more than to strip off my clothes again and push him onto the bed and have my wicked way with him.

I don't know how long we kissed before he tore his mouth from mine. We were both panting hard. His eyes were only a little bit cloudy. My lips felt wonderfully swollen. I made an unhappy sound.

"Gregg *will* come looking for us," Price said hoarsely. His hands moved over me like he was trying to memorize every curve.

"Might be worth getting caught in the act," I said, licking the corner of his mouth. Never let it be said that I went down without a fight. "Especially since you didn't blow us off to Oz on your magic tornado."

He snorted. "Is that a euphemism?"

"Just a little one."

"Now you're killing my confidence."

I seductively nudged my hips against his, feeling his hard length like an iron bar in his jeans. "Somehow I doubt that."

He kissed me again, this time hard and fast, then stepped back. "You're nothing but trouble."

I grinned cheekily, happiness curling through me. I waggled my brows. "Never claimed not to be."

He backed up. "Get your shoes on. Let's get downstairs."

I sighed dramatically. "If you insist. But I expect a complete performance, later. Opening act, the big Broadway show, and encores. Plenty of them."

He chuckled, grabbing my hand and lifting it to kiss the inside of my wrist. "As many as you want."

"I'll hold you to it." Now, if we could just find a little nookie time in between our life-and-death showdowns.

We went back into the living room. I laced on my boots while Price roamed restlessly.

"You don't have to wait for me," I said. "I want to clean up in the bathroom before I go down."

He just gave me a "get real" look and said, "Hurry up."

I went into the bathroom and started gathering up my discarded clothing. I made the mistake of looking at myself in the mirror. I'd forgotten to comb my hair. I looked like a drowned yeti.

I attacked the mess with a brush, wincing as I yanked out tangles. It wasn't like I didn't need a haircut with the way my escaped magic had mowed it. Emphasis on *cut*.

I couldn't find any way to make it look good. Different lengths flopped all along the top and left side of my head, and then I had a place on the other side where I was pretty much bald in a streak that ran from my part to my ear. Why Price had kissed me instead of rolling on the floor laughing, I'll never know. I yanked it all up into a ponytail, which hid a lot of the damage, and made a mental note to find a hat to wear for the next six months.

I finished gathering up my dirty clothing and headed into Patti's room to dump them into her hamper. She'd rather wash them than let them molder in my hamper. Who knew when I'd get to washing here again.

I twisted the handle on the door and shoved it open with the tip of my toe. The gloom inside didn't smother the rustling sound and small thump following my entrance.

"Someone there?" I asked. As soon as I said it, I realized that a) it was stupid to ask since anyone who shouldn't be there wasn't exactly likely to answer except with an attack, and b) it had to be Cristina. Before I could do or say anything else, Price yanked me out of the way and slapped on the light switch. He had his gun out.

"It's Cristina," I yelled before he could go into full Rambo mode.

The tension in his back didn't relax at all. "Wait here."

Gun raised to eye level, he stepped inside, sweeping from side to side. The bed was rumpled, but no sign of Cristina. She must have slid off the other side. She was probably under the bed by now. I couldn't tell. The bed skirt offered good camo.

I followed Price into the room and went toward the bed.

"Cristina? It's okay. I'm Riley and I'm with Price. We're the ones who rescued you from Ocho. You can come out."

No answer. I exchanged a glance at Price, who still hadn't holstered his gun. He started toward the bed, and I held up a restraining hand. Cristina had already been through too much, and we didn't need to add to it. Not just from Ocho, but coming to the diner and getting jumped by another set of goons. The girl had to be going out of her gourd. Anyway, I was certain it was her, even if Price wasn't.

"We aren't going to hurt you," I called out in a reassuring voice.

When she still didn't respond, I shrugged at Price. "She doesn't want to talk to us. That's fine." I faced the bed. "I'm going to put some laundry in the hamper and then we'll go downstairs. I'm sure your family will be here soon."

I deposited my dirty clothes and towels, and then motioned Price out. He waited until I cleared the door and followed me through, pulling it shut behind us.

"It might not be her," he growled as soon as the latch snicked.

"Who else could it be?"

"You're willing to bet Patti's life on it?"

My breath hissed between my teeth. He knew exactly which buttons to push. All of a sudden, I wanted to go back in and ransack the room. I took a breath and let it out. The logic hadn't changed in the last two seconds, and it was as sound now as then. I gave a firm shake of my head.

"Let's go eat. I'm starved."

He gave me a long look and then nodded and holstered his gun.

"Give me a minute," I said and returned to my bedroom. I pulled a plastic box out from under my bed. It was full of all sorts of odds and ends—Legos, glass beads, coins, rocks, bolts, tire weights—basically whatever innocuous object I could find that would hold magic. Stone and metal worked really well. Plastic was pretty good. Cloth and paper are pretty much like pouring chicken noodle soup into a napkin.

I dug through and found a leather necklace with a shark-tooth pendant. I'd found it in the street one time while walking. I grabbed it, and then a stretchy pink plastic bracelet, and a couple of quarters. I slid the latter two into my socks. I'd be able to activate them when I needed them and wouldn't spend them in the meantime.

I slid the bracelet onto my wrist and held the necklace out to Price, who'd once again shadowed me. I guess I was not to be trusted out of his sight. That would probably annoy me to no end later, but at the moment it made me feel warm and gooey inside. If only because he'd been avoiding me so hard the last few weeks. That, and I liked seeing how he worried for me.

"Can you put this on me?"

He took it, turning it in his fingers. "Interesting fashion statement. I particularly like the way it goes with that god-awful dime-store bracelet."

"They're nulls," I said. No duh. Like he hadn't figured that out. "People don't pay attention to the cheap and the ugly. They figure if you're going to make a null, you're going to put it into something pretty or really substantial. Anyway, I can't afford a lot of bling and this works just fine."

I don't know why I felt the need to defend myself. My methods had kept me alive and out of enemy hands my whole life. It's not like I was embarrassed.

He grinned at me and turned me so that he could fasten the clasp at my neck. "Remind me to buy you something blingy. Something with a lot of sparkle like your eyes." His fingers brushed my nape and a delicious chill ran through me.

He finished and settled his hands on my shoulders. His lips pressed against my skin. He gave a little lick, and my lady parts all clenched up tight with need. I tipped my neck to the side to give him better access. He took advantage, nuzzling and nibbling up my neck to nip my earlobe. "I'd like to see you in diamonds and sapphires and nothing else."

I about melted. "You're not playing fair."

I felt him smile against my skin.

"I know."

"Cristina is in the next room and your brother is downstairs."

"That didn't bother you a few minutes ago."

"You're starting fires you can't put out."

A chuckle. "Am I?"

"You know you are." I twisted out of his grip and shook a finger at him. "Be careful. Turnabout is fair play."

He traced my cheek with a finger. "All you've got to do is walk into a room to tease me."

"Then lucky for you, I'm on my way out of this one. No teasing at all." I stuck my tongue out and headed for the door, swishing my hips seductively. I was grateful for Price's playfulness. He'd found a way to lighten what had been a harrowing day, and it wasn't even noon yet. Touray was waiting downstairs, and I hadn't any doubts that whatever he had to say would be worse than bad. His tension, his posture, his eyes all had the look of a man about to start a war.

Chapter 16

Gregg

GREGG WATCHED the flow of people through the diner, examining each and mentally cataloging them. He didn't see any threats, but trouble rarely made a habit of announcing itself. Tyrell's men certainly hadn't.

He scowled. How had they tracked him in dreamspace? That question worried him most of all. The ability to travel, to be where he wanted without warning, was his best weapon.

His mind crowded with things he needed to do. He grabbed a napkin and reached for a pen in his pocket. He didn't have one.

Riley's friend Patti came zipping out from behind the dining counter like a miniature tornado. She handed out drinks to another table, then paused in front of his.

She thunked down an oversized mug. "Drink that."

He eyed it. "Thanks. You got a pen?"

She pulled one out of her apron pocket and dropped it, then skittered off. Gregg reached for the cup. Coffee steamed inside. Dark roasted and black as sin, just the way he liked it. He took a sip and blinked. It was laced with a healthy dose of whiskey. He took another sip and smiled in reluctant appreciation.

Just then, Patti jogged past, tossing small pad of paper onto the table. The woman was twenty-five pounds of dynamite packed into a five-pound canister. The air around her practically crackled with the energy she gave off.

Gregg started writing notes and lists of what he had to do and who he had to contact, and what he'd need from Tyrell. He glanced outside. Sooner or later Randall and Bruno, his two new knee-breaking bodyguards, would show up. They'd caught him here once; the diner would be one of the top places on their list to look for him.

The thought made him itch. Tyrell had sent a team after Clay and Riley, and once the bastard had a hold of them, Gregg doubted he'd let them go, especially once he figured out Clay's talent. Gregg couldn't allow that.

He drummed his fingers on the table, and then made his decision. He took his phone out and punched a number. It rang once. The other side picked up, but no one spoke.

"I'm in," he said.

"Good," Vernon said. "I'll be in touch soon." He paused. "How is my daughter?"

Gregg stiffened, scowling. "Why ask me?"

"She does not care to speak to me and my other children refuse to speak of her."

"You're a dreamer. Take it out of their heads."

"I'd prefer to avoid that. Since Riley is attached to your brother, I assume you know how she's doing."

Smooth, but something in the explanation sounded off. Especially from a man who'd tried to kill Riley. He shouldn't be bothered about rummaging in her siblings' heads for information. "She's fine," Gregg said finally, unable to pin down exactly what was bothering him. "Don't ask me about her again."

He hung up and dropped his cell onto the table. Riley wasn't going to like him allying with Vernon. In fact, she was going to be seriously pissed. That meant Clay was going to be unhappy. Too damned bad. They'd both have to get over it and get with the program. Too much was at stake. He couldn't let Tyrell take the city or run his life. Still . . . this business was going to be tricky. He didn't trust Vernon any more than Tyrell. If he was going to come out on top, he'd have to play both sides against the middle and hope everything didn't blow up in his face.

First things first: take control of Savannah's organization within the next seventy-two hours. That was good for him whether or not Tyrell and Vernon were involved.

He was on the phone with one of his top lieutenants—Mark Kinsey—a few minutes later, when Patti deposited a plate of biscuits and gravy in front of him, with a rib eye and a crispy mountain of hashbrowns.

He held the receiver away from his mouth and frowned. "I didn't order this."

"Take it or leave it," Patti said, already moving away.

Gregg watched her flit away, an unfamiliar bemused expression sliding over his face.

"What's wrong with you?" Riley asked, sliding into the booth opposite him. Clay followed, sliding his arm around her. He hadn't done much more than wash his face and hands. She'd showered. Her hair was still wet beneath her black knit cap. Dark circles surrounded her eyes and a snaking cut wriggled across her forehead and down her cheek.

"How did you get that?"

She touched the wound and shrugged. "Craziest thing. Electric eel came out of the drain when I was going to the bathroom."

He narrowed his eyes at her.

She just gave him a shit-eating grin and bent over the table, her voice dropping conspiratorially. "In case you didn't get the message, it's none of your damned business."

He clamped his teeth together, his jaw knotting. "Everything about you is my business. As long as you're with Clay." He looked at his brother, but Clay shook his head, refusing to interfere in the argument.

"Doesn't mean you get to paw through my underwear drawer," she retorted, then nudged her chin in the direction of his phone. "Aren't you talking to someone?" She gave him another one of those grins.

The look he shot her should have sent her cowering, but she only smiled wider. Gregg concentrated on his call.

"I'm here," he confirmed. "Got questions?"

"No, sir," Kinsey said. "I'll pull all the intel we can get and start moving personnel into place."

"I want a briefing in two hours."

He hung up and set his phone aside before digging into his food, wanting to bite someone—specifically Riley—but that wasn't an option.

"You going to tell us what happened to you?" Clay asked finally, after Gregg had plowed through half of the biscuits and gravy and Patti had dropped off a carafe of coffee and a pitcher of fresh cream.

Gregg swallowed, washing the bite down with the whiskey-laced coffee. He set his cup down. "Not here," he said. "Why don't you tell me how you got out of that hellhole?"

Clay gave him a long look and then recounted the story, though he never explained Riley's whiplike wound. As he spoke, he snugged Riley closer until Patti delivered heaping plates of pancakes, omelets, hashbrowns, sausages and bacon, along with a bowl of fruit.

"That should do the trick," she declared, surveying the bounty with satisfaction. She looked at Riley. "Don't even think of walking out of here without talking to me, girlfriend."

"Not a chance," Riley agreed.

"Better not be."

Once again, Patti scuttled off. Gregg marveled that she could walk on the stilts she called shoes, much less dance through the customers carrying armloads of food. He scanned the crowd. Mostly first responders and cops. They looked haggard and pissed beneath a grime of dirt and smoke.

"This place is doing a good thing," he observed.

"That surprises you?" Riley asked.

He considered the question. "A little. There's a lot of money walking out the door. It's hard to afford."

"People have to help each other how they can. First responders are willing to sacrifice their lives. Feeding them is how Patti and Ben do their part."

"They are unusual."

Riley sipped her coffee and set it aside. "Not really. People in the city take care of each other more than you think. You just don't see it from where you sit."

Gregg's brows lifted. "Where I sit?"

"Up in your Tyet tower. You have no idea what real people's lives are like."

Unfortunately, she was right. He was insulated from the way ordinary people lived by his money and the need to protect himself. Riley practically lived on the streets. She worked for the people. "Maybe you can teach me."

She lifted a brow at him. "Me?" She shook her head. "Try actually talking to people, walking around, shopping in grocery stores and shoe stores and hardware stores. Go to the post office, the coffee shop, and the mall. You know, the natural habitat of the native species."

That shit-eating grin was back. Gregg's own lips twitched in response. He supposed he deserved that.

"You sure you want to keep her?" he asked Clay.

"Have to. Can't just let her loose on the unsuspecting world," his brother replied.

Riley elbowed him in the side. "You'll pay for that."

The smile Clay gave her was intimate and possessive. "Promises, promises."

Their interaction made Gregg smile. She was good for Clay. He suppressed a sigh. Part of him envied their connection. What would it be like to trust a woman like that? To have her so devoted to you she'd literally lay down her life for you? Inwardly he snorted. He had a whole city depending on him. He didn't need a girlfriend getting underfoot. *But Riley wasn't just a "girlfriend," was she?* He was starting to think that if soulmates existed, she was Clay's. The two were bound together practically on a cellular level, or so it seemed. Crazy how fast that had happened. A few months ago, they didn't even know each other.

The thought gave him a pang. He'd never had to share his brother before. He wasn't sure he liked it.

Up until around three months ago, he and Clay had been as close as they had ever been. Things with Savannah and the FBI had started heating up, and Gregg had pressured Clay to leave the police force and join his organization full time. Clay had dug in his heels, unwilling to give up what he considered his calling. He finally relented enough to act as an enforcer for Gregg, but he picked and chose his jobs, never taking on anything that he found morally repulsive. Right up until Riley, and then Clay had sacrificed his career as a cop for her without a moment's hesitation. He'd never done anything like that for Gregg.

"What do you two have planned, now?"

They exchanged a look. Riley's expression was slightly pained, while Clay's was forbidding. Gregg tried not to let their wordless communication bother him. It did, however, underscore that Clay had a split allegiance, now.

"Riley needs rest," Clay said. "I want her to see Maya, too. As soon as possible." He frowned at her as expecting protest. He got it.

She rolled her eyes. "Maya isn't going to be able to do anything. And I don't need rest if you don't."

"Yes, you do, and you're going to get it if I have to chain you down and force-feed you tranquilizers. This is serious. "

Clay flicked a glance at Gregg before glowering at Riley again. "Her magic is giving her trouble."

She flushed. "Lying around in bed won't fix anything."

Gregg ignored her. "What kind of trouble?"

"It hurts to use. Enough that she can't control it."

"Shit."

"You said it. I'm hoping Maya will have some ideas."

"Ahem. I'm sitting right here and I can take care of myself, thank you very much." Her glare could have stripped paint.

Clay pounced. "How? Like that?" He pointed to the laceration crawling out from under her blue sweater.

Now Gregg knew how she'd been cut up.

"I'll figure it out."

"*We* will, and it won't hurt to talk to Maya. And don't bother telling me you don't want sleep. You're not that good a liar."

"Sure. I want sleep, so long as you're in bed with me." She gave him a smug grin. "What's good for the goose and all that crap. But enough about me." Riley focused on Gregg. "Let's talk about what happened to you."

"Start from when you got grabbed," Clay said, leaning over the table.

Gregg had already given his brother the outline of all that had happened when the two had been waiting for Riley to call and tell them where to find her.

"Tyrell was behind it." His hand tightened on his fork. The sturdy stainless steel bent. He loosened his grip with an effort.

"Jackson Tyrell? The trillionaire who's been fighting the whole magic-talent registry thing that Senator Rice is lobbying for? He's the guy Vernon said was behind the destruction of the Marchont building after we escaped."

Why? Gregg didn't know, but he tucked that news in the back of his mind to consider later. "It's likely the same person."

"What did he want from you?" Riley asked. "And how did he know to lie in wait for you here?"

"No idea how, but as to the why, he wants me to take the city for him. I've got five days to take control of Savannah's business. If I do it in three, he'll tell me how he knew to wait for me here." He paused.

"I told him how I left the two of you at Ocho's and he ordered up a strike team to rescue you." He looked at Riley. "He knew about you. Didn't say it outright, but I'm willing to bet if he finds you, he'll lock you away for safekeeping. You need to stay nulled. He's got at least the one strike team ready to move at a moment's notice and a stable of travellers to take them wherever they're needed. With any luck, nulls will keep them from using magic to find you."

Gregg couldn't see how they would if the same magic that allowed Tyrell to find him at the diner could find Riley just as easily.

Clay scratched the dark bristles along his jaw. "And you? Are you going to take the city for him?"

"I don't have a choice." Gregg shoved his plate away. The food had turned sour in his stomach. Besides, he'd bitten his cheek in the fight with Tyrell's two henchmen. Eating made it hurt worse.

He shrugged. "I'll play his game for now." He scraped his lower lip with his teeth. The next news wasn't going to sit well, particularly with Riley. "But I'm also going to take Brussard up on his offer to give me the resources I need to take over Morrell's operation and the city."

For a moment Riley just stared, her mouth dropping. "My *father?*" She squeaked. She shook her head. "That's a really bad idea."

"I agree, but he's got resources I'm going to need to take on Tyrell."

"If he doesn't cut your throat in the meantime. Or dump poison in your coffee. Or just rip out your mind." Riley's body had gone rigid, and her eyes gleamed with icy disgust. "You think he's better than Tyrell? He's not. You think you can handle him? You can't."

Gregg jerked forward, black anger rising hard. The rage he couldn't vent on Tyrell came frothing out.

"I know I can't trust your father worth a damn, but the enemy of my enemy is my friend, and I'll be damned if I'm going to give up Diamond City without a fight. I'll use whatever and whoever I have to to make sure I win."

His words flew like bullets. She didn't back down. Instead, she leaned in, her nose nearly touching his.

"Find. A. Different. Way."

That took Gregg aback. He blinked in irritation. Who was she to tell him to do anything? His expression must have made his opinion of *her* opinion all too obvious.

"I'll think about taking your advice when you get a clue about what the fuck you're talking about," he snapped back, feeling goaded. He agreed with her, but he was stuck, and playing both men against the middle was the only way out he could see.

Riley drew herself up straight. "Your funeral," she said, her lip curling. She looked at Clay. "Let me out. I need to call Taylor and the boys."

Clay stood to let her up. "Where will you be?"

She relented. "I'm just going into the back where it's quiet."

His brow furrowed. "I don't like when I can't see you."

She snorted. "Get over it. The world's full of disappointments." But as she spoke, she was looking at Gregg.

She spun and stalked away.

Clay watched her disappear behind a swinging door, then blew out a breath and slid back into the booth. "You know you can catch more bees with honey than with gunpowder, right?"

Relief shuddered through Gregg at his brother's wry tone. Clay *hadn't* taken Riley's side against him. He hadn't realized how much he'd feared Clay would.

He rubbed a hand over his face. "Maybe. But that takes time and I'm fresh out. She'll get over it." Gregg waved his hand as if to dust the scene away. A stinging pain caught his attention. He pulled up his sleeve. Dried blood stuck it to his arm. He tugged it loose and folded back his cuff. On his wrist was a three-inch cut. Thin, like a scalpel had made it. It curved in a C shape.

"Where did you get that?" Clay asked.

Gregg frowned at the cut. "I have no idea."

"Maybe Tyrell's thugs did it."

"I don't think so." Gregg's mind raced, remembering all that had happened after. He'd been bound. Nothing could have happened then. There'd been the tasing and beating in the car, but Dreadlocks had focused on his face. The slice to free him from his cuffs had been clean. So when could he have gotten the cut? A sinking sense of foreboding, along with unfettered rage, rolled through him. Tyrell had sicced a dreamer on him, taking away memories. There was no other explanation.

"I need Cass."

Clay's face went hard, his mouth twisting. "Go. Travel to her. Better yet, bring her here. I want to be here when she works on you."

"Not here. Tyrell assigned the two bastards who kidnapped me to be my so-called bodyguards. They'll be looking for me. Won't be long until they come here. Them, or someone else in Tyrell's network. I don't want him finding out that I know he's been fucking around in my head. Cass can work on me in private at the Lachia house. I'll pick up Cass. You can meet us there."

He slid from the booth, digging his wallet out, and tossed five one-hundred-dollar bills on the table. His contribution to feeding the first responders.

"What if he's got a bead on you and is already waiting at Cass's place?"

"Then I'm fucked. I'm hoping he trusts the dreamwork and figures he doesn't have to watch me too closely. Anyway, the clock's ticking and I don't have a choice. See you at the house. I hope."

Gregg opened up to dreamspace and travelled into the void, cursing Jackson Tyrell's soul to hell as he went.

Chapter 17

Riley

I MARCHED INTO the back room, yanking my phone out of my pocket as my teeth ground together. Tyrell was bad enough, but now Gregg was climbing into bed with Vernon? Was he insane? That wasn't just stupid, it was suicidal.

Certainty settled over me. Now, more than ever, I couldn't trust Touray. He had his own agenda and didn't care how many bodies he left in his wake, or what he might have to sacrifice to get what he wanted. Price was the only one he worried about, and even so, I was sure that sooner or later Touray's plots were bound to get him killed. Hell, Touray was probably the reason the FBI had picked up Price in the first place. They likely figured they could leverage one brother against the other.

Touray could do what he wanted, but I wasn't going to wait to find out just how he was going to get me and my family killed. We needed to start protecting ourselves from him and his new partners. I was done being a little boat tossed around at the mercy of the waves. I was going to become one of the motherfucking waves.

I stabbed the speed dial for Taylor. Surprise, surprise, my hands didn't shake. As pissed as I was, not to mention terrified, I was keeping my shit together. I probably deserved a trophy.

Her phone rang once, and she picked up like she'd been waiting for my call. "Riley? Are you okay?"

Not even a little. I didn't say it, nor did I explain anything. I didn't want Price or Touray walking in and overhearing me. "Meet me at my place. Bring everybody."

"When? What's wrong?"

"Now. I'll explain when I get there."

I hung up before she could ask anything else. I stood there for long moments, staring blankly at the coats hanging on hooks along the wall. Was I really going to attempt this? Six months ago I would have laughed at myself, or checked into a loony bin. A lot had changed in six months, though. I had to protect the people I cared about, and the only way I could think of was to fight fire with fire. That meant founding my own Tyet. It was the only way to protect my family and friends, short of nuking Tyrell and Vernon from space.

The audacity of my plan made me shake. Start a Tyet? Run one? Me? Riley Hollis? The tracer who'd spent her time scurrying around the city's shadows so nobody would notice her?

The entire idea was patently ridiculous. As bad as Mickey Mouse running for president. But what choice did I have? It wasn't like I had to do it alone. Taylor knew her shit. She'd run her own business for years, and she'd flown in Iraq for mercenary companies. She could more than handle herself, and she knew management. Leo and Jamie did too, with their own businesses, plus they had the magical talents to help me enforce laws. I snorted. Laws. God, was I serious? But I was. It was the only way. I needed my own damned army.

I considered Dalton. He had skills, too. I needed him, or someone like him. He knew the underworld of the Tyets, who the players were and their politics, and he knew Vernon. He likely knew a lot about Tyrell, too. I just didn't know if he was going to be willing to give up the information. Neither did I know if I could trust him, but I didn't have a choice. I refused to do anything as evil as asking Cass to flip a guarantee switch in Dalton's head so I didn't have to worry about it. Not that she would. But still. There were lines that I would not—could not—cross. Fucking in people's heads was one.

That's when Arnow's name came to mind. Instantly I shook my head at myself, but my brain refused to back down once I latched onto this idea. My brain was all in. I scrunched my eyes shut. Was I really thinking about reaching out to Arnow? The FBI agent knew as much or more than Dalton about the local Tyets, and she knew the ins and outs of the local criminal justice system. If I was going to be honest with myself, I needed her. Plus, I still owed her. I'd promised to trace her missing people. That was one way to convince her to help me. If she got on board, it would speed the process up and then I could help her. Once my magic healed up.

I refused to consider that it might not.

Before I could argue myself out of it, I dialed the FBI agent.

"Special Agent Arnow," came the other woman's sophisticated voice. She sounded like she'd been educated at Vassar, which likely she had. She also sounded like she had a stick sideways up her ass, which she also likely had.

"Come to the diner," I said and then hung up before Arnow could demand an explanation. This would go better in person. Plus, there was the bonus of driving her batshit crazy. Two birds with one stone. My lips curled in a smile.

Just then Price appeared in the doorway. He looked angry and worried, like he was the bearer of bad news. My stomach tightened, and my smiled faded. My tongue clung to the roof of my mouth. How was I going to tell him what I was up to? I wanted and needed him by my side, but I couldn't ask that of him. I couldn't ask him to choose between me and his brother. I had hoped it wouldn't come to this so soon.

I reached to lace my fingers through his. He tugged me forward until he could wrap the other arm around my waist, pulling me against him. His body was hard, the muscles knotted tight with tension. He pressed his forehead to mine, eyes stormy.

I was a total bitch for being grateful for anything to delay me from telling him of my plans. "What's wrong?"

"Gregg went to get Cass."

I didn't have to ask why. It only made sense to get screened by a dreamer after a kidnapping. But Price didn't look like this was just precaution. My stomach twisted. "This is more than a checkup, isn't it?"

"Gregg has a cut on his arm he can't remember getting."

Crap. "Cass will take care of it," I said confidently. She'd yanked out all my dad's twists and traps. If she could do that for me, she could do it for Touray. I wondered who'd been screwing around in his head. Vernon or Tyrell?

Price stepped away, turning to pull me back into the dining room. "We need to go meet him. It'll take us a while with the traffic. We should get going."

I dug my feet in, pulling back. "I have to go see Taylor and my brothers."

My stomach churned. It wasn't exactly a lie, but it neither was it the whole truth. I swallowed my guilt. I couldn't put Price between me and his brother. Maybe I could figure out a plan that would let me establish a power base and not screw over Touray. Once I had something concrete, I'd tell Price and let him figure out what he wanted to do. Right now, he needed to be with his brother.

I almost threw up then. Did I honestly think I could keep him from having to choose? No. It didn't have to come to that. I could figure this out. I wasn't going to compete with Touray. I just wanted us to be able to protect ourselves.

Right. It wasn't going to be that simple. If Touray pushed against me, I'd have to push back. Sooner or later it was bound to happen, what with him working for both Vernon and Tyrell.

I squeezed my eyes shut, forcing away tears. God, what a mess.

"Riley, what aren't you telling me?"

Price's voice held warning. I looked at him. His penetrating gaze was shrewd. He'd been very good at his cop job. How had I thought I could hide anything from him?

"I can't trust your brother," I said. "Tyrell would be bad enough, but Vernon? No way. If it became necessary to throw me or my family under the bus, Touray would. For the greater good, as he sees it."

The pressure in the room dropped, and my ears popped. The door behind Price slammed shut, and wind picked at the coats hanging on their hooks and teased my hair. I pushed the loose strands behind my ears. No need to ask how he felt. Price had his personal emotional barometer going on.

"So what—you were planning to just take off? Disappear on me?" His voice had gone deadly soft, the edges of it like jagged metal.

I shook my head. "No. I really *am* going to go see my family. I want tell them what's happened and talk to them about what to do. And yes, I may have an idea in mind, but if I tell you, you'll have to tell your brother. If you don't, you'll feel like you've betrayed him. Anything I do to protect me and my family at this point is probably going to go against him in some way. Hell, just putting myself on the opposite side of the fence is a problem, if only because he needs me to trace Kensington's blood to the hidden workshop. As soon as we figure something out, I plan to tell you and let you decide."

My fingers twisted together as I tried to explain. Ha. Fat chance. I was standing here telling him I wasn't going to disappear, but at the same time, we might not be able to have a relationship. I couldn't imagine having to choose between

Price and Taylor or Leo or Jamie. I wouldn't be able to. I loved them all too much. And yet, what if I had to? What if the only choice *was* to choose?

"Decide?" Price repeated in a deadly soft voice.

I just looked at him. He knew exactly what I meant. I'd already told him back at the cabin I didn't think I'd come out the winner when it came down to me and Touray.

The muscles in his jaw knotted. His eyes fogged white. The wind around us whirled faster. I didn't try to touch him. What comfort could I begin to give? It would be all right? That was an empty promise. The odds were that everything was most definitely not going to be all right.

Finally he spoke, his voice dripping condemnation. "So you've already figured what I'll do. Without even talking to me."

"Could you ever forgive me for forcing you to pick between me and your brother?"

"It won't come to that."

"I don't want it to, but I can't live in a fairy tale."

"He wouldn't hurt you. He's promised me. Gregg knows how much I love you. He knows I'd never forgive him if he went after you."

I nodded. "But he might do something like lock me up—for my own good. Or maybe tamper with my head. Or blackmail me into doing something I don't want to do. He's not above threatening my family or Patti, even. You know I'm right. He's a driven man and he's not going to let me or anybody else get in the way of saving this city. I admire that. I really do. But I also don't want any of my family to become a casualty of his war."

"It might not go down that way."

"True. But now that he's working with Vernon, I can't take the chance. My father has plans for me and we both know he doesn't have any lines that he won't cross to get what he wants. Touray may not be able to stop him; hell, Touray might not want to." I shook my head. "The only way to be sure is to take charge of my own safety."

I looked at him, somehow hoping he had a different argument or maybe a better solution. No such luck. His expression had turned haunted and bleak.

"It's okay," I said, a gargantuan knot aching in my throat. Pushing words past it was excruciating. "I understand and I know you're all he's got. You've got to stick by him. He's counting on you just like my family is counting on me. It sucks, but it is what it is."

Price jerked forward, grabbing my arms and dragging me against him. Grooves cut deep around his mouth.

"I *will not* let you go," he rasped.

He kissed me. It was hard and desperate and primal. I snaked my arms around his neck, locking myself tight against him and gave as good as I got. I tasted salt and realized I was crying.

I don't know how long it went on before he tore his mouth away. My lips were bruised, but I didn't care. His breathing was ragged. He slid a gentle hand over my cheek, brushing his thumb across my lower lip.

"We'll figure it out," he promised.

"Sure."

"Don't give up on me. Not yet."

"I'll never give up on you. But I know you couldn't live with yourself if you betrayed your brother. I understand and it's okay."

His arm around my back tightened. "It's not *okay*. I couldn't live if I lost you," he said.

I gave him a weak smile. "People don't die of broken hearts. You'd survive."

"Would you?"

I'd be a hollowed-out shell of myself. I already felt that way, knowing where this could go.

"Sure," I said again with zero conviction.

He brushed my lips with his. "Liar," he whispered.

Price set me away from him, letting go reluctantly. "Go. I'll find out what Tyrell did to Gregg and I'll call you."

"We're going to my place," I said. He wouldn't be able to find it without help. Nobody could, except my brothers and Taylor. Not even Patti knew how to get there. I'd showed Price a map once. He'd get close, but the glamours hiding it and the turn-away spells would keep him away. If not, there were bands of confusion spells and bramble spells that would do the trick.

"Good. That should be safe. Call me when you get there."

"Yes, Dad," I said, making a face in an effort to lighten the mood. "I'll make it in by curfew, too."

A knock sounded on the door leading into the dining area, and then Patti put her head in. "You two okay?"

"Fine," I said. I looked at Price. "I'll talk to you soon."

He looked like he wanted to say something, but then just nodded. He pressed a kiss to my lips and then shoved passed Patti. A sharp breeze followed him.

I wrapped my arms around my aching stomach as I watched him go. *We're not over*, I told myself. *We're going to figure it out.* If only I believed it.

Patti came in and scanned the room. "What a mess."

I followed her gaze. Paper of all kinds littered the floor, along with rags, bags of premeasured coffee, and dried beans from a bucket that had tipped over—all had spun wild on Price's angry wind.

"Sorry. I'll help you clean."

"Yes, you will." She retrieved a couple of brooms from the utility closet, along with a big dustpan and a garbage bag. It only took a few minutes to straighten up. Luckily Price hadn't gone full tornado.

"You going to tell me why you look like your dog died?" Patti asked as she tied off the bag.

I took her broom and the dustpan and put them away before facing her. "I've got something in the works. I'm going to need help with it. I've called Arnow, Taylor, Leo, and Jamie to meet me at my house. I know you're busy here—"

"I'm coming," Patti said.

"Good. Thanks."

She snorted. "About time you asked. Glad you figured out that you can't do everything alone, or even with Mister Big, Bad, and Beautiful by your side."

"I'll have to tell Price you think he's beautiful."

"Like he doesn't know. The man is a walking *GQ* ad. His brother isn't half bad to look at either. If only he'd keep his mouth shut, he'd be nearly a perfect man."

I chortled. "Please tell him so. I want to be there when you do. With a camera."

"I doubt I'd be the first woman to tell him," Patti said. "Wouldn't be the last, either. Did you know he left five hundred dollars to pay for breakfast? On what planet is that normal? I'm tempted to keep the change and shove it up his ass when I see him again. I don't need charity, especially from him."

"Maybe he wanted to kick in on the costs for feeding the first responders," I suggested. It was something Touray would do, though whether that had been his reasoning was anybody's guess. The possibility didn't mollify Patti in the slightest.

"Don't need his help," she said, putting her hands on her hips. "He can find his own way to give back. When does Snow Bitch get here?"

"How do you know Arnow's coming here?"

Patti rolled her eyes. "Because I'm not stupid. You wouldn't have told her how to get to your place, and even if you had, she couldn't get close to it with all the protective spells."

"No idea how long it will take her to get here."

"Then go nap. I'll come get you when she arrives."

Just the word *nap* made me want to fall over. I nodded and went back upstairs. Cristina's door remained shut when I came in the apartment. I locked the front door and kicked off my boots before falling onto my bed with a groan. I passed out before I could even think about crying at sending Price away.

"SHE'S QUITE THE queen of the bitches, isn't she?" Patti asked, having just woken me up.

"I'm standing right here." Arnow appeared in the doorway. She towered over Patti, who had replaced her stiletto heels with a pair of blue Doc Martens. Arnow still wore lady stilts. She was in her FBI uniform, which consisted of a gray pencil skirt, a cream silk blouse, and a gray blazer, all designer and probably hand-sewn by Italian monks. Her ash-blond hair was pulled up in an elegant chignon. On me it would have been called a bun, but something as mundane and messy as a bun didn't even live in the same zip code as Arnow.

To be fair, she didn't always look like an ice queen with a pointy stick up her ass. I'd seen her in jeans and wearing a ponytail and no makeup. Looking at her now, I could hardly believe the episode hadn't been a bad drug trip.

Her gaze took me in. "What the hell happened to your hair? Did rabid badgers attack you with hedge clippers?"

I sighed. "Magic did it." I had no intention of disclosing that losing control of my own magic had done the deed.

Arnow's eyes narrowed. "Sit down. I'm not going to be seen in public with you looking like that."

"I'll wear a hat."

"Yes, you will, but first, I'll get you close to presentable."

She sent Patti for scissors. I had high hopes Patti would stab them through Arnow's neck, but no such luck. She handed them over, and Arnow pushed me down into a chair, then set about snipping and clipping while making disgusted noises. When she was done, my head felt too light and the air on my neck was chilly. I went into the bathroom. I looked like a copper-headed Tinker Bell with big boobs and no wings. I went in search of my hat.

"I look stupid," I said, pulling the knit cap on and eyeing Arnow balefully.

"Of course you do, but what else is new? At least you no longer look like a lawnmower got loose on your head. You're welcome, by the way."

"I'll be sure to thank you at half past never," I grumbled. I grabbed my boots and started to lace them up. "Where's Cristina?" I asked, noticing the open door on Patti's bedroom.

"Her family came. They said to tell you thank-you."

"Good." One less headache to deal with.

"What am I doing here?" Arnow demanded. "Or are you planning to finally do the trace job for me?"

"I can't," I said, looking up at her.

The cold indifference on her face cracked away, replaced with burning fury. "We had a deal. Every minute that goes by cuts our chances of finding them alive."

"I know. But I said I *can't*, not that I won't."

Her pale brows winged down. "What does that mean?"

"My talent is kind of wonky at the moment," I said and brushed my fingers over the cuts on my face. "It's what happened to my hair." So much for keeping it a secret.

Patti scowled at me. "You didn't tell me that."

"I haven't had a lot of time."

She didn't look mollified, but moved on. "It's still a traffic nightmare out there and the subway is shut down. How are we going to get to your place?"

"Wait a damned minute. I'm not going anywhere. I came because I thought you were ready to hold up your end of our bargain," Arnow said.

I finished tying my boots and pulled the cuffs of my pants down over them. I propped my elbows on my knees and looked up at her. "I need your help, and I think you're going to want in on this."

She snorted in a most unsophisticated way. "Why would I help you when you can't keep your promises?"

"Because I will as soon as I'm able, and because you don't like Gregg Touray, and because I'm about to attempt to take over Savannah Morrell's empire." As soon as I said the words, I realized I'd been planning that since the moment I'd heard Touray was working with Vernon. Starting a new Tyet was ridiculous. Taking one over? Also ridiculous, but more possible.

Arnow stared, her mouth falling open. Finally she managed, "Take control?" She laughed with genuine amusement. "Savannah will swat you like mosquito."

"She would if she could, but since dead people don't move so well, I'm not worried about her."

Arnow froze, her face going slack. "Dead?"

"That's the word."

A strange look washed over her face, then her cold mask returned. She gave me a head-to-toe disparaging look. "Aren't you supposed to be the poster child for anti-Tyet groups everywhere?"

"I hate them. But you've got to fight fire with fire and right now, there's an inferno about to run us all over."

"Details," she demanded.

"I'd rather talk to everyone at once. We're going have a war counsel. That's why I called you."

"Who else?"

"Besides you two, my sister and brothers, and Dalton."

I was surprised when she didn't laugh at our very motley crew.

"What about your loverboy?"

A needle of hurt ran through my heart, and for a second I couldn't breathe. I drew a breath, letting myself get used to the pain. It wasn't going away. I'd have to live with it.

"He's visiting his brother." Which sounded like he could be in on this with me, even though that wasn't going to happen. Not in this lifetime.

Arnow shook her head. "Do you have any idea what you're getting into? This isn't running a grocery store. It's a criminal organization. You're going to be getting dirty. You don't have it in you."

"Let me worry about that. Are you in?"

"I'm an FBI agent," she reminded me, but I could tell she was just giving herself time to think.

"An agent who worked for Savannah. Now I want you to work for me. With me, because you're right, I don't know a damned thing about running a Tyet. You do."

Her lip curled. "I suppose if I refuse you'll never get well enough to trace my people. Is that the deal?"

I probably shouldn't have been insulted. I resisted the urge to tell her to fuck off and just shook my head. "That has nothing to do with this. I'll look for your people as soon as I can trace again. I'm hoping it won't be long."

She blew out a breath and looked away. I exchanged a glance with Patti, who shrugged.

Arnow finally turned back to look at me. "I guess I don't really have a choice. Not if I want you to stay alive long enough to trace my team."

Relief washed through me. Until I'd laid out my argument, I hadn't realized how much I really did need Arnow's expertise. "Good. Then let's get out of here."

IT TOOK US NEARLY three hours to get home, mostly because we started out in Arnow's car and slogged through traffic awhile, then parked it. To avoid tails, we walked a meandering, looping path on a mazelike route, finally ending up in a run-down industrial area on the north side of Downtown. It had fallen out of use because of the flooding that happens every spring and the need to put in extra supports and infrastructure if they wanted to build anything. Since the only building anybody had ever suggested for the area was low-income housing, nobody cared to spend the kind of money necessary to make it truly safe. So the city used the area to warehouse all sorts of junk they didn't want anymore. Every so often they held a surplus auction to liquidate what they could, then they stockpiled again.

I refused to expose my family's private subway system to Arnow. The less she knew about that the better. Bad enough Vernon and Dalton knew about it. I admit I had incredible respect for the way she maneuvered in her skirt and heels. She might as well have been wearing tennis shoes, the way she got around.

"These shoes are Louboutins," she seethed, gracefully hopping over a slushy puddle.

"How does an FBI agent afford those?" Patti asked.

"I'm frugal."

"You're on the take," I corrected.

She shrugged. "And I'm frugal."

"I thought that word meant cutting coupons, eating peanut butter and ramen every night, buying generic, using one-ply toilet paper, and shopping at dollar stores," Patti said. "I can't picture you doing any of those."

"Your lack of imagination doesn't interest me," Arnow said loftily. "How much longer must this idiotic adventure go on?" she asked me.

"Getting close."

I'd made her carry one of my trace nulls, even though she claimed to have her own. Not that I didn't trust her, but I didn't trust her, and I didn't trust whatever sources of magic she used. For all I knew, somebody had worked tracking spells onto her nulls.

I led my two companions down an alley between the backs of several decrepit warehouses. Rusted chain-link fences topped with sagging razor wire surrounded them. The ground was thick with gray, rutted, rippled ice and clods of snow. Overhead, power lines crackled and hummed.

Patti looked up. "Should I see an oncologist after this?"

"No, but you might develop the ability to climb walls like a spider," I said.

"I could live with that."

Chapter 18

Riley

I LIVE IN A PLACE called the Karnickey Burrows. Aside from the fact that there's no good reason to come near there, people generally stay away because they say it's haunted and cursed. I've done my best to reinforce their beliefs.

The urban legend about the place started in the bad old days. A jealous rivalry got completely out of hand and led one jilted man to release a magical virus into the Burrows—a cramped city-within-a-city constructed inside a narrow, snaking canyon in the crater's wall. The virus killed every single soul inside, including Karnickey, who built the place. After that, the Burrows was left abandoned. Not that it was prime real estate. The towering trees and steep, high canyon walls made the place gloomy for all but a few hours on a sunny day. As far as the city was concerned, it was next to useless. It wasn't worth the price of magic to develop it.

My place was near the mouth of the entrance, though you couldn't see it, thanks to my brothers' brilliant construction. I could light the place up like a Christmas tree and no one would see it.

I had several routes inside, and I took the one that had us climbing up a zig-zag of rock stairs and back down on a switchback that hugged the side of the canyon before becoming a steep flight of steps down to the bottom. The going wasn't as hard as it could have been. I'd bought spells to keep the ice and snow melted. Illusion spells made the path indistinguishable from the terrain around it, and turn-away and briar spells made everybody avoid the entire area.

The Burrows' original buildings had largely crumbled or been destroyed by nearly two centuries of flash floods and heavy weather. Not that they'd been built that well in the beginning. Jamie and Leo had stabilized the rubble with steel webbing and created a solid wing of wall to divert floods away from my house. I caught the scent of cedar woodsmoke from my fireplace. I never got tired of that smell. I breathed in a deep breath.

Mine wasn't your traditional house. In fact, from the outside, it looked pretty much like just another giant pile of rocks. Leo and Jamie had mortared walls together with steel, then added lumpy protrusions and extra rubble to reinforce the illusion of piled debris. A slab of basalt the size of a king-sized bed leaned drunkenly against my front wall, hiding the door.

We went up the narrow path and under the slab.

"This is where you live?" Patti asked, sounding delighted.

"Looks like a bomb went off," Arnow said balefully.

Patti took a hissing breath, and we both stared at the FBI agent.

"Wow. You've raised tactlessness to an art," I said.

Arnow had the grace to look contrite. "Sorry," she said.

"Sure. *Sorry* fixes everything, right?" Patti asked. "You going to apologize for your bomb-happy boss blowing up a bunch of people in the city, too?"

"I had nothing to do with that."

"Yes, you did. Everybody who let her keep doing what she was doing had their fingerprints on those bombs. Hell, not only *let* her, you helped her."

Arnow's silence went on so long I didn't think she was going to reply. "We all do what we have to."

"You didn't have to. Everybody's got choices."

"You're an idiot if you believe that tripe."

I led the way under the concealing slab and opened the door, pushing it inward. It was made of intricately laced copper wire over a steel core. My brothers had wanted to make me something pretty. Various dragonflies in colored titanium fluttered frozen over the front and back of it.

The sounds of voices met us along with the scent of coffee. We stood in a little foyer paved with slate. On one side was a wall with a series of hooks and shelves beneath for shoes. A door on the other side led into my laundry room. I also stored firewood there.

Opposite the front door was an arched opening leading into the main living area—open concept, except for the massive hearth and round chimney rising up from the middle. On one side was my spacious kitchen, stocked with almost nothing besides ramen, peanut butter, frozen Pop-Tarts, and probably an ancient bottle of ketchup. A door off the kitchen led into my basement.

On the other side was my living room. The niches in the walls held candles as far up as I could reach. I didn't have much by way of furniture. Mostly I used a lot of thick throw rugs and piles of pillows, with a couple of mosaic-topped tables. Hauling furniture to the Burrows wasn't easy, especially when you wanted to avoid attention.

Between the kitchen and the living room, a spiral stairway rose to my workspace and bedroom on the second floor. Beneath it, a door led out into my spacious bathroom, containing a wide sink, a toilet, a giant shower, and a natural hot tub. Broad mullioned doors slid apart to reveal my tiny little courtyard, which held a trickling waterfall and shallow pool, not to mention a few tons of a snow.

I pulled off my coat and unlaced my boots, leaving them by the front door. Patti and Arnow followed suit, Arnow shrinking a good four inches with the loss of her platform heels. I had to admit that I admired her ability to trek so far and over such rough terrain in them. Maybe that was her superpower. Well, her second one. Her first was being an incomparable bitch.

I hadn't been home in nearly three weeks. Usually walking inside made every muscle in my body relax. This was my sanctuary. Or had been. Now it was my headquarters. It could never be a home again until Price was here with me. My stomach twisted. If that ever happened.

We entered the living room to find Taylor pacing. Dalton propped a shoulder against the wall, watching her. Jamie and Leo sprawled out on cushions. Empty plates and cups sat beside them. Jamie snored. Leo frowned at a restless chunk of steel he was attempting to turn into something.

As we stepped inside, he dropped his project and flung himself to his feet in one elegant movement. I swear he was made out of springs.

He jumped over Jamie and grabbed me in a hug. "It's about time you got here." He pushed me arm's length away, studying me. "What the hell happened to you?"

"Long story that we don't have time for. We've got bigger worries."

I hugged Taylor, who dragged me away from Leo. Jamie got to his feet and wrapped his arms around both of us and then Leo piled on. We stood there a moment, and then I fought free, a knot burning in my throat. I was so lucky to have them.

I cleared my throat and smiled. Not very well. I probably looked like I'd eaten slugs. "I smell coffee. And what have you all been eating? If it was anything from my cupboards, we need to get you to a tinker, ASAP."

Jamie snorted. "As if. We know better than to expect anything but coffee here. We brought our own. Stocked the larder. And yes, there's plenty of cream. I don't even want to know how long you'd had that carton in your fridge. I think a new plague might have been growing inside it."

"Thanks. I think." I didn't cook. What was I going to do with a lot of food?

"If we're going to be here a lot, we want to be able to eat," Leo said.

"You going to tell us what this is all about?" Jamie asked after greeting Arnow and Patti.

"Yep," I said, taking the coffee Taylor made me and sitting on the floor, stuffing a cushion between my back and the wall. The others sat as well, all except Dalton, who maintained his silent position holding up the wall. He reminded me of a carrion crow, brooding and watchful.

Tersely, I went over Touray's latest kidnapping, ending with his alliance with both Tyrell and Vernon. Silence reigned when I finished.

"Your father is setting up Tyrell," Patti said finally.

I frowned. "Why do you say that?"

"He's too smart and too well connected not to know Tyrell is trying to move into the city. When Vernon killed Savannah, he had to know it would create a vacuum that Tyrell would jump to fill. He must have figured Tyrell would go to Touray, so Vernon made sure to get to him first."

I hadn't considered that angle.

"But what if Tyrell hadn't picked Touray to be his henchman?" Taylor asked.

"He'd have made a deal with the one Tyrell chose," Arnow said. "But Patti's right. Touray was the best choice. Next to Savannah, he's got the biggest network, and is most capable of making a takeover happen."

"The big question is—what does this have to do with you?" Jamie asked, eyeing me.

"I figure it's got to be the Kensington artifacts." I looked at Dalton. "You care to weigh in?"

His silver eyes told me nothing. "Your father plays the long game."

Leo snorted. "Thank you, Mr. Obvious."

"He also never plays just one angle. What you see barely scratches the surface."

Taylor folded her arms. "I don't suppose you want to give us more details about what he's up to?"

I could tell she didn't expect much. She was right.

He shrugged. "He plays his cards close to his chest."

Both Jamie and Leo rolled their eyes, while Taylor just looked away. Dalton's tightened facial muscles broadcast that he didn't like her reaction, but not so much he was willing to give any more detail.

All right, then. Moving on.

"Here's what I think is coming," I said. "Sooner or later Vernon and Tyrell are going to war against each other. When they do, I'm betting they are going to want the Kensington artifacts in order to build a weapon the other can't beat."

"Why do they want Diamond City so bad?" Patti wondered.

"I'd like to know that, too," Jamie said. He held a dart in his hand and threw it at the wall. It landed and melted away, running down to the floor and back to him. He collected it, reformed it, and threw it again.

"Maybe they just want the diamonds," Leo said.

"What for?" Arnow asked. "They don't need the money. They practically print it. It has to be something else."

"Which brings us back to the artifacts," I said. "But why make their moves now?"

I hated not having answers to all the important questions. I shook my head. What I did know was enough. "The *whys* don't matter right now. The fact is that sooner or later somebody is going to want help with the artifacts. Can you imagine the size of their boners if they find out I'm actually a Kensington? If the artifacts are linked to the family genes, they'll need me more than ever."

"You're a Kensington?" Patti and Arnow asked in startled unison.

I nodded. "I just found out a few weeks ago. Mom told me."

"Isn't your mother dead?" Dalton asked.

"Yes," I said, not explaining how it was possible that I'd spoken to her. I have to admit, his confusion delighted me.

"Anyway, the point is that sooner or later they are coming after me, which means they'll come after you, since anybody with half a brain in their heads knows I'd do anything for you guys." I glanced at Arnow and Dalton, and added dryly. "Most of you, anyhow."

"What do you want to do about it?" Jamie asked, as if on cue.

"We are going to beat them both to the punch."

Silence.

"Maybe you'd better explain," said Leo, pinching his lower lip.

"We are going to take over Savannah's organization." I didn't tell them step two. Stealing Touray's artifacts and finding the rest ourselves. That could come later.

More silence, which I supposed was better than hysterical laughter. Everybody just kept eyeing me with various expressions of surprise and contemplation. All but Dalton, who remained stone-faced.

Jamie broke the silence first. "We're going to what now?"

"It's the only way we can protect ourselves. Otherwise, we have to go underground, or leave the city. Maybe even leave the country, though I'm not sure there's anywhere on earth that would be safe."

"And you want to do this in three days—before Touray or Tyrell can do it first," Arnow said. Of everybody, I'd expected her to jeer at me for this idea. It probably should have worried me that she didn't. Instead, she got down to business. "What's your plan?"

"That's what I need you for. You worked for Savannah. You know her organization. I'm betting you know something about Tyrell, too. Same goes for Dalton. Plus he knows what support Vernon is likely to give Touray." I looked at him. "Assuming you're willing to give that information up?"

His only answer was a tight-lipped nod. Dalton had told us that he was on our side, that he'd stopped working for Vernon. Even if the latter was true, I was asking for help outside the scope of his personal mission to find out who was behind the experiments and stop them. I was asking for him to betray Vernon. I didn't know if he'd cough up what he knew, or if he'd be selective. Not that I had a choice about it. It was him or nothing.

"So that's my idea," I said, looking at everybody. "I know it sounds insane, but I can't see any other real choices. What do you guys think?"

"You're right. It is insane," Leo said. He held his hands steepled together and looked up at the ceiling.

"So you don't want to help me?"

"I didn't say that." He grinned rakishly. "I've got your back. Always."

"Me, too," Jamie said. "But this isn't going to be a cakewalk. And when we get control of the operation, we're going to have to keep running it. Have you thought about that?"

"Like I said—we need a plan." I silently blessed him for saying "when" instead of "if." "But you, Leo, and Taylor have experience running your own businesses."

"Running a Tyet isn't exactly the same thing," Arnow said, rolling her eyes.

"I have to start somewhere. It's not like there's night school for Tyet lords. Besides, business skills will help."

"I'm not sure you've got the balls to run your own organization," she said. "You might have to kill people. You will certainly have to threaten them and back those threats up with action. Can you do that?"

I could have said yes, but even I wouldn't have believed me. The thought of threatening innocent people, of deliberately hurting anybody—even someone as evil as Ocho—was sickening. And killing people? To what—make a point? Convince them of my determination? Everything inside me shrank from the idea.

There were other ways. Tampering with minds. Using haunters. A hundred other magic possibilities for coercion. My stomach actually lurched as I considered those options, and I tasted my breakfast.

I swallowed, meeting Arnow's gaze defiantly. "You know I won't. I'll find another way."

"And if there are no other ways? You're naïve *and* stupid if you think you won't have to get your hands dirty. This is a bloody, violent world you're about to walk into. You'll get ground to hamburger in nothing flat if you don't get with the program."

"I'll deal with that when I have to," I said.

Arnow shook her head. "Not if you want me on board. If I decide to join you in this insanity, I need to know our ship won't sink because you don't have the stomach for violence. They should be worried, too," she said, gesturing at everybody else. "We're putting our lives on the line. My career, too. Are you going to have our backs or what?"

One thing about Special Agent Bitch Arnow that I could admire—she was a pit bull. Right now, I hated her for it. I tried to find an answer that would satisfy her, but Patti beat me to the punch, leaping to her feet and jamming her hands down on her hips in fierce defiance.

"You don't know Riley that well, but I think you know she'll protect her own with everything she has. I don't really know why, but you're on that list. This whole adventure is a risk. Hell, it just might be a suicide mission. How is that different from every other day in Diamond City? Besides, aren't you supposed to be tougher than titanium nails? It's time for you to pull up your big-girl panties and get on the bus. Riley will figure out how to do this without turning into a clone of Savannah Morrell. Either you believe in her or you don't. If you don't, feel free to let the door hit you in your bony little ass on the way out."

Cold and aloof, Arnow folded her arms, staring down at Patti, who radiated fury like a high-voltage wire. I didn't interfere. I was kind of interested in Arnow's reaction. If she left, I'd be up shit creek without a paddle. But then again, I was already deep in the creek. Losing her would just make things a little bit more interesting.

Finally, she turned away, ignoring Patti and looking at me. "Fine. I'm in. But there's one piece of her operation I want complete control of."

The whole thing about looking a gift horse in the mouth? That's where I was, and we didn't have time to waste. "Which piece?"

"I'll let you know when it's time." Her brows rose in challenge, daring me to trust her enough to give her a blind promise.

Since I couldn't see how I was going to do this without her intel, I nodded. "Sure." But then I added a caveat. "As long as it doesn't involve hurting people."

"Everything involves hurting someone," she said, her face shuttering.

Before it did, I caught a flash of a wild emotion I couldn't read. Since she didn't look like she was going to be any more forthcoming, I moved on. Whatever part of Morrell's operation Arnow wanted, I'd deal with it later.

Dealing with things later is becoming my mantra.

"What should we do first?" I asked.

"Two things. The first—get into her house and into her files. I don't know exactly where she kept them, but she had dirt on everybody. Plus we need her business records—the secret ones the IRS never sees. She'll have notes on everything—she was meticulous."

I nodded. That was doable. Leo and Jamie could sense things through metal runs, like wiring or pipes or ductwork. It depended on the type of metal, but in a building, they could easily find hidden rooms, vaults, and that sort of thing. All they'd have to do is let the electric wires in the mansion guide them. That is, if we could safely get inside and out again.

"The second thing is you need to get her lieutenants on your side. There are seven of them, and they run different pieces of the operation. Of course, any one or all of them will want control of the whole pie, so you're going to have your hands full convincing them."

"Do you know where to find them?" Taylor asked.

"There's a meeting. Tonight."

"Tonight?" I repeated.

"That's convenient," Jamie drawled. "Maybe they can meet here. We'll have pizza and beer."

Arnow flashed a deadly look at Jamie. "Word of Savannah's death hasn't gone wide yet. They want to talk, figure out what happens next."

"Or they want to kill each other," Dalton said. "Clear the competition."

"They called a truce."

"How do you know about this?" I asked. "Did they send out a bat signal? Post it on craigslist?"

"They invited me."

I frowned. "You? Why? I mean, you're an informant for Savannah. That's pretty close to bottom rung in the organization."

"They probably want intel on the FBI." She hesitated. "And I was a lot more than just an informant."

That last hooked all of our attention. We looked at her expectantly. I could sense a struggle beneath her icy mask. Arnow's mouth thinned, and she crossed her arms.

"I was pretty much raised in the organization," she said. "I was sold to Savannah when I was around seven years old."

"Sold?"

A chorus of voices echoed back at her. She gave a little shrug as if it didn't matter, but I could tell it was a lie.

"You're surprised? She took in pretty girls and raised us to be educated, sophisticated, and poised, and then had us perform various tasks for her."

"What kind of tasks?" I had to ask, but I thought I knew, and my stomach hurt just thinking about the girls.

The corners of her mouth lifted in a swift, humorless smile. "The usual."

Her aquamarine gaze dared me to push. Something shifted inside me, and suddenly I was looking at Arnow through a different lens altogether. She'd come to her icy mask and ruthless determination through Savannah's machinations. How many girls had Savannah enslaved that way?

"That's what you want to take control of," I said, understanding dawning.

"I will tear her trafficking trade down to the ground and make sure all the girls end up in good homes and the women get choices in their lives," Arnow affirmed. "Boys, too."

That's what she'd meant when she said not everybody had choices.

"Count me in," Taylor said, her body tight with disgust.

"Me, too," I said. Arnow radiated tension, and she clearly didn't want to talk about it. I could empathize. I skipped back to the original subject. "But you still haven't explained why Savannah's lieutenants invited you to their shindig tonight."

"She grew to value my abilities. She assigned me certain delicate tasks and gave me access to areas of her business they were not privy to," Arnow said, and before I could ask for specifics, she continued. "I don't know exactly what they want from me."

"But you have some ideas," Leo said.

Arnow shrugged. "Doesn't matter. The main thing is they're meeting and you need to attend. It's going to be your only chance to have them all in one room at one time. You'd better come up with a hell of a good offer to get them on your side. Otherwise, you're going to be screwed."

No shit, Sherlock. "Tell me about them," I said.

"You got paper? Pens?" Taylor asked. "We're going to want to make notes."

"Upstairs. I'll get them."

"Meantime, I'll put on more coffee," Jamie said.

"Have you anything to eat?" Arnow asked. "I haven't had anything since breakfast."

"Kitchen's open. Follow me. I'll make you an omelet."

"I could eat, too," Taylor and Leo said in a hopeful chorus.

Jamie gave an exaggerated sigh. "I suppose everybody else is hungry, too."

"I wouldn't say no," I said, starting up the spiral staircase.

Patti shrugged, and Dalton just nudged his chin in what might have been a nod.

"I'm on it," Jamie said. Arnow followed him into the kitchen.

Upstairs, I collapsed onto my bed, staring blindly at the opposite wall. I could feel myself shaking and clenched my body to stop it. The quakes continued, growing in strength.

Did I really think I could possibly convince a bunch of big, bad Tyet thugs to let me order them around? What was I going to do—smile at them pretty and offer them Girl Scout Cookies and old scotch? *Sure, that would work.* About as well as saying, "pretty please with cherries on top." I needed some kind of leverage, and I didn't have any.

Price would have had some ideas. He wasn't here. I wrapped my arms around myself and bent over, pressing my forehead against my knees. I had to *think*. How could I do this?

I didn't hear Taylor come up. The bed compressed as she sat beside me and rubbed a hand over my back.

"Second thoughts?"

"More like fifty or a hundred," I said, my voice muffled.

"You can pull the plug on this right now, no harm, no foul."

I sat up, twisting to look at her. "And then what? We run? We live like cockroaches?" I shook my head. "We've got to draw a line and this is our best chance of success." Which, given my lack of ideas on convincing Savannah's lieutenants to let us waltz in and take control of the operation, really sucked. We couldn't blow this, or we'd be fighting an uphill battle for the rest of our probably very short lives.

"So then we do it."

I snorted. "Easy to say."

"We'll figure it out."

I made a sound that wasn't exactly agreement and started to get up to find the paper and pens. Taylor held me back.

"You haven't said anything about Price. What does he think?"

"I haven't exactly told him yet."

"Oh. Okay."

"I was supposed to call him when I got here."

"You going to?"

"I . . . should."

"But?"

"I'm not ready to hear he's got to stick with Touray, that we can't be together."

"He won't say that."

"Won't he?"

Taylor stood, stroking a hand over my hair. "Price loves you. Don't sell him short. We'll get through this. All of us together. Call him."

With that, she went back down the stairs. I fished my phone out of my pants pocket and thumbed it on. I made a habit out of not using my cell anywhere near my house, in case someone might track it, but inside was safe enough thanks to protection spells. I punched the speed dial for Price's number before I could chicken out.

He answered almost before it rang. "About fucking time," he said, his voice harsh with worry. "It's been hours."

"I slept," I said. "And then it took a while to get here."

"You're all right?"

"I'm good. What about your brother?"

"Cass worked on him. He's sleeping." A beat of silence. "What's going on?"

Did I tell him? If I did and he passed the information on to Touray, then we'd probably be screwed. If I didn't. . . . My lack of faith would cut him deep. I couldn't do that to him, to us.

"We're going after Savannah's territory," I said. "Before Touray or anybody else can get to it."

He didn't laugh or call me mentally incompetent for even thinking we could do it. He didn't say anything at all.

"Are you there?" I asked after thirty seconds or so of dead silence.

"Yeah."

"Okay."

I waited, knowing what was coming next. He was between a rock and a hard place, his loyalties sliced in half. If I had to pick between him and one of my siblings—it would be impossible to choose. Plus, if Touray failed in his deal with Tyrell, who knew what the psycho business magnate would do to him? Not just Tyrell. Vernon wouldn't like it either. How could Price walk away?

"I should probably go," I said miserably. Maybe I could delay the inevitable a little longer. "I'll call you later."

"When?"

"I'm not sure. There's something we've got to do tonight. It could take a while." Forever—if Savannah's lieutenants decided to end me before I could make a pitch.

I could tell my answer frustrated Price. I could almost hear the crack of the phone as he crushed it in his hand. For both our sakes, I was playing the vague game. It turned my stomach the same as lying. If he asked for specifics, I wouldn't hold back.

"What are the chances that you'll get hurt doing this thing later?"

"Let's just say I'm making sure my will is up-to-date," I said with gallows humor.

Price did not find it funny. He swore eloquently. "I should be with you," he said finally when he ran out of colorful descriptions of people and animals sticking things in inappropriate and painful places.

"I'd like you here," I confessed. "But you can't be two places at once and Touray's your brother. He needs you. You've got to back his play."

"*You* need me."

Underneath the cold iron in his voice, I heard uncertainty and accusation. I rubbed my forehead with my free hand, a headache starting to pulse behind my eyes.

"Jesus, Price, of course I do. This isn't about whether or not I need you or want you. It's about what *you* need and what your brother needs. I'm not going to be a wedge between you."

"Has it occurred to you that it's not up to you?" he asked. "Or did you just decide what was what and to hell with what I might think?"

Fist to the gut. I gasped to retrieve my breath. He didn't wait. His words lashed me like a whip.

"Either we're partners or we aren't. Either you're all in with me or we're done. You'd better think about just what I am to you. Call me when you decide."

The phone went dead.

I don't know how long I sat staring down at my cell. My head spun, and I didn't know what to think. I had a hole in my heart, and pain spilled out of it like a broken dam. On top of that, I was pissed. First, I didn't like ultimatums, and his last comments sounded like one. I wasn't wrong about wanting to protect Price. I didn't want to be the thing that tore him and Touray apart, and I couldn't imagine how it could go any other way if Price joined my crusade.

On the other hand, he was right, too. He was entitled to make his own choices. I'd be hot as hell if he tried to decide what I could and couldn't do.

I sighed, my fury draining away in a sudden rush. I rubbed my face, weariness grinding against my brain. I couldn't even manage my love life, and I thought I was going to run a Tyet? I was delusional. Complete nut job.

I started to call Price. He needed to know how much I loved him.

"You'd better come down," Patti said. She'd come halfway up the stairs, and just her head showed above the floor. She looked anything but happy.

My fingers froze before I could hit the speed dial, ice sliding through my veins. "What's wrong?"

"Agent Snowbitch just got a text. Morrell's lieutenants moved their meeting to my diner. They told her to find you. You're the guest of honor."

Chapter 19

Gregg

"TELL ME EVERYTHING."

Gregg had woken up with hammers pounding on every square inch of the interior of his skull. He downed two fingers of scotch and poured another. His thinking was fuzzy, and he could hardly remember fetching Cass or what had happened after. It annoyed the fuck out of him.

"What did that bastard do to me? What did *you* do to me?"

The blond woman who sat folded like a jackknife in the chair across from him lowered her coffee cup, resting it on a bony knee.

"I helped you," she said acerbically. "Which you asked me to do, so you don't need to sound like such an ungrateful asshole. Though let's face it, not being an ungrateful asshole would be stepping out of character for you."

Gregg wasn't in the mood to fence with her. "Tell me what you found and how you fixed it and why I'm having such a hard time remembering anything since I left the diner."

"You'll remember in a day or maybe two. The loss has to do with how your memories were realigned by the dreamer who worked on you, and how I had to untangle them. Whoever did it is damned good, not to mention creative. I haven't seen or considered making alterations that way."

"I'm not interested in your schooling," Touray said when she paused to sip from her cup again. "Explain."

She yawned and sipped her coffee again. "It's nice to see your brother. He looks like a bear with a herpes breakout, though. You might want to talk to him."

"Cass!" Gregg's fist hit the table. "What did they do in my head?"

"Your memories got sort of stitched together in a fold. The dreamer essentially took you back in time about a half hour or so, hiding everything that had happened between those points inside the fold. You'd have no way of knowing you lost anything, since he flawlessly seamed it up with a memory marker they established before they started.

"A memory marker?"

"Tyrell stabbed you in the thigh with an ice pick so the dreamer would know exactly how far to fold."

Gregg frowned, looking down at his legs, half expecting to find the wound.

"He had you healed so you wouldn't know," Cass said in a "no duh" voice.

Gregg gritted his teeth, though he deserved the ridicule. Cass had a tendency to grate on his nerves, but she was one of the best in the dreamer business, and she couldn't be bought by enemies. Once she committed to a job, she didn't betray her clients. That trustworthiness was gold in his line of work. The fact that she was also willing to cause dire harm to any clients or enemies of clients who came after her—whether to use her or get revenge—that permitted her to remain an independent contractor. Otherwise, she'd have been forced to work for someone like him full time.

"If you fixed it, why can't I remember the lost time?"

"Because the work was brilliant. The fold was designed to dissolve. In a few weeks, I don't know if I'd have even been able to tell anything happened and those memories would be gone forever. The process was already under way. I stopped it and smoothed the fold back out, but your brain is still trying to catch up. You'll be able to remember within a few hours or so. Everything since you left the diner will take longer, because I ruffled some things when I dismantled the memory fold. Anyhow, it will take your gray matter a little bit to settle the memories so you can access them."

"What can you tell me about that missing half hour?"

"You were given compulsions."

Ice drove down through Gregg's gut. "Compulsions?" he repeated hoarsely. "To do what?"

"One was to report in to your new boss at least once a day, whether to ask for resources, information, or to report progress. It was to be your idea."

Gregg's jaw knotted as he clenched his teeth. "What else?"

"To report to him on Riley. He wants her."

"And?" His chest felt like steel bands clamped him in a tightening grip.

"To soften you up to the bodyguards he's sending to you. You're supposed to quickly grow to rely on them and make them your trusted lieutenants."

"Anything else?" If Tyrell had been present, Gregg would have ripped the man's head off. Not that this wasn't cleverly done and smart. He'd have done the same if their positions were reversed. But how had he gotten the wound that alerted him to the tampering?

"He told me not to check on whether my brain had been messed with," he guessed aloud.

Cass nodded. "That's the thread that stitched the memory fold closed. A sort of 'don't look here, nothing here to see' suggestion. But there's one more thing."

"Why do you make it sound like it's worse than all the rest?" Gregg asked, foreboding tightening the bands around his chest.

"Maybe because it is?"

"Quit beating around the bush and tell me already," he snarled.

"He planted a trigger. Once it cemented in your head—which would take it a few days because of your instinctive resistance—he'd be able to say the trigger word and you'd obey him without question, and you'd be frothing at the mouth to do it. It's not a one-use trigger, either. He could use it as often as he liked."

"Jesus."

"Ain't got nothing to do with this kind of crap," Cass said. "You should probably be talking to the devil."

"Did you get it out? Did you get all that shit out?" He waved his hands at his head.

She shrugged. "Think so. I'll want to go back in and have a look in a day or so." She picked up a paper from the end table beside her. "Here. This is everything I told you. The trigger word is *Jettatura.*"

An uncomfortable prickling sensation circled Gregg's throat, and then faded. He jumped. "What the hell was that?"

Cass nodded satisfaction. "Good. I unhooked the trigger and dismantled the compulsion, but I was betting you didn't want Tyrell to know you'd discovered what he'd done. Now, anytime you hear the word, you'll get that needle feeling around your neck. You won't be able to ignore it, which means you'll be able to properly react."

Gregg considered her. "Smart thinking."

"It's not perfect. The only person you're supposed to react to is Tyrell. If anybody else says it, it shouldn't matter. I couldn't be sure I could tie the warning just to him since he's in the middle of the memory hash. But then, it's not like a lot of people are going to be shouting it in the streets."

"What does that mean? Jettatura? Is it even a real word?"

"Wikipedia says it is. Says it means 'bad luck' or 'casting the evil eye.' Appropriate, don't you think? Anyway, if you don't want your new boss to know you broke his mind-hack, you should have a good look at that sheet and remember to behave appropriately."

She yawned and set her coffee aside. "I need something to eat. And a ride home. *Not* travelling, thank you very much."

"The kitchen will make you anything you want, and after that, I'll arrange for your transport. And Cass, thanks." He held up the paper.

She unfolded from her chair and stood. More than slender, she looked almost emaciated. The toll of using too much magic. But then, he didn't remember her ever looking particularly healthy, though she ate like a horse. Her short blond hair stuck out in every direction, and the intensity of her penetrating gaze made him want to duck away.

"Aw gee. Aren't you sweet. And you didn't even break your face saying thank you."

"You look like shit."

Cass cocked an eyebrow at him. "Who's fault is that? Anyhow, I'm planning a two-week vacation of nothing but food, sleep, hot baths, and trashy books."

"When do you want to check up on me again?"

"Once the fuzziness clears and your mind sharpens again. Should be no more than forty-eight hours. I'll come back then."

"What do you expect to find?" Talking about himself, about his own brain getting tampered with, in such a clinical way, was surreal.

"Leftover debris, mostly," she said. "Fake memory fragments that don't attach anywhere and intrude on the real memories. Too many of those cause psychosis and nervous breakdowns."

"What's too many?"

"Depends."

"On?"

"You. The fragments. The memories. How old everything is—pretty much everything. Now, you'd better check on your brother. The big bad wolf is threatening your house." She winked and headed out the door.

Gregg watched her go, lost in thought. He ran a hand over his face, trying to push away the feeling of cobwebs layering his mind.

It didn't work, but he hadn't expected it to. He checked his watch. It had been around one when he'd left the diner to fetch Cass. Now it was approaching five o'clock. The countdown clock was ticking. He needed to rev up taking over Savannah's organization.

He stood, reaching for the phone on the table beside him. He touched a button, and it rang through to Julie, one of his assistants.

"Do you know where my brother is?" he asked without a greeting.

"Out back in the courtyard."

Gregg didn't bother with a reply. He hung up the phone, donned a thick jacket, and headed downstairs.

When he stepped outside, the wind struck him like a blow, making him stagger. It was cold and harsh, scraping at the skin of his face and shredding the steam of his breath. He plunged his bare hands into his jacket pockets, hunching his shoulders to help fend off the knife-edged wind from his ears.

The house formed a U shape, with the courtyard in the middle, the open side overlooking the caldera. The building was on the south side of the Midtown shelf and surrounded by thirty acres of trees, all inside a wall made of brick, iron, and magic.

The courtyard itself was paved in flagstone with an artful variety of fountains, planting beds, pergolas, benches, and an artificial creek running through it. Gregg kept the snow cleared all winter and often came outside for air and a chance to clear his head.

He grimaced. Clear his head. According to Cass, that wouldn't happen for another twenty-four to forty-eight hours. He didn't have time to wait it out.

Clay was nowhere to be seen, but Gregg heard a thudding sound echoing through the chill dusk. He strode across the flagstone, skirting the broad fire pit with its surrounding rock benches, and heading down the snaking center aisle. The wind continued to blow, a sharp wave of air that felt eerie and unnatural in its constancy. He paused at the railing to look out over the vista. Below, the dark shadows filled the caldera, while on the opposite side, sinking sunlight bloodied the edges of the mountains. The panorama was heartbreakingly beautiful.

With a grunt, Gregg abandoned the view. Turning around the south side of the house, he followed the continuing thuds and Clay's trail of footsteps in the snow. The towering evergreen trees soughed and tossed with the relentless sweep of the wind.

He found his brother beneath a tall pine. Clay had stripped off his coat and was swinging an ax, chopping determinedly at the trunk. He'd been at it awhile, having notched out one side and begun on the opposite.

"You aren't going to drop that on yourself, are you?"

Clay didn't stop the smooth rolling motion of his arms and back. "Suicide by tree? There are easier ways."

"We don't need firewood."

"Didn't think we did."

"So you suddenly decided to become a lumberjack? Or has it been a deep and abiding dream you never told me about?"

Clay took an extra hard swipe at the tree. The ax bit deep, and he released the handle, leaving the blade stuck in the wood. He swiped a forearm over his forehead. Sweat matted his black hair to his head. He examined his palms. A series of blisters had begun to form. "I'm getting soft."

"Hardly. What's going on?"

A sardonic smile came and left his brother's face. "I fucked up," he said, then changed the subject. "How are you? I saw Cass. She told me what she found."

"I'm a little foggy. Cass says it should clear up soon."

"Good."

"Are you done chopping? Because we've got some work to do and it's damned cold out here. You might want to put your coat back on."

Clay reached for the ax handle, jerking it free of the tree and readying himself to swing again. "I'll be in later."

"When?"

"Later," Clay repeated, punctuating the word with a hard swing. Woodchips flew.

"I need you now."

"I go inside now and I'll do a *Wizard of Oz* on the inside of your house. Knock it flat." He yanked the ax free and cocked back for another strike.

"And chopping down my trees will stop that?"

"Isn't hurting." Swing. *Crack!* Chips. Yank.

"We can't organize from out here."

"Can't organize in a tornado either." Swing. *Crack!* Chips. Yank.

"You want to tell me what's going on? You weren't having out-of-control issues earlier."

"I told you. I fucked up." Swing. *Crack!* Chips. Yank. Cock. Swing. *Crack!*

"This has something to do with Riley," Gregg guessed. Clay had iron control and a will of stone—except when it came to her. Then all bets were off. "What did she do?"

"You got wax in your ears? *I* fucked up." Clay paused long enough to swipe again at the sweat rolling into his eyes.

"Could you get more specific? I don't really have time for twenty questions."

Clay stiffened and looked up as he rested the ax head against the ground. He bit hard into his lower lip. Wind swirled hard around them both and then swept up and tight like a cocked fist. A moment of silent stillness, the air pulled taut as a bowstring. It snapped loose and rushed past Gregg, hitting the pine like a god-sized sledgehammer. A loud *crack* ruptured the silence. Wood chips exploded like shrapnel, and what was left of the tree leaped a good thirty feet before crashing to the ground, taking with it other tree limbs and saplings.

The wind collected again. Clay's face twisted, and he snarled with effort, thrusting the handle of the ax away from him. Before Gregg could say anything, wind slammed against a cluster of trees, snapping them off and sending the tops flying in a hail of wood chunks.

"I suppose it's less effort than using the ax," Gregg observed, trying not to feel nervous. "You're starting to be able to target it."

"Right. Like aiming an ocean at a snail."

"Nobody learns to ride a bike on their first try."

"Nobody slaughters innocent people with bikes."

"Neither will you."

"But I could."

Gregg snorted. "I don't think so."

Clay bent and picked up the ax. "Chopping helps me concentrate and keep my shit together. You're distracting me."

"Why don't you tell me what's going on with Riley so we can fix it and get to work. We're burning daylight." He glanced up. The light had turned more gray than not. The days were getting longer, but they were still short.

"I'm—" Clay paused, then faced his brother, his face losing all expression. "I'm not going to be able to help you."

Gregg frowned. "Because of your talent? We'll figure out how to work around it until you get control. What?"

Clay had begun shaking his head before Gregg finished his first sentence.

"Because you're working with Vernon, and because Tyrell is interested in the Kensington artifacts, and by extension, Riley. She wants to make sure she can protect herself and her family. She's taking a shot at Savannah's organization."

It took Gregg a few seconds to process that information. He shouldn't have been surprised. He'd be doing the same in her position, doomed as her effort was. He chuckled and shook his head. "She'll fail. Anyway, I've already told her I'll protect her."

"She doesn't believe it. She's not willing to put her fate or her family's fate in your hands."

Gregg's amusement drained away. "And you're going to help her." He couldn't help his feeling of betrayal and fury at both Riley and Clay. Her for coming between them, his brother for letting it happen. He spit on the ground, but it didn't take away the bad taste in his mouth. "Guess blood isn't as thick as they say," he drawled. "Why are you even still here wasting my time?"

Clay just looked at him. "Because you deserve to hear it directly from me, and because I don't know where she is. I may have broken it off with her."

Gregg just blinked, torn between curiosity and angry resentment. Curiosity won. "May have broken it off with her?" he repeated. "You're walking out on me for a woman you broke up with." He shook his head. "You're going to have to explain that one to me."

Clay smiled self-mockingly. The wind around them spun dagger sharp. Gregg pulled up his coat collar and dug his hands deep into the pockets. It didn't stop the cold from biting through his jeans.

"She planned to keep me in the dark. She didn't want to make me choose between the two of you, so she figured what I didn't know wouldn't hurt me. I got it out of her, and then got pissed and told her to call me if she decided she wanted me to be in her life. After that, I hung up. That was somewhere around an hour and a half ago. I haven't heard a word."

He reached for the ax, picking it up and looking around for another tree. "So now that I've notified you, I'm waiting and hoping to hell she hasn't given up on me."

"Why don't you just call her? Or better yet, go find her?"

"I tried to call. She didn't answer. And I don't know where she is."

"Then go ask her friend—Patti—the one who owns the diner. She'll know if anybody does."

"She won't tell me anything that Riley doesn't want me to know. Those two are as tightly bound as a virgin to her chastity belt."

"So that's it? You're just going to wait around, chopping down my trees?" Gregg spat again. "Sitting with your thumb up your ass isn't usually your style. But if that's your plan, the least you could do is be useful."

Clay readied himself to swing the ax. "I don't want to know your plans. I'll have to tell Riley. Bad enough I'm choosing her side. I'm not going to spy on you, too."

Gregg watched as Clay began chopping again. He made himself set aside his anger and betrayal. Losing his brother's help in this mess was annoying, but it didn't cripple him. He could still get the job done. He didn't want to do it without Clay, but he could. Riley? She was going to be putting herself at serious risk and for nothing. She'd never succeed, and would probably get herself killed trying.

The fact was that Clay loved her. Totally and blindly. If she managed to get herself killed, it would gut him, especially if he let her undertake this stupidity by herself. Gregg was capable, with seriously deep pockets now that he had Tyrell and Vernon backing him. He also knew what he was doing. She was going to get eaten alive.

Anyhow, being on different sides in this wasn't going to hurt his relationship with Clay, not if he didn't let it. Their bond was strong enough to weather this and a lot worse. They'd been on opposite sides before, with Clay being a cop. This would be the same.

"Better go find her," he said. "You don't want to wait for a call." *One that might not come.* He kept that to himself. Didn't matter anyway. Clay needed to be at Riley's side. "You were a cop. You know how to hunt down people who don't want to be found. Go do your thing before you knock down all my trees."

Clay stopped, his back rigid. Finally, he turned around, leaning the ax handle against the tree and picking up his coat.

"We're good?"

"Always."

Clay nodded, then pulled Gregg into a hard hug, thumping his back with an affectionate fist. Clay pushed back and quirked a pained smile. "See you when I see you. Watch your six."

"Back at you. And keep everybody safe. That family is a giant pain in the ass, but I like them. Even Leo."

"I'll be sure to send him your love."

Gregg laughed and headed back to the house. Clay set off in the other direction, out of the trees and around front to find a car. Gregg kept a small fleet with the keys inside.

MIDNIGHT CAME before Gregg found his bed. He stripped and showered, brushing his teeth under the hot spray, and then tumbled onto the mattress with a groan. The last hours had been grueling, like getting pecked by rabid ostriches while a proctologist jammed a hand up his ass. But things were in motion.

Savannah had compartmentalized her organization, with a CEO for each section, all of them reporting directly to her. It would have been simplest to just get them to offer him their loyalty and transfer ownership that way. But simple didn't equal easy. Those CEOs, Savannah's top lieutenants, all wanted to rule the roost. They'd be scrabbling to take over. If they hadn't gone to war with each other yet, they soon would.

Gregg planned to take advantage of the confusion. He had techs working to disrupt the money flow. Without the lubricant of money, the wheels of their separate franchises would seize up. No one worked for free, and while they could strong-arm some support, that wouldn't get them far. Not with Gregg ready to sweep in with all the man power and funds he needed to buy every last soul in the city. Between the carrot of money and the stick of bloodshed, he'd take Savannah's organization by Tyrell's three-day deadline. The toughest part would be rounding up her seven lieutenants. Getting rid of them fast would definitely help things.

He stared up into the darkness. It all seemed too easy. He and Savannah had been fighting for supremacy in Diamond City for years. She often had the upper hand, with more money and a better network of informants permeating every level of government, law enforcement, and private business. He had better ideas—more creative—and took nothing for granted. Theirs had been a war of bites, each gnawing away from the other. With Savannah gone, however, her organization was a snake without a head, flopping wildly with little purpose, and perfectly situated for a hostile takeover.

He considered Riley. How did she think she was going to take over Savannah's operation? Walk in and ask? Not that she wasn't smart and resourceful. She and her family had taken down the FBI building where Clay had been held. They'd been tough. But this? Ridiculous. Hopefully Clay would talk some sense into her, get her to sit this one out until the dust settled.

Dismissing thoughts of Riley, he returned to his own plans. He'd called Tyrell for no apparent reason, pretending to be driven by the planted impulse Cass had removed from his brain. He'd also let Randall and Bruno in when they'd finally arrived at the gates, though he'd kept them as far on the periphery of his plans has he dared.

The mental fog had started lifting, and he remembered most of what had happened when Tyrell had taken him. The dreamer who'd fucked with his head had been a woman—older, with a long, crooked nose and frowsy gray hair. She'd sniffed a lot, he remembered, and her fingers had been cold and bony as she laid them across his forehead.

Gregg shuddered at the memory, hate and fear rolling back over him like ocean waves. The wound on his wrist had come when he'd tried to fend her off. He'd sliced himself on the medical table he'd been strapped to after freeing his arm. Because he'd been wearing his coat, Tyrell hadn't noticed. He smiled. He'd been able to punch the dreamer bitch before he was immobilized again. Served her right.

If not for the dumb luck of cutting himself, he might never have known Tyrell had fucked with his brain. The idea revolted him. He needed to figure out some surefire way to warn himself if he ended up in that situation again. Something he could wear on his body or maybe a tattoo spell.

He was barely aware of the tickling sensation at first. Deep down in his brain, an itch he couldn't scratch. Gregg shook his head to clear the feeling, but it only increased. Now it uncurled itself like a spider, legs stretching outward, extending into his brain.

Gregg sat up, grabbing for his phone. Cass. His hand spasmed open. The phone fell. He reached for it but stopped halfway, then folded both hands in his lap, staring straight ahead.

Muscles twitched and jerked as the spider took control of his mind. It wriggled and settled itself. Threads spun from it, weaving through his brain. Trapped in his own body, Gregg didn't move. His heart raced, and then suddenly slowed as forced calm settled over him. His jaw relaxed, and he lay back down. His eyes closed.

The web continued to build inside his skull. His mouth opened and closed. He touched his right index finger to his nose and then his ear. He cupped his balls. Something itched along his side. It grew in intensity, and though underneath the controlling web his consciousness twisted and clawed, he remained still. At last the itching died.

He got to his feet and walked around the room, picking up a lamp, a cup, a picture, a statue. Each time he grew more fluid, the movements growing more natural as his body responded with increasing speed to the commands from his colonized mind.

He jogged in place, then dropped and performed six push-ups. Up on his feet and spin, then squat and a somersault. Back on his feet, Gregg began to speak, slowly at first, a little slurred.

"What time is it? Where is the bathroom? How much does it cost? Supercalifragilisticexpialidocious. She sells seashells by the seashore. The rain in Spain falls mainly on the plain. Peter Piper picked a peck of pickled peppers."

Gregg's tongue grew nimble, the words turning quick and crisp. He walked to the mirror, looking at himself. His chest and feet were bare, black flannel pajama pants tied loosely around his hips.

"I own you now, puppet," he said, meeting his own dark gaze in the silver glass. "There's nothing you know that I don't. Nothing you can stop me from doing. Don't worry. We're going to take down Tyrell. I've been after him a long time. You did well getting rid of your brother. That will make things go easier. What's that? You plan to fight me with everything you've got?"

Gregg gave a little laugh and smiled at himself. "I expected nothing less. The strong ones never succumb easily. So you know—I've never been dislodged yet. I'll be riding you like a jockey until I'm done with you. After that? Well, it all depends. But that particular problem is far down the road. I have plans for you. Many plans."

With that, he winked at himself, then took himself back to bed, curling up under the covers. Within seconds a heavy lassitude overtook him, and he was smothered under clouds of gray cotton.

Chapter 20

Riley

"WHY DO THEY want to meet me?" I asked for the fifth time as we approached the diner.

Dalton led the way, with Arnow, Taylor, Patti, and me behind. Leo and Jamie brought up the rear. All of us carried guns, along with a few other small magics I used for defense and escape when I was still doing hack tracing for a living. That was less than four months ago. It seemed like yesterday and forever. I think I'd aged a couple hundred years since then.

Guilt ate at my heart. I hadn't called Price back. I needed privacy for that, and time—neither of which I had at the moment. Anyway, I wasn't sure he was all that eager to hear from me. *Right.* He was probably having a cow. I couldn't help but think he deserved it a little. I mean, really? A fucking ultimatum? I'd gone through hell to get him away from the FBI. I'd risked my family, and my stepmom had lost her life. And he needed more proof?

Not fair, the not-a-raving-lunatic-bitch side of me said. *He is worried and helpless and I cut him out. I'd be just as pissed.* I sighed silently.

"Obviously they want you to do a trace," Arnow said exasperatedly, glaring at me. She'd given me the same answer the previous four times I'd asked.

"But who? And why now?" Patti mused. "Shouldn't they be worried about defending their business? They have to know that with Savannah dead, there are going to be attacks from all sides."

"Whoever they want to find must be pretty damned important," Taylor said. She looked at Arnow. "You know them—you've got to have *some* ideas about it."

Arnow frowned. "Savannah didn't let me in that far. I know them, yes, but not well. The real question is what are they going to do when they find out you can't trace?"

She gave me a raised brow look, and I could almost see the air quotes around *"you can't trace."*

"Do you ever get off the bitch train?" I asked. "No, don't answer that. I already know you don't."

"Back at you, sweetheart," she drawled. "Don't pretend your shit don't stink. You aren't exactly Mother Teresa. I notice you aren't answering the question."

"I'll bluff." My stomach tightened. It was a risk, but necessary. I needed to convince the lieutenants to let me be their boss. I had one thing they wanted. Now I had to leverage it. I had to hope they wanted it bad enough to give me control, and then I had to figure out how to carry out my end of the deal.

I racked my brain again for ideas on how to cure myself, but once again, I found nothing popped. Maybe I should have called Maya, but she was on Gregg's payroll. Wait. I couldn't be the first one to have this kind of magic burnout. It *had* to have happened to someone else. Maybe I should google it.

If only it was that easy.

We approached the diner from the opposite side of the street. The lights were on, and people sat at booths. Helena and Marie bustled from table to table with pots of coffee.

"Looks normal enough," Leo said and glanced at Patti. "What do you think?"

"I think nobody is eating and every bloody one of them looks like they'd kill their own mother for a buck. We need to get the hell inside," she said grimly.

"She's right," Taylor said. "Your waitresses don't look so happy, either."

"Can you tell anything?" Jamie asked, turning to me.

I hesitated, then made myself drop into trace sight. Fire streaked through my muscles, pulling like claws. I clenched my jaw, digging my fingernails into my palms, like I could somehow counterbalance the pain. It worked about as well as a paper umbrella in the rain. All the same, it didn't break free as it had in Ocho's hideout. Not yet. I had to make this quick.

I scanned the diner. "They've activated some binders. Looks like the diner's security web is off." Good thing, too. Binders tended to play havoc with active spells.

Binder spells and nulls frequently get used in the same situations, but work differently. Nulls eat active magic. They suck it right up, but leave the drained spells intact. They also hide trace by essentially taking the magic from it. Binders, on the other hand, lock down magic. It's still there, but it can't function until the binders go off. Like batteries, they only last so long before they run out of juice and the magic they've bound down pops back, though the spells usually get short-circuited. Banks and hotels use nulls to keep magic out and binders to keep anybody from using magic in most areas.

Patti's got a kind of binder talent that gives her the ability to physically bind things in place. So if she didn't want a car going anywhere, all she'd have to do is bind it to the ground. The binding wouldn't last long—maybe ten minutes.

Feeling my control eroding, I pulled myself out of trace sight. My heart raced, and little zaps of energy popped and sizzled in my body, making me twitch. I clenched my teeth and jammed my fists deep into my pockets.

If I could barely go into trace sight, how the hell was I going to do a trace?

I gave Patti a pointed look. "The outer ones are supposed to stay on all the time."

Years ago, I'd woven a significant web of nulls into the building, dividing them into an exterior zone to keep anyone from breaking in with magic, and a rarely used inner zone to disable any malignant magic that got activated inside. The outer field was supposed to run twenty-four/seven. The binders looked like amoebas next to my nulls. If Ben hadn't shut the security web down, it would have fried the binders. Now it was too late. The security web couldn't be activated with the binders running.

Patti made a face. "Ben doesn't like them. Says they interfere with his cooking."

"That's bullshit. I made sure nothing would interfere with him. I like eating here too much."

"I know that, and you know that. I've told him so a billion times, but he's stubborn. He shuts the whole thing off whenever I'm not looking."

Patti scowled and took a couple of steps forward. "Those goons better not have hurt him. I'll rip their throats out myself."

"You'll have plenty of help," Taylor said darkly, then looked at me. "Ready?"

Not on a bet. "Let's do it." I stepped off the curb, then turned around. "Jamie, you and Leo should stay here with Dalton." All three of them opened their mouths to protest, and I lifted a hand up. "There's nothing you can do inside. You won't be able to use magic and, trust me, they outgun us. Better if you hang back so that if something goes wrong, you can help us."

I eyed them all with steady determination. This was the first test of how we'd work as a team, with me in charge. Me in charge. Ludicrous. Yet no one laughed.

"All right," Dalton said. He flicked a look at Taylor and back to me. She didn't notice. "Try not to fuck this up."

Those were the most words I'd heard out of him at one time all night. I gave him a cocky smile. "I always do, Mr. Sunshine."

He murmured something I didn't hear.

"What did was that?"

"I said maybe you should do better than just try," he drawled, his silver eyes fixing me.

"Gee. Why didn't I think of that?" I turned to my brothers, ignoring Dalton's muttered curse. "And you two?"

"They'll stay," Taylor said. "If they don't, I'll kick their asses."

"You can try," Leo said, but he was hardly paying attention to her. He and Jamie exchanged a long look, then Jamie nodded.

"We'll stay."

"For as long as it takes," I added. "No busting in because you're tired of waiting."

"No busting in," Leo affirmed after a few long seconds. "For twenty minutes. Then all bets are off." The other two nodded agreement.

"A full half hour," I countered. I wasn't going to get my brothers to agree to any more time than that.

Another exchange of looks between all three, and then Leo nodded. "But ladies? Be careful and do *not* get stupid." He directed that last at me.

I stuck out my tongue at him for lack of an adult response and turned my back. "Let's go."

I marched across the street, deciding that since we were expected, skulking was unnecessary, and would waste precious time.

"How many guns do you think are pointed at us right now?" Taylor eyed the rooftops surrounding us.

"At least a dozen. Probably more," Arnow replied. "Not to mention seven small armies. It's a safe bet that each of the seven lieutenants brought protection."

She'd already given us overview sketches on each one. The one thing I hadn't expected was that they didn't get along well with Savannah. According to Arnow, when they were in a room together, you could cut the tension with a knife.

Two goons in black suits opened the doors as we stepped up onto the sidewalk in front of the diner. If they'd been wearing sunglasses, I'd have sworn they were Jake and Elwood Blues. Neither said a word to us.

Once we were inside, a woman stepped forward, wearing black fatigues. She looked like she'd been a drill sergeant in a past life. Her silver hair was two inches long and stood up straight on her head. Her body was powerful, and she looked like she should have been strutting up and down while recruits did push-ups in the mud.

"Ladies," she said in a raspy smoker's voice. "Put your things on the counter. That includes your cell phones, weapons, and any other devices you might have."

"Patti! Are you okay?"

Ben, Patti's business partner, stood up from where he'd been sitting in a corner booth. A lanky guard grabbed him and pushed him back down onto the seat, holding him firmly with a hand to the shoulder.

Relief washed through me. He wasn't hurt. I don't know what would have happened if he had been. Patti looked angry, but the pinched look around her mouth relaxed a little.

"Are you okay?" she asked.

"He's fine," the drill sergeant said, then tapped the counter with hard little bounces of her fingers. "Let's not keep everybody waiting. Put your things on the counter."

Patti looked the woman up and down. "That man is my business partner. If anything happens to him I will take you apart piece by piece." Her pointed finger punctuated the words with little jabs in the air.

The woman snorted, looking down her nose at Patti's diminutive figure. "Sure. Anything you say, I'll even get you a stool so you can reach me better."

Patti's cheeks went livid. Before she could say anything, I put a hand on her arm. "Save it," I said. "Ben's okay and we have business. You can teach her a lesson later."

"Anytime." The drill sergeant smirked.

"Better make sure there's a tinker handy. I don't plan to leave much of you intact," Patti told her.

We took off our coats and handed them over. I'd stashed my phone inside one of its zippered breast pockets. I'd stuffed my nulls and other magical defenses inside the roomy outer pockets. I pulled my gun and its pancake holster out of my rear waistband and set it on the counter beside my coat.

A quick frisk by Sergeant Bristle-Brush-Head, and she pointed to the booth where Ben sat. "You two wait with him," she told Taylor and Patti.

I didn't budge. "No."

"That's the rules."

"Then you'd better change them."

She eyed me, then went into the back room. A moment later she came back. "Let's go."

Point for me. Hopefully the rest of this went so well. *And maybe pigs would fly.*

She led us into the back room where a day or so ago I'd met with Emily and Luis.

All the tables had been pushed together to make a rectangle. Seated around one end were Savannah's seven lieutenants. They looked up as we entered. Nobody looked happy. They'd been discussing something heatedly. The tension was so thick I almost needed an oxygen mask.

"They're here," our escort announced unnecessarily.

We stopped at the opposite end of the table, but didn't sit. I recognized five of the lieutenants from the pictures Arnow had pulled up on her phone on our trip over. She hadn't had any of the other two.

The closest one on the left was Lewis Fineman. He had brown hair going to gray, with a round chocolate-milk face and a soft belly. I guessed him to be about my height, maybe a little bit taller. He reminded me of one of those TV dads who are slightly bumbling and not the brightest bulbs in the box. But his eyes were shrewd, and I knew better than to underestimate him. Any of them.

Next to him sat one of only two women. So much for equal opportunity employment. I recognized Ruth Blaine from her photo. She looked close to forty, her body voluptuous and firm like she worked out. Her chin showed a curved white scar on the right below the corner of her lip. She had to like having it, otherwise she'd have had it tinkered away.

Beside her sat Laura Vasquez, the other woman on the crew. Slender and vampire pale with bright red lips and a close-cut cap of slicked-down black hair, she wore a red suit jacket with a bow tie and a flowered shirt. I could almost hear Taylor shudder at the outfit.

Turning the corner of the table, I came to Bob Wright. He'd had a career as a big shot criminal attorney before crossing into the dark side. He wore a gray suit with a blue power tie. His thick salt-and-pepper hair rippled back from his face in elegant waves. The TV definition of distinguished looking. I'd put money on him getting regular tinkering to keep bald spots at bay.

The guy beside him surprised me. He wore a tee shirt with a stick figure humping the word "it." All right, I admit, that amused me. His face and arms were tanned, and he had long blond hair pulled up in a man-bun, totally destroying any illusion of competence. Maybe that was the point. Lure people into a false sense of security that he was harmless. He wasn't. By definition as one of Savannah's lieutenants, he had to be a shark. I guessed he was younger than me, which meant he had to have impressive skills and was an overachiever.

The next guy looked about as wide as he was tall and not an ounce of fat on him. His sweater strained to cover his bulk. He had Robert Redford hair and a full beard. I put him at around fifty years old.

Carter Matokai filled out the seven. Japanese in descent, he had high cheekbones and slashing eyebrows beneath a broad forehead. He wore his hair in a buzz cut. He was probably in his early to midthirties.

"Welcome. Thank you for coming." That from Bob Wright. He stood and gestured at the chairs. "Be seated. I hope you'll forgive our haste and lack of manners, but time is of the essence."

We did as requested, even as Wright went around the table, introducing everyone. Man-bun's name turned out to be Tracey Erickson, and the hulk was Emerson Flanders.

"You're probably wondering why we wanted to see you," Wright began as he sat.

"You want me to do a trace for you," I said, forgetting that I'd planned to stay silent while they explained.

He nodded. "We do. We wish to hire you immediately."

"Who are you looking for?" That from Taylor.

Wright flicked a surprised look at her then back to me. "Perhaps you might introduce your companions," he said. Matokai made an impatient sound and Vasquez drummed her nails on the table. They were antsy. Worried, even. This trace must be seriously important.

I played along with Wright, trying to figure out my own strategy. Until I knew what they wanted, I wouldn't know what my leverage was.

"Arnow you know," I said, gesturing toward her. "That's my sister, Taylor Hollis, and this is Patti Knotts, half owner of this diner."

They all nodded in greeting with each introduction, which felt surreal. It seemed so ordinary, like a business meeting instead of a gathering of some of the most deadly people in Diamond City.

"To answer your question," Wright said, looking at Taylor, "we desire you to locate several missing family members."

The answer left out as much information as it included. "Maybe you can explain," I said.

"Not necessary," Carter Matokai said.

"Sure," I said. "Then when I'm following their traces, I'll walk right into some sort of ambush or maybe tip off the wrong people that I'm coming. I'm sure that everything will turn out fine. I mean, it's not like someone might kill them because you decided to hunt them down." The sarcasm is strong with me.

The seven of them exchanged speaking looks. Taylor leaned close to me. "This is more important than they want you to know," she whispered. "I think you may have them over a barrel."

I'd arrived at pretty much the same conclusion. The question was, how desperate were they and what were they willing to pay to get the hostages back?

"You understand that your relationship with Clayton Price makes us uneasy about giving you details?" Wright said at last, breaking the silence.

"Sure. I totally understand." I stood up. "I wish you good luck and I'll get out of your hair."

"Please, Miss Hollis, I'm sure we can find common ground," Wright said, blanching slightly.

Tracey Erickson thumped the table with his fist. "Just tell her already. We don't have time for this crap!"

Another exchange of looks, and then the air seemed to go out of them all.

"Savannah took members of our families to guarantee our loyalties," Ruth Blaine said, taking over from Wright. "We have no idea where they are, who is looking after them, or if they've been abandoned or killed." Her eyes glittered with desperation. "I want my son back."

I don't know what I'd been expecting, but this was worse. Sympathy put my ass back in my chair. "How long has she had him?"

Blaine closed her eyes, her lips pinching together as if the pain was overwhelming. Collecting herself, she replied. "She took him when he was two. He's sixteen now."

I blinked. "You haven't seen him since he was two?"

"Oh no, my dear," said Fineman. "Savannah didn't want us to forget how much we loved the people she took. We saw them every month, sometimes more if she was particularly happy with our work. Then came months where we couldn't see them because of our failures." His mouth twisted. "On occasion, she went further and rewarded us with bits and pieces she'd cut off them."

I wiped a hand across my mouth, staring wide-eyed. I don't know why I was surprised. This is how Tyets worked. I'd been kidnapped and tortured by a drug lord; my own father had fucked around in my brain so that thinking certain thoughts would have killed me if Cass hadn't been able to fix me. Hell, Savannah had just blown up a bunch of buildings, killing who knows how many people, just to make a point with Touray. Evil was her calling. Evil was what the Tyets were all about.

Not mine. I would not become that sort of filth. I'd rather be dead.

"We'll pay you whatever you want," Flanders said, speaking up for the first time. He sounded just like the grizzly bear he looked like.

The perfect opening. Under the table, Patti grabbed my hand. Taylor grabbed the other. It's like they knew what I had to do and were telling me they had my back. I never doubted it.

"All right. Your invitation came at a good time. I planned to find you and make a proposal. People are out to kill or control me. People like Jackson Tyrell, Gregg Touray, other Tyets, and the government. I need a power base so I can protect me and my own. I don't have time to build my own from scratch. That's where you come in. I want you to give your loyalty to me and let me run this Tyet. You do that, and I'll bring your people back to you."

Wow, that sounded ridiculous. Like teaching donkeys to talk and growing money on trees. I kept my expression impassive and channeled Touray, eyeing each of them with an arrogant confidence I didn't feel.

Ruth Blaine laughed harshly. "Just like that. We put you, a nobody with nothing to back you up but trace talent, in charge of the strongest Tyet in Diamond City? The hell we will."

"Shut up," snapped Erickson. "We need her."

"So you're willing to just turn around and make the same stupid mistake with her that we made with Savannah? Let her hold our families over our heads? It's stupid. We'll find another tracer," Blaine returned.

"Not one as powerful as she is." Flanders ran his fingers through his thick red-blond hair. "With Savannah dead, who knows what might be happening to my Rachel. This woman is our best chance for finding her before—" He broke off, teeth scraping white dents across his lower lip, his face flushing red as he swallowed convulsively.

I thought quickly. "From what I know about Savannah Morrell, you're fresh out of time. I'd bet Savannah had standing orders that said if anything happened to her, execute the hostages. She'd have assumed one of you killed her, or failed to protect her. When word of her death makes it to the hostage locations, game over. You need me and right now." I spoke boldly, despite the fact that I could barely drop into trace sight for a few seconds. How was I going to actually find the hostages?

I didn't want to feel guilty, but I did. I hated when innocent bystanders became victims of Tyet machinations, and here I was, doing exactly what Savannah had done. Using their family members as leverage.

I told myself I didn't have a choice, and besides, they'd probably done the very same thing to others. Turnabout was fair play, wasn't it?

I disgusted myself. I also didn't back down.

"We'll do it," Fineman said finally, and again that exchange of speaking looks. He held each of their gazes until they cowed to him.

I'd have to remember that. I also didn't believe him in the slightest. He was telling me what I wanted to hear to get what he needed. A bridge I'd have to bomb later. Or I could use Savannah's Seedy Seven's hostages against their good behavior. I wouldn't be able to live with myself, but to protect my family, I might have to do it anyway.

I wanted to be sick.

Vasquez nodded, folding her hands together in front of her. "Fine," she snarled.

Going around the table, each of the others added their grudging assent. None of them sounded happy about it, but none dug their feet in.

Now all I had to do was figure out a way to heal up so I could actually find the hostages and Arnow's three missing operatives. And do it in the next few hours.

"I'm surprised—given your relationship with his brother—that you're not taking shelter under Gregg Touray's wings." Fineman's brows rose, asking a silent question.

Thinking about Price made my heart hurt. Did the fact I hadn't called back make him think I was ending things? Dear God, I hoped not. This was not the time to worry about it. It would, however, be the first thing I dealt with when this meeting was done. I forced myself to focus on the men and women sitting opposite to me.

Since the cliché had it that honesty was my best policy and it certainly couldn't hurt at this point, I decided to be candid. "I can't be sure he'll be able or willing to protect us down the road."

Touray would run into a burning building to help the people of the city. He would, and had, walked into a trap set by Savannah in order to save victims of a massive car accident, ending up in her private prison cell. He'd made protecting Diamond City his life's mission. His sacred calling. I'd never believe my name wasn't on his expendables list, not when it came right down to it. And even if he had left me off, Taylor, Leo, Jamie, and Patti wouldn't be so lucky.

"*I* have to take care of my own," I added.

That was met with solemn nods of understanding and agreement. So we had at least one thing in common. Could I build on it?

"Touray might think twice about attacking us if she was driving the bus," Vasquez mused speculatively.

"I wouldn't bank on it," I said, hoping that this time honesty didn't shoot me in the ass. "Jackson Tyrell is backing him to take over Savannah's empire. He's got to do it fast and he wants this badly. He's not going to let anything stand in his way, least of all me." I smiled. "Unless I push him back. Hard." I didn't mention Touray's deal with Vernon. Tyrell would find out about that soon enough, but I didn't want to help him learn about it. That would only hurt Touray, and I didn't want to do that if I didn't have to.

"Who is Jackson Tyrell?" Erickson asked.

"Don't you read the papers? Watch the news?" Wright shook his head in disgust. "Maybe if you looked away from your computer screen occasionally, you'd learn something about the world."

"I'm here, aren't I? No screen in sight. So teach me something, Grampa," he said, slouching down in his chair.

Wright groaned and gave a shuddering sigh. I could almost see him grabbing a cane and shaking it at Erickson while muttering about kids today.

"Tyrell is a gazillionaire philanthropist in a class all alone," he said. He looked at me, shaking his head. "You're wrong or you're lying. He won the Nobel Peace Prize. He practically lives under a media microscope. The idea he'd be Tyet affiliated is ludicrous. Someone in the public eye like him can't just hide that."

I thought about explaining about the deepwater Tyets that kept themselves hidden and ran countries, and the Consortium, which had come high enough to the surface that Arnow had discovered their existence. In the end, I decided I didn't have time. It wouldn't make much of a difference anyhow. They'd want to see proof I didn't have. "I'm neither wrong nor lying, but have it your way. You'll eat the truth sooner or later. But Touray now has all the money and man power he could want to take over the city."

Blaine gave a dismissive wave, unimpressed. "We expected him to come, and every other vulture in the city. We're prepared."

"With Tyrell's backing, he's going to have almost unlimited resources," I said. "He can hire anybody, bribe anybody, and buy anything he needs or wants. I'll bet my right hand you didn't plan for that."

I leaned back and crossed my arms, thrusting out my chin. "If you don't take me seriously, you're going to get slaughtered. Since that will be bad for me, I'd really appreciate it if you pretend that I know what I'm talking about. Which brings me back to the hostages. Did you bring something each of them touched?"

I was sure they'd come prepared, and I was right. They reached into pockets and purses. I stiffened at the seven bloodstained ping-pong balls they set on the table, each contained in a plastic bag. On the other side of Patti, Arnow sucked in a sharp breath.

When the three members of Arnow's off-the-books strike team had been kidnapped during a mission to capture a serial killer, the kidnapper had left behind ping-pong balls with the names of Arnow's team, and a message: *Welcome to the game. Take up your paddle and play.* They'd been sitting in pools of blood from each of the victims. The similar MO couldn't be a coincidence.

"Maybe we can kill two birds with one stone," I murmured.

Arnow turned her head, holding her hand in front of her mouth so that only I could hear her words. "If you can." Her eyes skewered me. She really cared about her missing people.

Patti stood to collect the baggies and set them on the table in front of me.

"What's up with the balls? Weren't toothbrushes and socks good enough?" The Seedy Seven didn't need to know a serial killer might be involved. At least not yet.

"You'd have to ask Savannah," Flanders growled. "She's always used them. Liked to roll them on the table, and tossed them at us to make sure we remembered what was at stake for us."

"What a bitch."

"On that we can agree," Blaine said. The others nodded.

I took a breath and blew it out. "Let's get down to the brass tacks. The trace will go faster if I know where to target," I said. "Arnow says Savannah kept detailed records of just about everything. They might give us details on location, and possibly more importantly, how they are guarded. Finding them's only half the battle. We'll still have to get them back alive."

"Someone inside has decided to make a stand against us, likely her husband or one of her flunkies. We've already sent teams to break into the manor," Flanders said. "It'll take a while. The place is zipped up tight and the security magic is significant."

"I'll get you in," I said before I shut myself up. My habit was to stay hidden, to keep people from knowing what I could do. That had kept me alive and free in the past, but that was then and now was a whole lot different.

"How?" demanded Vasquez.

Patti snorted. "How do you think? Nulls."

The Seedy Seven eyed me speculatively. Well, more like skeptically. Knocking out Savannah's security would take the magical equivalent of nuke.

Luckily, I had just that.

I had several nulls that I'd been powering up for years. The one I had in mind was the smallest. It would easily handle the dense magic of Savannah's manor and a hell of a lot more, though I had no idea how big the nulled zone would end up being. Maybe a mile, maybe twenty, maybe fifty. I was guessing somewhere around the latter. Wherever it hit would be thrown into chaos. So much of the city and daily life depended on magic. The null would suck dry every active spell as far as it could reach until it reached its limit. I hoped there wouldn't be a lot of collateral damage, but I couldn't worry about that right now.

Silence had fallen at Patti's declaration. Now Taylor leaned forward, knocking hard twice on the table.

"Let's cut to the chase. This is how it's going to work. Riley does your trace, and in exchange you give her the head chair at the table for a year with your full support and cooperation. If, after a year, you want to move on her, you can." She smiled, and it wasn't friendly at all. "We don't plan to go down easily."

"Second, we get you into Savannah's manor. It will serve as the base of operations for the organization, as well as a safe house for anybody who wants or needs it, starting with you and your families.

"Finally, if you live up to your side of the bargain, Riley will owe each of you one magical favor of her particular brand of magic, which you can collect anytime after the end of the first year. Any one of you violates the contract, and the deal is off. Then you'll find out just how dirty we can fight."

I clenched my teeth to keep my jaw from falling open. My sister had balls. Not only that, she'd come up with a deal that should keep us all safe for a year—providing the Seedy Seven agreed to it. By then, hopefully we'd manage to guarantee ourselves continued control.

"That's preposterous!" Matokai sputtered.

Despite the fact that they'd already agreed in principle, a chorus of agreement followed his pronouncement, followed by a general melee of angry retorts and then an argument about how much they needed me, which quickly devolved into brainstorming on how to force me to cooperate.

I was not going to let that happen.

I watched a couple of minutes. Anger steeped inside me, growing hotter and more explosive by the moment.

"We need to think about getting out of here. If they decide not to play nice, they'll use me, Taylor, and Arnow to force you to trace for them," Patti said in a low voice. "We can probably take them down—I doubt they allowed each other to have weapons in here and I'm betting most of them don't know how to fight."

"That's not going to help a lot against the guards outside who *are* armed," I said.

"We could use these assholes as human shields," Taylor suggested.

Arnow shook her head. "To take them down fast, we'll have to knock them out at the very least. Can't fireman carry a body shield. Leaves too much of yourself exposed. Not to mention the fact that most of the bodyguards won't care who becomes a casualty, as long as it isn't their particular boss."

I considered our options. It had been a calculated risk to attend the meeting. Leo, Dalton, and Jamie couldn't do anything with the binders up that the Seedy Seven had brought with them, though I expected they'd be charging in soon. Our half hour was almost up. I couldn't see the three of them getting far. Not against a full room of guards and no magic.

I glanced around. No windows, no back doors. There'd never been any before, either, but that didn't mean Patti and Ben hadn't miraculously installed one since I was here last.

I could see only one possibility.

Somehow I needed to unleash the magic stored in the security web, and I couldn't just activate it. The binders made that impossible. On the other hand, just summoning magic wasn't the same as activating it. Maybe because it was a function of a person's spirit. I don't know.

Theoretically, I could summon the power out of the null field, then release it all at once. None of that would be active. And if it wasn't active magic, I had hope that I could handle it better than at the skating rink. Here, I'd just be holding a lot of magic for a while, then letting it all go in one big burst. I could do that. I snorted inwardly. I *had* to do that.

The wash of passive power output should overwhelm the binders, since they didn't care what sort of magic they attacked.

What did I have to lose by trying?

I decided not to answer that, since the first step involved me opening myself to the trace. If I couldn't manage to maintain the connection, the plan was doomed before I started.

I took a breath and let it out and opened myself to the trace. I expected the pain that crawled over me in popping jolts of laser energy. My hands began to shake. *Suck it up*, I told myself. *You've been through a hell of a lot worse, and failure is a really bad option.*

Taking another breath and holding it, I summoned my null magic back to me. Good news: because I'd built the field, it responded easily. Magic flowed into me.

It *hurt.*

What's worse than agony? I didn't know the word for it, but I'd sure as hell found the experience. I'm pretty sure I'd gone to hell, not that any of the seven talking heads noticed anything. Their argument was growing more heated. They really didn't like each other. The sensation of spinning broken glass filled my insides. A flock of steel-beaked woodpeckers pounded against my skull. It took everything I had to stick to the right side of consciousness. All the same, elation buoyed me.

A person can only hold so much magic inside herself before she goes up in flames. Or explodes. Literally. I'd never in my life tried to contain this much magic at one time. It had taken me weeks to first establish the null web, and I'd been adding onto it for years. Now all that magic came gushing back to me like an uncorked fire hydrant.

I didn't know how to deal with the pain. It kept getting worse. I blindly gripped the arms of the chair, determined not to fail. I would not let my family and friends down. Not now, not ever. I could do this. Just a few more seconds.

I reached the point where I felt swollen and overfull, yet the magic kept coming. What should I do? Did I have enough? Could I release what I had as the field continued to fall apart?

I couldn't risk it. Once the binders shut down, the uncontrolled leftover magic would wreak havoc. I couldn't risk Patti, Taylor, Arnow, Ben, or the waitstaff. I wouldn't. I had to direct all of the magic or none.

I think I moaned as I took another look at the unraveling null field. I'd barely made a hole in it. If this was a marathon, I'd run maybe a third of a mile and I still had twenty-six to go.

I wasn't going to make it.

I had to.

I'd heard somewhere that the definition of insanity was to keep repeating the same action and expecting a different result.

I had to shift gears.

Flickers of ideas scattered like light from a mirror ball. Nothing I'd ever done offered any hope of a solution. Once I'd started unraveling the spells, I'd opened a floodgate I couldn't close. No turning back. That was another rule of magic.

Use the Force, Luke.

As if it were that easy. I was the force in this equation, and the threads of my control were snapping one by one.

Was this what it was like for Price? Power so overwhelming he didn't know what to do with it? All he could do was try not to let it rise up inside him.

The only way to win is not to play.

Screw that.

I dug deeper inside myself, gripping my shredding control with all my might. That's when a very simple, very stupid idea struck me.

I just had to speed things up. I could hold the magic for a few seconds, couldn't I? Sure I could. A few seconds was nothing.

If I survived, I'd have to see a psychiatrist. I appeared to have gone over the edge of insanity. Far, far, *far* over the edge.

I opened myself wider to the inward flow of magic and drew down on it as hard as I could.

It flooded through me in a torrent, pushing and tugging at all the sinews that held my body together. My spirit was another kettle of fish. It felt like acid eating through silk and leaving behind tattered rags. I snatched at bits of myself that tore off and tried to float away, only to lose more. Little rainbow moths that fluttered toward escape.

Even as I started to panic, another part of me grabbed me by the throat and shook me. My own schizophrenic wake-up call. A self-applied slap in the face.

I didn't have time to die today. I told myself to get my shit together and straighten up and fly right and get to work. I needed to tell Price we were a team. I needed to find Arnow's people. I needed to take over Savannah's syndicate. I needed to do a lot of things yet, starting with finishing the destruction of my nulls and pulling myself together. Literally.

What I didn't have in strength, I made up for in sheer stubbornness. *Imagine the null field is Vernon attacking you again,* I told myself. *Are you going to let him win? Are you going to let him keep fucking with you? No? Then shut him down. Grind him into dust.*

A vague idea suggested itself. Probably stupid, definitely dangerous, but then I was already in the middle of a stupidly dangerous idea, so what did I have to lose?

I took hold of the inward flow of magic. I began wrapping it around myself.

Feet, legs, hips, torso, arms, head. I turned myself into a mummy of magic. I did it again. And again. I contracted the layers, pulling them into my flesh, into the marrow of my bones, and wrapped again. After the first few times, the pain actually started to diminish, almost like the layers acted like actual bandages with healing salves and soothing balms, except for my magical self instead of my physical self.

Cool.

I didn't know how many times I rinsed and repeated. By the time the inward flow of energy dwindled and stopped, I glowed incandescent in trace sight. Not only that, instead of feeling like I'd fallen into a woodchipper, I felt good. Better than that. Like I'd just touched the sun. Like I'd climbed Mount Everest. Like I'd flown to the moon and back.

I conducted a mental inventory of myself. Ripples of energy slid beneath my skin, washing over my muscles and warming me to my core. Sparks floated through my veins and danced in my lungs. It felt exhilarating and intoxicating.

All the magic I'd wrapped around myself and drawn inside remained. More than that. It had melded with me. I pulsed like I was one big magic battery. The biggest plus was that my magic no longer seemed like it wanted to kill me.

Time to finish the showdown.

I rose back to awareness. The room was far too quiet. The Seedy Seven were staring at us, looking expectant. I was pretty sure they'd said something I was supposed to respond to.

"Threats?" Taylor sneered from beside me. "It's a fair deal. We both get what we want."

"What you want doesn't matter," Wright said imperiously. "Miss Hollis will conduct the trace or watch the other three of you die a horrible, painful, and very *slow* death." He smiled smugly.

"Think again, asshole," I said, and then dumped all the collected energy out of myself.

I felt the moment when the binders stopped working. My loosed magic crackled in the air. I drew it back in, almost without thought. Nice.

"Binders are down," I said casually, like announcing dinner was ready.

The Seedy Seven didn't seem to grasp what I'd said. Taylor, Arnow, and Patti did. They leaped into action. Which is to say, all hell broke loose.

Chapter 21

Riley

MY THREE COMPANIONS lunged up, sending their chairs flying. Patti was fastest. She'd almost reached Flanders when an invisible force pushed her back a few feet. Several of the Seedy Seven shouted, and the doors burst open, bodyguards pounding inside.

Taylor halted her charge, twisting to face down three guards. She moved fast as a flame, flickering forward and back, kicking and spinning and punching. For every four or five blows she struck, one of her opponents landed one, mostly glancing.

Patti went after another four. She had multiple black belts, and with every touch on her opponents, she locked down feet and hands with binding magic, allowing her to subdue them quickly.

The Seedy Seven stood and clustered behind the table. They looked confused and more than a little irritated. More guards charged through the doors.

I managed to get to my feet, but my body felt awkward, lagging behind what I told it to do. I caught my balance against the table. A guard made a swipe for me. I succeeded in dodging, but my feet tangled and I ended up on the floor. I rolled under the table and out the other side, finding my feet again. Only now things had taken a turn for the bizarre.

Out of nowhere, Matokai started throwing green ceramic bowls of something gooey and orange. Then every object in the room grew a pair of yellow bat wings and started bumbling around into walls and whatever else got in the way. The wings weren't large enough to launch the chairs or tables, but they shook and bumped, hitching a few inches in random directions.

A bowl flew at me, dumping its contents down my shoulder. I yelped and jumped up, expecting acid or molten lava. Instead I smelled sugar and ... butterscotch? The big bad Tyet lord was flinging bowls of butterscotch pudding?

I swear to God, I was in an *Animaniacs* fight.

Flashes of bright strobing colored lights swarmed around Taylor and Patti. I blinked and squinted, barely able to see anything with the spots dancing across my vision. The table beside me flipped sideways on its own and skidded forward, stopping dead after four feet. Patti didn't notice it as she took several steps back to line up her next attack. She bounced against the wood and tilted sideways. A bowl of pudding hit her in the side of the head and she staggered, swiping the gooey stuff away from her eyes and shaking her head. Two more bowls followed in rapid succession, one hitting her jaw, the other flying wide.

I leaped at Matokai with every intention of breaking his arms. He stood on the other side of Flanders. The blocky man caught sight of me and turned to face me squarely. He took several fast steps forward, closing the distance between us. A guy his size shouldn't move that quick. I was too late to halt my forward momentum. If he got his hands on me, he'd wrap me in a bear hug and break all my ribs, or put me in a choke hold.

I dove low at his legs. Hooking his left leg with my arm, I landed on my belly and pulled myself in a sharp circle, using his leg to twist myself onto my back. I let go, stopping slightly behind on his right. I'd pulled him off balance and now jammed my foot against the inside of his left leg. He *oofed* and toppled toward me. This wasn't my first takedown, and I'd already scrambled backward out of the way of his falling bulk.

I rolled to my feet, avoiding Flanders's meaty hands as he grabbed for me. I kicked him in the jaw, and his head snapped back. He slumped facedown on the floor. One down.

Someone snatched my shoulder from behind. Wright. I twisted and his hand slipped and grabbed a fistful of my hair. What there was left of it, anyhow. Wright jerked me back. I turned under his arm and jammed my shoulder into his stomach. He grunted, letting go of my hair and clamping down on my neck with his arm. Before he could slug me with his other fist, I punched him in his family jewels. His arm around my neck contracted, and he made a high-pitched sound.

I shoved him and he let go, staggering backward, his thin face screwed tight with pain, one hand cupping his genitals. I kicked his leg and drove an elbow into his kidney. He dropped to his knees, and I snapped a kick up under his jaw. He dropped to the floor.

I spun around and stopped. Taylor stood panting beside Patti, who wiped away the blood on her chin with the back of her hand. Arnow had a choke hold on the bristle-haired woman who'd frisked us. As I watched, the woman went slack. Arnow held her another thirty seconds, and then dropped her. She bent to retrieve the pumps she'd kicked off during the fight. Everybody else was either unconscious or caught in metal shackles, or both. Jamie and Leo stood in the doorway, faces tight with concentration and fury.

Dalton shoved between them and stopped, his gaze going straight to Taylor. He visibly relaxed when he saw her. *Interesting.*

The strobe lights continued to pop.

"Whoever is doing that, stop it now before I do something you'll regret," Taylor snapped. The lights vanished.

Though the strobes had stopped, dark spots continued to hop across my vision. Not a very useful talent, but certainly distracting.

Just then the bands circling Vasquez's feet and arms popped free and jumped away from her. She must have been responsible for throwing the table, too. She clearly had distance limits on her talent. Better than conjuring bowls of butterscotch pudding, though. I wondered how many people Matokai let in on that humiliating secret. A whole lot of talents weren't particularly useful, but I'd have thought these seven would have something more potent to work with. Clearly, I was mistaken.

I eyed Vasquez. What did she think she was going to do now? But she just righted a chair and sat gracefully, crossing her legs and adjusting her bow tie before folding her hands and resting them on her knee.

"I believe you've made your point," she said to me.

I glanced at the rest of the conscious seven. Their expressions were more thoughtful than angry.

"I hope I have. I've heard that slower children need more than one lesson."

I bent and gathered up the bags of ping-pong balls that had scattered during the fight, then glanced at my watch. Almost ten o'clock.

"At three a.m., we'll be setting off the null at Savannah's compound. It'll stay active for less than a minute and kill all active magic in a ten- to fifty-mile radius."

Probably wouldn't last more than a few seconds. As soon as it was activated, its power would rush from ground zero as far as it could, gobbling magic as it went. The equivalent of a magical nuke.

Ignoring the startled gasps elicited by my announcement, I continued. "Once it exhausts itself, we'll need to move and reestablish the security grid before Touray or anybody else can strike. They won't be expecting the null, so their magic will get knocked out. As long as our team's ready, we should be able to pull it off long before they get their shit back together. You've got five hours to get your people in place.

"Once the compound is secured, your priority is to dig up information to help me trace the hostages. I expect you to guard my people like they're your own family. They are in charge." I pointed to Arnow and Taylor. "You run everything through them. You've got questions, you've got problems—you check with them. They are the central command. That's nonnegotiable."

"Where will you be?" Vasquez asked.

"Tracing the hostages. With luck, they're in the city or nearby. If not, I'll be taking a road trip. I'll still have to follow their trace on the ground. But going east could lead me to Baltimore or Cincinnati or Denver. If you can dig up a more targeted location, I'll find them faster. I can fly in to a spot rather than driving. If they are overseas, specifics become crucial to a timely rescue."

I faced them. Flanders had regained consciousness and struggled to sit up on the floor. Wright still wasn't moving. "So that's the plan. Are you in?"

"If you say yes, you're agreeing to the terms we laid out," Taylor said. "No exceptions, no deviations."

I nodded. I didn't want them coming back later and saying they only agreed to work with me until I got the hostages back for them.

"We agree," Blaine said. She scowled at the others. "All of us."

"What about Wright? Is he going to go along?"

"He will," Fineman said. "He won't have a choice."

The rest nodded again.

"Good," I said, clamping down on a mix of stunned surprise, elation, and terror. "I'll tell you again—take it as gospel—Touray has unlimited resources now. Money, man power, magic. He's going to come fast and he's going to come hard. He's probably already begun his assault, so you'd better get going."

"Let everybody go," I told Jamie and Leo.

When the seven were loose, I told them to call off their goons outside the building. They made the calls, and then we headed for the door. I stopped and gave a half turn. "One last thing. You're responsible for cleaning up and repairing the diner, for covering lost revenue, and for keeping it secure until I can reestablish a null field." I walked out before they could respond.

Bodies littered the front area of the diner, where my brothers and Dalton had plowed through. Ben stepped between the prone guards carrying a couple of heavy-duty meat tenderizers, ready to play whack-a-mole if any got frisky.

I grabbed him in a hug. "Sorry about all this. Are you okay?"

His hug was just as tight. "I'm fine. No worries."

Patti hugged him next. "I'm going with Riley. It may be a while."

Ben shrugged, shaggy brown hair falling across his eyes. "Kitchen needs a spring clean, anyway. May as well get on it now."

"They're going to keep this place secure and get the necessary repairs," I said. "If you've got renovations you want to make, may as well do them, too. I'll cover the cost."

Both Patti and Ben snorted disgust at that. "As if," Patti said.

"It's a good idea, but we'll cover it ourselves," Ben said.

"Damned right," Patti added.

"I ought to contribute since you feed me for free and I live here half the time," I protested.

"You also put up a top-notch null field for nothing and we're not taking any money so just shut up now," Ben said with his crooked grin.

"I guess this means you'll be looking down the barrel of huge Christmas presents, then," I said.

"Buy me an island in the South Pacific," he said. "Or a castle on the Rhine."

"Won't you be surprised when I do just that?" I asked and then sailed off before he could reply. My mike-drop exit was ruined when I stumbled over the outstretched hand of an unconscious bodyguard. I sighed and kept moving. Arnow, Patti, and I retrieved our coats and weapons and headed out the door.

Once outside, I halted. "That went better than expected."

"How the hell did you shut down the binders?" Jamie asked. "That was epic."

Arnow saved me from answering.

"You don't really think they'll just let you take charge, do you? For a year? If you do, you need a trip to the mental ward."

I sighed exasperatedly. "Of course not. But I also don't think we're going to give them any choice." I said it with a lot more certainty than I actually felt. Like ninety-eight percent more.

She gaped. "You've got to be kidding. We're way outclassed here. We don't have the weapons, the money, or the army to take over." She pointed back at the diner. "They are humoring us until they get what they want, and then we'll end up at the bottom of a deep mineshaft. These people don't have integrity.

You can't expect them to keep any bargain they make."

"You don't think I know that? I'm not actually the brainless idiot you think I am."

I ignored her muttered "could have fooled me."

I put my hands on my hips. "All right. What did you want me to do?"

She glowered. "You should have punished them, demonstrated that there's a price to pay for double-crossing you."

"And what do you think that should have been?"

"I don't know. Carve off a couple ears. Put collars on them. Something. You can't be a pushover. You have to show strength at all times."

"Noted." I disagreed. Humiliating them wouldn't help. I wanted loyalty. I needed their respect, and sure, a little healthy fear wouldn't hurt. Whatever Arnow thought, I didn't have time for head games right now. I turned to Leo and Patti.

"I need you two to fetch the null from my place. It's upstairs in the niche by the fireplace. A tire rim off an old Ford pickup with a kind of a weird praying mantis sculpture welded on top of it. It's heavy. Dalton and Taylor go collect whatever weapons you think will be useful. Arnow, go with Jamie to Savannah's place. Figure out a plan and coordinate with the seven."

"What are you going to do?" This from Arnow, who had folded her arms. She'd gone from mere irritation to anger.

"I'm going to chase down the hostages and your missing people. You've got their balls, right?" Their trace had been nulled when the balls had been made, but now that my magic was back to normal, I could trace them even so. The strength of my abilities had been growing in leaps and bounds in recent months. I'd begun breaking through barriers of impossibility and finding I could do a lot more than I ever knew.

"Of course. But I'm going with you."

"You can't. You're the only one of us who knows anything about Savannah or the inside of her compound. You have to help take it over and then see what you can find out about the hostages."

"They'll have to do without me. You don't have a clue what you're getting into, and I do. Remember my team got taken while I was hunting a vicious serial killer, one that was obviously working for Savannah. These ping-pong balls are not a coincidence. If he gets ahold of you, you're dead, and then Alex, Ryan, and Laurie are doomed. So I'm going. May as well get used to it and stop wasting our time arguing."

I drew a heavy breath and blew it out. Clearly, I wasn't going to be the kind of Tyet dictator Savannah had been, though the thought of stabbing Arnow through the eye held a certain appeal at the moment.

I rubbed my forehead. "Fine. Then I guess we go to my place so the boys and Patti can pick your brains."

We'd all crowded into Dalton's SUV on the way over from my place, dropping it about a half mile away when we hit thick traffic. Since we needed to split up, that left us a vehicle short, and the subway wasn't running yet.

We could borrow Ben's car, or we could go another route.

I raised my voice and turned to look past the diner. "Do you have room for five passengers?"

Five heartbeats passed, my companions eyeing me and then followed my gaze up the sidewalk.

A shadow stepped out of the darkness just inside the alley.

Price.

My heart thudded even though I'd realized he was there almost as soon as we'd come out of the diner. He carried an active null, but that only made his trace harder to see, not impossible, not for me, not anymore. I made an automatic habit of scanning for trace whenever I might be walking into trouble. I figured the Seedy Seven might have left backup outside or maybe someone else had followed them. I'd found Price's nearly instantly.

He strolled toward us. As usual, he was dressed head to toe in black. I couldn't read his expression. It was remote and entirely neutral. Like a robot. Even the perpetual breeze that swirled around him had quieted to nearly nothing.

He nodded to the others and slanted an unfathomable look at me. "I'm driving a Wrangler."

My stomach balled. He'd pretty much told me he was done with me if I was cutting him out of my plans. But if that was true, why was he here and not with his brother? I was beyond confused, not to mention terrified I'd totally fucked things up beyond repair.

"Tight," Jamie said, breaking the strained silence. "We'll be sitting on laps." He looked at Leo. "You can have the ice queen."

"Gee, thanks," Leo said.

"You're very welcome. Patti can ride on my lap," Jamie said with a grin.

"Maybe I want to sit on the ice queen," Patti said tartly. "Or in Riley's lap. Ever thought of that? You two aren't the prizes you think you are."

"How would you know? Gotta ride the train to know how good it is," Leo said, waggling his brows.

I was pretty sure this exchange was for my benefit, to let me adjust to Price's unexpected presence. God, I loved these people. Well, maybe not Arnow and Dalton.

Patti scanned Leo up and down with slow deliberation. "I recognize a no-good, broke-down lemon when I see one." She glanced at Arnow. "What about you? You think that train is as hot as he thinks it is?"

Arnow repeated the examination, first with Leo and then Jamie. Both of them flushed as she took her time. "I think you give them too much credit," she drawled. "They should sit on each other's laps, since they think so highly of themselves."

"Brilliant plan," Patti said, clapping her hands together.

I smiled weakly. Price's careful indifference was driving me nuts. I'd know more about how he felt if I grabbed his trace, but I had a feeling I might not like what I found out. I needed to talk to him, but we didn't exactly have time for a heart to heart. Or privacy. I did not want to air my dirty laundry in front of everybody else. My family would take it as an invitation to participate.

I comforted myself with the fact that Price's presence had to mean something good.

"Now that that's settled, Dalton and I should go," Taylor said. "We'll meet you at your house in an hour or so."

With that, the two of them strode away.

"Jeep's up the street," Price said and led off in the opposite direction.

When we crossed Casey Avenue, which dead-ended into the front of Price's former precinct, I hustled to catch up with him, falling into step beside him.

"How'd you know I'd be here?"

"I didn't."

"So . . . ?" I prompted.

"I came to question Patti on your whereabouts."

Such a cop answer. "And?" I prompted, feeling like I was pulling teeth.

"The place was bottled up tight."

"So you decided to wait?"

"So I decided to wait."

Had he known we were inside? I wanted to ask, but we'd reached the Jeep.

I ended up in the front seat beside Price, with the console dividing us. In the back, Patti sat on Arnow's lap with Leo in the middle and Jamie on the other side.

"You know, there's an FBI safe house not too far from here that we could use. We don't all have to go pick up the null," Arnow said. "Be easier than hiking in and out of your place in these shoes, plus it will have a change of clothes for me."

"That's a good idea," Patti agreed. "Let's do that. You and Price can fetch the null while the rest of us get squared away on Savannah's compound."

Leo looked like he was going to object, and she elbowed him in the side. He scowled at her, but subsided.

"Good idea," Price said, and that was that.

I guessed we were going to have a chance to talk by ourselves. I looked forward to it and wanted to vomit at the same time.

Arnow directed us on the route. Nobody spoke. I guessed the peanut gallery in the back seat was waiting for me to let them know if they could speak freely. They didn't know if I wanted to reveal our plans to Price, if I thought we could trust him or not.

He'd come to find me. That was all I needed to know. I started talking, detailing everything that happened since his phone call to me all the way up to us walking out of the diner. I didn't leave anything out. When I was done, Patti and Arnow offered up extra explanations to Jamie's and Leo's questions. Price never said a word, never reacted in any way. I was considering prodding him with a knife to see if he was really Price or a wax doll.

We pulled up outside a secluded house in Midtown. It was a little south of the main artery cutting through the city. A fringe of trees planted inside an iron fence screened the house from sight. The gates responded to Arnow's touch and swung open. We drove up the winding drive.

The house itself was a gray Cape Cod with white trim. Three dormer windows faced the driveway above a curved front porch. The place was crowned with a steep slate roof. An open expanse of unmarked snow surrounded the house.

The drive hadn't been plowed since the last snow, but the Jeep didn't mind, and we motored right up to the garage door.

"Better text Taylor and give them the address," I said to no one in particular.

The others hopped out. Price waited until Arnow opened the door and everyone retreated inside, and then put the Jeep in reverse and turned it around. This time, the gates opened automatically.

Price remembered the map I'd shown him weeks ago and headed back into Downtown. The silence stretched. I figured out pretty quick that he wasn't going to be the one to talk first.

"I was surprised to see you," I said finally. I wasn't ready to jump into the deep end of this conversation yet.

"I figured."

This was going to be either a really long conversation or a really short one if he stuck with two-word answers.

"I was surprised that you didn't come into the diner to find out what was going on."

"Were you?"

I had a feeling he was doing it on purpose just to needle me. I eyed him, but his profile gave nothing away. I looked back out on the road. Traffic had smoothed somewhat. Detours had been set up to unsnarl the worst of the problems. And at this time of night, people had gone home.

We went down through the Excelsior Tunnel and turned north toward Karnickey Burrows.

I needed to quit being a chicken and just cut to the chase. "You gave me the impression that if I didn't call you, I wouldn't be seeing you."

"Did I?"

Like he'd forgotten or I'd misinterpreted his very specific words.

"Yeah."

He shook his head. "Couldn't have. If I had, you'd have called me back in seconds." He dipped his hand in a pocket and pulled out his phone, thumbing it to life. "Nope, no missed calls, no messages." He tucked the phone away again. "You must not remember correctly."

Passive aggressive much? Okay, I couldn't blame him. I'd be pissed as hell right now if I were in his position. I sighed. "I was still wrapping my head around that phone call when I found out about the meeting with the Seedy Seven. I planned to call you when we were done."

"When you were done," he repeated, and this time his tone was colored with a light coat of derision. Finally. *Some* kind of emotion. "You know what? You should probably shut up now before I put my fist through my dashboard."

He slowed to take a corner, shifting down with unnecessary violence. We skidded, and the tires caught traction again.

"You're the one who gave me an ultimatum," I said, sitting back in my seat and folding my arms. Apparently I was twelve again. "I was just trying to do the right thing."

"Your idea of the right thing and my idea are very different."

"So you're just going to take up arms against your brother? Because sooner or later it's going to come down to a fight if I get control of Savannah's business."

He hit the brakes hard. We slid sideways and jolted to a stop against a snow-piled curb. The Jeep rocked. Price twisted to face me. Darkness hollowed his eyes.

"Well, you fucked up because I choose you, whether you like it or not. Phone call or not. Fight with my brother or not. Understand?"

My mouth dropped open at the violent intensity of his voice. He waited, and when I said nothing, he blew out a soft breath that spoke volumes of disgust and put the Jeep back in gear.

"Is it so difficult to believe I'd pick you?" he asked after a couple of minutes.

My brain was still trying to reboot. "I never imagined you would," I said with blunt honesty.

He started swearing.

"It's not that I don't think you love me," I said when he paused to take a breath.

"Then what is it? Because I sure as hell don't understand. You know, you *have* to know, what you mean to me after all we've been through. There's nothing I wouldn't do for you. Why is it so hard to believe?"

"Because it's your brother—"

"And he's a big boy who knows exactly what he's doing and has no illusions about the nature of his business. He wasn't particularly surprised when I told him I was going to find you and help you. He also told me to keep you safe. You and your family. Even Leo."

The last choked a laugh out of me. Leo and Touray had not gotten off on a good foot.

"Is that it? The whole reason you cut me out?" Price asked, and his voice had returned to the cool reasonable cop tone like he was interrogating me and didn't want me to know it. "Nothing else?"

I was baffled. "What else?"

"Who knows what thoughts are racing around in that brain of yours."

I could tell it was more than that, though. Price was digging with a purpose. Suddenly I was worried. "Even if you did pick me, I thought you'd resent me and be angry and hurt and guilty. I couldn't do that to you."

"So you thought you'd rip my heart out instead."

"You'd get over me."

I flinched when his head whipped around. He looked away long enough to slot the Jeep into a parking spot this time before he turned back to me, leaning forward so that I wanted to slide down in my seat.

"Get over you?" he repeated in a voice so angry I could practically smell the smoke drifting off it. "That's what you thought? Let's be clear. I love you. Desperately and completely. I'm not just going to get over you. I'm not even sure I can live without your stupid, ridiculous ass."

I averted my gaze. "My dad got over me. He loved me, too. Or he acted like it," I said in a small voice. The words actually hurt my throat, airing a truth I'd refused to think about, much less say. But Price had felt that tiny piece of me I'd held back.

Price grabbed my chin in a firm grip and forced it up, waiting until I looked back at him.

"Your father is a psychopath. I am not. I will not be compared to that rotten piece of shit. I love you. Forever. In this world and the next and the next. What else do I need to say to convince you?"

I stared at him. He stared back, unmoving, waiting for me to absorb his words, challenging me to believe. I couldn't have looked away if I wanted to.

Losing Price terrified me. Before him, I hadn't known I could feel like this about any man. That I'd be willing to. After my mom died, I'd clung to my father. He'd been my everything. Then he'd vanished. That had broken me in ways I'd never fully realized. Not until now.

After he left, I'd had Mel, Leo, Taylor, Jamie, and Patti. I'd loved them, but carefully. I'd kept a piece of myself back, just like I had with Price.

Deep down, I'd always expected to lose him. I'd hedged my emotions against the inevitable, trying to protect the fragile inmost part of me that had nearly shattered to bits when my father had abandoned me. I'd recovered from that—enough to live my life, anyhow. I didn't think I could recover from losing Price.

But the moment had come when logic said he should have walked away. He should have chosen Touray. But he hadn't. He'd picked me. All I had to do was believe him. Believe that he meant it and that he'd keep picking me forever.

A lump grew in my throat, too big to swallow or speak around. Tears overflowed my eyes and trickled down my cheeks. Finally I nodded.

"I need the words, Riley. That you can't live without me any more than I can't live without you. I need you to say you're going to hold on to me as tightly as I'm planning to hold on to you."

The hand holding my chin trembled ever so slightly. The idea that he could possibly need my reassurance boggled me. That's when I realized how different he was from my father. Vernon hid everything. Price exposed everything—the good, the bad, and the ugly. I never had to doubt him.

I slid my fingers over his, gripping tightly, swallowing hard so I could speak the words he needed to hear.

"I love you," I said huskily. "End-of-time kind of love. I couldn't have stayed away from you. I'd have kidnapped you and locked you up so you couldn't get away." I smiled brokenly. "I can't live without you."

He kissed me then, deep and powerful, like sealing a bargain. I held nothing back, trying to show him what he meant to me. By the time he lifted his head, we were both breathless and I at least was shaking.

"To be continued," he said, releasing me reluctantly.

"I hate waiting for sequels."

Price put the Jeep back into gear. "I'll make it worth the wait. I promise."

"I'll hold you to it."

As soon as humanly possible.

"YOU'VE GAINED control of your talent," I said later as we waited outside the gates of the safe house. I'd texted Arnow to let us in.

"Some. I'm learning."

He'd held my hand most of the way back like he couldn't stand not touching me. I knew the feeling. He lifted it to his mouth and kissed the inside of my wrist.

"I decided I had to stop letting it cripple me. It's my talent. It's not going away. If I don't learn to use it, I'll end up tromping through Diamond City like Godzilla through Tokyo."

"More like the big bad wolf going after pigs one and two."

"Except this wolf could wipe out three's house just as easy, plus the entire pig village and the next-door goats and sheep."

I laughed. "Fair enough. At least the cows and horses will be safe."

The gates opened then, and we drove through. The garage rolled open as we drove up to the house. Price pulled in next to Dalton's SUV. He and Taylor had beaten us back. Arnow pressed the button to close the garage door and came down the three steps from the house to look inside the back of the Jeep.

"*That's* the mother of all nulls? It's ridiculous."

"It holds a lot of magic, and it was convenient. A client gave it to me as a thank-you for a trace job."

"I don't think he meant it as a thank-you. That thing is atrocious."

"It's cute."

"Which only proves you lack taste. Not that we needed more proof."

"You're just pissed because you don't have one."

"Right. That's it. I desperately want a rusty piece of junk made out of nuts, bolts, spark plugs, wrenches, and whatever else the so-called artist scrounged out of the dump. Is that a bedpan?"

"Yep. Clever how he cut it in half and attached it with the butter knives, isn't it?"

"That's one word for it."

"If you're lucky, I'll get you one for Christmas."

Arnow groaned. "Please don't. I'll have to pay to get it hauled away."

"I think I'm going to have fun redecorating Savannah's house. I'll bet it would look great decked out in garage-sale chic," I said, grinning at her. "We could put up tapestries of 'Dogs Playing Poker' and—oh! A velvet Elvis."

Price chuckled.

Arnow scowled. "You do that and I promise Savannah will crawl out of the grave and haunt you until the end of your days."

"I ain't afraid of no ghosts."

"You also don't have the sense God gave goldfish," she retorted before marching back into the house.

"I hate it when she gets the last word," I said, sighing. I did notice Arnow now wore FBI-issue navy cargo pants and a pair of tennis shoes.

"Depending on where we go, we might have to stop at a Walmart and find her some boots," I said, then giggled at the idea of Arnow shopping in a discount store. The woman would likely go into seizures at the mere touch of off-the-rack discount clothing. Heck, she'd probably curl up and die just walking in the door.

"Not the hill you want to die on," Price said wryly as we both got out. "And trust me, she'd kill you for that."

"Might be worth it."

"You really do like to live dangerously."

"You're only just figuring that out? Where have you been the past couple of months?"

"In a lovesick haze, apparently."

"I must be spectacular, then, if you didn't notice all the pain, suffering, and general mayhem."

By then we were at the door to the house. Price stopped me in the doorway, snatching a quick kiss. "Spectacular pain in the ass," he murmured against my ear, and then went inside.

I also hated when *he* got the last word.

EVERYBODY HAD gathered in the living room, including Taylor and Dalton. The mouthwatering scent of pizza permeated the room, and my stomach cramped.

"Pizza?" I asked hopefully.

"We stopped for it. I'll get you some," Taylor said.

"I could use seconds," Leo said. "And another beer."

"Then get off your ass and get them yourself," came Taylor's tart reply.

The furniture had been pushed back to allow Jamie and Leo to render Savannah's compound in 3-D according to Arnow's descriptions. Piles of pots and pans were heaped beside the fireplace, along with the scattered detritus of all the things they'd already stripped of metal.

"A couple of Barbies and you two could have a good time," I said, examining the metal model. "That's amazing. Is it accurate?"

"No, I lied and everything is skewed." Arnow glared at me. "Of course it's accurate."

Okay, I'll admit. That one was dumb. Someone hand me a *stupid* sign. "I meant is it complete? Are you all done with Arnow? We should get going. As soon as we eat," I amended.

"What time is it?"

"Just after midnight," Patti replied.

"Then eat fast and we can grab a couple hours' sleep," Price said.

I didn't argue. I'd had maybe four hours' sleep in the last couple of days. I wasn't turning down a nap. "Okay."

"Okay?" he repeated. Like me being reasonable was surprising. Shocking even.

"That's what I said."

I grabbed a beer and the plate Taylor had made me from the kitchen and plopped down on the big sectional couch. Price fetched his own meal and sat beside me, his thigh snugged up to mine.

The others went back to planning, Leo and Jamie making additions and filling in details on the model as they talked. From what I could tell, they had things well in hand. Taylor and Dalton offered the most suggestions for how to proceed. Patti made a list of what would be needed from the Seedy Seven.

"The key will be getting inside and getting the security web back working before anybody else can come in," Dalton said. "It would help to know what kind of numbers we're working with and what talents."

Arnow took a pen, paper, and her phone. She scrolled through her contacts, stopping to write down numbers. She handed the page to Dalton. "Those are the contacts for Savannah's lieutenants. You can text them your questions."

"Not Savannah's anymore," Taylor said.

Arnow growled. "Fine. Riley's lieutenants, then."

"Ours," I corrected. "All of us. You're just as much a part of this as we are."

That surprised her. She froze a moment, and then gave a faint nod.

"Anyhow, I like the Seedy Seven for them. Or maybe the Seven Dwarfs. Though can they all be Grumpy?" Leo said.

"Seedy Seven?" Patti snorted. "That's the one." Her gaze dropped to my empty plate. "Time for you to hit the hay." She took my plate and Price's, then pointed imperiously toward the stairs. "Go."

"You'll wake us in two hours?"

"I won't let you oversleep," Arnow said.

I hesitated, then nodded. She knew better than I did that time was of the essence.

The master bedroom was at the end of the hall. It had a giant bed and an attached bathroom. I went to wash my hands and face, and found packages of toothbrushes and toothpaste in the top drawer between the double sinks. I handed Price a brush and then went about cleaning the fur off my teeth.

I peeled down to my underwear and tee shirt and slid in between the sheets, yelping at the chilled linen. Flannel had been too much to ask for. Price stripped to his birthday suit and climbed in beside me. He snuggled me against his warmth, dropping a light kiss on my lips. It was a testament to how tired I was that I only considered jumping his bones for a second before deciding I'd rather sleep.

"I've missed this," I said, "more than you know." It seemed like a hundred years since he let me sleep with him.

"Trust me, I know," he said, pushing my hair away and nibbling down my neck to my shoulder.

My body flamed hot, and I pinched my thighs together. "If you don't stop that we won't be getting any sleep," I said.

He sighed, his breath fluttering across my cheek. "Since when are you the voice of reason?"

I laughed. "Next time we have a couple of weeks alone in a mountain retreat, you'll know better than to keep running away from me." I wiggled my hips where they nestled against him. I felt his cock harden.

He tightened his arm around my waist. "Stop that."

"You started it."

"And I'm ending it. Did I say you were the voice of reason? I was wrong."

I laughed softly and twisted my head to kiss the inside of his arm pillowing my head, then settled down to sleep.

Chapter 22

Riley

DAWN FOUND US on Highway 133. The trace from the ping-pong balls led east. Since Arnow's people had disappeared in Denver, I was hoping that's where the trace would lead us and not to France or Egypt or somewhere equally as difficult.

"She'd want to keep them pretty close so she could produce them easily," I said, more to convince myself than anything else. But if she used travellers to move them, Savannah could have stashed them anywhere on the planet and still had easy access.

We fell silent a few minutes.

"Do you think they've started yet?" I asked. Arnow had woken us up just before 5:00 a.m. Activating the null at 3:00 a.m. like I'd first told the Seedy Seven hadn't been feasible with the plan Taylor, Leo, Patti, Jamie, and Dalton had devised. I couldn't complain about the extra sleep, but everybody else had gone to rendezvous with the Seedy Seven before we woke up. I was annoyed I hadn't had a chance to see them before they left. I'd texted when we got on the road, but it wasn't the same.

"Maybe," Arnow said. "They had to go over the plan with the seven and then get their troops in place. They wanted the cover of darkness if they could get things going by then." She shrugged. "We'll hear soon enough."

I chewed my lower lip. Worry twisted my stomach and made the coffee I'd drunk boil up my throat. I swallowed.

My phone rang. I snatched it up, looking at the screen. Cass.

"You're up early," I said by way of greeting.

"I'm up late," the other woman corrected. "Been trying to reach you. Finally got ahold of Ben at the diner and got your new number."

I winced. "Sorry. I meant to let you know."

"You've had other things to deal with. I've called to add to your problems."

Foreboding tightened my chest. "What's wrong?"

"You know Touray had his head messed with, right?"

I glanced at Price, who frowned back at me. "Yeah. He's okay, now, right?"

"I—maybe. Maybe not. I want to scan him again in a day or so, see if I can dig a little deeper. There was a lot of damage and I had a tough time seeing past it. That's why I'm calling. Even though Touray remembers a woman working on him, I could swear it was your father."

"Vernon?" I clenched my hand on my phone. "Why do you say that?"

"That's the problem. It's nothing all that concrete, just a feeling. The work, even though it was entirely different, reminded me of what he did to you. Same sort of vibe. He's had a chance to learn a whole lot of new tricks in the last ten years, so it's not surprising the technique would be different. But it still felt like him."

"You're saying my father is on Tyrell's payroll," I said slowly.

Price jerked the wheel and steadied it.

"I'm saying that I think he's the one who messed with Touray's mind."

"For Tyrell."

"Seems like a reasonable conclusion."

"Shit."

"I thought you should know."

"Did you tell Touray?"

She hesitated. "No. I thought you and Price should know first. Can you see what he wants me to do about his brother? If there's more your father's done—and there is, since Touray remembers the dreamer being a woman—then likely there're land mines waiting, just like Vernon left in your head. Touray's also working with your father against Tyrell, isn't he? I mean, that's what he was thinking when I did the scan. But if Vernon is working for Tyrell, too—"

I could hear the silent shrug.

"I'll talk to Price. In the meantime, maybe you should go to ground. If Vernon finds out that you know what he's up to, he's likely to come after you."

"I'd like to see him try."

"Cass, I'm serious. He's bad news."

"So am I. Don't worry about me."

Since I wasn't going to win the argument, I gave up. Hopefully she was right. "All right. Thanks for the heads-up. Oh, and you should probably know that we're trying to take over Savannah's organization before Touray or anybody else can."

For once, I'd made Cass speechless. I could hear her sputter. "You're what?" she shrieked when she scraped her wits together.

"I'm pretty sure you heard me," I said, unable to help my smile. It wasn't often anybody caught Cass off balance.

"That's—you're—since when? Why?" Then just as quickly. "Never mind. I got it. You're afraid your father is coming after you and your family, and you want to have the means to protect yourselves, especially now that he's allied with Touray. Not a bad idea, but can you pull it off?"

I filled her in on our activities.

"Might work. Maybe I should go lend a hand. I mean, you *do* plan to let me join up with you, don't you? Did my invitation get lost in the mail or something?"

"I wasn't sure you'd want to. You like being an independent contractor."

She was silent a moment. "You're the only person in the world I trust completely," she said finally. "I don't want to be on the outside."

"Then you're in," I said, stupid tears welling in my eyes, my throat clogging with emotion. Wonder, mostly. Shock, too. "I'll text you Taylor's number. She and Dalton are running the invasion."

"You're crazy, you know that?"

"Yep."

"Where are you?"

"Heading out of town. On a trace. If we can find who I'm looking for, we'll have a chance to win Savannah's team to our side."

"Price is with you?"

"Yep."

"Good. Stupid to push him away. You're made for each other."

"So he tells me."

"He gets to be right once in a while. Kick him in the ass for me. I'll talk to you later."

She hung up.

"What's wrong?" Price asked as I lowered my phone.

I didn't prevaricate. "Pull over, first. It's not good news and it's safer for all of us if you're outside when you hear it."

He gave me a sidelong glance to see if I was serious. When he saw that I was, his mouth tightened, grooves digging deep around his lips. He slowed and jerked over onto the shoulder, shutting off the engine and hitting the parking break.

I launched myself out of the door and went around to the front. He met me. Arnow got out and stood behind me. I got right to the point.

"Cass thinks Vernon's the one who tampered with your brother's mind for Tyrell," I said baldly. "If that's true, then Vernon works for Tyrell."

Price didn't react as I'd expected. He remained stoically calm. "What makes her think Vernon did it? That doesn't match Gregg's memory."

"She said that it feels like what Vernon did to me. She said there's so much raw damage that she can't be sure right now. She wants to go in again to see if she can find out more."

Price was silent as he absorbed that. Abruptly he walked away, crossing the road. I wanted to follow, but I wanted to give him a chance to collect himself, too. I waited.

"What's your father's game?" Arnow said, coming to stand beside me.

The air started to churn, picking at my hair and biting through my jeans. Price stood stiffly, looking out over serried ridges painted pink and orange in the dawn light.

"I have no idea."

"If he's working for Tyrell, then why is he supplying resources to help Touray fight against their boss?"

"That's the question. Maybe he's like Touray. Maybe he doesn't like working for Tyrell and is plotting a way out." I couldn't believe it was as simple as that. Not with Vernon.

I kept my eyes on Price. He stood like a statue, but all around us the trees started to toss and moan as an angry wind swept through their crowns. On the ground, powdery snow skirled and danced over the road.

"Is he going to be okay?" Arnow asked.

"You mean, is he going to lose control and kill us? Maybe." I climbed up on the hood of the Wrangler and sat with my legs dangling over the front. The heat from the engine warmed me.

"Comforting." Arnow climbed up beside me. "Did you bring popcorn?"

I almost choked and swiveled to look at her. "Was that an actual joke? Did you rupture anything? Should we call for an ambulance? Hit you with a defibrillator? Oh, tell me I can hook you up and shock you. Please, Mom? I'll be super good and I won't ask for anything next Christmas. I promise." I held three fingers up in a Scout promise sign.

She slanted me a disgusted look. "One day someone is going to wrap your face in duct tape."

"You just can't handle the truth."

"I'm not sure you've ever met the truth."

I opened my eyes innocently. "Of course I have. We're friends with benefits."

That broke her. She snorted and smiled.

I bumped my shoulder into hers in odd camaraderie and turned to watch Price again.

The truth was, I wasn't worried. He wasn't going to let us get hurt. His control had been growing, and like me, he was too stubborn to risk hurting people he cared about.

The wind intensified, the eye we sat inside shrinking. Snow, rocks, and other debris spun up off the ground, turning the walls of the tornado murky. I remembered I needed to send Cass Taylor's cell number and did so. I wanted to text Taylor myself, but she didn't need me bugging her. She had her hands full.

"Do you think they can do it?" I asked Arnow. "Take Savannah's compound, I mean."

"Chances are good. Your null cuts the odds of failing quite a lot and then the Seedy Seven"—her mouth curved on the name—"they don't want anybody else taking over. At least a few of them wouldn't mind taking the throne themselves. The first step in that plan would be to take the compound, so no matter what, helping take the compound works in their favor."

I nodded. "That's what I thought."

"What are you going to do when they turn on you?"

"Convince them it's in their best interests not to," I said.

"How are you going to do that?"

"I'll let you know as soon as I figure it out."

"Comforting," Arnow said again, a little less acidly than the first time.

"One thing at a time."

"Try not to get a bullet in your head before you sort it out."

"Working on it."

I shivered. The air around us was still, but even so, the temperature hung around zero, and the warmth from the Jeep's engine was quickly fading.

"How long do you think he'll keep this up?" Arnow pulled the hood of her coat up over the black knit cap on her head.

Since there was no polite answer to that, I held my tongue like a grown-up. It hurt me deeply, but I did it.

All of a sudden, my ears popped and the air twisted. In the blink of an eye, the bottom edge of the tornado lifted up, drawing up into a spinning disk far above. Bits of things pelted us. Branches cracked and evergreen needles filled the air like darts. Arnow and I pulled the edges of our hoods together to protect our faces. It wasn't necessary. A solid wall of nothing drew around us. The flying debris crashed against it and dropped to the ground.

"Neat trick," Arnow said.

"Told you," I said, pride for Price resonating through my entire body.

"No, you didn't."

"Sure I did. You just can't remember. You should see someone about that. Inexplicable memory loss. Maybe you've got Alzheimer's."

"I swear I'm going to start carrying duct tape."

I watched the wind above us. It was a giant pulsing saucer whirling in place. As I watched, it condensed, growing denser and darker as the debris bunched tighter.

It had shrunk to maybe thirty or forty feet in diameter when all of a sudden it took off like a flying saucer. It streaked away across the distance. I stood up on the hood, watching as it cut a swathe through the tops of trees and then hit the side of a mountain. There was a kind of explosion as trees flattened in an imitation of a crop circle.

Abruptly the shell of protection surrounding Arnow and me dissolved. I looked down at her. "I guess that's it."

I jumped down to the ground, and she slid off the hood to stand beside me. Price continued to stare at the destruction for a long moment, then he turned around and strode purposefully back to us. That neutral badass mask had slid back down over his face. His eyes burned with laser intensity. He'd found control, not calm. Again, pride for him flared inside my chest.

He came to a halt in front of us. "Let's go."

I nodded. "Won't take us long to get back to the city."

"We aren't going back," he said.

"We aren't?"

He shook his head. "No."

"I've got to admit, that's not the response I expected," Arnow said. She eyed the destruction he'd wrought.

"Get in the car. We're wasting time."

Price climbed into the driver's seat, and we got in.

"Are you sure about this?" I asked as he started the Jeep and put it in gear.

"Hundred percent," he said as he pulled out on the road, checking his mirrors as he did.

"Could you explain it to me? I'm confused."

He blew out a tense breath. "Vernon and Tyrell both have their hooks in Gregg. Going back is only going to reveal that we know what they've done. The best thing for Gregg, for all of us, is to do exactly what we're doing. Establish a power base to protect ourselves from whatever they come up with next. We do it fast enough, we can pull Gregg and his organization in before Vernon and

Tyrell can do anything worse to him."

He made sense. But it had to be gutting him to know his brother was being manipulated and used while he was standing by doing nothing. If it were me, I'd be crawling up walls. It was the right choice, but that didn't make it easier.

"It's the smartest thing to do," Arnow said, and there was a gentle note to her voice.

Was that sympathy? From the ice queen? The apocalypse must be happening.

"Glad you approve," Price said sardonically.

"So we have to assume whatever Touray knows, Vernon and Tyrell know, too," I said, thinking out loud. "Which means they know we are going after Savannah's organization. What are they likely to do about it?"

"Laugh their asses off," Arnow said. "They probably think we're puny minnows and they are sharks and they won't do a damned thing beyond what they were already planning to do."

"I agree," Price said.

I did, too. "Why do you think Diamond City is so important to them all of a sudden?" I wondered.

"Good question," Arnow said. "I'd like to know that, too."

"Let's worry about the hostages," Price said. "That's our job right now."

I could tell he didn't want to talk about Touray anymore. I took his hand in mind, holding it tightly. I couldn't fix things, but at least we were in this together.

Chapter 23

Gregg

GREGG POURED HIMSELF coffee and dove into his breakfast. A stack of papers sat on the table beside him. On the other side were two tablets. The one Tyrell had given him, and his own. He shoved Tyrell's out of the way and started scanning reports.

He was performing triage. During his absence, his three senior lieutenants had stepped up to run things. He needed to finish getting himself up to speed on current activities. Taking over Savannah's organization not only meant getting control of her territories and businesses, but he had to absorb them quickly. It would lessen the chance of rebellion from those who might want to resist if he took the uncertainty out of the merger by stabilizing their day-to-day routine.

He was also curious to find out if Dimitriou, Castillo, and Kinsey had started laying foundations to stage a coup. He wouldn't blame them. Without knowing if he'd ever come back, they'd have been smart to make plans. All three had welcomed him back with open arms, which either meant any thoughts of taking over depended on him not returning, or they weren't ready to make a move yet. Taking over Savannah's organization would give them more power and more rewards, which would soothe them, at least for a while. Plus they deserved it for keeping things running in his absence.

At seven, he gathered his things and retreated to his office. Randall and Bruno followed him. He glared at them.

"I'm in my own house. You can back off."

"No, sir," Randall said. "We protect you wherever you go, at home and abroad."

"What do you think is going to happen to me here?"

"Knife between the ribs," suggested Bruno.

"Is that something you think could happen or something you hope for?"

They didn't respond. Annoyed with their hovering, Gregg travelled to his office. The doors were locked, the room sealed against eavesdropping or other spying.

He sat at his desk and reached for his phone. He tapped in a number and waited. After two rings, the other end picked up. A woman spoke, her voice smoothly professional.

"What can I do for you?"

"I want to put a contract out on Alexander Dimitriou, Liv Castillo, and Mark Kinsey."

"Of course. Specifics?"

"Should be public and should look intentional. Two hundred grand apiece, completed by Tuesday. Ten grand bonus for every day earlier than that. I'll fax pictures."

"Very good. Do you have specific hitters in mind?"

"Open contract."

"Yes, sir."

"You can handle demonstration of performance." Not that smart people crossed assassins by claiming kills that they didn't make. It happened occasionally, but those people didn't survive long.

"As you wish. We will need a deposit of full payment funds plus our service fee before we make any assignments."

"You'll have it within the hour."

"Very good. Always a pleasure."

The Operator hung up. Gregg fired up his computer and made the transfer, including the maximum bonus money. The unused portion would be refunded or banked against future jobs.

He sat back in his chair, staring up at the ceiling, considering, then went back to his computer. A couple of minutes later, he reached for the phone again. The Operator picked up after two rings.

"What can I do for you?"

"I have another job. Five hundred thousand. Forty-eight-hour clock. Open contract, you handle proof of performance."

"Target's name?"

"Cassandra Dix."

A slight pause on the other end. Gregg smiled. It wasn't easy to take the Operator off guard.

"We will need a deposit of full payment funds plus our service fee before we make any assignments," she said, recovering.

"I've already sent it."

He hung up. It was really too bad to lose such a valuable tool, but Cass was too dangerous to tolerate. He didn't need her now, anyway. Not with Vernon on his side.

Dismissing all thought of Cass, he went back to work.

Chapter 24

Riley

"YOU SHOULD SLEEP," Price told me after glancing over his shoulder at the slumbering Arnow.

"I don't want to miss it if the trace lines change direction." Not that I could sleep anyhow. I couldn't stop thinking about Touray, about the invasion going on back at Savannah's, and about what Vernon might be up to. How did I fit into it?

"I need to talk to my mom."

"Now?"

"You know, if I followed one of the hostage's trace through the spirit world, I could find out where they are and come back. Wrapping myself in null magic at the diner seems to have fixed me. I can totally handle it."

He started shaking his head before I got halfway through. "Too dangerous. You don't know what you'd be walking into. If you got caught, we wouldn't be able to find you or them."

He spoke like he wouldn't go nuts if I went off by myself into danger. Impressive. I'm not sure I'd manage any level of calmness at the prospect of him in the same situation.

"You've thought about this." Of course he had. He had a cop brain.

"I knew it would occur to you sooner or later, especially now that you're back to having functional magic. I was planning to make you take me with you if I couldn't reason with you."

I was willing to put it on the back burner. For now. "Consider me reasonable."

"I don't know if that's scientifically possible."

"Probably not. But I agree. It would be stupid to try it without a compelling need."

"Hallelujah. She isn't as dumb as she acts," came a sleepy voice from the back seat.

Arnow sat up and looked out the windows. "Where are we?"

"Thirty miles east of Glenwood Springs," said Price.

"Denver is looking more likely," she said. "Makes sense, since that's where we were investigating the murders."

I turned to look at her. The side of her face had a red mark where she'd propped it against the seat. Strands of ash-blond hair had pulled loose from her ponytail and haloed around her face. She wasn't wearing makeup. She almost looked like a real girl.

"What?" she demanded when I kept looking at her.

"Almost didn't recognize you for a minute. Is that dried drool on your chin?"

She rubbed the spot before she could stop herself, then glared at me. "Mind your own business."

"Turns out you are my business. Seems like God really does have a sense of humor. Something I've been meaning to ask you. Why didn't you know about the hostages? What were you to Savannah, anyway? Because you sure know a lot of things for someone low on the totem pole, and you know too little for someone higher up."

She looked out the window a long moment, considering, then turned back to me. "Like I told you, Savannah bought me when I was around seven. She had a stable of nearly three dozen girls, ranging from young ones like me, all the way to eighteen. She had a private school on the compound that we attended, as well as an extracurricular school, I guess you'd call it. If you failed to carry high scores in either, you were sent away. We never heard from those girls again.

"We were raised in luxury. On top of the usual school subjects, we were taught to be genteel, to walk and speak correctly, to dance, to appreciate wine and exotic foods, and to do all the things a debutante might be called upon to do. When we turned fourteen, we began lessons on how to be a woman, how to please lovers of both sexes, how to seduce and charm. We were also taught how to remember information exactly.

"Savannah would have parties where we served food and drinks and mingled, and if a guest selected us, we would entertain them privately. Once we reached eighteen, we were sent to college at an Ivy League school. Like before, good grades were mandatory. After college, we returned to act as hostesses at the weekly parties where we would seduce targets and wriggle information out of them through whatever means necessary. Some of us were assigned to begin long-term affairs with particular targets."

Hearing about her life made me want to throw up. "Savannah was an evil bitch."

"Yes, she was," Arnow agreed, looking out the window again. "I was part of her after-college stable for couple of years. Then one day she decided I needed to join the FBI and be her eyes inside. She made sure I got accepted into Quantico and that's when I began my double life."

She paused. "I liked being an agent. It was hard to juggle Savannah's demands, but I managed to keep my connection to her quiet in the Bureau. If I hadn't, she'd have yanked me back to party duty."

The bitter expression on her face showed just how much she'd hated that idea.

"Why didn't you leave? Quit working for her?"

She gave a harsh laugh. "I liked breathing."

"She was a real prize, wasn't she?" I said, then a memory triggered. "That's one of the places you knew Touray from, wasn't it? Her parties. You *entertained* him." My gaze zeroed in on Price. "Did you go to them?"

His lip curled. "A couple of times. I didn't like them and I wasn't interested in the . . . amenities." He glanced in his rearview. "I didn't know the . . . staff . . . was unwilling."

"Not everyone was. Savannah paid well and provided luxurious living with a monstrous allowance. For a lot of us, that made it worth it."

"But you and Touray . . ."

Thinking about Touray and Arnow in bed was surreal. I couldn't imagine it.

"He was better than most," Arnow said with a shrug, but her voice betrayed anger and resentment. "He would give me information for Savannah and I'd give him what she wanted him to know. It was a game."

"I'd rather play Russian roulette," I muttered.

"At least he didn't get off on rape fantasies," Arnow said, but I'm not sure she knew she'd said it aloud. She'd turned inward, caught up in memories I was sure would give me nightmares.

"Someone should have put that bitch down years ago," Price growled with another look in the rearview.

"Amen to that," I said.

Arnow blinked and turned her focus back to me. "If I could have, I would have. Ending her is one good deed you can chalk up to your father."

I snorted. "It was just a snake killing a scorpion. He's no better."

"Maybe," Arnow said, sounding doubtful. "Savannah was pure evil, on par with the devil himself."

"My father might just be the devil."

"Then let's make sure the two of them spend eternity in hell together."

We exchanged a look of perfect accord. Both of us had suffered betrayal, torture, and threats of death from one of our parents. I had a feeling that little Arnow had looked to Savannah like a mother only to find out she was Lady Macbeth.

She seemed to read my mind, folding her arms and giving me a disparaging look. "Don't think this makes us BFFs."

"Only in my nightmares," I said. "The really bad ones."

A COUPLE HOURS later we pulled into the suburbs of Denver. We'd stopped to gas up once and fuel ourselves with energy drinks, chocolate, and jerky. Well, I did. Arnow eyed my bounty disdainfully and grabbed coffee, trail mix, and a little bottle of orange juice. Price followed my example with the energy drink, but went for a sandwich out of the fridge.

"You know that's probably crawling with salmonella," I said as we stood in line.

"I'll risk it."

"Suit yourself, but I am so going to tell you I told you so when you're puking on the side of the road."

He bent and kissed me, probably to shut me up. He didn't lift his head until the pimple-faced cashier cleared his throat.

"You want to buy those?"

Price handed him all our items, including Arnow's. "Pump five, too."

"You know that you just sent me the wrong message, don't you? I mean, if you wanted me to stop. Kissing me is more reward than deterrent."

"Duct tape," Arnow advised Price as he chuckled. "Buy it by the pallet. You'll need it."

I was feeling jittery by the time we came down into Denver. I shouldn't have topped my Red Bull off with a 5-Hour Energy bottle. At least I was awake.

We still hadn't heard anything from Taylor. I wasn't sure when we would. But then, I didn't know when they'd have started their attack, and I didn't know how long it would take to secure the compound, and then find the information we were looking for. Realistically, it could take days.

We didn't have days.

"Where to now?" Price asked.

I considered the trace trails from the bloody balls. Those of the seven hostages hadn't been nulled and flowed away in steady lines. The trace of Arnow's three contractors was more difficult to read, but seemed to follow the same path. I just hoped the trail ended near Denver and we weren't heading for the East Coast.

"Keep following the freeway."

I turned to Arnow. "Tell us about the killer you were tracking. Why were you off the books with it? How is he connected to Savannah?"

She unbuckled her seat belt and sat forward. "The FBI circulates reports from offices across the state about current cases. Mostly to keep everybody updated on the existence of other investigations in case something we're working on overlaps. Mutual cooperation sort of thing.

"A little over ten months ago, a series of killings started up along the east side of the range in Denver, Boulder, Fort Collins, Pueblo, and so on. Bodies were discovered in groups of three. In every case, the killer transplanted bits of each person onto another. It started with small things—patches of skin, fingers, toes, eyes, and ears. It didn't take long before he started getting more extreme—whole limbs, organs, everything. Within a couple of months, he upped the ante again. He'd perform the transplants, and after, he dismantled his victims with precise butchery. He'd lay out the parts of all three bodies in single circles, always in the exact same order. In the last warehouse where he captured three of my squad, we found nine circles."

I frowned. "There hasn't been any news about that."

"That's because the FBI's work hard to keep it under wraps. Even after we stopped investigating."

"Stopped investigating?" Price tossed a startled look over his shoulder.

Arnow took a harsh breath, her shoulders tense. "Every agent in the state was on the lookout for something that might point to the killer. Forensics had found no DNA, no fingerprints, nothing. Then all of a sudden, the investigation shut down. Anybody who asked questions got shipped out to Timbuktu. All references and files got erased off the computers. Giant cone of silence."

"Why?"

Arnow snorted at me. "Because someone with a lot of power and money decided to make it happen."

"The Consortium," Price murmured.

"I thought so."

The Consortium was a kind of mega power Tyet that operated deep below the radar. I hadn't known they existed until Arnow revealed them to me. I frowned. "Thought so? Past tense?"

Arnow got a look on her face I couldn't interpret, but didn't answer. "I'd kept copies of everything I could get before the case got shut down, and followed the local investigations as well as I could. They kept a pretty tight lid on things and it seemed to me their digging was shallow. I caught a break when four months ago, he started leaving messages."

"Messages?" Price repeated. "What kind?"

"They looked like demented screeds. He'd leave pages covered with them, or scrawl them on walls and floors. Whatever was handy."

"What did they say?" I asked.

"I've only seen three. But he's obsessed with the Holy Mother, that he'd failed her and she'd turned her face away from him. He was going to earn back the Holy Mother's blessing. He babbles about the ascent of man in heaven, of the gifts bestowed by the High One on the chosen people, and how he planned to bring the High One's blessings to all."

"And the High One is God?" I asked.

She hesitated. "Could be."

"You don't think so?" Price asked.

Again Arnow didn't answer; instead, she changed the subject, much to my aggravation. I told myself to be patient. She must be getting to a point.

"Savannah didn't just keep a stable of girls. She kept boys, too. They learned a lot of the same skills we did. There was one who seemed to be a particular favorite of hers. Matthew was older than me—fourteen or fifteen when I got there. Like all the other boys, he was handsome as all hell.

"Savannah used to take him on special trips. We never knew where. He worshipped the ground she walked on. He was her golden boy. He looked the part, too. Blond, tanned, muscular. Smart, too. She sent him off to college like everybody else. He came back right before I left for Vassar, but something was different. He'd changed. He'd hardened.

"During college, I'd come back for summers and have to work the parties. The second year he and I hooked up on the sly. That lasted to the beginning of August, when we got found out. Savannah was furious. She sent me back to school. I never saw Matthew again. I thought maybe she'd killed him." Her voice faded. She looked out the window, swallowing hard.

The memory was clearly painful, and part of me wanted to reach out to her. The rest of me told me if I did, she'd chop off my hand. I kept both of them in my lap.

After a minute, she continued. "I had such a crush on him. He made me feel—special. Like I mattered. He was confident and funny and always breaking the rules and getting away with it. He had a habit of sneaking into where he didn't belong. He'd always leave something behind to prove he'd been there, like a secret signature.

"Sometimes he'd carve it, sometimes he'd write it with a Sharpie marker. It looked like three wide *X*s sitting sideways on top of each other."

"Like the *XXX* for porn?"

She nodded. "Only tipped sideways."

She fell silent. I made myself wait a whole minute before I prompted her again.

"What about the killer?"

She sighed, looking upward and blinking, like she fought back tears. "That was his signature. The killer. He signed the screeds with it. He wrote it on the bodies. When I saw it, I knew it had to be Matthew, and he had to be working for Savannah, but I had no idea why or how she could be connected to the Consortium." Arnow paused. "I hated her more than you can begin to imagine. I've spent every day of my professional life trying to figure out how to bring her down. *I* wanted to be the one to kill her."

"If it makes you feel any better, you can kill my father," I offered.

Price snorted, then looked at Arnow in the mirror. "So that's when you decided to hunt him down?"

"He needed to be stopped and nobody but me had any real idea of who he might be or his connection to Savannah, and she or someone else had clearly managed to short circuit the investigation." Arnow rubbed her fingers over her lips. They trembled. "If Matthew's discovered that she's dead, who knows what he'll do to the hostages. The nature of the murders says he's unhinged. And then there's my people. What's he doing to them?"

"They're alive." That much I could tell from looking at their trace. I hadn't tried to get an emotional read on them. There wasn't much point to knowing without being able to be right there to help.

Arnow's lips twisted in an attempt at a smile. "Alive. But in what condition? And for how long?"

Since I had no good answer for that, I circled back to the big questions. "Why would Savannah want him to kill those people? And what's up with all the religious stuff?"

"I've wondered if the Holy Mother and the High One referred to Savannah."

"I can buy one, but both?" Price asked.

"Unless there's another player we don't know about."

Neither Price nor I responded. There could very well be another hundred players we didn't know about.

"If Savannah was behind the murders, she had a reason," Price said. "Savannah was nothing if not ambitious and she didn't let much get in the way of her goals."

"*If?*" Arnow laughed. "Nobody gets away from Savannah. He's working for her or he'd be dead."

"When were you going to tell me about him?" I asked.

"You didn't need to know. All you had to do was find them. I'd take care of the rest."

Arnow clearly had a personal stake in this guy. Maybe she thought she could save him.

"It's not your fault," Price said.

Arnow threw herself back on her seat. "What's not my fault?"

"The killings."

She scoffed. "Of course they aren't. I had nothing to do with them."

Price didn't let it go. "You're blaming yourself for getting caught with him way back when. You're thinking Savannah punished him by turning him into a killer, and that it broke him."

"Fuck off."

"You don't deny it."

She rubbed her hands over her face and scraped her fingers over her scalp. "The guy I knew couldn't torture people this way. She did something to him. Twisted him somehow. This isn't his fault."

"It's not your fault, either," I said.

She gave me an unconvinced look, but didn't say anything.

"Is there anything else we need to know?" Price asked finally.

"Nothing concrete."

He looked at her in the rearview. "But you've got a theory."

"I'm pretty sure he uses a mix of talented and untalented people in every murder. Usually the one who gets the Frankenstein body replacements is the normie. They found evidence of Sparkle Dust on his most recent victims."

"So what's he trying to do?"

Just the mention of SD made me cringe. Instantly addictive, it allowed people to experience a magical talent for the first time, or if the user already had a talent, a new one. With continued use—and everybody continued—the stuff turned you into a wraith. Your body faded from the outside in until you died. Almost no one came back from using it. No one that I knew of at all, except me and Taylor, who'd been force-fed the stuff.

Then there was Josh, Taylor's ex-fiancée. Like us, his kidnappers had forced him to take it. Unlike us, he'd ingested a lot more SD. Cass and Maya had done all they could to cure him, but I hadn't seen him since the night we'd rescued him. The night he'd tried to kill me. Who knew if he'd managed to keep off the stuff?

"I have no idea what Matthew's doing or why," Arnow said. "Is this some sort of twisted religious ceremony? Maybe satanic? Or something Savannah ordered him to do?"

"Do you have any pictures?" Price asked.

Arnow dug in her pocket and brought out her cell. She brought up her photo gallery and passed it up to me. I held the phone so Price could see and thumbed through them. There were only a few, and each one worse than the last. I had to look away after the first couple or I'd have been spewing the contents of my stomach all over the car.

"Anything you've seen before?" Arnow asked.

Price shook his head as he changed lanes. "That's all you've got?"

"When the investigation was live, the SAC didn't share pictures. He didn't want those getting into the papers. I got these from the local LEOs before they buttoned up."

"Fucking politics," Price said with a knowing shake of his head.

"You know better than anyone that corruption in law enforcement is high and you never know who you can trust," Arnow said in a resigned voice. "We both were dirty. I still am."

"Sounds like you haven't had much choice," I said. I have no idea why I wanted to comfort her.

"We all have choices," she replied.

WE FELL QUIET for a few miles.

"Better start going more south," I said as the trace bent a little more sharply. That was positive news. The closer we got, the quicker we got off target. "South and east."

"Valley Highway is close," Arnow said.

Price took the off-ramp. We passed through a few miles of industrial ware-houses before the vista returned to businesses and houses. The recent snow made everything appear fresh and sparkling clean beneath the brilliant sun.

Half an hour later, we hit a traffic jam, and I started twitching in my seat. Price reached over and laced his fingers through mine, but didn't offer any reassurance. There wasn't any. Every second that ticked by was a second the hostages and kidnapped agents didn't have. Not real agents. Vigilantes. Bounty hunters. Arnow paid them with any money they found doing the job, and they collected any available rewards. I had a feeling she dipped into her savings to pay them, too. My guess is she had a healthy bank account, working for Savannah. Especially given the designer labels on her clothing.

It really sucked to find out that under her ice-and-steel exterior, the iron maiden had a gooey center. Or at least a little warm blood and something resembling a heart. Made me start questioning my opinions of other people, like Dalton.

We inched along for nearly forty-five minutes. An accident between a car and a pickup had closed two lanes. A pair of tow trucks were hooking up the crumpled vehicles by the time we passed by. A half dozen police cars and two fire trucks completed the scene.

After that, we sped up a little, but still drove well under the speed limit. I pulled out my phone and texted Taylor a one-word question: *Update?*

I stared at the screen but no immediate reply was forthcoming. Gritting my teeth, I dropped my phone in my lap and tapped impatient fingers on the arm of the door.

Every few miles I checked the trace to see if we were still on track.

"We need to go more east," I said after we started passing the Denver Tech Center. "The angle of the trace is shrinking."

Price nodded and started heading for the next exit, which was East Orchard Road. We drove past clumps of shops and a Starbucks, and into a vast land-scape of cookie-cutter neighborhoods. Eventually we dead-ended into a broad swathe of open fields. On the other side, far in the distance, the march of houses resumed.

"Which way?"

"Straight," I said.

"South, it is," he said and turned parallel to the field.

"Do you recognize the area?" I asked Arnow, who leaned between the seats to see better.

"Vaguely, but mostly from the maps. It's Cherry Creek State Park. They're close, right? Any idea how far away they might be?"

I gave a little shrug.

"But they're here in Denver somewhere?"

Arnow's sound of frustration made me take pity on her. She was on edge, and I actually sympathized with her. Maybe because she wasn't acting like her usual ice-bitch self. Maybe it was because I'd started not hating her.

"It doesn't work that way. There's no way to tell how far away anybody is. I have to follow until I find them."

"Fucking useless," she muttered, flinging herself back on her seat.

Aaaand there she was again, the Agent Ice Bitch.

Almost immediately she popped forward again. "What happens when you're tracing someone who gets in a car or a train or an airplane. Or goes overseas? Or travels?"

"The trace is still there. It's like a ribbon following their track. It settles down onto the ground, no matter how high up in the air they are when they leave it or whether they cross water or quicksand or whatever. Travelling works pretty much the same way, the trace falling into the real world once the person exits from dreamspace. It can take awhile to settle, but eventually I can follow."

"How long is awhile?"

I just shrugged. I had no idea.

She made a disgruntled sound.

"So what you're saying is, we'd better find them before they are travelled away, or it'll take you awhile to find them, and also they might not be in Denver."

"He's close. Otherwise the angles of the trace wouldn't be narrowing. And I doubt he's going anywhere. He's got a place to hole up and he knows the area," I said by way of offering comfort.

"Unless he got bored or drunk or some voice in his head told him to get the hell out of Dodge."

"We know if he has the hostages—and given the ping-pong balls, I'm leaning toward believing he does—then he'd have to move at least ten people," Price mused. "Which wouldn't be easy to pull off. My bet is Savannah sent travellers whenever she wanted the hostages back in Diamond City. It's not likely he could just order them up himself, which means he'd have to use ordinary transportation to move his captives. That means leaving a trace for Riley to follow now rather than later."

Price made sense, and Arnow nodded. None of us speculated on what Matthew might do to his captives when he learned of Savannah's death.

Every mile wound my stomach up tighter. Between worrying about what was happening in Diamond City and what we might find at the end of our journey, I thought my head might pop off.

"Next time, fewer energy drinks," Price said, glancing at me as I squirmed and fidgeted, checking my phone for texts every ten seconds.

"What do you think is happening back in the city?"

"I think that they are doing their jobs and that they're too busy to report in," he said, so calmly I wanted to kick him.

"Or they're all dead."

"Nobody's dead."

"And you know that because?"

"Your family is too stubborn and obnoxious to be dead, and even if they decided to start throwing themselves on bombs, Savannah's Seedy Seven would stop them. They aren't going to let anything happen to your family until you find the hostages and bring them home. Anyway, you know you've been checking their trace."

His quiet composure and the fact he was right annoyed me to no end. "So you're telling me to relax."

"We're about to beard a serial killer in his den. I don't think relaxation is on the menu."

"So which is it? Take a chill pill and relax? Or go to DEFCON 5 and prepare for war?"

"How about shut up and let the man drive already?" Arnow groused from the back. "Better yet, Price, let's stop at a hardware store and get some duct tape."

I twisted to look at her. "Remind me again why we brought you with us?"

"Apparently you needed a babysitter."

"One of these days I am so going to kick your ass," I grumbled.

"You can try, little girl. Keep your insurance up-to-date."

"What do I need insurance for? I have Dalton and his bottomless box of heal-alls."

"He knows how damage-prone you are."

"He's not the only one," Price said. "I've got a box of them in the back. Thinking of buying stock in a heal-all factory."

I stared. "You, too?"

"You're surprised? Do you want to count how many times you've been mangled, maimed, shot, or otherwise wounded since we met?"

"You haven't exactly been Mister Healthy, either."

"Exactly. So we're prepared for the inevitable."

His fast agreement only slightly mollified me, but since he conceded the point, I was forced to shut up.

We passed a new housing development near the Aurora Reservoir, and then civilization ended. Ahead were the vast eastern plains of Colorado.

"Still east," I said before anybody could ask.

Price checked the GPS. "County Line Road is a little south of here. We can take that or go back north until we hit Highway 70 again. About halfway to Kansas, it drops down lower than this and heads due west. It's a better road and plowed. County Line is going to be a lot slower going." He looked at me. "Which do you want?"

"County Line," I said without any hesitation.

I waited for one of them to question my reasons, but both remained silent. Price put the Jeep in gear and turned. As he did, the angle of the trace widened. "They're close," I said.

"How do you know?"

"How close?"

Arnow and Price spoke simultaneously.

"Triangulation and I'm not sure. I'd guess no more than twenty to fifty miles."

"Triangulation?" Arnow asked, leaning up between the front seats again. "What do you mean?"

She actually sounded interested instead of combative.

"Draw a line in the direction of the trace from where we turned. Now draw another line from where we are right now to where the trace goes. Wherever they cross is where Matthew is holding the hostages. The fact that the angle is widening pretty quick as we drive means that the two imaginary lines intersect nearer to us rather than farther. Does that make sense?"

She nodded, looking pleased. "It does. And here I thought you were just a talented idiot."

"I've got hidden depths."

"Maybe you shouldn't hide them quite so well," she suggested.

"Maybe you should kiss my ass."

"If we find my people alive, I just might." Her voice darkened, the humor evaporating. She glanced out over the treeless expanse of white washing away from us. "It won't be easy sneaking up on him."

"The terrain isn't as flat as it looks," Price said. "There are a lot of hills and gullies. Most people out here build their houses down lower to stay out of the wind."

"And if he's on top of a hill with a clear line of sight for miles?"

"Then I'll blow us up a snow screen and he'll never see us coming," Price said.

"Can you?" I asked. "I mean, can you do it without causing a full-on blizzard or ripping his hideout to bits?"

He nodded. "Pretty sure."

"It's only been what—two or three days since you flattened the safe house."

"You destroyed the cabin?" Arnow asked. She looked at me. "Do your brothers know?"

I couldn't remember if I'd told them or not. "Given the situation, they'll understand."

"Sure. Whatever lets you sleep at night. If I were you, I'd be looking out for payback."

She was right, but they were family, so I made a token effort to defend them. "How would you know? You barely know them."

"I know them well enough. They may not be particularly upset, but honor will require vengeance of some kind. Probably with a dose of humiliation mixed in."

She actually did know them pretty well.

Price groaned. "I can hardly wait."

"We'll keep them too distracted," I said.

"You do that," Arnow said with a grin. "I'll ask them to let me be a witness. It'll be fun."

"You are not nice."

She snorted. "Like that's news."

We turned onto County Line Road. The first few miles were relatively clear, then they turned rough. Snow had melted and frozen in ruts, and then more snow had fallen. Repeat the cycle over a few months of Colorado winter, and our pace slowed to a crawl.

"I could walk faster than this," Arnow complained after twenty minutes with a top speed of just under thirty, though we only hit that maybe twice. The rest of the time we crawled along at around ten or fifteen.

"Feel free," I said, but I wasn't paying that much attention to her.

A few more miles along, and the line of trace straightened to due north. "This is it," I said. "We need to turn left as soon as possible."

Price stopped the Jeep, and we looked out. I couldn't see any roads crossing the broad fields rolling away on the left side of the road.

"I don't suppose you've got a couple of snowmobiles in the back with the heal-alls," I said. "Or maybe some snowshoes?"

"Afraid not. I've got chains, though. Plus kitty litter, salt, and a shovel. We should be able to handle a cross-country drive, if we're careful."

He tapped on his GPS. "I don't see any paved roads. There are probably dirt access roads. We just have to find one."

He put the Jeep in gear again. Not much farther, we came up on a set of mailboxes on the right. On the left side was a promising possibility. The gravel access road looked like it had been plowed at some point, but not for a week or two at least.

We pulled off onto it. Price stopped, and we hopped out to put the chains on. With all three of us, it only took ten minutes to get them hooked into place, and then we started off again.

The trace lines leaned a little to the west now. We'd overshot, but not by much. We had to be within a mile or two if my mental geometry was correct, and it usually was.

I started fidgeting again as we jounced along. I kept trying to sort out plans, discarding them all. I didn't have enough information to plan a birthday party, much less take on a serial killer.

We'd been driving up and down rolling hills. We came to a split in the road, and Price eased left and drove up a long rise. As we topped it, a ranch yard nestled against the hills below came into view. Split rail fences surrounded twenty acres or so. Inside the fence perimeter were corrals, barns, three giant loafing sheds, and on the northern end, a white-trimmed blue two-story farm house big enough to hold a family of forty.

"That's it," I said.

Price put the Jeep in reverse and rolled back down the rise until we couldn't see the ranch yard anymore. We retraced our way up the hill on foot and ducked down behind some snow-covered scrub bushes and rocks to get a better look.

There was little sign of habitation. A thin stream of smoke rose from one of the house chimneys. Several herds of cows and horses huddled together under the big three-sided loafing sheds. A couple of pickups were parked near one of two massive steel pole barns, but I didn't see any sign of actual people.

"How are we going to get close?" I asked.

"Can you pinpoint where they are?" Price asked.

I focused my trace sight. "They're either in the house or the white barn by the trees." I pointed. "I can't get more specific until we get closer."

"There's no good cover for an approach," Arnow said. "Especially if he's got cameras or alarms set up, which he will, along with a range of other security. Savannah was nothing if not careful."

"We could knock on the front door," I said jokingly.

I was about bowled over when Price nodded. "Might be our best shot."

"Seriously?" Arnow looked both outraged and thoughtful. Like a startled chicken that couldn't decide which direction it wanted to run. I kind of felt the same way.

"If he lets us in, then we bypass security," Price said.

"We also lose the element of surprise," I said.

"The question is, how do we get in otherwise?" Arnow asked.

"I can take down the null fields, which should overwhelm any binders—the same as at the diner. If you blew up a little storm, we could walk right in."

"If he doesn't have other booby traps. He's bound to be at least a little paranoid," Price said.

"We'll have to deal with those as we find them," Arnow replied.

"Maybe we should split up." I looked at Price, who was already shaking his head. "What do you think?"

"This is really a piss-poor way of running a Tyet," Arnow declared before Price could speak

I frowned in confusion. "What are you talking about?"

"You're supposed to be in charge. That means you tell people what to do. You don't ask. You don't take refusals. You want to divide up? Then tell this giant jackass to toe the line." She poked Price's chest. "Make it an order, not a request. You'll never survive if you don't start acting like you're the boss."

She was probably right. She was definitely irritating. Like a hedgehog in my underwear.

"Right," I said. "Because everybody knows I know next to nothing about running one, so of course they'll line up to listen to my stupidity as I spew ridiculous orders. What I need to do is ask questions and learn. Are *you* seriously going to let *me* tell *you* what to do?" I looked at Price. "What about you? Do you think I need to be more domineering? Tyrannical like Savannah?"

He fought a smile and lost. "Not that I mind you bossing me around, but it's not your style. You trust people to be smart, loyal, and to give their all. You also know you don't know everything and you listen, even when those people annoy the fuck out of you. Like . . . Dalton," he added with a wink at me and a none-too-subtle jerk of his head at Arnow.

"I saw that," she snapped. "And anyway, you're wrong. You have to be strong to run a Tyet."

"Who said Riley isn't strong? I said she has a different approach and you prefer it. Admit it. You want to have input. You want to be heard, and taken seriously."

"Sure, I do, but that doesn't mean that's the way things ought to run."

"I disagree," I said. "And since I'm in charge, I'll run things the way I want to." I gave her a shit-eating grin, and continued. "What I want is to get in there and rescue the victims before Matthew kills them in the name of whatever twisted gods he's determined to impress. I'd also like all of us to stay alive. I think our best bet is for me to pull down the security nulls, and for Price to spin up a storm to cover our entrance. If we split up, Matthew can only target one of us at a time."

"I don't like us splitting up," Price growled. "You and I will go in together." His sapphire eyes brooked no argument.

Arnow rolled her eyes. "See? You can't run a Tyet by committee. You can't let people step on you and second-guess you all the time."

I didn't pay any attention to her. Arguing with Price would waste time, and I'd still lose. I couldn't blame him. Both of us still felt too raw from the emotional roller coaster of the past few days, not to mention the dangers. Plus, if Price and I really were going to be partners, then I couldn't be the boss. Well, maybe occasionally. I could think of a few situations where being the boss would be a whole lot of fun. I put that fantasy away for later consideration.

"If Price and I went in the front door, we could distract Matthew so that you could slip in the back without him noticing. With any luck, he'll think it's just the two of us."

Arnow made a sound of disgust, but then gave grudging agreement. "That could work."

"Then consider it an order," I said sweetly. "You take the Jeep. Price and I will hike down under the cover of the storm. As soon as he creates the white-out, drive down as close to the house as you can get. He'll keep the road clear for you."

Price made a sound and then shook his head.

"What?"

"You've got a lot of faith in me."

"Of course I do."

He made the sound again as if that was the most ridiculous thing he'd ever heard. I ignored him and spoke to Arnow again.

"Once the security net goes down, we'll follow you as fast as we can. Remember that you're supposed to wait for us before you go inside."

Her brows rose. "Sure."

"Please don't dive headfirst into trouble without backup." Surprisingly, to me anyhow, I didn't want Arnow getting killed.

"Like you always do."

"I've turned over new leaf. I drag my friends and family into trouble with me now," I said, looking haughtily down my nose at her.

She cracked a reluctant grin. "You're such a pain in the ass."

"People say that. Personally, I don't get it. You, on the other hand, really *are* a pain in the ass."

"I do my best," she said.

"You're best is damned good."

"I think so."

"Let's get going," Price said, and went to the back of the Jeep.

He dug in one of the duffel bags in the back and pulled out a couple of rose quartz spheres, handing them to me. After a moment's thought, he got out two more.

"Take these, too. You're likely to need all four."

I put a heal-all in each of my front pants pockets, then zipped the other two into a pocket inside my coat. Price stashed away several others, and passed a couple to Arnow.

"There are more here, so don't be afraid to use them on the wounded. Remember you can activate them and leave them in your pocket. Do it if you get hurt."

"Yes, sir," I said, giving him a little salute.

I already had my .45 in its holster and tucked into my rear waistband. Price had his Glock in a shoulder holster. I didn't know where Arnow's weapon was, but certainly she had at least one.

Price pulled out zipper bag and handed them to Arnow. "Flash bombs," he said. He pulled another case out and passed it to her. "Some other surprises. They're all labeled."

He took out another case and slung it over his shoulder before shutting the rear door. "Let's do this."

Chapter 25

Gregg

"THERE'S TROUBLE at the Morrell compound." Mark Kinsey spoke to Gregg, but also continued to listen intently to the phone held to his ear. "I'll get back to you." The lean man set his phone on the table in front of him.

"The place is under attack. Someone dropped a nuclear null and killed all the security magic, not to mention every other scrap of magic for who knows how far. A small army rushed in. It's likely the attackers belong to Savannah's lieutenants, but a redheaded woman appears to be in charge. Description fits Taylor Hollis." He pointed to a picture of her on the whiteboard, one of many filling the space.

"Not Riley?" Gregg said in genuine surprise.

"No, sir. At least nobody's seen her yet."

"And Clay?"

"No sign of him."

Gregg looked at Vernon, who sat at the other end of the table. Between them the wood surface was littered with papers and photographs.

"We need to move."

Vernon nodded, his brows furrowing. "I'd appreciate if you kept my children alive."

Gregg snorted. "I'm not interested in harming any of them." He looked back at Kinsey. "Make the call."

The other man punched a number into the speakerphone on the table. A moment later Dimitriou and Castillo picked up.

"Status?" Kinsey asked.

"Ready," said Castillo first, followed by Dimitriou.

"Move in," Gregg said. "Try not to kill any members of the Hollis family."

"Yes, sir."

"And your brother?" Kinsey asked.

Gregg grimaced. "I'd prefer him breathing, but do what you've got to do."

"Anything else," Kinsey asked.

"Go get started," Gregg told him.

Kinsey nodded, cutting the connection before departing, casting a frowning look back at Gregg before he closed the door.

Vernon refilled his coffee cup, stopping short of the rim. He topped it off with whiskey before passing the bottle to Gregg, then lifted the cup in salute. "To the hard choices."

Both men drank.

"I didn't think you had it in you," Vernon said, eyeing Gregg over the rim of his cup.

"Didn't have what?"

"The stomach to do what's necessary to get the job done."

Gregg swirled his whiskey-laced coffee in his cup. "I love my brother more than life itself, but I've a responsibility to the people of the city and I can't let personal feelings get in the way of driving the vermin out once and for all."

"Some might say you're one of the vermin."

"Some would be right, but I'm also the only one capable and willing to do the job. Maybe one day someone like me won't be necessary, but that time is not now. Anyway, Clay isn't stupid. He's going to take care of himself and Riley. I'm not worried about him."

"I'd better get going," Vernon said, setting aside his cup and rising.

"What about my new bodyguards out there?"

"I took care of them. They won't cause me any problems."

Gregg frowned. "When?"

"First thing. I don't want Tyrell knowing I'm involved quite yet."

"So it doesn't matter now if they see you?"

Vernon shook his head. "They'll know they've seen me before, and they'll know I'm familiar and a friend, but they'll forget about me as soon as I'm out of sight. Next time they see me, it'll be the same."

"And if they decide to contact Tyrell while they still have eyes on you?"

The corner of Vernon's mouth quirked. "They won't."

A chill ran down Gregg's back. God, but he hated dreamers. They had their uses, but the fact that they could reach through walls and fuck with someone's brain made his blood run cold. He'd made sure he was nulled up tight before Vernon arrived. All the same, he should probably have Cass scan him again sooner rather than later.

Vernon rose. "I look forward to hearing about your success on taking over Morrell's compound. If I might make a suggestion . . . ?"

Gregg nodded.

"You might want to think about putting Riley somewhere safe. For her own good. She's one of a kind. Eventually you will want to find the rest of the Kensington artifacts. She's the only one who can trace down his workshop. I understand this could cause a rift with your brother . . ."

"I told you, personal feelings can't get in the way of saving the city."

Vernon nodded, satisfied. "I'll leave you to it, then," he said and left. In the outer office, an escort waited to guide him out.

Gregg sat a moment, tapping his fingers thoughtfully.

"That went well," he said out loud to no one at all. "We'll need to make sure Brussard doesn't scan you, though. He's very good. One of the best. He could really throw a wrench into my plan. Now, time for you to report to Jackson. He'll be waiting. We don't need him growing suspicious of either of us."

Gregg reached for his phone and dialed.

Chapter 26

Riley

"KISS FOR LUCK?" I asked as Price and I prepared to start our invasion.

"We aren't supposed to need luck."

"We don't. I want you to kiss me."

He frowned. "You don't have some ridiculous idea that you want to kiss me in case you don't make it, do you?"

That busted the mood. "I hadn't thought that, but thanks for putting it in my head. Realistically we are going after a psychopathic serial killer," I said. "One of us could get shot or knifed or something."

A shudder ran through Price, and his expression went taut, his nostril's flaring. A sharp wind picked up, scraping powdery snow into the air. "Don't remind me." He shook himself, twisting to face ranch yard. "Let's get this over with."

"Hey, I'm not going to let this nut job do anything to me," I said, grabbing his arm.

He lifted my hand off his arm and linked his fingers through mine. "You can't promise that, Riley," he said soberly. "Don't pretend you can. We're doing this because we're the only ones who can. I'm here because I don't want to be anywhere but at your side. But don't pretend you're superwoman. You aren't bulletproof, any more than I am, any more than your stepmother Mel was. Death is out there and in this business, we court it every day."

"I know that. But if I remembered it too well, I'd never get out of bed in the morning. Bad things happen. They hurt." I thought of Mel, of the makeshift funeral we'd conducted. Hurt was an understatement of epic proportions. Tears burned my eyes. I swallowed the ache in my throat. "We all have to keep going, and we can't let the evil people win. We have to make our sacrifices worth it."

I sniffed and straightened my shoulders. "Time's wasting. Let's get to work."

A whirling wall of white had grown up around us. I couldn't see the ranch yard. My luck, I'd start walking and end up end up in Kansas. I looked at Price. "Lead the way."

He held me snared in his gaze, tugging me around to fully face him. "Don't let yourself be one of the sacrifices," he ordered softly, then dropped a fast kiss on my lips. A moment later, he led me into the storm.

I dropped into trace sight almost immediately. Magic poured off Price. It filled the air like an indigo aurora borealis. His body glowed, veins of magic writhing over and through him. They covered him so thickly he might as well have been made of magic.

The pressure shifted, and my ears popped. Price cleared a path for us to walk on, the freed snow whirling into the air.

We stumbled downhill toward the ranch yard. A thick web of spells wrapped it—for more than just security. Multiple rings nested inside one another: nulls, binders, more nulls, more binders, more nulls. Inside those were bands of other magics. I'd guess something malignant and painful if intruders made it through the exterior rings. Inside the innermost ring was something else. Probably a reinforcement of the split rail fencing to keep the animals from blundering into the dangerous spells.

The interior held an array of magics. Most were probably helpful spells— warmers for the barns and water troughs, fire-suppression systems, mouse and rat deterrents, and who knew what else. The main house was another story. It glowed like a small sun. I couldn't begin to say what sort of magic it held.

Price's breathing roughened as we drew closer to the security wall.

"How are you holding up?"

His hand tightened momentarily. "Managing."

This was a larger storm than he'd had to control before. He could easily lose hold of it. Manipulating weather on a small scale was tough enough, but Price needed to cover the entire ranch yard and farther. That meant moving a lot of air, dealing with changing high and low pressures, keeping the wind rotating, and who knew what else. The bigger the storm, the more difficult it was. Plus he had to keep the road clear for Arnow.

The only thing I could do to help him was to tear through the security wall as quickly as possible.

I let go of his hand and reached into the trace dimension, taking hold of his burgundy-blue trace and wrapping it around my wrist. I could feel his emo- tions—elation, worry, determination, love, and an all-encompassing element of protectiveness. There was also an underlying wildness akin to the wind blowing outside. Like he was out there flying with it. Or it somehow sang inside him.

That's right. My boyfriend is part wind. But not a blowhard, or an airhead.

Good thing he couldn't hear me. He'd have groaned in pain at my idiocy.

I slogged as fast as I could through the snow to the edge of the first null wall. The noise of the storm made it impossible to hear Price if he yelled anything at me.

This was going to be a little bit of braille, a little bit of art, and a whole lot of luck, all wrapped up in mulish stubbornness. If you looked it up in the dictionary, I'd be the poster child for mulish stubbornness. Well, me *and* Leo. I was going to go out on a limb and say his picture came first.

I didn't have time to do the summon and release I'd done at the diner. I was going to have to do something far more dangerous and dig in claws and tear the magic apart. I was counting on the layers of the wall being linked. Most times they were to make them both easier to charge and more effective overall. Un- less someone with my level of trace talent attacked. Then the connections be- came a liability, because I only needed to shred the outer wall apart to cause a chain reaction. Price's storm could speed the process, since wild weather had the effect of short-circuiting magic, requiring regular charging and spell mainte-nance.

The real trouble would come when everything broke apart. A lot of wild magic would get released in an enormous explosion of power. I wouldn't be able to collect it the way I had in the diner. It would come too fast and too hard.

My main goal was to survive, and keep Price alive.

I sent off a little prayer for whatever extra help God or the angels could give, and then I went to work.

With no ceremony at all, I raised my hands and skewered as deep as I could into the null wall, clawing and tearing as hard as I could.

Power slammed me. If I hadn't been anchored to the null wall, I'd have been thrown into the air. Crushing pain smashed into me. Instinct alone kept me going. I kept yanking and tearing the outer null wall until I felt it lose cohesion. It exploded, and this time, nothing stopped me from being flung away like a rag doll.

I fell through a whirl of frigid snow, landing hard on my back, my breath bursting out of me. Magic exploded, one after another, a chain reaction of spell failure, each one burning brighter and hotter. I couldn't breathe. Somehow I was connected to the magic and power coruscated through me. Instinct had me winding it around myself like kite string around a reel. Globs of it clung to me like giant cancers. All of it burned. All of it ate away at me, at my body, at my soul, and there was nothing I could do but endure. I sure as hell didn't plan to die.

I'm pretty sure I went on an acid trip. Literally. I was swimming in the stuff. Drinking it. Every thought I tried to have melted to nothing. Pain mowed me down like a runaway freight train and just kept pummeling me, one endless car after another churning me under steel wheels, slicing and dicing and crushing. I couldn't catch my breath or regroup.

My brain finally kicked into first gear and notified me that I should take con-trol of my own magic. No duh. It whirled and churned inside me. Loose brambles of it lashed me, cutting and biting. That hurt. Not as much as the acid or the freight train, but supremely unpleasant all the same.

Nothing worth having ever came easy. Right. Whoever said that was an id-iot. Except that seemed to be the story of my life these days. I was so *tired* of being out of control. All. The. Time.

Anger boiled up in me, giving me a thin cushion against the hurting. I wanted to kick something. Hard. Kick my own ass, maybe. Taylor would tell me to do it instead of just wallowing in pain. Leo and Jamie would just grab pop-corn and hunker down for the entertainment, offering catcalls and an unhelpful advice. Brothers.

I imagined all three and felt a wave of warmth roll through me. Joy at having such a family. They'd always love me no matter what, always have my back. I'd dragged them into an insane life, and they'd come along merrily, like their own lives hadn't been upended and turned inside out. Normally I felt guilty about that, but the warmth washed it away. Or maybe it just turned up the lights so I could see that all three of my siblings were there because they wanted to be. Sure, I was the catalyst, but I hadn't dragged them anywhere they didn't want to go. Not only that, they were actually excited about this insane adventure. I'd discounted those feelings, thinking they were pretending just for me, or it was like Christmas and that excitement would pass, but now. . . . They had a purpose. Something bigger than themselves, and it felt good. For me, too.

Maybe that was what changed. I felt a little bit like the Grinch, my heart growing three sizes. Only the change was far more than that. It was like I'd suddenly grown-up, like that moment when you realize for the first time that you're an adult and you're responsible for your life. Not only are you responsible, but you're actually capable.

Anyhow, something changed in me. Suddenly everything stopped seeming so overwhelming and impossible. Something inside me unfolded, and I just knew what to do with the magic, with this enormous talent that flowed in my blood.

I quit thinking of it as separate from me. I quit thinking of it as something I had to be afraid of. Birds weren't afraid of flying; whales weren't afraid of diving deep into the ocean. They'd been born with the ability to make use of their bodies. Magic was my body. I was made to handle all that I'd been given.

That realization let me let go of my fears and just let nature take its course. Innate intuition took over. I nudged my power into flows and skeins. I let it slide around and over and through me, tugging it back and into a kind of chaotic order. Arnow probably would have had it regimented, sorted, and no coloring outside the lines. That wasn't me. I was wild and silly and impetuous. I liked things unpredictable. I liked living on the edge.

My magic's personality mirrored mine. Knowing that, I realized I didn't have to fear it. It couldn't be stronger than I could handle. Not if I embraced it and let it be what it needed to be.

I gathered the torrent of escaping magic in, smoothing out the edges and clumps. The pain began to fade. I still felt like there were a couple dozen balls covered in steel spikes spinning around inside me. Old habits, old fears, old ways of dealing with my talent. I grabbed them one by one. They dissolved, flowing through my mental fingers like silk. Power layered around me, wrapping me around and around the way it had in the diner. It felt right, not constricting or suffocating. It was light as foam and warm as sunshine on a July afternoon. I wondered if I could teach Price to stop fighting his talent.

Soon I didn't even have to tell it what to do. A part of myself that was as automatic as breathing took over. I swelled with power. By the time I held it all, I felt like a giant ball of gleaming ribbon. I hadn't tried to take all the magic inside and tuck it away—something that had nearly killed me too many times before. A person could only hold so much. Instead, I'd wrapped it around me. Without the terror and desperation I usually felt, I'd been calm and confident. The power responded the way the rest of me responded. My heart slowed and became evenly paced, my muscles relaxed, the knots in my stomach loosened and fell apart. The flailing brambles of magic turned to silk and smoothed over me in a soothing cocoon of warmth and electric ripples.

I came back to myself slowly. I'd been so lost in my task, I'd lost track of Price. A spike of fear drove through me. How had he fared?

I realized then that he held me in his arms on the ground. He was saying something, though I couldn't make it out. My head still sang with notes of power. Around us, a storm raged, but we stood in a bubble of calm, permeated only by the howl of the wind.

I wriggled and sat up, putting my arms around him and burrowing my face into the crook of his neck. His heart thudded frantically in his chest as his arms tightened around me.

I put my lips next to his ear, speaking loud enough to be heard over the storm. "The key is to enjoy the ride." I started laughing. I couldn't help myself. I'd finally come into my own.

Chapter 27

Gregg

"GIVE ME THE UPDATE," Gregg ordered as he finished typing out a text. Stupid how most of his time in this surge against Savannah's old operation was spent behind a desk like some bean counter. He felt more like traffic cop than a general. Nevertheless, someone had to make sure that all the balls stayed in the air and sent forces where they were needed. The military would call this a time-on-target attack, where all the weaponry hit at the very same time. Except he'd had to rush the planning and implementation and now had to call up and redirect resources as needed. That meant sitting in front of the computer and a half dozen phones with a dozen assistants scurrying about like tweaker mice.

Kinsey stood behind the chair opposite Gregg's desk. He didn't speak, and after a moment, Gregg looked up. Kinsey's expression was stupefied.

"What happened?"

"Dimitriou and Castillo are dead."

It took a second for the words to register. Gregg thrust to his feet, his chair rolling away to crash into the wall behind him. "What? How?" He punched down on his desk. The wood cracked from the force. Pain told him he'd broken knuckles, maybe bones. A snarl peeled his lips from his teeth. "Tell me what happened."

Kinsey shook his head. His eyes were bloodshot and rock hard. "Snipers. Simultaneous head taps, both. Professional job."

"It's time I got out there," Gregg decided. He glanced at his secretary sitting at a small desk on the opposite side of the room. "Karen—where's Mason?"

The middle-aged woman started at his bellow and tapped quickly on her keyboard. "Midtown. At Morrell's Boreal residence."

"Get him for me." Gregg tapped his fingers impatiently on his thigh.

"With assassins out there, you shouldn't expose yourself," Kinsey said. "You're the one they really want."

"I'll go into half-travel mode. Right now, I need a firm hand on the wheel up there. My people need to see me and know I'm still in charge. If we don't take Savannah's compound down before a competitor gets entrenched, we'll be in for a long siege and I don't have time for that."

"He'll be on the line in the moment, sir," Karen said.

Gregg answered when one of his cells rang. Each was set up to receive calls on the same number, but instead of someone getting a voice mail or busy signal when he was on the phone, the next cell in the linked lines would ring; if Gregg was busy, an assistant would pick it up.

"Mason, here."

"Get up to Morrell's main compound ASAP. Dimitriou and Castillo have been killed. Hits, both."

One thing Gregg liked about Mason—he could think on his feet and didn't waste time or let obstacles stop him.

"Yessir. I'll leave Naples in charge here. We've breached and are clearing now. Should be mostly mop-up."

"I'll meet you there." Gregg hung up.

Kinsey blocked his path. "I'm coming with you."

"I need someone to coordinate here."

"Petra can handle it. I've already sent for her." Kinsey's craggy face brooked no arguments.

"Fine. Wear body armor—including a helmet. I don't want to lose you, too."

"You, too. Half-travel mode won't save you from a traitor getting you when you think you're safe."

The idea that someone might be a traitor burned through Gregg. "It damned well better not have been an inside job," he snarled. "If I find out it was, the culprits will wish they'd never been born. I'll make them suffer in ways they can't even begin to imagine."

Everybody in the room stared at him, the tension thick. His gaze scraped over each of them. Most paled, and a few turned green like they were going to be sick.

Kinsey was not so easily cowed. One of the reasons Gregg trusted him. He told the truth as he saw it and didn't sugarcoat it. "If someone wanted to make a big play, taking you down and grabbing up Morrell's holdings would be the way," he said, drawing Gregg's attention. "Chances are their intent is to lure you out from cover, but they could easily have a plant inside, or it's possible one of us decided they want to be the one giving orders."

Gregg couldn't imagine who. He made a point of doing right by his people. He wanted to get their loyalty willingly, not scare it out of them. He'd always thought it made for a stronger organization. Maybe he'd been too soft. Maybe he could learn a thing from Savannah.

The thought surprised him. A question to ponder later. Now he had to get up to Savannah's compound and salvage the operation.

"I've got Crockett and Tubbs out there," Gregg said, referring to Bruno and Randall. "They've got a stake in keeping me alive. They'll make sure no one stabs me in the back."

Kinsey scowled but didn't object. Not that Gregg would listen. He had work to do. He was about to take on Clay, Riley, and her family. He only hoped he didn't have to kill them all.

CITY TRAFFIC MOVED like sludge. Gregg fought the urge to travel to the compound and leave his entourage to catch up. It took a good hour to even get close. They stopped and parked and hotfooted it the last mile. Gregg was accompanied by Randall and Bruno, Kinsey, and a dozen soldiers. Each was well-shielded against magic and wearing body armor. Gregg slipped halfway into dreamspace, where bullets couldn't touch him.

The neighborhood surrounding Savannah's estate was all too familiar. Was it only days ago Savannah had let him loose from her prison with the null around his wrist? It seemed like a year. Taylor and that bastard Dalton had rescued him that night as he'd run from his waiting enemies. Now he was their enemy. That seemed wrong, too.

A blinding pain knifed through his head. Gregg staggered and caught himself against a tree trunk, his body solidifying as he jerked out of dreamspace.

"Boss?" Kinsey asked. "Something wrong?"

Gregg dropped to his knees, grabbing his head in both hands. An animal sound erupted from him. Hands hooked under his arms and lifted him.

"Let's get him out of here," Kinsey said.

"No," Gregg rasped. "On to Savannah's." The pain in his head receded slightly, allowing him to think. "I'll be fine."

Kinsey gave him a doubtful look but just nodded, redeploying half their soldiers to take point, with the other half watching their flanks. He fell in beside Gregg with Randall and Bruno just behind.

"What happened?" he asked.

"Don't know."

"You should get checked out."

He should. By Cass. The moment the thought flickered into his mind, pain speared through his skull again. His sight went black. He continued to walk blindly forward, even as his gorge rose and his balls shriveled up inside his body. The hurt should have dropped him into unconsciousness. Somewhere he knew that. But it didn't, and so he was forced to feel it. Forced to endure.

"Maybe later," he said vaguely in answer to Kinsey's comment. "After we get this business settled." He waved ahead of him, hoping he was gesturing in the right direction.

"I'll remind you."

"You do that."

When he focused back on their mission, the pain receded. If he tried to think about why, it came back, so he didn't. Not now.

Getting to their frontline command center was relatively easy. Before they'd been killed, Dimitriou and Castillo had set up a phalanx to make sure they had a clear path to safely come and go and bring in supplies. Gregg's soldiers made sure that interlopers didn't trespass into the territory they'd staked out. Not alive, anyhow. Gunshots perforated the day, echoing off the mountains. All the same, they walked right in without incident.

The command post had been established across the street from Savannah's estate on the parklike backyard of another big estate. The redbrick wall had been knocked over and some of the debris piled to create a makeshift bunker. Nulls and binders didn't stop conventional attacks.

Behind it sat a semi, its trailer serving as a mobile command unit. Several tables with a scatter of notepads, cell phones, weapons, and an assortment of magical items. Several people spoke on phones and others on radios. A substantial arsenal had been organized inside an area fenced in by vans stuffed with supplies and gear. A wall tent had been erected just beyond to hold bodies.

Parked behind the still-standing section of wall were an array of vehicles, including a dozen four-wheelers and snowmobiles.

Gregg glanced over the setup and then eyed the open expanse behind. A hundred yards away behind a screen of trees, he could see the gray tile roof of the mansion that belonged to the wall and grounds.

"Sir!" A dark-skinned, iron-jawed woman with a short high-and-tight jarhead haircut trotted down the stairs of the semitrailer.

Gregg had to search his memory for her name. Strange. He was usually much better with details and prided himself on remembering names. He finally dug it up out of the depths of his brain. Angel Curtis from San Diego. She was smart and disciplined and loyal. Former Marine. Dimitriou had relied on her a lot.

"What's the situation, Curtis?"

She'd caught his look at the empty snowfield behind them. Dozens of tracks crisscrossed it.

"We cleared the house and set sentries and UPMs. Shouldn't have any problems with that back door."

UPM stood for Urban Perimeter Mine. There were any number of varieties. Generally they would send up warning signals when the perimeter was broken by mundane or magic means, plus either temporarily freeze intruders in place, or otherwise disable them. They had to be set in overlapping patterns and spread over a band of at least twenty feet in order to be effective, since the magic they expended wore out within a few minutes. A handful of sentries could take out any intruders before they made it through the band, protecting vulnerable flanks while freeing up man power for forward action. They were useful in a lot of urban situations when you didn't want a lot of carnage.

"Mason get here?"

Curtis shook her head. "Not yet, sir."

"What's our status?"

"Magic's up and working, but that null they used crippled us. And then there's that."

She gestured back to Savannah's. It took a moment for Gregg to see what she was talking about. A wire net rose just on the outside of the wall. It shot up a good thirty feet and then curved outward. The filaments were so fine they looked like fishing line. The work of Riley's half brothers, no doubt.

"It's sharp. Put a hand on it and it slices you to the bone," Curtis said. "It's covered in razor barbs as well. Looks like Savannah's people joined forces and are making a united stand. They didn't suffer from the null blast. They were expecting it."

"We get anybody inside?"

"Yes, sir."

He nodded, considering. Time was getting far too short for comfort. His deadline was looming. It was time to bring in the big guns. Literally.

"Here's what we're going to do," he said, and laid out his plan. His goal was to breach the metal net in so many places that the brothers couldn't rebuild it before Gregg's team could deploy enough binders, which they'd start putting into place immediately. After that, he'd send in an army of people with mundane weapons to overwhelm the defenders. He had an entire army already staging just outside of the city limits, not far from Savannah's, all courtesy of Jackson Tyrell.

As the name crossed his consciousness, a spasm ran through his brain, shaking him to his fingertips, almost like a mini seizure. He shied from thinking about it. He couldn't afford the distraction of the pain.

"Kinsey—start moving the rest of our forces up here." He glanced at the field behind him. "This place should work for staging. Let the sentries know you're coming and have them dismantle the UPMs. Curtis—when Mason gets here, you two get a deployment plan and move everything into place. I want to strike in no more than two hours, so hustle. There'll be bonuses all around when we get this done. In the meantime, I want you to gather a strike squad and bring four of the big binders."

"What are you going to do, Boss?" Kinsey asked with a worried frown.

The corner of Gregg's mouth lifted in an unpleasant half smile. "I'm going to do a little reconnaissance." The perks of being a traveller. He could slide partway into dreamspace and walk through Savannah's compound like a ghost. All he had to do was make a hole in the perimeter. With luck, he could find Riley's brothers. Taking them out of the picture would definitely better the odds in Gregg's favor.

Having their marching orders, Curtis and Kinsey swung into high gear, galvanizing their people to action. Mason arrived on a snowmobile as Curtis and the six-member strike squad joined Gregg. Bruno and Randall tagged along.

He knew exactly where he wanted to hit. A scenic corner in the back of Savannah's compound made the perfect entry point for him. A wide creek ran under the wall on one side, and back out on the other. A footbridge led across to a private gazebo where Savannah sometimes entertained, or more likely, her staff fucked their clients.

The corner was about as far from the main house as it was possible to be, and Gregg was willing to bet it wasn't well guarded.

He was right.

Running water eroded magic. This part of the security wall should have been getting recharged a couple times a week. He was willing to bet it hadn't been charged since before Savannah's death, which made it a weak link. He couldn't make a full-on assault here, but he could get himself through.

Curtis ordered the four big binders put into place, then waited for Gregg's signal. He nodded to her and turned to Bruno and Randall. "Have a cup of coffee, boys. I'll be back."

Before they could protest, he slid halfway into dreamspace and strode through the wall. As he'd expected, the binders worked like a charm. They wouldn't last more than fifteen or twenty seconds, but it didn't matter. He'd breached the security wall. Now he could travel with impunity.

He stepped fully into dreamspace, porting himself into the room where Savannah had held him prisoner. It was empty, the door open. Not that a locked door would have mattered to him now. He returned to ghost mode. Nobody would see him, and he'd see and hear everything.

Before he could move, he flickered and solidified. Maybe there were binder fields at play somewhere in the mansion. He summoned more magic and stabilized himself.

Drifting purposefully through walls, he began his search of the mansion. The upper floors with the bedrooms were largely empty. The main two floors bustled. The squatters had established their command center in the small ball-room. People hunched over banks of computers, some watching security footage, others scanning the web and social media for helpful information. Others messaged informants, while a bank of four wore headphones, typing and talking at the same time as they coordinated outside the compound.

At a long table in the middle of the room sat Savannah's lieutenants. Taylor stood at the head of the table. She spoke with firmness and control. She looked comfortable leading them, and while she treated them with respect, she made it clear she was running the show.

Gregg couldn't deny he was impressed, not to mention incredibly turned on. Was there anything more sexy than a beautiful woman with strength and smarts? Not to mention eyes that could drive a man to his knees.

Down, boy, he told himself. Even if being Riley's sister didn't put her way off-limits, she was the enemy.

A sly voice whispered back in his mind: *She's a grown woman—why should she be off-limits? Why not take her prisoner and work out a mutually delicious deal for parole?*

The idea whirled in his mind, overwhelming his senses. He tried to push it away, but it netted him, sending pulsing waves of desire rushing through him. His cock hardened and strained at his pants. Even halfway into dreamspace, he could feel the aching need for release.

Take her. Snatch her right now. Haul her upstairs and bed her. Ride her hard. Drive her wild until she's begging. You know you want to. You've always wanted to. The sly voice urged, stroking his primitive desire higher.

Gregg felt himself starting to flicker again. He summoned more magic to steady himself. Fire consumed his body. Nothing else seemed to matter. All he could think of were the things he wanted to do to her. With her. He couldn't tear his gaze from Taylor's delicious curves and intoxicating lips. God, to have those around his cock. . . . He nearly exploded.

A spark of sanity ignited in his brain. He flung himself fully into dreamspace and back into his prison cell. He staggered as he landed, panting as if he'd run a marathon. Sweat dampened his back and sides, and his cock was a bar of iron. He hadn't felt this hungry for a woman since his first time. Maybe not even then.

He frowned. Why the sudden overwhelming urges? Taylor was beautiful, but so were plenty of other women. He'd never—

Pain.

Gregg dropped to his knees, gripping the sides of his head, his vision blurring. A whine escaped him, and his body convulsed as the pain drilled deeper into his skull.

His desire for Taylor should have melted, but it didn't. The pain from his head stoked the blistering ache of unfulfilled hunger. Dizzying sparks raked through him.

Abruptly the agony in his head withdrew, pricking him lightly with needles as if to remind him it remained ready. Gregg pushed himself up until he sat on his heels, his breath coming hard between his lips. He tried to think about what had happened, but a dagger cut into his mind, and he recoiled. Instead, his thoughts turned to Taylor. Warm delight answered, soothing the pain away. He thought of Mason and Curtis and fell backward as a shotgun blasted inside his skull. Taylor again. The pain receded and pleasure swirled around his balls and over the head of his cock, making him shudder.

What was happening to him?

Laughter. *Call it behavior modification.*

A maelstrom of horror, terror, and fury crashed into Gregg. He had a brain jockey. A dreamer had taken hold of his mind and had control of him. Instinctively, he summoned up his training to fight the dreamer's hold. A smothering blanket settled over his mind in instant response.

Now, now. None of that.

"Who are you?"

A dry chuckle. *All you need to know is that I'm your master. I give you orders, and you obey and reap the reward, or you fight me and pay the consequences. Either way, you will do as I tell you.*

Was it Vernon? Gregg could think of no one else. But why?

Ah, Vernon. Or should I call him Sam? Whatever he chooses to go by these days, rest assured, I am not him.

"What do you want from me?"

Right now? Take Taylor—rape her if she refuses you. Revel in her until they hunt you down and throw you back in a cell. Your brother will be very angry with you, as will Riley. They will not soon forgive you.

"Why?" Gregg gasped, barely able to form the words. Disgust balled in his gut. Rape Taylor? He couldn't.

But you can, and you will, if that's what it takes. Another dry chuckle. As for why—*the wrench doesn't need to know why it turns the bolt. Do as required and you will feel pleasure like you've never experienced in your life. Do not, and . . .*

A flash of agony so savage his body seized. The pain intensified, and he thought he would pass out or die. But that wasn't permitted. He must remain conscious and suffer. Learn his lessons like a good boy.

For the first time in his life, Gregg prayed for death.

Oh, no, my friend. You are far too valuable for that. Now go do as you're told. Fuck the woman. Enjoy her. Then get yourself caught.

"Who are you?" Gregg asked again, desperate to know who his enemy was.

I knew you were a persistent bastard. I like that in an employee. All you need to know is that I give you orders and you obey.

The bastard didn't want Gregg to know his or her identity, didn't want someone like Cass picking it out of his brain.

A laugh. *Indeed. But we won't have to worry about her much longer now, will we?*

"What have you done?"

It's not what I've done. It's what you've done.

Bile rose in Gregg's throat, and he spat on the floor before lunging to his feet, his muscles cording with the violence of his emotions. "What did you make me do?" He rasped, his vocal cords scraped bloody by the hard edges of the words.

Let's just say the deaths of Dimitriou, Castillo, and Kinsey weren't all that unexpected.

"What? No, Kinsey isn't dead."

Yet.

Doubt and self-loathing churned in Gregg's gut. Had he called in hits on them? On Cass, too? She was practically family. They all were.

And yet you are at war with your only brother. How much can family really mean to you?

Gregg roared and struck the wall with his fist. His hand went through the drywall and met a plate of steel on the other side of the studs. He reveled in the pain. It was his. He'd caused it, no one else. No damned puppet master hiding inside his fucking brain. Gregg wrenched his fist out of the hole, and he pounded it again and again until it was a bloody pulp, his bones shattered into bits.

The rage seemed to loosen the hold of the dream jockey riding him. Or maybe the bastard didn't care if Gregg hurt himself. He might even enjoy the spectacle.

Gregg stood thinking, his arms dangling, blood dripping to the floor as he panted. He was a bear caught in a trap. He'd be damned if he'd be a pawn in someone else's game. As if he had any choice. His mouth tightened, and arctic determination settled over him. He'd find a choice and shove it up this mother-fucker's ass.

Taunting laughter. *Try.*

"You can count on it," Gregg said and then without a clue what to do, he stepped into dreamspace.

Chapter 28

Riley

THE WIND AND SNOW continued to whirl around us as we made our way down the hill, though it had lightened from a category-holy-shit blizzard to just a don't-want-to-be-out-in-it storm. Price pushed a wedge through the drifts in front of us, cutting a path down to the earth.

"What are the odds Arnow waited for us to go in?" I walked behind him so that he didn't have to work so hard making a wide path.

"What would the odds have been of you waiting if people you cared about were inside?"

He had a point.

"Maybe we should hurry."

I'd made sure that Arnow's trace clung to me. Now I reached into the trace dimension and grabbed hold of it and twisted it around my wrist. Instantly I could read her emotions.

"She's not in trouble," I said, feeling only steely determination, a deep-seated rage that probably would burn until the day she died, topped off by a whole lot of worry. The second something bad happened to her, I'd know.

I was also monitoring the traces of the hostages. I hadn't grabbed their traces. I didn't want to get stuck in their suffering or their deaths if the killer started cleaning house. Either one could be debilitating to the point of turning me useless for days. This was a really bad time to turn into a paperweight.

The split rail fencing around the compound had vanished. I had to take Price's word for it that we'd crossed inside. I could see the shadows of the loafing sheds hulking up out of the white gloom. That meant he'd protected the animals. A wash of relief ran through me. Thank you, God.

A jolt hit me from Arnow's trace. Shock. Pain. A lot of it. I recoiled and gasped. Anger roared up inside her, and then her emotions settled. No, she flattened them. I could feel them beyond a layer of iron control.

"Something's happened to Arnow," I told Price.

Price's answer was to break into a fast jog. I kept up easily, though my attention focused on the Ice Bitch. Oh hell. Had I started actually liking her enough to be worried about her? What was next? Dogs and cats living in sin?

"I ain't afraid of no ghosts," I muttered. Serial killers on the other hand . . .

"What?" Price glanced back at me.

"Can't we go any faster?"

He quickened his pace. The wind-wedge running ahead of us sent up a white smoke of snow, coating my head and face. I blinked away the stuff crusting on my eyelashes, ducking my head to avoid the worst of it.

Price slowed before I noticed, and I thumped into him. We stood just outside the front of the big blue farmhouse. It looked like it had been built to look turn of the century. The roof was slate, and there was a pair of French doors leading out onto the wrap-around porch.

"I'm letting the storm go now," Price said. Like it would be that easy.

All of a sudden, the wind went wild, zinging and skipping in every direction. Snow spun and danced, then sputtered up in a cold geyser, then whipped into a tight whirlwind before exploding outward. I twisted and ducked, but it still knocked me face-first onto the ground. When it finished with me, I got to my feet and looked for Price. He stood a few feet away. His hands were clamped into fists, his jaw thrust out, all the muscles in his body knotting. A jolt ran through him. His mouth twisted. Short breaths blew out of his nose as his obvious effort increased.

I had a feeling he was facing the same wild magic situation I had with the security wall. I wanted to offer advice, but didn't dare distract him. Just noticing me could shatter his concentration. So I drew my gun and stepped in front of him as a shield in case Matthew appeared. Then I waited.

The air vibrated, and ripples ran through it. Breathing was strange, to say the least. Arnow's trace stopped giving me clues to her well-being or lack thereof. She'd shut herself down cold. I had to admire that kind of control. I was a walking stick of TNT just looking for a spark. She was titanium sitting in a bath of liquid nitrogen.

Did that mean I deserved a prize for being able to pop her control? That probably shouldn't have been something I took pride in, but I did. I'm petty like that sometimes. Not that she didn't gloat like a hyena in a butcher shop when she got under my skin. So it worked out.

I examined the front of the house, scouring the windows for signs of movement. I felt incredibly vulnerable. I didn't do frontal assaults. I was the sneak in the shadows. I didn't have an attack magic—at least none that I'd successfully managed. Everything I did was strictly defense. Even holding a gun and trained in hand-to-hand, I knew backdoor attacks always worked better than the ram-through-the-front-door kind. Most of the bad guys had guns too, and just as much training.

I twitched when I saw a curtain move on the second story. I raised my gun, but the movement didn't repeat. Maybe I hadn't seen it at all. Maybe my brain was in overdrive, and I was seeing danger where there wasn't any.

The sound of three quick, muffled gunshots made me jump halfway out of my skin. Price didn't seem to have heard. For a moment I wavered between leaving him unprotected and going in after Arnow and the hostages. Not that he was really unprotected. He had the power of an incredible talent.

"I'm going inside."

He didn't react to that, either. I hesitated, and then slogged through the snow up onto the porch. The last blast from Price had buried it under several feet of snow. I kicked aside enough to pull open the screen door, and then twisted the handle on the front door.

Why had I been expecting it to open? I reached into my pocket for my ever-present set of picks and had the door open in under thirty seconds. It wasn't that good a lock. But then, it wasn't really what had been protecting the place. That had been the security net.

I glanced back at Price. It occurred to me that I might not see him again. "I'm going inside" was a crappy way to say good-bye forever if I ended up with a hole in my skull. Not that I wanted to make any sort of grandiose exit. That would totally jinx me. I rolled my eyes at my idiocy. How old was I anyhow?

Old enough to know I was waffling when I should be moving. If I made Matthew worry about me, he wouldn't have time to worry about Price. That settled it.

The door creaked when I nudged it open. I'd expected it. An extra alarm for those of a paranoid bent. The house was dark inside, lit only by the light coming in from the windows, which wasn't much.

Once inside, I went into cat burglar mode, gliding across the wood entryway to an arch leading into the rest of the house. I peered out into the room beyond. It wasn't so much a room as a giant kitchen/dining room/living room/game room setup. On the right wall was a massive stone fireplace with leather couches and chairs surrounding it. I could smell the leather and the fragrance of burning cedar. On the right stood a pool table. A dining table long enough to seat twenty marked the entry to the kitchen.

It shone with wood-clad appliances, white counters, and warm pendant lights with blown glass shades. A set of French doors led off into another room. Between the broad windows hung elk, moose, and deer heads. The entire space screamed "elegant hunting lodge for the rich and famous."

I saw no signs of life. Not even crumbs on the counter or a wadded napkin on the table. Crouching, I slid from shadow to shadow, listening for anything out of place. The wind outside continued to sough. The fire crackled and set-tled, the flames burning low on the glowing coals.

I quickly discovered that the large open living area was misleading. The big place was compartmentalized into a ton of rooms, hallways, and stairways going who knew where. I opened myself to the trace, feeling my power swirling up inside me, potent and ready.

The energy of Arnow's trace was dulled and vaguely clotted. The cold calm had lifted some, and I could feel pain, frustration, anger, and fear. I doubted the last was for herself. She didn't scare easily. Even though I'd only known her a few months, the only thing I'd ever seen her scared of was letting her people down and getting them killed. It was the thing I liked most about her. Maybe the only thing, but it was a big one. She wasn't the selfish bitch I'd thought she was. She was driven by demons I couldn't begin to imagine, and she still would kill herself to protect her own.

It was my own little acre of crazy that demanded I not only had to help her, but maybe die trying. Or maybe it was that I'd decided she was one of my little flock and that meant we'd all die for each other, though at this point, I wasn't so sure she would agree to performing her part of that deal when push came to shove.

Loyalty is something you earn. Fair enough. Time to put my money where my mouth was and start earning some loyalty.

I moved my search deeper into the house. It wasn't very old, so the floors didn't creak, but it paid to be careful anyway. I passed a couple of stairways going up, and then went through a solarium with three walls made out of windows and a fireplace in the one that wasn't. The grate was cold and the room chilly, the windows crusted with frozen condensation. Several dozen dead plants decorated the room.

I went into one of the two doors leading off the opposite side. That's when things started getting creepy. The walls and ceiling were painted stark white and covered with words and symbols drawn in rusty red. The smell told me the ink was blood. The wood floor was scarred with carvings and burns, the symbols almost seeming to writhe as I looked them.

Stepping inside that hallway took all I had. My claustrophobia kicked into high gear. I felt like I was walking into Satan's mouth. A fun house ride taking me straight to hell.

To distract myself, I wondered what had driven the boy Arnow had described to such monstrosity. Duh. Savannah Morrell. She could have driven Gandhi to murder. The major question was what exactly did Matthew want and how were we going to stop him?

A lot of trace ran along the corridor. I recognized the ribbons of the hostages, Arnow's vigilantes, and Arnow. That still left several dozen. I crouched, reaching into the frigid cold of the spirit dimension and ran my fingers over them like guitar strings, not long enough to know a whole lot about any of the people, but I figured I'd know which belonged to Matthew the Twenty-First-Century Ripper the second I touched his trace.

It still wasn't what I expected. I expected that it would feel like the heart of evil—malevolent and oozing corruption. This killer felt desperate, angry, hurt, vengeful, and heartbroken, and running all over the top of that cocktail was a giant dose of despair. If I hadn't known better, I'd have thought the guy on the other end of the trace was maybe fourteen or fifteen. Sixteen tops. Only he was at least seven years older than Arnow, and I figured she had a couple or so years on me.

I took hold of his trace and twisted it around my other wrist before pulling my hand out of the deathly cold spirit realm. I couldn't help thinking of my mother. I'd promised to go talk to her. She'd been trying to corner me for months, but every time I felt good enough to go into the spirit realm to go hear what she had to tell me, I was in the middle of a catastrophe. I sent a mental apology and promised myself that as soon as I survived this rescue and got the hostages back and got things nailed down with Savannah's lieutenants, I'd go see my mother and finally find out what she needed to tell me.

The fact that whatever she wanted was probably nothing I wanted to hear didn't exactly encourage me to hurry. All the same, I'd been practicing adulting, and ignoring the existence of a potential problem wasn't going to make it go away.

Resolutely, I pushed aside thoughts of my mother and stepped out into the hallway. Even though I knew all the scribblings probably weren't magic, I still half expected to erupt in a ball of fire. Nothing happened. I shuddered, and sweat broke out all over me as I moved deeper down the dark hallway. The stench of blood and carrion grew stronger with every step.

Contributing to my unease was the fact that the only light came from the open door behind me. That faded to nothing when the hallway hooked to the right, leaving me in darkness with the smothering stink of death. I realized I was starting to hyperventilate, and made myself count as I breathed in and out until I got myself under control.

I stood there, knowing what I had to do and unwilling to do it. I did *not* want to use my hands to guide myself. I shuddered at the idea of running my fingers along the bloodstained walls, and then remembered I'd tucked a flashlight in the side pocket of my cargo pants. Standard issue equipment for me, along with the Chinese baton I'd finally replaced. I pulled them both out, and flicked the baton to full length, and turned on the light. Relief at having light lifted my fear slightly.

The hallway went another fifty or so feet. There were two doors on either side, but they were both padlocked and covered with the bloody writing. At the end was another door, this one painted red and lacking any of the scribbling. The trace went through it.

I glided down and twisted the knob. The door swung silently open, revealing a set of stairs descending into inky darkness. Of course. The bad guys always retreated to the basement. So cliché. Why couldn't they do their dirty work in bright shiny rooms with windows and fresh air? Somewhere a person could move and breathe?

That's when the smell hit me. Death. Feces and vomit. Piss, stale cigarettes, and the jarring scent of cinnamon and cloves. Before I could curl up in a terrified ball, I made myself walk down the stairs. At least the steps weren't scrawled with any of the writing from the hallway. Stupid as it was, that shit unnerved me. Intellectually I knew that such writings weren't magical at all. Still a part of me wondered if God and Satan knew that, too.

I breathed through my mouth, but that only made me taste the air, and I had to swallow hard to keep myself from throwing up. Wasn't any worse than being in the Bottoms, I told myself. It smells just like this. Well, except for all the rot of death, but close enough.

I stopped at the foot of the stairs and ran my flashlight around the small space. It was maybe fifteen feet by fifteen feet. Metal shelves lined the walls. They held a range of disposable plates, silverware, and cups, plus a load of prepackaged and canned foods, including one entire shelf devoted to ramen noodles. It could have been my pantry, as little as I cooked.

Several refrigerators and a couple of upright freezers hummed along the wall beneath the stairs and the wall adjacent to it. I scanned the rest of the space, finding yet another door. This one was made of steel, with the bottom half a solid plate, and vertical bars across the top. There was no place to stick a key, which meant no way to pick the lock. I wrapped my fingers around one of the bars and pulled, hoping the magic sealing it tight had been disrupted along with the security net.

It swung silently open, and I breathed out a slow breath. So far, luck had been in my favor. It couldn't last. It never did.

And yet—

I stepped inside, leaving the iron door wide behind me. Beyond was an industrial-styled kitchen with stainless steel everything and a cement floor. I shined my light around. Pots and pans gleamed on shelving racks. The place smelled of bleach, which was almost a relief after all the carrion smell.

The only color in the room was a picture that had been painted directly on the wall above the sink. Even though the strokes were crude, its lines were powerful and emotionally stirring. It showed a pair of Kokopellis playing flutes and dancing. The larger was black, the smaller purple. Behind was a background of red mountains with an orange sky above and a bright yellow sun. From it, I had a sense of wild joy and rage. The bottom corner held one of the odd vertical triple-*X* images in black. It looked like our killer considered himself an artist. At least this time he'd used paint and not blood.

I crossed to the other side of the kitchen and paused between a set of steel cabinets and the double ovens. An opening led out into a darkened dining area containing four picnic tables. How big was this dungeon, anyhow? As big as the house? The dull murk within was slightly illuminated by light coming from one of the two doors leading out on the opposite side. I crept across the room on cat feet, pausing again in the shadows beside the lit doorway. Beyond I could hear noises. The rumble of a man's voice, a jingling-scraping sound, and music. Country-western with twangy guitars and metal slides. Old-style stuff.

I peered around the corner and saw that the space beyond broke off in three directions: left, right, and forward. The light came from the left. A stubby little hallway opened up into what appeared to be a larger room. I dodged across the little space and edged my way down to the doorless opening and peered around.

Low ceilings sagged over a spacious room. Or maybe they didn't, and that was my claustrophobia talking. The walls seemed to press inward, too. All the furniture had been pushed back against the walls, which were covered in more of the hallway writing intermixed with paintings similar to the one in the kitchen, except the theme of these seemed to be fire and brimstone and the apocalypse. Angels with bloody wings chopped people apart with shining swords. Jesus stood on a mountain flinging lightning bolts from glowing hands. A lamb with sharp teeth and a bloody mouth attacked a bat-winged demon.

Ten people knelt in a semicircle facing an altar. The seven hostages were easy to pick out. They look terrified and healthy. The other three—two men and a woman—had to be Arnow's team. They had not fared as well. Their faces were mottled with cuts and bruises, and they slumped, their backs bowed as if under a tremendous weight. None of the ten were bound. Had they been drugged?

The altar was half-assed. It consisted of a wood table with a white sheet draped over it plus seven unlit fat white and red candles set around the edges, and last, but not least, Arnow splayed out on top.

Like the others, she wasn't bound, and like the others, she didn't move. I sucked in a tight breath. Crimson splotched her chest and smeared her hair, her chest rising and falling as she took a breath and spoke to her captor.

I couldn't hear what she said. Matthew ignored her. He paced around the interior of the semicircle, mumbling and then shouting. He kept turning to look at thin air and talk to it. Was he schizophrenic? On drugs? Either way, that was an extra layer of trouble. Because I needed more.

Another scan of the space assured me that he didn't have support staff. That took skill—keeping ten different people subdued—even if they were drugged. Plus he'd bested Arnow. He wasn't going to be a pushover for me to deal with. I frowned. Arnow should have handled him easily. Unless he had a talent and had surprised her.

Physically, he was thin, with hanks of greasy black hair hanging to his shoulders. It was clearly dyed. His skin was vampire white except for dark smudges of five o'clock shadow. The front of his black shirt clung wetly to his body. I had a feeling the liquid was blood—either his or Arnow's.

I was tempted to wait for Price to join me before I made a move. Together we'd have a good shot of taking this bastard down without hurting anybody else. But this guy was getting more agitated by the second. He started to shout at a point just beyond the end of the altar, stabbing the air with his fingers. He whirled and shouted at Arnow, then slammed his hands down on top of the altar table beside her head. The candles jumped, and two thumped to the floor.

Then all of a sudden he started speaking in a calm voice. I strained to hear his words over the jangle of the music. What I could make out didn't make a lot of sense. Something about consecrating afflictions, affixing of punishments, the law of God, serpents rising, and a bunch of other stuff. The words came faster as he grew agitated. They rattled from his lips fast and hard.

Still jabbering nonstop, he raised Arnow's bound arms up over her head and pushed them down as far as they'd go. She didn't fight him. In fact, except for breathing and talking a little, she didn't seem to move at all. That worried me.

Matthew the Ripper retrieved the fallen candles and set them in place, then pulled a lighter from his pocket and lit them and their five brothers. He stood very still, then, engrossed in looking down at Arnow. Time to make my move. With his back to me, I wouldn't have a better chance.

I pocketed the flashlight and my baton and drew my gun. Holding it up at eye level, I stepped out into the room to square up my shot. I didn't make a sound. I know it. Even if I had, the music should have covered it. Yet somehow Matthew knew I was there. He stiffened, tipping his head to the side, and then whirled to face me.

His eyes gleamed white in his thin face. His nose jutted narrow and sharp over thin lips. He strode toward me, the litany of nonsense he spoke never breaking.

"Don't make me shoot," I ordered. "Get down on the ground."

He didn't waver. He stepped between two of the hostages—a young man— maybe Blaine's son—and a silver-haired woman.

It's not that easy to shoot at someone, even when you know they mean to kill you. You can practice with targets all you want, but shooting a person isn't the same. I'd been girding myself up to make this shot ever since we left Diamond City. Not only to pull the trigger, but not to hesitate. I squeezed my finger, aiming center-mass high so I wouldn't hit the hostages. The gun bucked in my hand, and Matthew grasped his chest, stumbling backward from the force of the impact. He bent over. The froth of words stopped.

Then he straightened and tossed aside my bullet. What the fuck? He had to be a tinker. One more powerful even than Maya. No wonder nobody had spoken or moved. He'd messed with their bodies.

He started walking toward me again. His dark gaze was piercing and utterly cold and blank. It was like looking into the pitiless eyes of a shark.

I squeezed off two more rounds, and again he clutched his chest and stumbled backward. Again he bent and held himself still. The two bullets bounced onto the floor. He straightened and charged toward me, leaping over the hostages.

A fucking tinker. He was a fucking tinker.

Change of plan. I ratcheted off another couple shots and launched myself at him. I kept pulling the trigger. I doubt he could have healed a head shot, but odds were against me making one of those with the way he was moving. I'd hit his heart at least once. He should have been dead.

I was only a few feet away, tensing myself for whatever he'd try, when something grabbed my foot and yanked it up from behind. I toppled. Training and muscle memory kicked in. I somersaulted over one shoulder as I connected with the floor, bowling myself at Matthew. He leaped up, launching off my back as I rolled under him.

I came to my feet and spun around. He was already coming back at me. He didn't have a weapon, but then he didn't need one. He just had to touch me, and he could shred apart my heart or blow an artery in my brain.

My gun was still in my hand. I raised it and took aim at his head. Before I could pull the trigger, the weapon twisted out of my hand and struck me in the jaw. Pain exploded. What the fuck? Was one of the hostages helping him somehow? Using telekinesis? Or maybe he had a partner in a corner I hadn't seen. I didn't have time to figure it out. I ducked and dodged under Matthew's outstretched hands and jumped inside the altar circle.

He followed me. He'd gone silent, concentrating entirely on chasing me. I kept moving, jumping back out of the circle and running around to put Arnow and the altar between us.

I could hear her labored breathing.

"Riley? Kill him. Don't mess around."

"I'm doing my best."

"Do better."

What was I going to do? Maybe I should have waited for Price. Was he in the house yet? If so, I just had to delay until he could get here and then we could tag-team this bastard to death.

The Ripper wasn't going to give me that kind of time.

Standing at the foot of the altar table, he grasped Arnow's ankle.

"I'll kill her."

That was the whole threat. All the "surrender or else" stuff was implied. For a guy who'd been boiling over with words a few minutes ago, it seemed awfully terse.

I decided delay was my best tactic, at least until I could come up with something better.

"Why are you doing all this?" I waved at the altar and kneeling hostages without taking my eyes off him.

He didn't take his eyes off me either, but neither did he answer.

"Get him." Arnow's voice was thin.

I risked a swift glance at her. Blood trickled from a dozen wounds on her face, running in thin rivulets into her hair. Not dire. Not life threatening. At least not yet, but it would be if I didn't surrender. Her gaze on me was unwavering. She didn't speak again. Matthew must have taken her voice.

I didn't doubt he'd kill her if I didn't do something—and quick.

"Cat got your tongue?" I asked, turning my attention back to Psycho-Boy. "Or did you use up all your words for the day?"

He made a menacing sound deep in his throat.

I nodded sympathetically. "I've had those days. Makes you want to crawl back into bed. I'm sorry about shooting you, by the way, but to be fair, you *are* a serial killer and you were about to do terrible harm to Arnow here, and while she's not my favorite person on the planet, I do like her better than you, plus let's face it, you're too dangerous to just let run around, kinda like a rabid raccoon."

My mind raced as I spoke. He wasn't going to give up. Rabid seemed a pretty accurate description. I couldn't see anything human in his eyes.

"What's that business with the stacked diamonds? You sign your kills and your pictures with it."

I nearly jumped out of my skin when he answered. "My initials. My name is Matthew Morrell." He spat the words.

I blinked, my mouth dropping open. Morrell. As in Savannah Morrell. He was her son. I could see the resemblance now that I was looking for it. And then I understood that the stack diamond symbol was really two *M*s turned sideways, belly-to-belly.

"Your mother's dead."

Wrong thing to say. Or maybe really right. He sucked in a breath and leaped at me.

I snatched a candle and threw it at him. He swung a hand to bat it away, but it never got close to him. It rebounded at me like a bullet, smashing against my chest like a missile. I went ass over teakettle. The air exploded from my lungs as I landed. I used my momentum and swung my legs over my head, rolling over backward and shoving up with my hands. I landed back on my feet, my chest aching.

He was nearly on top of me. I lifted my baton, but it wrenched from my hand and went flying through the air. It clanged against something and the music shut off. That left hand-to-hand. So as long as I stuck with kicking and elbow blows, I wouldn't make skin on skin contact and open myself up to his tinkering. Right. Because he wouldn't be doing his damnedest to touch me. Plus the whole telekinetic thing someone was using on me meant my clothes could get ripped open at a really unfortunate moment. I was surprised they hadn't stripped me already.

I didn't have time to think it out. I decided to go for surprise. I made to dodge aside, waiting until he began to shift to block me. Once he was committed, I lunged back on one leg and whip-kicked around, nailing him in the meaty part of his thigh. That move hurt a lot. I knew from hard experience.

He grunted and staggered away. I whirled, getting both feet on the ground and driving at him. I rammed his shoulder with mine, but before I could finish the move by sweeping his feet out from under him, my shoelaces knotted together, and I fell like a tree.

I bounced, knocking my chin hard into the floor before rolling away. I didn't get far. A couch lifted up and landed in my path. I fought to get my boots off, but they clamped my feet like hungry mouths. My coat sleeves swallowed my hands so I couldn't get at the laces to unknot them.

Invisible hands looped my ankles and dragged me upside down in the air. Shit. I twisted at the waist to see where Matthew was. At the same time, I belatedly evoked the null tattooed on my stomach. I dropped to the floor like a sack of hamburger. I attempted another somersault roll, but I ended up crashing onto my back in a reverse belly flop. For a second, all I could do was lie there and gasp like a beached whale.

In the meantime, Matthew had climbed to his feet. The right side of his face was starting to swell, and he was going to have a serious black eye and fat lip. For a moment I thought I was winning. That I'd freaked him out enough that he'd forgotten to tinker himself back into good shape. Then I realized he barely glanced at me, and instead he stared off into thin air just over my left shoulder.

"I don't need your fucking help," he snarled. "The Lord that is Risen will aid me and if I fail, then it is God's will."

A moment of silence. Confused silence on my part, but I think I was the only one.

"What do you mean the helicopter rescue joke?" Matthew asked, scowling confusion.

I knew that one. A man in a flood climbs on top of his roof. A guy in a boat comes by and offers him a ride. The man says, "No thanks, God will save me." Then a guy on a Jet Ski comes by followed by a helicopter, both offering to help. He gives them the same reply. The man ends up drowning and at the Pearly Gates, he asks why God didn't save him. God says, "I sent you a boat, a Jet Ski, and a helicopter. What else did you want?"

I stood up, wincing at the way my body throbbed. "It means whatever alien space rabbit you're talking to right now was sent by God to help you, or so he seems to be claiming. Personally, I'm thinking both you and Space Harvey have Satan to thank."

His gaze fell on me again. Looking into his eyes was nothing like looking at Maya or Price when they went all white eyed. Looking at Matthew was like looking into the basement of hell where all the really scary monsters live.

"I am a warrior against Satan," he said, his back straightening and his chin lifting with obvious pride.

"Sure you are. That's why you get your rocks off torturing and killing people. God's well-known for that."

"You joke, but the Lord on High sent Abraham to kill his own son. He destroyed Sodom and Gomorrah. He sent plagues to destroy Egypt and flooded the world, killing all but Noah and the chosen of the ark. He sent the Crusades to cleanse the earth of idolatry. He wiped witchcraft out of Europe with the Inquisition. He is all-knowing and all-powerful. He is just to those who serve him, and merciless against evil. He called me to serve in his divine army. I will die before I fail him."

"Feel free," I said. "Anytime. Now would be good."

He didn't seem to hear. He'd looked away again, his gaze falling on Arnow and the makeshift altar. He walked back toward her, seeming to forget about me completely.

"What are you doing?" I blocked his path, forcing him to stop.

"Freeing Sandra's soul so that it may be cleansed of its taint."

Sandra. He'd recognized her, then. He knew her. Except he didn't. Not really. Nobody did, because she'd been raised to wear so many masks that she probably didn't even know who she was. "Sandra's not her name."

That took him aback. "What is her name?"

"Hell if I know. Personally I think it's either Esmerelda or Bertha. Or possibly Agnes."

He considered, and then shrugged. "Sandra's true name doesn't matter. Only her soul."

"Bullshit."

He cocked his head at me. "What use are names?"

"You're the one that leaves your initials everywhere. You tell me. And what about Jesus? God? Satan? Solomon? Mary? Are you going to tell me those names aren't meaningful? It's not like you're going to start calling God 'Larry' or 'Lance.' That would be blasphemous, wouldn't it?"

I had his full attention now. "What's yours? Why are you here?"

I smiled ever so sweetly. "How about you call me God? I'm here to send you to hell where you belong."

I barely saw his hand move. It shot out, and he snatched my jaw in a powerful grip. He twisted me around, wrapping his other arm around my neck.

"You are Lucifer's handmaiden. You must die. Now."

I'm pretty sure he did something tinkery then. I didn't wait for him to realize it hadn't worked, thanks to my belly null. I slammed my head backward into his face while simultaneously jamming my elbow into his ribs. He made a *huffing* sound, and his grip on my neck tightened. He punched the side of my head with his free hand. Pain clapped my skull and pierced my eardrum. Everything on that side sounded watery and distant.

I reached back and raked my nails over his face, then grabbed his head and tried to gouge his eyes with my thumbs. He thrust me away, shoving me to the floor and then jumped on top of me, straddling my hips and snatching at my neck.

I grabbed his wrists and pulled them apart as I sat up and head-butted his mouth. Blood spattered my forehead. I let go of his wrists and smashed my palms over his ears at the same time. He gave a sharp scream as blood ran out his ears. I put both hands together and gave a powerful jab into his throat. He made a whistling wheezing sound. I shoved him off me and lurched to my feet. I kicked him in the ribs three times until he curled up in the fetal position.

"Nice work."

I looked up to see Price standing just a few feet away. His eyes were white, but the air around us was perfectly still. Too still for comfort. He was volcanic, but managing to keep himself under iron control. I wasn't sure how long he could hold it. I felt the pressure building and thickening, making it hard to breathe. Normally I'd have asked what took him so long, but this was probably a bad time for jokes. Anyway, it couldn't have been more than five or ten minutes since I got down here. He hadn't taken all that long, especially given the shitstorm he was dealing with.

"Got anything to tie him up with?" I swiped at the blood dribbling down my nose from a cut in my forehead. From Matthew's teeth, I supposed. My cheek and jaw ached from where he'd hit me. I might have had a loose tooth or two as well.

Price dug a pair of riot cuffs out of his pockets.

"Actually, give those to me first." I explained the telekinetic stuff that had been happening and then summoned my null magic. It flowed powerfully. I fed it into the cuffs, turning them into a null. I handed them to Price, who pulled Matthew's arms behind his back and fastened the cuffs on his wrists. He wouldn't be tinkering anybody anytime soon.

I went to Arnow, who hadn't moved. I poured my magic over her, trying to disrupt the spells he'd put on her. She still didn't move. Whatever Matthew had done to her, nulling magic wasn't going to fix it. For all I knew, he'd cut her spinal cord or something.

"We'll get you help," I promised as I pulled her arms back over her head and down to her sides. "You're going to be fine." A heal-all wouldn't fix tinker work. It had something to do with tinker magic making the physical modifications look natural, like a person had been born that way.

Price had joined me then. He pulled me into a hug and held me. We stood like that for a good minute before he loosened his grip. I expected a lecture on going off on my own, but he didn't say anything at all.

"I'm not sure anybody can walk," I said awkwardly, after a long moment of silence.

He didn't get a chance to answer. One second he stood in front of me, the next he was flying across the room. He smashed off the wall and dropped to the floor in a heap. I started to run to him, but the couch came sliding toward me. I dodged to the side, but it pivoted back around. I jumped onto it to keep from getting run over.

Chairs rose in the air and dive-bombed me. I ducked and lunged off my perch. One chair rammed my back, and the couch bashed into me, shoving me toward the wall. I pulled up my magic and pushed it out. It was unformed, but potent. It flooded outward, killing every bit of magic in its path.

The chairs fell with a clatter. I rolled away as the couch stopped. I held my magic in place, pushing into every nook and cranny of the room.

Price picked himself up. "What the hell was that?"

"I think we've got a poltergeist. I'm nulling the room." It was the only thing that made sense. They were spirits who hadn't crossed over who retained their magical talents. In this case, Casper had been telekinetic in life and now death.

"If it is a poltergeist, it's not your biggest fan," Price said.

"What do we do about it?"

"Talk sweet and give it a cookie?"

At least he was joking. That was positive. "I can't hold this field forever," I said. "When I drop it, Casper the not-so-friendly ghost will attack again." But the answer popped into my head almost as soon as I asked. I looked around for what I needed and didn't see anything workable.

"I need something metal or glass or stone. Something we can carry with us."

Price dashed out of the room and returned a minute later with a frying pan. Perfect. He handed it to me.

This next bit was going to be tricky. I needed to maintain the null field while simultaneously creating a null that we could use to protect ourselves as we left. At first I couldn't seem to manage. I'd concentrate too much on the frying pan, and the field would flicker and start to die. I'd bolster it back up, and the magic I'd woven around the frying pan would unravel. I didn't have a lot of practice doing both at once.

After a few minutes, I found my groove. I had to notice everything at once and let my instincts and muscle memory take the lead.

By the time I was done, I felt like I'd been through a taffy-pulling machine for a few hours.

I handed the pan to Price. "Invoke it," I said, my voice more croaking frog than human woman.

I felt him activate it, and I reeled the room's null field back into me. As I finished, I sagged, my legs wobbly. I caught my hands on my knees, letting my head dangle as I drew in several deep breaths.

Price went to check on the prisoners. None of them spoke. They looked at us with staring eyes and chalky faces. Arnow's three remained contorted. My stomach twisted as I realized that Matthew had tinkered them all. If I had to guess, I'd say he'd cut their vocal cords and then messed with their bodies to suit his sense of divine justice.

"I need to call Taylor and let her know we have them. And that we'll need tinkers."

"What are you going to do about proof of life?"

Savannah's lieutenants weren't going to just take my word that we had rescued their families. I'd expected to let the hostages talk for themselves and provide their own proof.

"Send pictures, I guess, then drive like a bat out of hell back to the city so they can see for themselves."

"We'll need another set of wheels," Price said.

"Two will have to do. We don't have any other drivers. We saw a couple pickup trucks earlier. Maybe there's something in the garage or a barn that will hold more people." I looked down at the prone man. "His full name is Matthew Morrell. Savannah's son."

GETTING EVERYBODY upstairs proved easier than I expected. Price lifted two at a time on wind gurneys. I made another big null out of a waffle iron. Two nulls meant I could leave one in the basement and one upstairs to protect Matthew's victims from the poltergeist. I decided it was the better part of wisdom to create a third one out of a soup ladle so that I didn't have to worry about Price when he moved the hostages.

Upstairs, I texted Taylor, sending pictures of each of the hostages. I told her they'd been tinkered not to talk or move and that we'd be needing medical help. I also told her to ask the lieutenants to think really carefully about which tinkers they could trust with the lives of their loved ones. Then I went in search of a vehicle.

Unfortunately, the poltergeist decided I not only needed company, I needed entertainment. First, it pulled the rug out from under me. Literally. I landed on my hands and knees. And I'd just used a heal-all. Now I'd have to suffer through the wormy feeling all over again.

"Would you just stop it?" I asked, standing up. A sconce ripped out of the wall in response. I drew up my power and pushed out a null field. The sconce dropped, dangling from its wires.

This totally wasn't going to work. Whatever was after me needed to be bottled, or we'd never get out of here. I'd be pleasantly surprised if it hadn't gone out and torn apart all the drivable vehicles.

I was out in the first big sitting room. Price had chosen the solarium for the victims as he transported them out of the basement. I turned in a circle.

"Why don't you just tell me what your problem is? Write it on a wall or something."

I retracted my null field to allow for a response. I got nothing. Of course not. Why would a ghost tell me what it wanted? Why not just bludgeon me to death to make its point? It was probably sticking its tongue out at me right now because I was too stupid to figure it out for myself.

Let's try this again. "Why do you want me dead? Come on, spill it. You know you want to gloat. It's time for the bad guy soliloquy part of this movie. You know, where you brag on your evil triumph so your victim will know just how awesome you are."

I waited. Still nothing. What else could I do? Aside from those nuclear-powered electronic gun things from *Ghostbusters*, how did one neutralize a ghost? Didn't shamans use sage? 'Course, I wasn't a shaman, nor did I have any sage handy. Didn't have a Catholic priest for any exorcism action either. So where did that leave me?

Tired, pissed off, with sore knees. So pretty much business as usual.

I rubbed my forehead. Why couldn't the serial killer have been the worst of my worries?

I paced. Fact: the ghost could travel outside of any null field. Fact: nulls didn't work well on moving cars, which meant once we got going, our annoying little pest could pop the tires or tear apart the engine, and we'd be stranded. Or worse. Fact: if Casper was strong enough, he could shove us off a cliff.

Maybe I should stay behind. Maybe it would stay focused on me and not follow the others. I snorted. Yeah, Price would go for that. And then for his next trick, he'd fly to the moon. Wasn't going to happen.

Twenty minutes later I still hadn't come up with a solution. Price came in.

"Did you find something?"

I shook my head. "The ghost is going to be a problem."

I could see the wheels spinning in his head as he put two and two together. He scowled.

"I don't suppose you have any bright ideas?" I asked hopefully.

He shook his head.

"You could go without me—"

He just gave me the *look*.

"I wonder if Google has any ideas," I said, desperation getting the better of sense. I tapped out a search on my phone. A whole bunch of websites popped up, with a Wiccan site topping the list. I read it and then stopped and reread it again. I grinned. Maybe I wasn't as far up shit creek as I'd thought. In fact, if my head had been fastened on right, I'd have figured it out a half hour ago.

"Just a second," I told Price.

"What are you going to do?"

"Send this bastard where he belongs." I dropped into trace sight. It wasn't that hard to find the ghost. He hovered over a lamp only a few feet away. He was mostly a white glowing apparition, but I could make out that he was beefy, with short hair and wearing jeans and a button-up shirt. His mouth pulled unnaturally down to the right. The rest of his face appeared mottled and wrinkled with what looked like burn or acid scars. Half his nose was gone, along with one ear and a patch of hair.

His trace was gray, but flickers of silver ran down it. I reached into the trace to grab it.

"I'll be back in a minute," I told Price, and then plunged myself into the trace dimension.

As usual, the cold slammed me like a fist. It dug under my clothes and pushed inward. All around me, jewel-colored lights and streamers flashed and rippled through an endless velvet night. I grabbed the poltergeist's trace with both hands and yanked, letting my power flow through my hands. A second later, the he popped into being in front of me, looking very surprised.

"You belong here, not the other side," I told him. "See you around."

"Thank you."

The sincerity of the two words caught me up short. "Excuse me?"

"I couldn't cross."

"Is that why you were throwing a tantrum up there? And why start hanging

out with Matthew?" I had started to shiver. This realm was for the dead and
meant to increase its population by one if I stayed too long.

"I was hexed."

"By who? Why?"

His body started to fade. His trace now rippled with gold, orange, and pink.
I wasn't sure what happened to the dead when they made the crossing. My
mother looked just like what she did when she'd died, except transparent.

"All is not what it seems," he said in whispery voice. "Watch for the serpent
in the garden."

With that, he floated away, a ball of colored light. My teeth chattered. I
needed to get out of here. I grabbed hold of my own trace and followed it back
to where I'd left Price.

He hadn't moved. The moment I appeared, he pulled me against him, rubbing his hands up and down my arms and back to help warm me.

"He's gone," I said, my voice muffled. My face was pressed into his chest.
He unzipped his coat and pulled me inside, his warmth and spicy scent envelop-
ing me. I snuggled closer, wrapping my arms around his waist.

"Good riddance."

"He said he was hexed and thanked me for helping him cross. He also said
that all is not what it seems and that I should watch out for a serpent in the
garden. Does that make me Eve and you Adam?"

His chest rumbled as he chuckled. "I bet you'd look hot in a couple of fig
leaves."

"So we don't need a serpent or an apple for you to want to jump my bones,
is what you're saying."

"I'm saying I love your apples and my serpent is always available for you."

I groaned, and he laughed again, then kissed me. It wasn't nearly long
enough, but then, I never got enough of him.

"We'd better go find transportation," he said.

I sighed and pushed away. "To be continued later." How much later, I didn't
know. There was still a war going on back home.

WE FOUND A NISSAN Armada in the garage, along with a BMW sedan and
a restored 1978 Chevelle.

The Armada had three rows of seats. I figured it could carry six or seven
people besides the driver. With Price's Wrangler, we could haul everybody,
though it would be tight. Not that we had a choice. I wasn't sure anybody could
sit up on their own, and I anticipated there was going to be a serious mess to
clean up when we got back to Diamond City, but it wasn't like we could sit
them all on a toilet before we left. I didn't even know if they were capable of
going to the bathroom right now, anyway.

It turned out, we didn't have to wait for things to start getting messy. More
than a couple people had wet their pants or worse. All we could do was get
them loaded and plan to drive fast.

Price kept giving me the side-eye as he loaded everybody up. I buckled them
in and shoved pillows I'd scavenged from the house around each to help keep

them upright. Arnow's three people couldn't be straightened. We put the third seat down in the Armada and fitted them in together, trying to make them as comfortable as possible. I kept telling everybody they'd be okay, that we were taking them to safety. I hoped they believed me.

We put Arnow in the front of the Armada with me. It unnerved me to see her so lifeless, but her trace told me she was anything but dead.

"What about you?" Price asked after we loaded the last person up. He touched my cheek lightly with his fingers.

"I could use a gallon of coffee and a six-pack of Red Bull."

"This is all I've got." He handed me a chocolate bar. I took it like it was the most precious thing I'd ever seen.

"If I didn't love you before, I would now."

"You're easy."

I smiled. "Only when it comes to you."

I'd had a one-word text back from Taylor in response to me telling her we had the hostages: *Good.* Nothing else. I itched to know more, but she didn't need me bugging her, and it wasn't like there was anything I could do, anyhow.

I drove the Armada and followed Price, since I didn't want to trust myself to remember the route back through Denver. Plus, he could use his talent to clear the snow off the road, which was necessary after his homemade blizzard.

We didn't get back to Diamond City until well after dark. As we approached, I realized that we hadn't planned where to go. I'd assumed Savannah's place, but with it being a war zone, that was less than a good idea. I'd have liked to go to Maya, but she worked for Touray, and I couldn't risk it.

I called Taylor.

She answered on the third ring. "Where are you?"

"Just outside the city. We need a tinker and somewhere safe to go."

"Bring them here. They want to see them in person."

I interpreted *they* to mean the Seedy Seven and *them* as the hostages. "Can we get through?"

"Touray's army tried to overwhelm us a couple hours ago. We held on, but they're still on the front steps. We'll need to travel you."

My father, Vernon, had kidnapped me once the one and only time I'd ever travelled through dreamspace. It wasn't exactly safe. I reminded Taylor.

"We don't have much choice."

I thought of Price and his talent. Maybe we could make things safer.

"Let me talk to Price," I said. "I'll get back to you."

I hung up and called Price back. "Pull over. We need to talk."

He turned into the parking lot of a scenic viewpoint. The snow lay a good two feet deep on the asphalt, but he swept it away with a blast of wind. I was impressed. He really was getting good at using it.

We both got out.

"What's up?"

"We have to go to Savannah's. Your brother's got the place surrounded. Taylor wants to send travellers, but—" I shrugged, and he nodded agreement. "I had this idea. I could push a null field out beyond the vehicles a ways and shut down nearby magic. I'd leave you space to blow up such a cloud of snow to keep anybody from seeing us. And if someone did launch something at us, you should be able to deflect it."

"Could work."

"You're not too tired?"

"Are you?"

The truth was that I felt damned raggedy and was starting to see double. "I'm good."

"So am I."

With the lies out of the way, I focused on the logistics of our plan. "It would be a whole lot easier if we weren't driving two vehicles. Do you think we could load everybody into one?"

"It won't be comfortable."

"It won't be for long."

"Let's take the Nissan. It's bigger."

With that, he used his talent to transfer everybody one by one while I texted Taylor the plan. I did my best to make the injured fit in the Wrangler with some level of comfort. We put five people in the very back, five more in the back seat with two sitting on laps between people, and Arnow in the front seat.

"Do you want me to drive?" I asked Price.

He looked me over. "I think I'm in better shape."

I couldn't argue that. "Are you going to be able to split your focus on the wind and the road?"

"I'll let you know when I get there."

"Or we crash."

"Or that." He pushed me toward the passenger side. "Get in. We're burning daylight."

"It's nighttime."

"Okay, we're burning moonlight."

I had the choice of sitting on Arnow or having Price lift her so I could slide under her. I chose the latter, though I tipped her so that her head rested on the console between our two seats. It was like holding a giant floppy Barbie. Her body held no tension. Within a few minutes, she started sliding down to the floor. I tried to hold her up, but couldn't. She folded down until her head rested on her knees.

We entered the posh outer neighborhoods of the Rim. It was quiet here, and well lit. The road was clear and dry, courtesy of magic. Price drove as straight a path as he could to get to Savannah's. It still took us a good forty-five minutes to get to the first roadblocks. I couldn't tell who'd put them up. Maybe the cops, maybe Gregg, maybe somebody else.

I called up my magic and formed the null ring around us, leaving ample room in the center for Price to do his thing. Luckily I could aim the null energy outward, or we'd have been screwed.

"When do you want to start your part of the floorshow?" I asked Price. I'd already called Taylor to let her know which gate we would be heading for. She promised to be ready to let us in.

"Now."

I'd sort of expected a gradual rise of wind picking up snow until we were at the center of another tornado. Instead, all around us drifts of snow shot into the air and hung there. I could see shadows of buildings and trees through the icy curtain.

"They can still see us."

"I'm not done."

"You might want to get on that."

"Don't tell me—you're hungry."

"As a matter of fact . . ."

"I've never met a woman who eats like you do."

"You mean like a horse. I have to maintain my voluptuous curves." I fluttered my lashes at him.

Price leered back, his gaze dropping to my chest. "I do love your curves."

"Then don't complain about how much I eat."

"I'm not complaining about how *much* you eat. I'm complaining about how often you need to be fed."

"I'd eat less if I used fewer calories." I tapped my lower lip thoughtfully. "Maybe I should give up sex. That would cut out an extra breakfast, lunch, and dinner every day," I mused.

"Never mind. I'll set up a buffet in the bedroom if you want."

"I thought you might say something like that."

By this time, the wind had pulled more snow up into the air, and it whirled around us in a slow, thick current. I could no longer see anything beyond us. He started driving again.

"Don't go too fast," I warned. "I don't know if I can maintain the field if you do."

"Copy that."

I tipped my head back and closed my eyes, pushing my magic as far as I could. The more margin we had where magic didn't work, the safer we would be. So long as nobody lobbed an RPG at us.

The minutes ticked past. I'd started pushing my feet hard against the floor. My fingernails cut half-moons into my palms. I began to pant, despite my efforts to keep my struggle a secret.

"You okay?"

"Keep driving."

He reached over and pulled my hand out of my pocket and enveloped it in his. I held on to him with all my strength.

He started to speed up, and I felt my control slipping.

"Too fast."

Immediately he slowed again, but now he began a muttered chant of invectives with the word *fuck* holding a starring role in most of them.

"Text your sister," he said finally, after we made several turns. I had already prepared the message. All I had to do was hit *Send.* I did. A couple of seconds later, I got her reply.

"It's a go."

"Hold on."

Price floored it. We plunged through the slow-moving wall of snow. At that speed, I couldn't hold my power. I let it go and slumped against the window, closing my eyes. I couldn't have opened them if I wanted to.

We skidded and swerved and sped even faster. The Nissan jolted over something. I jounced a good eight inches off the seat, my teeth clacking together as I landed. Price's hand came across my chest and pushed me back in a traditional momma seat belt. His hand stayed there as we went over several more bumps. Curbs maybe.

"Do you know where you're going?" The snow hid everything beyond the hood.

"I'm taking a shortcut."

Of course he was.

We humped and jerked across bushes. I heard the screech and scrape of branches and twigs against the doors as the front end of the Nissan rose up and plunged back down. I braced my free hand on the dashboard and wondered if it was too late to put on my seat belt.

We bogged down a little in deep snow, the tires spinning with a high-pitched whine. The SUV lurched and lifted off the ground, floating forward a few feet before dropping back down onto a road surface.

Price hit the gas again, and we sped forward. "Almost there."

I could have cheered.

Two minutes later, the SUV skidded to a stop. "You can relax now," Price said, looking at me with haggard eyes.

"I may never relax again."

"Try watching your girlfriend die in front of you."

I'd forgotten about that. Well, not so much forgotten as decided not to remember.

"Try watching your boyfriend get shot and try to bleed out in front of you."

Technically, he hadn't been my boyfriend when Savannah had shot him and used him to bait Touray into turning over the Kensington artifacts. We'd slept together, but I'd told him I wasn't interested that same night. It wasn't until a few weeks later that I realized how stupid I'd been. Of course, my realization came because someone had bombed his brother's place and Price had been caught up in it. Luckily, he'd only been slightly injured.

Our whole relationship was full of near-death experiences. "The sex is worth it."

"Worth what?"

Oops. I hadn't meant to say that out loud. I didn't get a chance to answer. The doors were yanked open, and Leo pulled me out of the car and hugged me. I hugged him back hard.

After a moment, he pushed me away to look me over. The snowstorm that Price had created had cleared, and lights shone around us.

"You look like shit."

"Appropriate, since I feel like shit."

He wrinkled his nose. "What is that stench?"

"Also shit. And some piss and vomit."

I didn't get to say much else. I got shoved aside as the Seedy Seven came running, along with a crowd of other people I assumed were family, or maybe bodyguards. I saw Leo pull Arnow out of the front seat and carry her inside.

I looked for Taylor, but didn't see her. Jamie stood on the other side of the vehicle, talking to Price. Getting the lowdown on our adventure, no doubt. We hadn't brought Matthew back with us. We didn't have room for him. We'd left him where we'd cuffed him, closing the barred door and pushing a refrigerator in front of it to keep him from escaping. Taylor had promised to send someone to retrieve him. If she'd sent a traveller, then he'd already arrived.

I yawned. I needed a bathroom and something to eat and a bed. I edged around the crowd toward the door. My legs were pudding. I managed about a dozen steps before I decided I'd better sit down before I fell down.

I found a low wall piled with snow and dropped onto it. I may have dozed off. Before I knew it, Price found me. He picked me up in his arms without saying a word, then carried me toward the house. Mansion. Whatever.

Right before we got there, we heard gunshots and shattering glass. Taylor screamed, and a body thumped onto the roof of the Nissan, collapsing it. A hail of glass pattered down after.

Price swung around. I started to kick myself free of his arms and then froze as I saw who had fallen and now lay twisted and bleeding on the Nissan's caved-in roof.

Touray.

Chapter 29

Gregg

GREGG'S HAND ACHED and body throbbed with unsatisfied desire that flamed higher as the brain jockey stoked it. Encouragement to cooperate, but it could be a double-edged sword. Gregg could use it to conceal his thoughts, if he could keep them deep enough.

Smug laughter. *Better men than you have tried. Better women, too.*

As if to both taunt and challenge him, the brain jockey dumped an avalanche of pornographic images featuring Taylor into Gregg's mind. Her naked on his bed, legs spread, her fingers buried inside herself. On her knees, her breasts hanging, her ass begging for attention. On the floor looking up at him, her tongue sliding out of her mouth as she took his cock between her lips.

The images looped endlessly. He couldn't shut them off no matter how hard he tried. His cock was stone hard, though he didn't know if the lust was real or stimulated by the brain jockey. He could barely move, it hurt so much.

You see? I have no need to worry that you are disguising your thoughts from me. I control you entirely. Now go get her.

Before long Gregg found himself returning to the war room to watch Taylor some more. He couldn't stop himself. He wanted her beyond reason. What before had been attraction had turned to a raging insanity of desire, thanks to the fucker in his head. Lust overtook his mind until he could think of nothing but having her in a dozen different ways.

Her phone pinged, and she answered it. Gregg could see her body tense at whatever she heard. He moved closer, telling himself he just wanted to know what had captivated her, but that was a lie. He couldn't keep himself away from her lush body any longer, not with the mind jockey stoking his lust.

She hung up and snapped out several orders. Her ever-present shadow—Dalton—nodded and jogged out the door.

"They're coming in," she announced, facing the table of Savannah's lieutenants.

Chairs scraped as everyone boiled into action. In moments, the group had vanished out the door. Taylor followed more slowly, typing a text as she went.

Excitement flooded him. This was his chance.

Gregg waited until she went through the door. Outside was a smaller room filled with furniture, three fireplaces, and a small stage at one end holding a piano with room for other musicians. Taylor hustled across, nodding to several people who loitered within. Then she headed down the curving marble stairway. She'd gone down a dozen steps and was momentarily out of sight of anybody above or below. Gregg swooped in and snatched her, pulling her into dreamspace.

He took her upstairs to a fourth-floor bedroom, lavishly appointed in a French country style. He laid her on the bed nearest the bay window overlooking the courtyard. Travelling was disconcerting to those without the talent and often resulted in disorientation and sometimes unconsciousness. It usually took a few minutes for passengers to reorient themselves.

Taylor wasn't quite out cold, but she had gone limp, her eyes bleary and confused.

Gregg watched her, his muscles knotting. Every primal instinct told him to strip her clothes off. He fought the urge. He was no rapist. He wanted her with an unholy ferocity, but he wanted her willing and eager.

A little petting wouldn't hurt.

That damned voice. Gregg lost the war with the pressure in his head and glided a hand up her thigh, over her hip and stomach to her breasts, and cupped one, rubbing his thumb back and forth over her nipple. It puckered into a tight peak. He heard himself moan as his balls tightened in response. He almost came in his pants. Abruptly he yanked his hand away.

Just in time.

"What are you doing here?" Her voice was a rough whisper.

"I want you," he said. "I've wanted inside you since the first moment I saw you."

Taylor sucked in a sharp breath. "What's wrong with you? We're in the middle of a turf war. You're the enemy and suddenly you're so horny for me you'd risk getting caught to drag me off?"

He grimaced. "Something like that." He kept his mind focused on her and only her. Unable to resist, he bent and put his mouth to hers, teasing her lips with his tongue, tasting her lush mouth.

She drew back. "We can't do this."

"I disagree." He kissed her again, and this time her mouth opened for him. He swept his tongue inside, tasting, feasting. His body shuddered, and he moaned low in his throat.

She twisted her head away. "This is a really bad idea. It's wrong."

"Why?" Gregg kissed up her jaw and nibbled at her ear, sucking gently on the lobe, feeling waves of smug satisfaction from his brain jockey and hating him with every last scrap of his tormented soul. "You want me, too," he murmured, covering her breast again. "Don't you?"

Before she could answer, he kissed her again. This time it lasted longer. This time she met him with a bold thrust of her tongue. He sucked on it. She answered his passion, sliding her hands around his head as if to keep him from pulling away. He broke the kiss, his lips lightly grazing hers. "You can't lie. You want me, too."

"That doesn't mean I'm going to fuck you."

He smiled at her, eyes heavy with desire. This felt good. Right even. He'd not lied when he told her he'd wanted her. "Why not?"

"Because this is insane. Price and Riley are on the way right now, and anyway, this doesn't make any sense. This isn't you. You're cold as ice and there's no way you'd want to have a little seduction trip with me while waging war. So either you've flipped your lid, or you're up to something. What's your game?"

She shoved him back, jumping up beside the bed and glaring at him.

Gregg rose to face her. The mind jockey hadn't expected a return of her resistance. But then, the bastard didn't know Taylor the way he did. Gregg felt him—her?—regrouping, even as his lust spiked again. Taylor tensed, her feet apart in a fighting stance. He leaned against the tall bedpost to show her he wasn't a threat. He wasn't here to force her. He wanted to seduce her. He wanted her willing.

I'll let you try, but if you can't get her naked on the bed in the next two minutes, then you'll take her, willing or not. She'll be the last woman you'll have for a long time, so use her well. Don't waste your time with her.

The voice seared through his brain like white lightning.

"Life is short," Gregg said by way of answering Taylor's question, continuing on the path he'd set for himself and refusing to acknowledge the voice in his head. "It's been made suddenly very clear to me how short."

She snorted. "So you decided you'd better hustle in here and get your rocks off with me? Right in the middle of a turf war? Please, bitch. I'm so not that stupid."

He loved her mouth. So tough, so lush. He couldn't wait to have her lips on him. He said so, watching as pink stained her cheeks.

He took a chance and stepped closer, his voice turning gravelly with hunger. "You don't think you'd be on the top of my list of things I don't want to miss if I die?"

She frowned. The pink faded. "When pigs fly. Anyway, you aren't the type to freak out over a near-death fright or whatever's happened to you. The only explanation that makes any sense is that you're playing me. Why?"

He sidled closer and shook his head. "I could have my pick of women, but you're the one that haunts my dreams. I always knew you were too dangerous for my own good."

She scowled. "What the fuck is that supposed to mean?"

He grinned and slid an arm around her, pulling her against him. She resisted, but he wasn't letting her argue. He pressed his lips to hers again. She opened reluctantly to his wicked assault. He wanted her naked right then more than he wanted almost anything else in the world. He lifted his head, putting his mouth near her ear, his breathing sounding harsh in his ears. "It means you could make me change my ways," he whispered roughly. "By the way, there's a hit out on Cass."

As soon as the words left his mouth, punishing pain struck. Too fucking late.

Gregg exploded into motion. With one hand, he thrust Taylor away. With the other, he drew his gun out and fired it at the window, lunging up onto the window seat and launching himself through the bullet-pocked glass. He heard Taylor scream.

Below, the courtyard was full of people surrounding an SUV. He plunged toward it, wrapped in a haze of unspeakable agony. He didn't care. He'd won. The motherfucker in his head couldn't use a dead man. Couldn't make him betray everyone who trusted him.

He'd known Taylor was attracted to him. Everything he'd said to her, everything he'd done in the last ten minutes, grew from his own real desire for her. He'd never meant to act on it. He preferred his women to come without ties of any kind. Since he didn't have a choice this time, Gregg had given in to the prodding of the brain jockey, letting his cravings for her swamp him, and disguising his real intent behind his own lust and the torrent of lascivious images the brain jockey had dumped in his mind.

The bastard had thought his control absolute, that if the lure of pleasure and threat of pain didn't force Gregg's unquestioning cooperation, then he'd make a puppet of Gregg. But the fucker hadn't counted on Gregg's fundamental and intrinsic fear of losing control of himself, of his mind. He didn't even have to think about killing himself to escape—it was instinct.

The fucker in his head had underestimated him. Gregg might be about to die, but he'd won. He was nobody's slave.

How do you like me now, asshole?

Chapter 30

Riley

TOURAY WASN'T DEAD, thank God. After his fall—a suicide jump, according to Taylor—I'd thought it was over. Nobody could survive that. But he'd still been breathing, albeit in bubbly, jerky gasps. The tinkers on hand had worked quickly and saved his life. He now lay in a coma in one of the bedrooms.

"What can be done is done," Maya told us when she arrived and checked him over. I didn't want anybody else for him. He needed to live and get whole. "A dreamer might be useful."

"But if he's physically healed, shouldn't he wake up?" Price pushed. He was holding himself together by his fingernails.

To anyone else, he probably seemed calm and contained. I knew better. He wore a mask developed over years as a cop and a Tyet enforcer. But his eyes gave him away. He'd aged a thousand years in the moment that Touray landed on the roof of the Nissan. Inside he'd shattered.

I stayed close, touching his shoulder or hand when he let me. I didn't speak. I knew all too well what he felt. So fragile that a touch could break him. So lost, so overwhelmed with terror and worry you can't even breathe. And so very, very helpless with nothing to do but watch and wait and hope. Nothing I could do or say would help, so I just stayed close.

"The brain works on a magic all its own," Maya said gently. "Pray, and see if Cass can help him."

She left us alone then. I'd already called Cass and sent an escort for her. She refused to travel, and I couldn't blame her.

"She's coming," I said. Like Price didn't already know. Like I hadn't already told him, but I didn't know what else to say. I blinked away the hot burn of tears. He needed me to be strong. Crying wasn't going to help at all.

Taylor came in a few minutes later. "Any change?"

I shook my head and then went into the hallway with her. "What happened?"

Her lips firmed, and she looked up and down the hallway, and then pulled me along to a bathroom, shutting the door behind us. Her arms folded over her chest.

"It was the weirdest thing. I was in the war room and you called and Savannah's seven cleared out to meet you. I was on my way when Touray showed up out of nowhere and snatched me. He took me up to that bedroom. I was out of it at first, and then realized he was seriously making moves on me.

I kept asking why. It made no sense. Why come here just to try to seduce me? Why now?

"He kept pushing, so I pulled myself together and told him to get lost. He started telling me how bad he wanted me and that he kept dreaming about me. Then all of a sudden, he grabbed his gun and started shooting at the window and jumped."

"Just like that?" If Taylor hadn't been the one telling me, I'd have thought she was lying. Never in a million years would I have predicted Touray would do something like this. It really didn't make any sense.

Her eyes widened with sudden emotion. "Oh fuck, there's something else. Just before he jumped, he said there's a hit out on Cass."

It took a second for that to sink in. Fear snatched me. "A hit?" And that's when things clicked together. Cass had said Vernon had done more to Touray's mind and she meant to see if she could figure out what. "That's why Touray wasn't acting like himself. He wasn't," I said, after reminding Taylor what Cass had said.

She nodded, tapping away on her phone. "That makes a hell of a lot more sense."

She sounded almost . . . disappointed? No, that was my exhaustion talking. Taylor despised Touray.

"We have to warn Cass."

"On it," she said, not looking up. "I sent a text to Cass and I'm telling Leo and Jamie to grab a traveller and go find her."

I decided I'd send her a text, too, and then I called. I got her voicemail. "Cass, go underground. There's a hit on you. Tell me where you are. I'll come get you."

I hung up, wishing I could do more. Wait. *I* could go get her. I could go through the spirit realm.

"No," Taylor said firmly when I voiced the idea.

"But—"

"No. You can't be everywhere and do everything, and you're needed here. You're the only one the Seedy Seven might take orders from. Until we can secure this place and your position in charge, you can't go anywhere. Leo and Jamie will find her."

I noticed she didn't say they'd find her alive. I couldn't argue with her logic, though. Well I *could*, but I wouldn't win. I changed the subject, hoping to distract myself.

"What about Arnow and the hostages?"

"Tinkers are working on them now. Don't worry, I've got everything covered. You concentrate on Price. Maybe get some rest."

She opened the door as she spoke. Dalton stood a few feet away, clearly waiting. She flicked him a look. "What's wrong?"

"I came to see if you needed me."

"If I wanted you, I'd let you know. Keep an eye on the war room for now. I'll be down in a few minutes." Her tone was brusque, even for Dalton.

"What was that about?" I asked as he stalked away.

Taylor frowned. "What do you mean?"

"I know he irritates the fuck out of you, but that was kind of harsh."

She glared at me. "What do you know about it?"

"Nothing. That's why I asked. Care to let the air out of your bitch balloon and tell me what's going on?"

She sighed, her voice dropping low so that I could barely hear her. "He . . . confuses me. And now with what happened with Touray. . . . Riley, he turned me on. I wasn't expecting it, but . . . shit." She ran her hands through her hair in frustration.

Oh. "So let me get this straight," I said slowly, trying to wrap my head around the concept. "You're into Dalton and Touray."

"No!" She looked up at the ceiling and blew out a breath. "Maybe. I don't know. I don't know what to do."

"You don't have to do anything. Not now." Not ever. I didn't say it. Who was I to tell her who to care about? "You've got time to figure it out. Just be careful. You can't trust either of them."

"I know." She shook herself and straightened her spine. "This conversation is now over. I've got work to do. Go be with Price. I'll send you guys up something to eat. When was the last time you got any sleep?"

"Sleep is for quitters," I said, opening the door to return to Price.

"Consider it a favor to me."

"After what you just told me? I'll have nightmares about you and your boy toys."

"Welcome to my world."

With that, she strode off.

WHEN AN HOUR went by without a word from Leo, Jamie, or Cass, I started getting antsy. Two hours, and I was climbing walls. I tried texting and calling, but no answer.

"How did your brother know there was a hit out on her?" I asked Price, not really expecting a reply.

"Because he posted it."

I stared at him, wide-eyed. "Oh my God. That makes sense."

Price's lips twisted. He sat with his elbows on his knees, his gaze fixed on Touray's slack face. "He must have come here to fight the mind control. Somehow he realized. Maybe the brain jockey taunted him."

Vernon. The brain jockey could only be Vernon. "I don't understand. Why would he come here? Are you saying he came to kill himself?"

"Taylor said he came on to her hard and heavy. Right?"

I couldn't interpret Price's look. "Right."

"That's why. Primal emotions like lust and hate can keep a brain jockey from seeing intent."

"Really? That works?"

He shrugged and looked broodingly at his brother. "It's something we were taught in order to resist dreamer interference. I think he picked Taylor because she'd know it didn't make sense, and it gave him a chance to warn us about Cass."

"So you think he jumped deliberately. He wasn't forced."

"I think he wasn't going to let himself be used."

Now that sounded like Touray.

Price's face contorted and he looked at me, eyes anguished. "What if Cass can't help?"

"Cass can't help," Taylor said from the doorway.

I turned to look at her. Her face was ashen.

"Cass was shot."

The End

Acknowledgements

As always, this book was made possible by the support and help of many people—too many to mention here, but I have to try. First, my editor Debra Dixon who gave me encouragement and helped me find my way through the enchanted forest to finish the book. This book wouldn't exist without her. Then I had my secret cabal on Facebook who gave me advice, suggestions, and help whenever I asked. My beta-readers were phenomenal, as were my colleagues and friends who helped me stay sane and find my path in this book: Lucienne Diver (agent extraordinaire), Christy Keyes, R.J. Blain, Devon Monk, Adrianne Middleton, Cynthia Dix, Megan Thyagarajan, Justin Barba and Dorri Kay. Thanks also to the Miscon gang and the members of SFNovelists. I also want to thank you, my wonderful readers, for liking what I write, for reviewing my books, for telling your friends, and for being so kind and generous whenever we interact. Thanks also to the amazing team at Bell Bridge Books. You've been terrific and I appreciate you so much. And finally, my long-suffering family who keep me grounded and believe in me, even when I'm bouncing off the walls. They mean everything to me.

I know I've forgotten some at this moment, but if I have, know that I'm hugely grateful for everyone that helped me write this book.

About the Author

Diana Pharaoh Francis is the acclaimed author of over a dozen novels of fantasy and urban fantasy. Her books have been nominated for the Mary Roberts Rinehart Award and *RT Magazine*'s Best Urban Fantasy. Find out more about her at www.dianapfrancis.com.

CPSIA information can be obtained
at www.ICGtesting.com
Printed in the USA
LVOW07s2325251117
557531LV00007B/531/P